TL
15
274
970

AIR FACTS AND FEATS

The Dream is Old... Fulfilment New

"*they cannot say indeed they have yet made an Eagle's flight, or that it doth not cost now and then a Leg or an Arm to one of these new Birds; but they may serve to represent the first Planks that were launched on the Water. . . . The Art of Flying is but newly invented, it will improve by degrees, and in time grow perfect; then we may fly as far as the Moon.*"

John Glanville: A Plurality of Worlds, 1688

AIR FACTS AND FEATS

A RECORD OF AEROSPACE ACHIEVEMENT

Compiled by
FRANCIS K. MASON
F.R.Hist.S., A.R.Ae.S., R.A.F. (Retd.)
and
MARTIN C. WINDROW
A.R.Hist.S., C.R.Ae.S.

With colour illustrations by
Michael Roffe

DOUBLEDAY & COMPANY INC.
GARDEN CITY, NEW YORK

Published in Great Britain by

GUINNESS SUPERLATIVES LTD.

24 UPPER BROOK STREET, LONDON, W.1, ENGLAND.

Printed in Monotype Baskerville Series 169
by McCorquodale and Company Limited, London, England.
Monotone and 4-colour half-tone blocks by Gilchrist Bros. Ltd., Leeds, England.

CONTENTS

Chapter		Page
1	Pioneers of the Air	9
2	Military Aviation	27
3	Maritime Aviation	98
4	Route-proving and Commercial Aviation	121
5	Lighter-than-Air	145
6	Rotorcraft	159
7	Flying for Sport and Competition	163
8	Rocketry and Spaceflight	174
	Appendices	
A	Addenda	189
B	Air Speed Records	195
C	Two remarkable aircraft	198
D	Aviation's worst disasters	200
	Selected Bibliography	203
	INDEX	205

INTRODUCTION

It is arguable that the supreme achievement in the history of mankind's journey from darkness to enlightenment has been the conquest of the air. The invention of the printing press, and the consequent communication of abstract ideas across the barriers of time and distance, is usually quoted as the seminal point in the development of modern Man; but those barriers were still daunting, and until aviation cut travelling times between nations and continents from weeks to hours, world-wide co-ordination in any field of endeavour was not really possible. Today a world shrunk by the scheduled air services is accepted as commonplace; it is easy to forget that it is a world founded on the dreams and labours of imaginative and gifted men over a period of two hundred years.

For more than a century, from the days when a handful of Frenchmen allowed themselves to be carried aloft in their flimsy balloons until the point was reached when a man could successfully be sustained in flight by a powered aeroplane, aeronautics was held within limits of progress ruled largely by the natural elements. In the years since the Wright brothers first coaxed their rudimentary biplane into the air over Kill Devil Hills in 1903, these limits have been swept aside by the colossal acceleration of scientific and industrial advance which has been characteristic of the twentieth century; and the last few years have seen the bonds which have tied Man to the surface and atmosphere of this planet smashed by that symbolic landing of which men have dreamed for centuries. The single lifetime of anyone who is today more than 66 years of age has spanned both the first flight of the Wright biplane, and mankind's first visit to the surface of the Moon.

This book seeks to record many of the outstanding achievements along the road between the Bois de Boulogne and Tranquillity Base. It is an enormous story of courage and persistence in the face of repeated frustrations, of vision and sacrifice in an environment of scepticism, of heartbreaking failure and of costly dead-ends. It is set against a background of peace and war, of sport, competition and exploration. So broad is the scope of Man's achievement in aviation that this first edition of *Air Facts and Feats* can only present a general framework and a proportion of specific records; it is intended that subsequent editions will be designed to distil achievement in various areas of endeavour, to place emphasis upon specific nations, and to explore in greater detail the fields of commercial and sporting aviation. Each successive edition will differ to a marked extent from its predecessor, and will of course be updated in the light of new records and achievements.

In selecting material for this book the compilers have been at pains to acquire the latest available data; but historical research is a dynamic process, and it is inevitable that there are occasional references which will become outdated before the appearance of a second edition—indeed, the compilers are aware that one or two have already been overtaken by events during the mechanical production of the book. It is hoped that a continuing editorial process will keep pace with new facts and feats, and maintain a balanced picture of future aerospace achievement—whether by man or by his machines.

ACKNOWLEDGEMENTS

The compilers wish to extend their thanks to the many organisations and individuals who gave generous assistance during the preparation of this book, and particularly to those listed below in alphabetical order:

Aero Spacelines Inc.
Ronald Barker
Beaumont Aviation Literature
The Boeing Company
British Aircraft Corporation (all Divisions)
J. M. Bruce, M.A., F.R.Hist.S.
Avions Marcel Dassault
General Dynamics Corporation
Grumman Aircraft Engineering Corporation
Lt. Col. J. Harsit, Israeli Defence Force/Air
   Force
Hawker Siddeley Aviation Ltd. (all Divisions)
Imperial War Museum
Lear Jet Industries Inc.
Lockheed Aircraft Corporation

Alex Lumsden
Ministry of Defence (R.A.F.)
Ministry of Defence (R.N.)
P. J. R. Moyes
N.A.S.A.
New York Post Corporation
North American Rockwell
Novosti Press Agency
Rolls Royce Ltd.
Society of British Aerospace Companies Ltd.
John W. R. Taylor
Johannes Thinesen
United States Air Force
United States Marine Corps
United States Navy

CHAPTER 1

THE PIONEERS OF THE AIR

The dream of flight is as old as Man himself. The element of water was conquered early in the human story, but the taunting freedom of the birds could only find an envious reflection in myth. It seems that Man's vision of flight has been most often identified, over the centuries, with direct imitation of the creatures which peopled his sky; as in our Western myth of Daedalus and Icarus, the concept of the "heavier-than-air" craft is clearly isolated. The other road to achievement was the "lighter-than-air" craft, which, as its title implies, rose aloft because the gas contained in its envelope was lighter than the surrounding air—provided that the "lift" afforded by the contained gas was greater than the structure weight of the craft. As will be shown in a later chapter it was the lighter-than-air craft, the balloon and the dirigible, which were to take man aloft first, more than one hundred years before his first successful, sustained flight in a powered aeroplane. It is with his attempts to produce a successful powered aeroplane that this chapter deals.

The nineteenth century was occupied for the most part by would-be aviators in the search for knowledge of aerodynamics, and for a formula by which this knowledge could be applied to a craft which would not only fly but also carry a man aloft. Leonardo da Vinci (1452–1519) had realised in his studies that to achieve forward flight through the air some method of paddling or winding one's way through the air was necessary, rather than a simple flapping of wings. He even went so far as to sketch a rudimentary form of helicopter in about 1500 which, as its name implied, incorporated a man-powered helical fan which when rotated would wind its upward path. But while Leonardo realised that simple up-and-down flapping of wings would not achieve forward flight, he persisted with sketches of ornithopters.

After the death of Leonardo there followed nearly three centuries of aerial fiction, punctuated from time to time by unsuccessful and scarcely chronicled attempts to construct models—usually gliders. It was not until the appearance of Sir George Cayley (1773–1857) that the modern form of aeroplane was evolved in model form. This great English scientist defined for the first time the principles of heavier-than-air flight, presenting for posterity a sketch illustrating a monoplane glider with lines of lift, thrust and drag. What is more, Cayley achieved man-carrying flight with his full-size gliders in the middle of the nineteenth century.

Cayley's lifetime also witnessed experiments by other inventors, notably Henson and Stringfellow (1812–1888 and 1799–1883 respectively), who, acknowledging the rudiments of fixed wing lifting surfaces, sought to propel their craft with steam engines—these being all the rage of their day. However, although the principles of aerodynamic lift were now partly understood, no fixed lifting wing surface had been designed that would support the great weight of a steam engine. And so the pendulum again swung back to "practical aerodynamicists", a trio of true pioneers. These were the German, Otto Lilienthal (1848–1896), the American, Dr. Octave Chanute (1832–1910) and Percy S. Pilcher (1866–1899), an English engineer.

Lilienthal it was who laid the foundations of flight in his classic book *Der Vogelflug als Grundlage der Fliegekunst* (The Flight of Birds as the Basis of Aviation), published in 1889. Although this work over-emphasised the significance of the ornithopter, Lilienthal sought to show that forward flight was achieved by a bird's outer wing feathers, twisting to produce thrust. Two years after his book's publication he set about a series of gliders with fixed wings, to which were attached a man whose legs dangled below and who ran downhill to achieve the forward speed to provide lift over the wings.

Both Chanute and Pilcher conducted their early gliding experiments with Lilienthal-type gliders before progressing to radical designs of their own, and this was the stage reached in flight at the turn of the century; the gliding experiments had nevertheless cost the lives of both Lilienthal and Pilcher.

To the persistence and indeed the survival of Chanute in America may be attributed the acceleration of efforts to achieve man-carrying powered flight in that country, for the next milestone was reached when the American Samuel Pierpont Langley succeeded in launching his steam-powered pilotless aeroplane *Aerodrome No. 5* over the Potomac River on 6th May 1896 for a sustained flight of more than one minute. Although Langley's experiments continued until 1903 and culminated in attempts (unsuccessful) to carry a man aloft, the race to achieve this feat was won by the Wright Brothers with a powered flight on Thursday 17th December 1903 by Orville in their *Flyer* at Kill Devil Hills, Kitty Hawk, North Carolina.

The activities of the Wright Brothers, Orville and Wilbur, were to dominate aviation for the next five years, and it was not until 1906 that powered man-carrying flight was achieved in Europe—first by the Dane Ellehammer and almost immediately afterwards by the Brazilian Santos-Dumont. Thereafter came a growing band of enthusiastic fliers, Voisin, the Farman brothers, Delagrange, Blériot, Cody, Levavasseur, Archdeacon, A. V. Roe and the rest, almost all of whom not only contributed to aviation by positive technical achievement but by successive failures eliminated much fruitless chaff from the growing harvest of Man's progress in the air.

The history of aviation before the First World War illustrates the heyday of unsophisticated advance. There was little in the way of material assistance from established industry or from national exchequers; aviation continued to flourish and advance as a sport, the competition being that to surpass the simplest of values, measured speed, endurance in the air, distance flown and altitude reached.

It is perhaps significant to remark that once flying took a hold upon Europe during the latter half of King Edward's reign the fierce international spirit of competition quickly advanced aviation as something more than a sport, while the tempo in the United States perceptibly slowed—both processes becoming more and more marked throughout the century's second decade. As will be shown in a later chapter, progress in America had become so retarded that by 1917 it fell to England and France to provide the necessary "know-how" to enable that great country to participate in the air war and bring her enormous resources in men and material to bear against the Central Powers.

The first man in the world to identify and correctly record the parameters of heavier-than-air flight was the Englishman, Sir George Cayley, 6th Baronet, 27.12.1773–15.12.1857.*. The following is a list of notable "firsts" achieved by this remarkable scientist:

(a) He first set down the mathematical principles of heavier-than-air flight (i.e. lift, thrust and drag).

(b) He was the first to make use of models for flying research, among them a simple glider— the first monoplane with fixed wing amidships, and fuselage terminating in vertical and horizontal tail surfaces; this was constructed in 1804.

(c) He was the first to draw attention to the importance of streamlining (in his definition of "drag").

(d) He was the first to suggest the benefits of biplanes and triplanes to provide increased lift with minimum weight.

(e) He was the first to construct and fly a man-carrying glider (see below).

(f) He was the first to demonstrate the means by which a curved "aerofoil" provided "lift" by creating reduced pressure over the upper surface when moved through the air.

(g) He was the first to suggest the use of an internal combustion engine for aeroplanes and constructed a model gunpowder engine in the absence of low-flash-point fuel oil.

---

* Sir George Cayley succeeded to the Baronetcy in a long and distinguished line of Cayleys whose origins are traceable back to Sir Hugo de Cayly, Kt., of Owby, who lived early in the twelfth century. Sir William Cayley was created first Baronet by Charles I on 26th April 1661 for services in the Civil War. The present Baronet, Sir Kenelm Henry Ernest Cayley, 10th Bt., of Brompton, Yorkshire, was born on 24th September 1896. It was at Brompton Hall, near Scarborough, one hundred years before that young George Cayley had carried out some of his early experiments with model aeroplanes.

The first person to be carried aloft in a heavier-than-air craft in sustained (gliding) flight was a ten-year-old boy who became airborne in a glider constructed by Sir George Cayley at Brompton Hall, near Scarborough, Yorks, in either 1852 or 1853. The glider became airborne after being towed by manpower down a hill against a slight breeze.

The first man to be carried aloft in a heavier-than-air craft was Sir George Cayley's coachman at Brompton Hall, also in 1852 or 1853. A witness of the event stated that after he had landed the coachman struggled clear and shouted "Please, Sir George, I wish to give notice. I was hired to drive, not to fly." No record has ever been traced giving the name of either the ten-year-old or of the coachman. The decennial census of 1851, however, records the name of John Appleby as being the most probable member of Sir George's staff. With regard to the young boy, Sir George had no son or grandson of this age at the time of his experiments, so it may be conjectured that the first "pilot" may have been a servant's son.

Cayley's model glider

The first model aeroplane powered by a steam engine was that designed and made by W. S. Henson (1812–1888) and John Stringfellow (1799–1883) at Chard, Somerset, England, in 1847. This 20-ft. (6·5 m.) span monoplane, powered by a steam engine driving twin pusher propellers, was launched from an inclined ramp, but sustained flight was not achieved. Henson subsequently emigrated to America, but both he and Stringfellow remained interested in aeronautics and pursued experiments with powered models. Contrary to opinions held until recently, none of Stringfellow's powered models ever achieved sustained flight.

The first scientist correctly to deduce the main properties (i.e. lift distribution) of a cambered aerofoil was F. H. Wenham (1824–1908) who built various gliders during the mid-nineteenth century to test his theories. In collaboration with John Browning, Wenham built **the world's first wind tunnel** in 1871 for the Aeronautical Society of Great Britain.

The first aeronautical exhibition in Great Britain was staged at the Crystal Palace in 1868 by the Aeronautical Society of Great Britain. The exhibits included model engines driven by steam, oil gas and guncotton.

The three most outstanding pioneers of gliding flight prior to successful powered flight were undoubtedly the German Otto Lilienthal (1848–1896), the American Dr. Octave Chanute (1832–1910), and the Englishman Percy S. Pilcher (1866–1899). Their achievements may be summarised as follows:

Otto Lilienthal, German civil engineer, published a classic aeronautical textbook Der Vogelflug als Grundlage der Fliegekunst *(The Flight of Birds as the Basis of Aviation) in 1889. Although he remained convinced that powered flight would ultimately be achieved by wing-flapping (i.e. in the ornithopter), Lilienthal constructed five fixed-wing monoplane gliders and two biplane gliders between 1891 and 1896. Tested near Berlin and at the Rhinower Hills near Stöllen, these gliders achieved sustained gliding flight; the pilot, usually Lilienthal himself, supported himself by his arms, holding the centre section of the glider. Thus, he could run forward and launch himself off the hills to achieve flight. During this period he achieved gliding distances ranging from 300 ft. (100 m.) to more than 750 ft. (250 m.). Although he had been experimenting with a small carbonic acid gas engine he was killed when one of his gliders crashed on the Rhinower Hills on 9th August 1896 before he could progress further with powered flight.*

Octave Chanute

Octave Chanute, American railroad engineer, was born in Paris, France, on 18th February 1832. Initial experiments with Lilienthal-type gliders during 1894–1895 convinced Chanute that stability and control would best be achieved by some form of wing-warping in preference to the pilot shifting his weight. He built five gliders during 1896, progressively reducing the number of superimposed wings from five to two (a biplane), the old man occasionally going aloft himself. During 1896–1897 at Dune Park, 30 miles east of Chicago on the shores of Lake Michigan, Chanute, in company with his associates, Dr. Ricketts, William Paul Butusov, William Avery and Augustus M. Herring, achieved more than 1,000 successful gliding flights without a single accident. Although Chanute never achieved powered flight, he was frequently consulted by the Wright brothers with regard to constructional techniques and materials.

Percy S. Pilcher, English marine engineer, built his first glider, the Bat, in 1895 and flew that year on the banks of the River Clyde. Following advice by Lilienthal as well as early practical experiments, Pilcher added a tailplane to the Bat and achieved numerous successful flights. This aircraft was followed by others (christened the Beetle, Gull and Hawk), the last of which was constructed in 1896 and included a fixed fin, a tailplane and a wheel undercarriage. It had a cambered wing with a span of 23 ft. and an area of 180 sq. ft. (7·0 m. and 16·72 m² respectively). Pilcher had always set his sights upon powered flight and was engaged in developing a light 4-h.p. oil engine (probably for installation in his Hawk) when, having been towed off the ground by a team of horses, he crashed in his glider at Stanford Park, Market Harborough on 30th September 1899, and died two days later.

The first man to achieve sustained, powered flight with an unmanned heavier-than-air craft

Samuel Pierpont Langley

was the American Samuel Pierpont Langley (born 22nd August 1834 at Roxbury, Massachusetts; died 27th February 1906, at Aiken, South Carolina). Mathematician and solar radiation physicist, Langley commenced building powered model aeroplanes during the 1890s, launching them from the top of a houseboat in the Potomac River near Quantico. His 14-ft. span models (*Aerodrome* Nos. 5 and 6*) achieved sustained flights of up to 4,200 ft. (1,400 m.) during 1896 and incorporated a single steam engine mounted amidships driving a pair of airscrews. In 1898 Langley was requested to continue his experiments with state finance and set about the design and construction of a full-scale version. As an intermediate step he built a quarter-scale model which became the world's first aeroplane powered by a petrol engine to achieve successful sustained flight in 1901. His full-size *Aerodrome*, with a span of 48 ft. (16 m.) and powered by a 52 h.p. petrol engine, was completed in 1903, and attempts to fly this over the Potomac River with Charles M. Manly at the controls were made on 7th October and 8th December 1903. On both occasions the aeroplane fouled the launcher and dropped into the river. In view of the success achieved by the Wright brothers immediately thereafter, the American government withdrew its support from Langley and his project was abandoned.

* Langley's use of the name *Aerodrome* was derived incorrectly from the Greek ἀερο-δρόμος (*aero-dromos*) supposedly meaning "air runner"; the word, however, is correctly defined as the location of a running event and cannot be held to mean the participant in a running event. Thus in the context of an *airfield* the word aerodrome, as originally applied to Hendon in Middlesex, England, is correct.

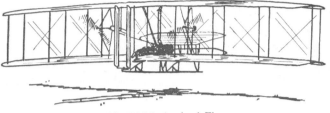

The Wright brothers' Flyer

The first aeroplane to achieve man-carrying, powered, sustained flight in the world was the *Flyer*, designed and constructed by the brothers Wilbur and Orville Wright, which first achieved such flight at 10.35 a.m. on Thursday 17th December 1903 at Kill Devil Hills, Kitty Hawk, North Carolina, with an undulating flight of 120 ft. (40 m.) in about 12 sec. Three further flights were made on the same day, the longest of which covered a ground distance of 852 ft. (230 m.) and lasted 59 sec. It should be emphasised that these flights were the natural culmination of some three years' experimenting by the Wrights with a number of gliders, during 1900–1903. Details of the powered *Flyer* were as follows:

Wright Flyer No. 1 (1903)
Wing span: 40 ft. 4 in. (12·3 m.)
Overall length: 21 ft. 1 in. (6·43 m.)
Wing chord: 6 ft. 6 in. (1·97 m.)
Wing area: 510 sq. ft. (47·38 m.²)
Empty weight: 605 lb. (274 kg.)
Loaded weight: Approx. 750 lb. (340 kg.)
Wing loading: 1·47 lb./sq. ft. (7·2 kg./m.²)
Powerplant: 12 b.h.p. 4-cylinder water-cooled engine lying on its side and driving two 8 ft. 6 in. diameter propellers by chains, one of which was crossed to achieve counter-rotation. Engine weight with fuel (0·33 imp. gal.), approx. 200 lb. (90 kg.)
Speed: 30 m.p.h. approximately (45 km./hr.)
Launching: The *Flyer* took off under its own power from a dolly which ran on two bicycle hubs along a 60 ft. (20 m.) wooden rail.

The first indigenous aeroplane to achieve a powered "hop" in Europe (and the first outside the United States of America) was the tractor semi-biplane powered by an 18-h.p. engine, designed, constructed and flown by the Dane, J. C. H. Ellehammer, in Denmark in 1906, when he achieved a sustained "hop" of 140 ft. (46 m.) ground distance.

The first accredited sustained flight (i.e. other than a "hop") achieved by a manned, powered aeroplane in Europe was made on 12th November 1906 by the Brazilian constructor-pilot Alberto Santos-Dumont, a resident of Paris, France, who flew his "*14-bis*" 722 ft. (241 m.) in 21 sec.; his aeroplane was in effect a box-kite powered by a 50-h.p. *Antoinette* engine, and this flight won for him the French Aero Club's prize for the first flight of more than 100 metres. A previous flight, carried out on 23rd October, covered nearly 200 ft. (65 m.) and had won Santos-Dumont the Archdeacon prize of 3,000 francs for the first sustained flight of over 25 metres.

The first aeroplane flight in Italy was made by the French sculptor-turned-aviator Léon Delagrange in a Voisin in 1907. At this time the French brothers Gabriel and Charles Voisin employed two pilots, the English-born Henry Farman and Léon Delagrange. Gabriel Voisin later remarked that the former possessed considerable mechanical and manipulative skill, whereas the latter "was not the sporting type" and knew nothing about running an engine. Delagrange was killed flying a Blériot monoplane in 1910, but Farman survived many years, having abandoned flying to pursue the business of aeroplane manufacture.*

Voisin biplane

The first monoplane with tractor engine, enclosed fuselage, rear-mounted empennage and two-wheel main undercarriage with tailwheel was the Blériot VII powered by a 50-h.p. *Antoinette* engine. This was Louis Blériot's third full-size monoplane and was built during the autumn of 1907 and first flown by him at Issy-les-Moulineaux, France, on 10th November 1907. Before finally crashing this aeroplane on 18th December that year Blériot had achieved about five flights, the longest of which was more than 1,600 ft. (about 510 m.). This success confirmed to the designer that his basic configuration was sound—so much so that despite a thirty-year deviation into biplane design, Blériot's basic configuration is still regarded as fundamentally conventional among propeller-driven aeroplanes of to-day.

The first internationally-ratified world aeroplane records of performance were those which stood at the end of 1907, both for distance covered over the ground and for flights which followed unassisted take-off from level ground. Thus although the Wright *Flyer* (1905 version) had achieved numerous observed flights across-country, these were not ratified by the F.A.I. for world record purposes as they were, more often than not, commenced by assistance into the air by external means. The records standing on 31st December 1907 were thus:

12th November 1906. Santos-Dumont (14-*bis*)   722 ft. (220 m.)
26th October 1907.   Henry Farman (Voisin) 2,530 ft. (771 m.)

The first aeroplane flight in Germany was made by the Dane, J. C. H. Ellehammer, in his triplane at Kiel in June 1907. A development of this triplane was flown by **the first German pilot,** Hans Grade, at Magdeburg in October 1907.

The first aeroplane flight in Austria was made by the Frenchman, G. Legagneux, at Vienna in April 1908 in his Voisin. **The first Austrian** to fly was Igo Etrich, who flew his *Taube* at Wiener-Neustadt in November of that year. His aircraft gave its name to the type of aircraft in fairly widespread use by Germany at the beginning of the First World War.

---

* Henry Farman was born in England in 1874 and retained his English citizenship until 1937 when he became a naturalised Frenchman. Having turned from painting to cycling before the turn of the century, he progressed to racing Panhard motor cars and at one time owned the largest garage in Paris. He died on 17th July 1958.

The first aeroplane flight in Russia was made by Van den Schkrouff in a Voisin biplane at Odessa in July 1908.

The first aeroplane flight in Sweden was made by the Frenchman Legagneux at Stockholm in his Voisin biplane in July 1908.

The first aeroplane flight in Rumania was made by Louis Blériot in his monoplane at Bucharest in October 1908. It has been said that Blériot's first flights outside France during 1908 represented the first serious threat to the acknowledged superiority of the Voisin biplane in Europe at that time. However, the Blériot aeroplane was still in effect a prototype, whereas the Voisin had already achieved a degree of series production, about six examples of roughly similar design having been completed.

The Voisin brothers

The first officially-recognised aeroplane flight in Great Britain was made by the American (later naturalised British citizen) Samuel F. Cody in his *British Army Aeroplane No. 1*, an aircraft based to some extent on the Wright Biplane of 1905. The flight of 1,390 ft. (460 m.) was made at Farnborough, Hants, on 16th October 1908 and ended with a crash landing, but without physical injury to Cody.

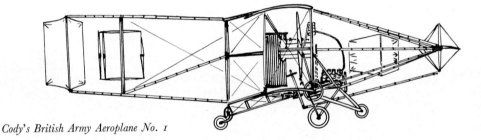

Cody's British Army Aeroplane No. 1

Despite the apparent growth of interest and participation in heavier-than-air aviation in Europe during 1908 it is true to say that the practical studies of the Wright brothers and those of Glenn H. Curtiss maintained America's technical lead until this period. However when in August 1908 Wilbur Wright gave his first public flying demonstrations in France (at the Hunaudières race course near Le Mans) between the 8th and 15th of the month the European aeroplane constructors and pilots were so greatly impressed by the performance and precision of control displayed by the Wright biplane that from this moment on the competitive development of aeroplanes in Europe suddenly accelerated. The American tendency to persist with relatively conservative development of the early Wright and Curtiss designs thus eliminated this lead within two years while European design surged ahead.

The first fatality to be suffered by the occupant of an aeroplane occurred on 17th September 1908 at Fort Myer, Virginia, when a Wright biplane flown by Orville Wright crashed killing the passenger, Lieutenant Thomas Etholen Selfridge, U.S. Signal Corps. Wright was seriously injured. The accident occurred during U.S. Army acceptance trials of the Wright biplane and was caused by a failure in one of the propeller blades which then severed a control wire sending the aircraft crashing to the ground from about 75 ft. (25 m.).

The first resident Englishmen to fly in an aeroplane* (albeit as passengers) were Griffith Brewer, The Hon. C. S. Rolls, F. H. Butler, and Major B. F. S. Baden-Powell, who were taken aloft in turn by Wilbur Wright in his biplane at Camp d'Auvours on 8th October 1908. Frank Hedges Butler had founded the Aero Club of Great Britain in 1901, while Baden-Powell was Secretary of the Aeronautical Society.

The first circuit flight made in Europe was flown by Henry Farman on 13th January 1908 in his modified Voisin biplane at Issy-les-Moulineaux when he took off, circumnavigated a pylon 500 metres away and returned to his point of departure. By so doing Farman also won the *Grand Prix d'Aviation* and the Deutsch-Archdeacon prize of 50,000 francs offered to the first pilot to cover a kilometre.

Henry Farman

The first passenger ever to fly in an aeroplane was Charles W. Furnas who was taken aloft by Wilbur Wright on 14th May 1908 for a flight covering 1,968 ft. (650 m.) of 28·6 sec. duration. Later the same morning Orville Wright flew Furnas for a distance of about 2·5 miles (4,000 m.) which was covered in 3 min. 40 sec.

The first passenger to be carried in an aeroplane in Europe was Ernest Archdeacon, the Frenchman whose substantial prizes contributed such stimulus to European aviation, who was flown by Henry Farman on 29th May 1908.

The first American to fly after the Wright brothers was Glenn H. Curtiss, who flew his *June Bug* for the first time on 20th June 1908. During this flight Curtiss covered a distance of 1,266 ft. (420 m.) and exactly a fortnight later he made a flight of 5,090 ft. (1,700 m.) in 102·2 sec. to win the *Scientific American* trophy for the first American to make a public flight over a measured course.

The first specification for a military aeroplane ever issued for commercial tender was drawn up by Lieutenant George C. Sweet of the U.S. Navy Department during October 1908 after having witnessed the U.S. Army trials at Fort Myer the previous month. The specification ran as follows:

"Each machine is to carry two persons, one an observer, of an average weight of 175 pounds each, and a sufficient supply of fuel at the start for a flight of at least 200 miles, for a period of four hours, at an average speed of not less than 40 miles an hour, and to remain continuously in the air during the trial. The machines are to be so constructed as to be able to alight without damage, on land or water; to float on the latter, when at rest, without wetting any of the air-

---

* The "resident" qualification is necessary here as of course the English-born, French-resident Henry Farman had been flying for more than a year by the time the four Englishmen were taken aloft by Wright.

supporting or controlling areas, and to be able to rise therefrom without appreciable delay under their own power, without the aid of special starting apparatus."

Having regard to the fact that this requirement was formulated at a time when aircraft were achieving flights usually measured in minutes rather than hours, and that no Englishman had yet flown in a British aeroplane for a measurable distance, this specification may have seemed far-fetched. Yet on the last day of 1908 Wilbur Wright achieved a stupendous flight of 77 miles in 2 h. 20 min. which won for him the Michelin prize of 20,000 francs—apart from breaking all his own records. A summary of the flights made by Wilbur Wright up to the end of 1908 is as follows:

17th December 1903	At Kitty Hawk	852 ft.	(260 m.)	
9th November 1904	Dayton, Ohio	3 miles	(1,610 m.)	Flew 105 times during 1904.
5th October 1905	Dayton, Ohio	24 miles	(38·6 km.)	Flew 49 times during 1905.
8th August 1908	Le Mans, France	—	—	Demonstration flight.
21st September 1908	Auvours, France	41 miles	(65·9 km.)	Flew more than 100 times at this location.
10th October 1908	Auvours, France	46 miles	(74 km.)	In 69 min., with M. Pain-leve as passenger.
18th December 1908	Auvours, France	62 miles	(99 km.)	In 114 min. Climbed to 360 ft. (120 m.) to estab-lish new altitude record.
31st December 1908	Auvours, France	77 miles	(124 km.)	In 2 hr. 20 min. 23 sec. to win Michelin prize and set up new world record.

As a measure of the Wright biplane's world supremacy at the end of 1908 the following is a list of the more significant flights made by other aviators up to that time:

Alberto Santos-Dumont
13th November 1906   Made the first flight (accredited) in Europe at Bagatelle, covering 720 ft. (219 m.) in 21 min.

Léon Delagragne
16th March 1907   Covered 30 ft. (10 m.) at Bagatelle in the first Voisin.
17th November 1907   Covered 500 ft. at Issy-les-Moulineaux.
29th March 1908   Covered 453 ft. (137 m.) with passenger (Henry Farman).
22nd June 1908   Covered 10·5 miles (16·8 km.) in 16 min. 30 sec. at Milan, Italy.
6th September 1908   Covered 15·2 miles (24·4 km.) in 29 min. 53 sec. at Issy-les-Moulineaux.

Henry Farman
26th October 1907   Covered 253 ft. (77 m.) in closed circuit for first time.
6th July 1908   Covered 12·2 miles (19·6 km.) in 19 min. 3 sec. to win Armengand prize.
30th October 1908   Covered 17 miles (27·3 km.) in 20 min. on cross country flight from Chalons to Rheims.

Glenn H. Curtiss
4th July 1908   Covered 5,090 ft. (1,552 m.) in 1 min. 42 sec. to win *Scientific American* prize.

The world's first woman passenger to fly in an aeroplane was a Madame Peltier who, on 8th July 1908, accompanied Leon Delagrange at Turin, Italy, in his Voisin for a flight which lasted 500 ft. (150 m.).

The first aerodrome to be prepared as such in England was the flying ground at Shellbeach, Isle of Sheppey, where limited established facilities were provided during the winter of 1908–09 by the joint efforts of the Aero Club of Great Britain, and Short Bros., Ltd.

The first sustained, powered flight by an aeroplane in Canada was made on 23rd February 1909 by J. A. Douglas McCurdy, a Canadian, over Baddeck Bay, Nova Scotia, in his biplane *Silver Dart*, which he had designed. He had made his own first flight at Hammondsport, N.Y., U.S.A., the previous December.

The first resident Englishman to fly an aeroplane in England was J. T. C. Moore-Brabazon (later Lord Brabazon of Tara) who flew three sustained flights of 450, 600 and 1,500 ft. (130, 180 and 450 m.) between 30th April and 2nd May 1909 at Leysdown, Isle of Sheppey, in his Voisin biplane. He had learned to fly in France during the previous year and on 30th October 1909 won the £1,000 *Daily Mail* prize for the first Briton to cover a mile (closed circuit) in a British aeroplane—a Short-Wright biplane. He also qualified to become Great Britain's first pilot, being awarded the Aero Club of Great Britain's Aviator Certificate No. 1 on 8th March 1910. After a lifetime in aviation, Lord Brabazon died in 1969; such an active life span in aviation can perhaps only be matched by the French pioneer aviator, Gabriel Voisin.

Moore-Brabazon, and the Short-Wright biplane

The first aeroplane flight of over one mile flown in Britain was achieved on 14th May 1909 by Samuel Cody who flew the British Army Aeroplane No. 1 from Laffan's Plain to Danger Hill, Hants—a distance of just over one mile—and landed without breaking anything. The Prince of Wales requested a repeat performance during the same afternoon, but Cody, turning to avoid some troops, crashed into an embankment and demolished the tail of his aeroplane.

The first man to smoke a cigarette while piloting an aeroplane was Hubert Latham who, during a flight in his Antoinette monoplane in the first week of June 1909 at Chalons, France, despite the full blast of a 45 m.p.h. slipstream in his exposed cockpit, rolled his cigarette, lit it and smoked it!

Conquest of the English Channel. In response to an offer by the *Daily Mail* of a prize of £1,000 for the first pilot (of any nationality) to fly an aeroplane across the Channel. **The first attempt** was made by an Englishman, Hubert Latham, flying an Antoinette. He took off near Calais at 6.42 a.m. on Monday 19th July 1909 but landed in the sea shortly afterwards following engine failure which could not be rectified in the air. He was picked up by the French naval vessel *Tarpon*. The occasion of this attempt was also the **first instance of wireless telegraphy being used to obtain weather reports**, the first report being transmitted from Sangatte, near Calais, to the Lord Warden Hotel, Dover, at 4.30 a.m. on that morning.

Despite working furiously to erect a replacement Antoinette, Latham was beaten by M. Louis Blériot. The Frenchman took off in his Blériot XI monoplane at 4.40 a.m. on Sunday 25th July 1909, and landed at approximately 5.20 a.m. in a field near Dover to become **the first man to cross the English Channel in an aeroplane.**

Latham did however make another attempt to fly the Channel two days later (on 27th July), taking off at 5.30 a.m. from Cap Blanc Nez. When only one mile from the Dover cliffs, his engine failed and once again he had to land in the sea.

Louis Blériot

The Blériot cross-Channel monoplane

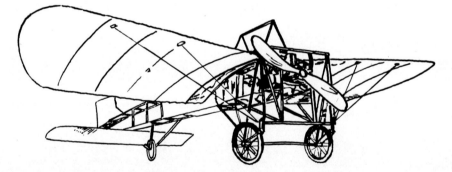

The first woman passenger to fly in an aeroplane in England was Mrs. Cody, wife of Samuel, who was taken up by her husband during the last week of July 1909 over Laffan's Plain, Hants, in the British Army Aeroplane No. 1.

The first passenger to be carried by an aeroplane in Canada was F. W. "Casey" Baldwin who was taken aloft on 2nd August 1909 at Petawawa, Ontario, in an aeroplane flown by John A. D. McCurdy.

The first International Aviation Meeting in the world opened on 22nd August 1909 at Rheims, and lasted until 29th August 1909. Thirty-eight aeroplanes were entered to participate, although only about a dozen managed to leave the ground; the meeting also attracted aviators and aeroplane designers from all over Europe and did much to arouse widespread public interest in flying.

The world's first speed record of over 100 km. was established by the Englishman, Hubert Latham, during the Rheims International Meeting (see above) between 22nd and 29th August 1909. Flying an Antoinette (powered by a 50 h.p. 8-cylinder Antoinette engine) he covered the distance in 1 hr. 28 min. 17 sec., at an average speed of 42 m.p.h. In so doing he won the second largest prize of the meeting amounting to 42,000 francs. First prize went to Mr. Henry Farman who, flying a Gnôme-powered Farman set up new world records for duration and distance in a closed circuit, covering 112·5 miles (181·04 km.) in 3 hr. 4 min. 56·4 sec., winning the 63,000 francs.

The first aeroplane flight in the world in which two passengers were carried was made at the Rheims International Meeting (see above) on 27th August 1909 by Henry Farman who, in his Gnôme-powered Farman biplane, covered a distance of six miles in ten minutes.

The first certificated woman pilot in the world was Mme. la Baronne de la Roche, a Frenchwoman, who received her Pilot's Certificate at Chalons, France, on 23rd October 1909, having qualified on a Voisin biplane.

The first aviation meeting held in Great Britain was that organised by the Doncaster Town Council on the Doncaster Race Course between 15th and 23rd October 1909. This meeting was not governed by rules laid down by the FAI, nor was it officially recognized by the Aero Club of Great Britain. Twelve aeroplanes constituted the field, of which five managed to fly. **The first officially-recognised meeting** was held at Squires Gate, Blackpool, between 18th and 23rd October 1909, being organised by the Blackpool Corporation and the Lancashire Aero Club; seven of the dozen participants were coaxed into the air.

The first manned flight by a glider in Australia was made on 5th December 1909 by the Australian artist-inventor-poet-journalist George Augustus Taylor at Narrabeen Beach, New South Wales. He made a total of 29 flights.

The first woman glider pilot in the world was Florence Taylor (wife of George Augustus Taylor, see above) who flew her husband's glider at Narrabeen Beach, New South Wales, Australia, in December 1909.

The first aeroplane flight in Ireland is believed to have been carried out by Mr. H. G. Ferguson of Belfast during the winter of 1909–10 in an aeroplane of his own design and manufacture which resembled a Blériot powered by an 8-cylinder 35-h.p. air-cooled JAP engine.

The first American monoplane to fly was the Walden III, designed by Dr. Henry W. Walden and flown on 9th December 1909 at Mineola, Long Island, N.Y. It was powered by a 22-h.p. three-cylinder Anzani engine.

The first flights by aeroplanes to be undertaken in Egypt were by a pair of Humber-built Blériot monoplanes flown by Capt. G. W. P. Dawes and a Mr. Neale. Both pilots crashed during practice for a flying meeting to be held at Heliopolis, Egypt, in January 1910; their aircraft were damaged and they did not in fact participate in the meeting.

The first aeroplane flights in Australia were achieved in January 1910 by Colin Defries, also well-known as a motor racing driver. He flew an imported Wright biplane for a mile at a height of 35 ft. (11 m.) over the racecourse at Sydney, New South

Wales. On the day after his first flight he made a further short flight, this time with a passenger, **the first to be carried by an aeroplane in Australia.** (It has often been said that Ehrich Weiss, better known as Harry Houdini the escapologist, was the first aeroplane pilot to make a *significant* flight; on 18th March 1910 he flew three times in a Voisin biplane at Digger's Rest, Victoria, achieving a maximum height of over 100 ft. (30 m.), while his longest flight exceeded two miles (3·2 km.).

The Aero Club of Great Britain had the prefix " Royal " bestowed upon it by H.M. King Edward VII on 15th February 1910. This body had already displayed considerable tact and administrative acumen in the control of flying in Great Britain, and it is quite clear that the King, in bestowing the Royal title upon the club, recognised the position of responsibility it would come to occupy in man's determination to perfect the aeroplane in the coming years. That Great Britain achieved and maintained the front rank in international aviation during the next thirty-five years was in no small measure due to the unscrupulous impartiality and efficiency of the Royal Aero Club, whose prestige won the respect of the whole world.

The first recorded night flight in Great Britain was made by Claude Grahame-White during 27th/28th April 1910 in his attempt to overhaul Louis Paulhan in the *Daily Mail* London–Manchester air race. During the course of this race Paulhan (who won) thus made the first London-to-Manchester flight and was **the first to fly an aeroplane over 100 km. (62·14 miles) in a straight line in Great Britain.**

The first aeroplane to be "forced down" by the action of another was the Henry Farman biplane of Mr. A. Rawlinson during the Aviation Meeting at Nice, France, at the end of April 1910. Mr. Rawlinson was flying his new Farman over the sea when the Russian Effimov passed so close above him (also in a Farman) that his slipstream forced the Englishman down on to the water. The Russian was severely reprimanded for his thoughtlessness and fined 100 francs.

The first British woman to fly solo in an aeroplane was almost certainly Miss Edith Maud Cook, who performed various aerial acts under the name of Miss "Spencer Kavanagh". She achieved several solo flights on Blériot monoplanes with the Grahame-White flying school at Pau in the Pyrenees early in 1910. She was also a professional parachute jumper and was killed after making a jump from a balloon near Coventry, England, in July 1910.

The first England-to-France and double crossing of the English Channel was accomplished by the Hon. C. S. Rolls flying a Short-built Wright biplane on 2nd June 1910. He took off from Dover at 6.30 p.m., dropped a letter addressed to the Aero Club of France near Sangatte at 7.15 p.m., then flew back to England and made a perfect landing near his starting rail at 8.06 p.m. He was thus **the first Englishman to cross the English Channel in a British-built aeroplane, the first man to cross from England to France in an aeroplane, the first man to make a non-stop double crossing, and the first cross-Channel pilot to land at a pre-arranged spot with damage to his aeroplane.**

The first world record to fall to an Englishman (apart from Henry Farman, and Hubert Latham who established an inaugural record, see above) was the duration record taken by Captain Bertram Dickson who, on 6th June 1910, remained airborne for exactly two hours with a passenger in his Henry Farman biplane at Anjou, France, thereby establishing a new World Endurance Record with one passenger.

The first British pilot to lose his life while flying an aeroplane was the Hon. Charles Stewart Rolls (born in London, 27th August 1877, the third son of the 1st Baron Llangattock), who was killed at the Bournemouth Aviation Week on 12th July 1910 when his French-built Wright biplane suffered a structural failure in flight.

The Hon. Charles Rolls

The first flight in Australia by an Australian in an indigenous aeroplane was made by John R. Duigan of Melbourne on 16th July 1910 at Mia Mia, Victoria, in an aeroplane constructed from photographs of the Wright's *Flyer*. On that day Duigan flew only 24 ft. (7 m.), but on 7th October he covered 196 yards (179 m.) at a height of about 12 ft. (3·5 m.).

The first Swedish pilot was Baron Carl Cederström who was granted a pilot's certificate at the Blériot flying school at Pau, France, in 1910. On returning to Sweden he was awarded Certificate No. 1 by the Aero Club of Sweden (*Svenska Aeronautiska Sallskapet*). He was lost, presumed drowned, while flying as a passenger between Stockholm and Finland in July 1918.

The most famous name in early Swedish aviation was probably that of Dr. Enoch Thulin, D.Phil., who gained his first pilot's Certificate in France and was subsequently granted Swedish Certificate No. 10. Before the First World War he abandoned full-time flying to concentrate upon aeroplane manufacture, establishing his Company at Landskrona in 1915. After the United States entered the War, the Thulins Company was probably **the largest aircraft manufacturing concern of any neutral country.** Dr. Thulins was killed in a flying accident on 14th May 1919.

The first aeroplane flights in the Argentine and Brazil were made in 1910 by Voisin and Henry Farman biplanes respectively.

The first mail carried in an aeroplane in Great Britain was flown by Claude Grahame-White on 10th August 1910 in a Blériot monoplane from Squires Gate, Blackpool; he did not reach his destination at Southport having been forced to land by bad weather.

The first crossing of the Irish Sea was made by Robert Loraine who, flying a Farman biplane on 11th September 1910, set off from Holyhead, Anglesey. Although engine failure forced him down in the sea 60 yards offshore from the Irish coast near Baily Lighthouse, Howth, he was generally considered to have been the first to accomplish the crossing.

The first air collision in the world is believed to have occurred at the beginning of October 1910 during an aviation meeting at Milan, Italy, between Capt. Bertram Dickson in his Henry Farman and a Frenchman named Thomas in an Antoinette monoplane. The French pilot escaped unhurt but Dickson was severely injured and never flew again.

Perhaps the greatest feat in learning to fly was that achieved by T. O. M. Sopwith (later Sir Thomas Sopwith) in 1910. Having purchased a Howard-Wright biplane and assembled it himself, he attempted to perform the first test flight (never having before flown); it crashed and was wrecked, but Sopwith was unhurt. This occurred on 22nd October. He promptly ordered another Howard-Wright and on 21st November made his second attempt to fly; he carried out some taxying before lunch, took off and made some circuits in the afternoon and qualified for his pilot's Certificate around teatime. He carried his first passenger the same evening. Within three weeks, and with no more than ten hours' solo to his credit, Sopwith then set up new British distance and duration records, and came second in the competition for the 1910 British Empire Michelin Cup awarded for the longest distance flown by a British pilot in a British aeroplane. He was awarded Aviator's Certificate No. 31.

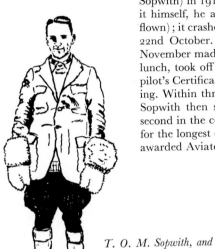

T. O. M. Sopwith, and Howard-Wright biplane

The largest single crowd to watch a display of flying before the First World War was almost certainly the concourse of nearly 750,000 Indians who turned out to watch M. Henri Jullerot of the Bristol Company in his Military Biplane at Calcutta on 6th January 1911.

The first flight in New Zealand by an aeroplane was made by a Howard-Wright (type) biplane piloted by Vivian C. Walsh at Auckland on 5th February 1911. With his brother Leo, Vivian Walsh imported materials from England with which to build the aircraft and installed a 60 h.p. ENV engine. Vivian Walsh also made **the first seaplane flight in New Zealand** on 1st January 1914.

The first Government (official) air mail flight in the world was undertaken on 18th February 1911 when the French pilot Henri Pequet flew a Humber biplane from Allahabad to Naini Junction, a distance of about five miles (8 km.) across the Jumna River, with about 6,500 letters. The regular service was established four days later as part of the Universal Postal Exhibition, Allahabad, India, the flights being shared by Captain W. G. Windham and Pequet. The envelopes of this first mail service were franked "First Aerial Post, U.P. Exhibition, Allahabad, 1911" and are highly prized among collectors.

Eleven passengers were first carried in an aeroplane on 23rd March 1911 by Louis Breguet over a distance of 5 km. (3·1 miles) at Douai, France, in a Breguet biplane. **Twelve passengers were first carried in an aeroplane** on 24th March 1911 by Roger Sommer over a distance of 800 m. (875 yards) in a Sommer biplane powered by a 70 h.p. engine.

The first non-stop flight from London to Paris was made on 12th April 1911 by Monsieur Pierre Prier in 3 hr. 56 min., flying a Blériot monoplane powered by a 50-h.p. Gnôme engine. Prier, who was chief flying instructor at the Blériot School, Hendon, took off from Hendon and landed at Issy-les-Moulineaux.

The first Swedish pilot to be awarded a pilot's Certificate by the Royal Aero Club of Great Britain was Lt. C. O. Dahlbeck who qualified at Hendon with the Grahame-White School on a Henry Farman biplane, being awarded Certificate No. 120 on 29th August 1911. Lt. Dahlbeck was holder of Swedish Certificate No. 3.

The first British woman to be granted a pilot's Certificate was Mrs. Hilda B. Hewlett who qualified on a Henry Farman biplane at Brooklands for Certificate No. 122 on 29th August 1911. Her son, Sub-Lt. F. E. T. Hewlett, R.N., was taught to fly by her, and was thus **the first and possibly the only naval airman in the world ever to receive his flying tuition from his mother.** His Certificate, No. 156, was gained on 14th November 1911. Young Hewlett was one of the first five officers of the Naval Wing, R.F.C., when formed in October 1912.

The first mail to be carried by air in Great Britain was entrusted to the staff pilots of the Grahame-White and Blériot flying schools who commenced carrying the mail between Hendon and Windsor on Saturday 9th September 1911. The first flight was undertaken on that day by Gustav Hamel in a Blériot monoplane, covering the route in ten minutes at a ground speed of 110 m.p.h. (177 km./hr.) with a strong tailwind. The service lasted until 26th September, having been instituted to commemorate the Coronation of H.M. King George V. The total weight of mail carried was 1,015 lb. (460·4 kg.) between the Hendon flying field and Royal Farm, Windsor.

The first Chinese national to receive a pilot's Certificate was Zee Yee Lee who was awarded R.Ae.C. Certificate No. 148 on 17th October 1911, qualifying on a Bristol Boxkite after receiving his training on Salisbury Plain, England. Lee later became chief flying instructor at the Military Flying School at Nanyuen, Peking. He was followed by Prince Tsai Tao, Wee Gee, Colonel Tsing, Lt. Poa and Lt. Yoa, at least two of whom gained Certificates in the U.S.A.

The first instance of a Government ordering the grounding of a specific type of aircraft occurred in March 1912 when the French Government ordered all Blériot monoplanes of the French Army to be prohibited from flying until they had been re-built so that their wings were braced to withstand a degree of negative-G. Five distinguished French pilots had been killed following the collapse of the Blériots' wings, but the ban was shortlived and the aircraft were flying again within a fortnight. The weakness was spotlighted by Louis Blériot himself who, despite the likely loss of prestige, published a short report explaining the weakness in his own aeroplanes. There is no doubt that his frankness increased—rather than detracted from—his very high standing in aviation circles.

The first American woman pilot to receive her Certificate was Harriet Quimby. She was also the **first woman to pilot an aeroplane across the English Channel,** doing so in a Blériot monoplane and taking off from Deal on 16th April 1912.

The first flight from Paris to Berlin was achieved by the Frenchman Audemars who flew a Blériot monoplane from the French capital to the German capital via Bochum in Westphalia during the spring of 1912.

The first flight in Norway by a Norwegian took place on 1st June 1912 when Lt. Hans E. Dons, a submarine officer, flew a German *Start* across Oslo Fjord from Horten to Fredrikstad. As a result of this achievement the Norwegian *Storting* (Government) voted the sum of £900 ($2,160) to send four officers to Paris to learn to fly. Within three months (in August) one of these officers had established a Scandinavian distance record.

The first American woman to be killed in an aeroplane accident was Julie Clark of Denver, Colorado, whose Curtiss biplane struck a tree on 17th June 1912 at Springfield, Illinois, and turned turtle.

The first crossing of the English Channel by an aeroplane with a pilot and two passengers was made on 4th August 1912 by W. B. Rhodes-Moorhouse (later, as 2nd Lt. in the Royal Flying Corps, the first British airman to be awarded the Victoria Cross on 26th April 1915) who, accompanied by his wife and a friend, flew a Breguet tractor biplane from Douai, France, *via* Boulogne and Dungeness, to Bethersden, near Ashford, Kent, where they crashed in bad weather. Nobody was hurt.

The first man to fly underneath all the Thames bridges in London between Tower Bridge and Westminster was F. K. McClean who, flying a Short pusher biplane from Harty Ferry in mid-August 1912, passed between the upper and lower spans of Tower Bridge, and then underflew all the remaining bridges to Westminster where he landed on the river. No regulations forbade this escapade, but the police instructed McClean to taxy all the way back to Shadwell Basin before mooring!

The first officer of the Royal Flying Corps Reserves to be killed while engaged on military flying duties was Lt. E. Hotchkiss (the Bristol Company's chief flying instructor at Brooklands) who, with Lt. C. Bettington, was killed on 10th September 1912 when their Bristol monoplane crashed on a flight from Salisbury Plain. The aircraft suffered a structural failure, after which the wing fabric started to tear away and the aircraft crashed near Oxford. Within three weeks the flying of monoplanes by the Military had been banned by Col. Seely, Secretary of State for War, and although the ban was to last no more than five months it gave rise to an extraordinary prejudice against monoplanes in British military flying circles that was to persist for more than twenty years. (It is usually recorded that Hotchkiss' Bristol crashed on Port Meadow, Oxford, but the memorial tablet, confirms that in fact the accident occurred half a mile west of Godstow on the right bank of the River Thames, just north of Port Meadow.)

Memorial tablet erected at Godstow, Oxford, to Lieutenants Bettington and Hotchkiss, who were killed on 10th September, 1912

The number of Aviators' Certificates which had been awarded in the world by the end of 1912 was 2,480, though the number of actual pilots was slightly smaller as some had been awarded certificates in more than one country. One or two others had received certificates in countries which were not members of the *Fédération Aéronautique Internationale*. The massive superiority of France at this time is evident:

1	France	966	10	Holland	26
2	Great Britain	382	11	Argentine Republic	15
3	Germany	335		Spain	15
4	United States of America	193	13	Sweden	10
5	Italy	186	14	Denmark	8
6	Russia	162	15	Hungary	7
7	Austria	84	16	Norway	5
8	Belgium	58	17	Egypt	1
9	Switzerland	27			
				Total	2,480

Two British pilots had been killed during 1910; six aeroplane occupants were killed in 1911, fourteen in 1912 and twelve in 1913. By the outbreak of the First World War forty-eight British subjects had lost their lives in aeroplanes.

CHAPTER 2 **MILITARY AVIATION**

"I hope these new mechanic meteors will prove only playthings for the learned and the idle, and not be converted into new engines of destruction to the human race, as is so often the case of refinements or discoveries in science."

Horace Walpole, 1782. (1717–1797)

The first military man to die in an aeroplane crash, and also the first aeroplane casualty in the world was Lt. Thomas E. Selfridge of the U.S. Army on 17th September 1908 at Fort Myer, Virginia; his pilot was Orville Wright, who was seriously injured in the crash.

The first aeroplane purchased by the American Government was a Wright Biplane, *Miss Columbia*, sold by the Wright Brothers on 30th July 1909. The price was $25,000, but a bonus of $5,000 was awarded as the specified maximum speed of 40 m.p.h. (64 km./hr.) was exceeded. The aircraft was constructed at Dayton, Ohio.

The first military firearm to be fired from an aeroplane was a rifle fired by Lt. Jacob Earl Fickel, U.S. Army, from his single-seat Curtiss biplane at a target at Sheepshead Bay, New York City, on 20th August 1910.

The first missiles dropped by an American were lead darts dropped by Glenn Hammond Curtiss on 30th June 1910 from a height of 50 feet (15 m.) during trials at Hammondsport, N.Y.

The first German active duty officer to receive a pilot's licence was Lt. Richard von Thiedemann, a Hussar officer. He made his first solo flight on 23rd July 1910.

The first explosive bombs dropped by American pilots were those dropped by Lt. Myron Sidney Crissy and Philip O. Parmelee during trials on 7th January 1911 at San Francisco, Calif.

The first American aeroplane armed with a machine gun was a Wright Biplane flown by Lt. Thomas de Witt Milling at College Park, Md., on 7th May 1912. The gunner, who was armed with a Lewis gun, was Charles de Forest Chandler of the U.S. Army Signal Corps.

The first serving officer of the British Army to be awarded an aviator's certificate in England was Capt. G. W. P. Dawes* who was awarded Certificate No. 17 for qualification on a Humber monoplane at Wolverhampton on 26th July 1910.

FORMATION OF THE FIRST BRITISH MILITARY AEROPLANE SQUADRONS

(The Royal Flying Corps came into being officially on 13th May 1912.)

Squadron	Date	Remarks
No. 1 (Airship and Kite) Sqdn.	13th May 1912	Formed out of No. 1 Airship Company, Air Battalion.
No. 2 (Aeroplane) Sqdn.	13th May 1912	Formed from scratch.
No. 3 (Aeroplane) Sqdn.	13th May 1912	Formed out of No. 2 Aeroplane Company, Air Battalion.
No. 4 (Aeroplane) Sqdn.	16th May 1912	Formed from scratch.
No. 5 (Aeroplane) Sqdn.	26th July 1913	Formed from scratch at Farnborough.
No. 6 (Aeroplane) Sqdn.	31st Jan. 1914	Formed from scratch at Farnborough.
No. 7 (Aeroplane) Sqdn.	May 1914	Formed from scratch.
No. 1 (Aeroplane) Sqdn.	May 1914	Formed out of No. 1 Airship and Kite Sqdn., R.F.C.

The first Swedish military pilot was Capt. G. von Porat of the Royal Swedish Engineers who, with two other military pilots, gained his military flying brevét at the Nieuport School in France in 1912 but did not qualify for a Swedish certificate. In 1914 he was injured in a flying accident and joined the aeroplane department of *Södertalge Verkstäder.*

The first German Air Service pilot to be killed on active service was Oberleutnant Reinhold Jahnow. He was fatally injured in a crash at Malmédy, Belgium, on 12th August 1914. He was holder of German pilot's licence No. 80, and a veteran of several reconnaissance flights for the Turks during the Balkan campaign of 1912.

The first Mexican military pilot was Maj. Alberto Salinas who learned to fly in the U.S.A. and was awarded pilot's flying certificate No. 170 by the Aero Club of America in 1912. He was also founder of Mexican Military Aviation in that year.

The first military aviation establishment in the Argentine was the Military Flying School at El Palomar, opened during the autumn of 1912; the first flying course commenced instruction on Farman biplanes on 4th November that year and was attended by twelve pilots. One of these, Sub-Teniente Manuel Origone, was killed on 19th January 1913 and was thus **the first military air casualty in the Argentine.**

---

* Capt. George William Patrick Dawes died on 17th March 1960 aged 80. He had served in South Africa between 1900 and 1902 when he was awarded the Queen's Medal with three clasps, and the King's Medal with two clasps. He took up flying privately in 1909 and was posted to the R.F.C. on its formation in 1912 and commanded the Corps in the Balkans from 1916 to 1918, during which time he was awarded the D.S.O. and the A.F.C., was mentioned in despatches seven times, and awarded the Croix de Guerre with three palms, the Serbian Order of White Eagle, the Order of the Redeemer of Greece and created Officer of the Legion d'Honneur. He served with the Royal Air Force in the Second World War as a Wing Commander, retiring in 1946 with the M.B.E. He thus was one of the very few officers who served actively in the Boer War and both World Wars.

The first Siamese military pilots were Maj. Luang Sakdi Salyavudh, Lt. Thip and Capt. Luang Avudh Sikikorn, engineers of the Royal Siamese Army, who obtained their pilots' certificates at Villacoublay, France, on 22nd October 1912, 12th May and 30th June 1913 respectively. Maj. Luang Sakdi subsequently took his military pilot's brevét. **The first flights by aeroplanes in Siam** were undertaken by these officers in December 1913 flying Nieuport and Breguet aircraft exported from France.

The first military aircraft acquired by China were six 80 h.p. and six 50 h.p. Caudrons ordered from France in March 1913.

The first night flight by a British military aircraft took place either on the night of 15th/16th or 16th/17th April 1913. Lt. R. Cholmondeley, of No. 3 Squadron, Military Wing, R.F.C., flew a Maurice Farman biplane from Larkhill to Upavon and back by moonlight.

The Sikorsky Ilya Mourametz

The first four-engined aeroplane in the world was the Sikorsky *Grand* of 1913. The Sikorsky *Ilya Mourametz* followed in February 1914 and was a biplane powered by four 100-h.p. tractor engines mounted on the lower wing. The *Ilya Mourametz V* dropped 600 lb. (270 kg.) of bombs on 15th February 1915 over the German lines on the Eastern Front.

●

The first four-engined bomber to see active service was the *Ilya Mourametz* (see above), designed by Igor Sikorsky, head of the aeronautical department of the Russian Baltic Railway Car Factory at Petrograd. By the time of the Russian Revolution 73 had been delivered to the military; some 400 bombing sorties were made by the type. It carried up to sixteen crew members and, as with the German R-Type bombers of 1918, routine servicing and minor repairs could be carried out in flight. It is believed that only one was ever shot down by enemy fighters.

The first French airmen to be killed on active service were Capitaine Hervé and his observer, named Roëland. During the colonial campaign in Morocco early in 1914 they made a forced landing in the desert and were killed by local Arabs.

The first military flying corps in Siam was formed on 23rd March 1914 by Chief of the Siamese General Staff, H.R.H. the Prince of Piscnoulok. A detachment of volunteer airmen was sent to France in 1917 but their final training was not completed before the Armistice.

The first military operations involving the use of American aeroplanes were those against Vera Cruz in April 1914 when several Curtiss AB flying boats were carried to the port aboard USS *Mississippi*. The first such military flight was undertaken by Lt. (Jg) P. N. L. Bellinger who took off in the Curtiss AB-3 flying boat on 25th April in order to search for mines in the harbour.

Curtiss AB flying boat

The first Air Service of the U.S. Army was established on 18th July 1914 when an aviation section was formed as part of the Signal Corps with a "paper" strength of 60 officers and 260 men. The entire equipment amounted to six aeroplanes.

THE FIRST WORLD WAR

The first British airmen to be killed on active service were 2nd Lt. R. R. Skene and a mechanic named Barlow, of No. 3 Squadron, R.F.C., on 12th August 1914. Flying from Netheravon to Dover to form up for the Channel crossing their aircraft, a Blériot two-seater of "C" Flight, landed because of engine trouble. Shortly after taking off again, the aircraft crashed into trees and both occupants were killed.

The first British aeroplane to land on the Continent after the outbreak of the First World War was a B.E.2A, No. 347, of No. 2 Squadron, R.F.C., flown by Lt. H. D. Harvey-Kelly. He left Dover at 06·25 hrs. and landed near Amiens at 08·20 hrs. on 13th August 1914.

The first bombs to be dropped upon a capital city from an aircraft fell on the Quai de Valmy, Paris, in August 1914. The pilot of the German *Taube* aeroplane has been variously identified as Leutnant Franz von Hiddeson and Leutnant Ferdinand von Hiddessen. A similar confusion obscures the date of the attack (either 13th or 30th August), and the number of bombs dropped (either two or three). One account states that two French civilians were killed and several injured.

The only British aeroplane fitted with a machine gun at the outbreak of the First World War was a Henry Farman biplane of No. 5 Squadron, R.F.C., flown by 2nd Lt. L. A. Strange, which the pilot had fitted with a Lewis gun in the front cockpit. On 22nd August 1914 Strange and his gunner, Lt. L. da C. Penn-Gaskell, unsuccessfully pursued an enemy aircraft over Mauberge. Strange was subsequently ordered by his commanding officer to remove both the gun and its mounting, on account of the deterioration in the aircraft's performance caused by their weight.

The first enemy aircraft forced down in combat by British aircraft was a German two-seater forced to land on 25th August 1914 by three aircraft of No. 2 Squadron, R.F.C.

The first aeroplane to be destroyed by ramming was an Austrian two-seater flown by Leutnant Baron von Rosenthal, rammed over Galicia on 26th August 1914 by Staff Captain P. N. Nesteroff of the Imperial Russian XI Corps Air Squadron, who was flying an unarmed Morane Saulnier monoplane scout. Both pilots were killed.

The first British air raid on Germany was by four aircraft of the Eastchurch R.N.A.S. Squadron. On 22nd September 1914 two aircraft took off from Antwerp to attack the airship sheds at Düsseldorf, two to attack the airship sheds at Cologne. Only the aircraft flown by Flt. Lt. Collet found the target—the sheds at Düsseldorf—and his 20-lb. (9 kg.) Hales bombs, while probably on target, failed to explode. All aircraft returned safely.

The first aeroplane in the world to be shot down and destroyed by another was a German two-seater, possibly an Aviatik, shot down over Rheims on 5th October 1914 by Sergent Joseph Frantz and Caporal Quénault in a Voisin pusher of *Escadrille V.B. 24*. The weapon used is believed to have been a Hotchkiss machine gun.

The first successful British air raid on Germany took place on 8th October 1914. Sqdn. Cdr. Spenser D. A. Grey and Flt. Lt. R. L. G. Marix of the Eastchurch R.N.A.S. Squadron flew from Antwerp in Sopwith Tabloids (Nos. 167 and 168) to attack airship sheds at Düsseldorf and Cologne with 20 lb. (9 kg.) Hales bombs. Grey failed to find the target, bombed Cologne railway station and returned to Antwerp. Marix reached his target at Düsseldorf, bombed the shed from 600 ft. (200 m.) and destroyed it and Zeppelin Z.IX inside. His aircraft was damaged by gunfire, and he eventually crash-landed 20 miles (30 km.) from Antwerp, returning to the city on a bicycle borrowed from a peasant.

The first aeroplane raid on Great Britain, by one aircraft, took plane on 21st December 1914. Two bombs fell in the sea near Admiralty Pier at Dover.

The first bomb dropped by an enemy aircraft on British soil, and the second aeroplane raid on Great Britain, again by one aircraft, took place on 24th December 1914. One bomb exploded near Dover Castle.

The first Russian woman to serve as a military pilot (and probably the first in the world) was Princess Eugenie Mikhailovna Shakhovskaya. Gaining her certificate at Johannisthal, Germany, on 16th August 1911, Princess Shakhovskaya made a personal request to the Tsar on the outbreak of the First World War that she be allowed to serve as a military pilot. In November 1914 she was posted to the 1st Field Air Squadron as a reconnaissance pilot.*

The first airship raid on Great Britain was carried out on 19th January 1915 by three German Navy Zeppelins, L3, L4 and L6. They took off from Hamburg and Nordholz. L6 was forced to return through engine trouble but L3 and L4 arrived over the Norfolk coast at about 20.00 hrs; bombs were dropped in the Yarmouth area, and several people were killed and scores injured. The two airships were both wrecked on the coast of Jutland during their second attempt on 17th February 1915, the surviving crews being interned.

---

* Princess Shakhovskaya survived both the War and the Revolution; indeed, she subsequently served in the *Cheka* (Bolshevik secret police) at Kiev, in the post of chief executioner—unusual work for a young woman of noble birth.

1. B.E.2a of the Eastchurch Squadron, Royal Naval Air Service, flown by Sqn. Cdr. Charles R. Samson in France and Belgium during the early months of the First World War. Samson formed an affection for *No. 50*, and it accompanied him to Tenedos when he was posted to command naval aircraft in the Dardanelles campaign; in the course of the campaign he continued to fly the B.E.2a on reconnaissance, artillery spotting and bombing missions against the Turkish forces. Details of Samson's career may be found in the text.

2. Nieuport 17 *B1566*, flown during the early summer of 1917 by Capt. William A. Bishop, D.S.O., M.C., of No. 60 Squadron R.F.C. Bishop, whose career is described in fuller detail in the text, is thought to have achieved nearly 20 of his 72 confirmed victories while flying *B1566*.

3. Sopwith Triplane *N5492* "Black Maria", flown during the spring and early summer of 1917 by Flt. Sub-Lt. Raymond Collishaw as commander of "B" Flight, No. 10 Squadron R.N.A.S. During 27 days of June 1917 Collishaw flew this aircraft to victory over 16 enemy machines, including the Albatros D III of *Jasta 11* flown by the ace, Leutnant Karl Allmenröder. *N5492* was eventually shot down in July while being flown in combat by another pilot. Details of Collishaw's career may be found in the text.

4. S.E.5A *B4863*, one of the aircraft flown during the summer and autumn of 1917 by Capt. James T. B. McCudden, M.C., M.M., as commander of "B" Flight, No. 56 Squadron R.F.C. Details of McCudden's career may be found in the text. During the winter of 1917/18 he is known to have flown S.E.5A *B4891*, fitted with the red-painted propeller spinner from an LVG CV two-seater which he shot down on 30th November.

5. Sopwith 7F.1 Snipe *E8102*, flown on 27th October 1918 by Maj. William G. Barker, D.S.O., M.C., attached to No. 201 Squadron R.F.C. Flying alone on the early morning of 27th October, Barker had shot down a German two-seater when he was attacked and wounded in the right thigh by a Fokker D VII. Barker's aircraft lost height in a spin; in the course of the next few minutes he passed through successive layers of a large German formation, being attacked on four separate occasions by groups of at least a dozen Fokker scouts. Before he finally managed to bring his damaged Snipe down for a successful forced landing, Barker had been wounded twice more (in the left thigh and the left elbow); had lost consciousness twice, and twice recovered and regained control of his aircraft; and had shot down three more enemy aircraft. This epic engagement led to the award of the Victoria Cross.

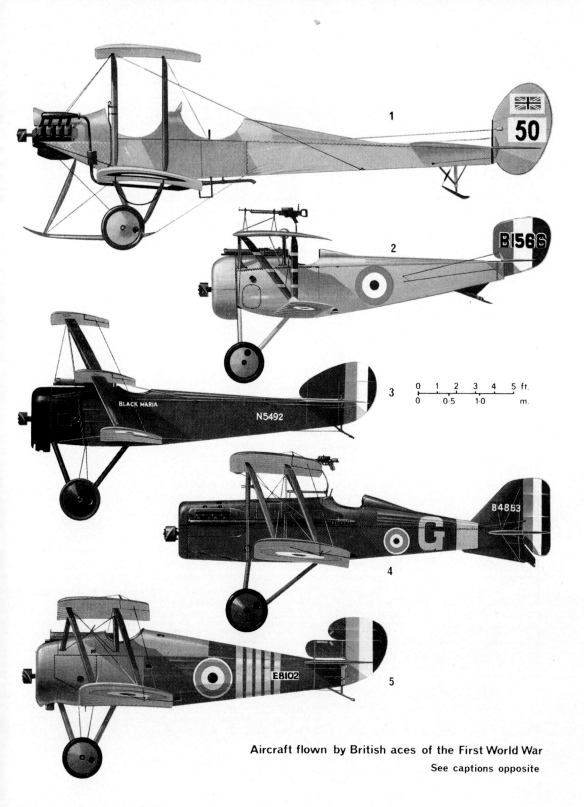

Aircraft flown by British aces of the First World War

See captions opposite

6. Fokker D VII flown during the spring of 1918 by Hauptmann Rudolf Berthold as commanding officer of *Jagdgeschwader Nr. 2*. Sixth in the roll of German aces, with 44 confirmed victories, Berthold suffered continual pain from a wound which rendered his right arm useless. He had the controls of his Fokker altered to compensate for his disability and continued to fly, scoring at least 16 of his victories during a period when his arm refused to heal and was rejecting splinters of suppurating bone almost daily. Active in the *Freikorps* movement in the immediate post-war period, Berthold led an anti-Communist band known as the *Eiserne Schar Berthold*. He was murdered—by strangulation with the ribbon of his *Ordre Pour le Mérite*—on 15th March 1920, after accepting a safe conduct offer from a Communist group in Harburg.

7. Siemens–Schuckert D III flown late in the summer of 1918 by Oberleutnant Ernst Udet as commanding officer of *Jasta 4*, based at Metz. This gifted pilot was credited with 62 victories, and in this respect was second only to Manfred von Richthofen; his amiable and rather flamboyant disposition made him a popular commander, although an early over-confidence sometimes led him into difficulties. He survived the war, and became well known as a stunt pilot, explorer, and international aviation "playboy". His extrovert nature and long friendship with many leading personalities in German aviation led to senior appointments under the Nazi régime; but he eventually found himself playing a rôle for which he was temperamentally unsuited, and a growing sense of estrangement culminated in his suicide on 17th November 1941. The monogram displayed on his aircraft referred to his fiancée, Fraulein Lola Zink.

8. Fokker Dr I, number *152/17*, sometimes flown by Rittmeister Manfred, Freiherr von Richthofen as commanding officer of *Jagdgeschwader Nr. 1* during the early months of 1918. (Details of Richthofen's career may be found in the body of the text.) Richthofen is known to have been flying this aircraft on 12th March 1918 when he gained the 64th of his 80 confirmed victories; his victim on that occasion was a Bristol F.2B, number *B1251*, of No. 62 Squadron R.F.C. brought down near Nauroy. The crew, Lieutenant L. C. F. Clutterbuck and Second-Lieutenant H. J. Sparks, survived the crash and were made prisoners.

9. Albatros D III flown during the spring of 1917 by Leutnant Werner Voss, whose 48 confirmed victories place him fourth in the roll of German aces. Voss became a pilot in May 1916 and served his apprenticeship in the famous *Jasta Boelcke*; he was a born flyer and fighter, but lacked the leadership qualities of Richthofen and Berthold. During the spring of 1917 he is believed to have served briefly with both *Jasta 5* and *Jasta 14*, and it is with the former unit that this Albatros is usually associated. In July 1917, at the request of his friend Richthofen, Voss was posted to command *Jasta 10* in *Jagdgeschwader Nr. 1*. During their lifetimes, Voss was second-ranking ace to Richthofen; he was finally killed on 23rd September 1917 in a prolonged dogfight between himself (flying Fokker Dr I *103/17*) and one Albatros scout, against seven S.E.5A's, including the whole of "B" Flight, No. 56 Squadron R.F.C., led by Captain J. T. B. McCudden. Voss was twenty years and five months old when he died.

10. Fokker E I, number *3/15*, flown by Leutnant Oswald Boelcke of *Fliegerabteilung 62*, based at Douai in August 1915. (Details of Boelcke's career may be found in the body of the text.) It it is believed that this was the machine flown by Leutnant Max Immelmann of the same unit when he gained his first victory on 1st August 1915.

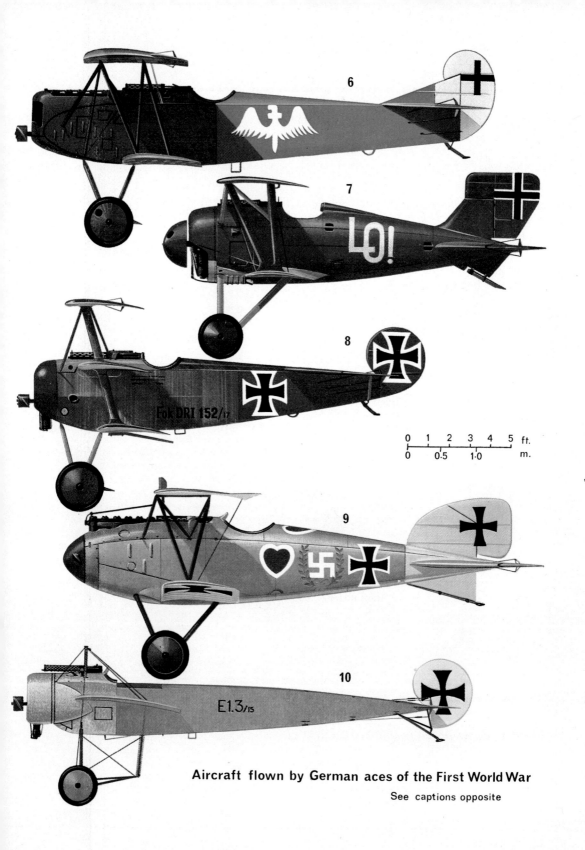

6

7

8

Fok DRI 152/17

9

10

E1.3/15

Aircraft flown by German aces of the First World War

See captions opposite

The first British bombing raid in direct tactical support of a ground operation occurred on 10th March 1915, comprising attacks on railways bringing up German reinforcements in the Menin and Courtrai areas during the Neuve Chapelle offensive.

The first air Victoria Cross was awarded posthumously to 2nd Lt. W. B. Rhodes-Moorhouse, pilot of a B.E.2 of No. 2 Squadron, R.F.C., for gallantry in a low-level bombing attack on Courtrai railway station on 26th April 1915.

2nd Lt. W. B. Rhodes-Moorhouse, V.C.

The first American aeroplanes used in actual military operations were eight Curtiss JNs of the 1st Aero Squadron, U.S. Army, which accompanied the punitive expedition under General John Pershing to Mexico in March 1916.

The first airship to be shot down was Zeppelin LZ37 on the night of 6th/7th June 1915. In company with LZ38 and LZ39, the airship set out from Bruges to bomb London but adverse weather later forced them to alter course for their secondary targets —railways in the Calais area. LZ37 was located and attacked by Flt. Sub-Lt. R. A. J. Warneford of No. 1 Squadron, R.N.A.S., flying a Morane-Saulnier Parasol from Dunkirk. Warneford's only means of attack were six 20 lb. (9 kg.) bombs; he followed the airship from Ostend to Ghent, being forced to keep his distance by fire from the airship's gunners. He made a single pass over the airship as it began to descend to its base at Gontrode, dropping all six bombs from about 150 ft. (50 m.) above it. The sixth exploded, and the airship fell in flames on a suburb of Ghent killing four people on the ground. Only one member of Oberleutnant Otto van de Haegen's crew survived. Warneford returned safely to base after making a forced landing to repair a broken fuel line. He was informed the following evening that he had been awarded the Victoria Cross; he died twelve days later when the tail of a Henry Farman pusher biplane collapsed in mid-air.

The first American pilot to be shot down in the First World War was H. Clyde Balsley who served with the *Lafayette Escadrille* on the Western Front and who was shot down and wounded near Verdun on 18th June 1916.

The first American pilot to be killed in the First World War was Victor Emmanuel Chapman of the *Lafayette Escadrille*, who was shot down near Verdun on 23rd June 1916.

The first Peruvian military pilots were 2nd Lt. Enrique Ruiz and Aspirant Guillermo Protzel who were seconded to El Palomar, Argentina, in 1916 and graduated with the fifth Flying Course. (Argentinian records however suggest that Guardia Marina Ismael Montoya and Guardia Marina Roberto Velazco (both Peruvians) also attended this course, and that Ruiz was killed on 13th March 1917 while flying a Blériot monoplane.)

The magnificent Albatros D I, first true fighter aircraft in the world

The first British unit to be formed specifically for night bombing operations was No. 100 Squadron, R.F.C., which formed at Hingham, Norfolk, in February 1917, and crossed to France on 21st March. A week later the unit received its first aircraft, twelve F.E.2bs, then being based at St. André aux Bois. Moving to Le Hameau on 1st April 1917, the squadron received four B.E.2es. The first operations were two raids on the night of 5th/6th April 1917 on Douai airfield, home base of the "Richthofen Circus". One F.E.2b failed to return; four hangars were badly damaged by bombs.

The first American, serving under American colours, to shoot down an enemy aircraft was Lt. Stephen W. Thompson, who destroyed a German scout on 5th February 1918 over the Western Front.

The most successful American pilot to serve exclusively with an American unit in the First World War was Capt. Edward Vernon Rickenbacker who was credited with the destruction of 22 enemy aeroplanes and four balloons.

(Left) Capt. Edward V. Rickenbacker

The first American, serving under American colours, to shoot down five enemy aircraft, (in American terms, an "ace"), was Lt. Douglas Campbell who shot down his fifth German victim on 31st May 1918. *(Right)*

The first combat aeroplane to enter production in the United States was the British de Havilland D.H.4. The first machine was completed in February 1918, and by 5th November the same year 3,431 had been completed. A total of 4,846 was built before production stopped in 1919. The D.H.4 (or DH-4) was the only American-built aeroplane to fly over enemy territory during the First World War (which excludes of course the operations against Mexico in 1916).

The fastest German aeroplane to reach combat status during the First World War was the Fokker D VIII parasol monoplane single-seat fighting scout, with a top speed of 127·5 m.p.h. (204 km./hr.) at sea level. It was powered by a 110 h.p. Oberursel U II 9-cylinder rotary engine and was armed with two synchronised Spandau machine guns. It reached front line *Jastas* in August 1918 but was withdrawn shortly afterwards owing to a number of accidents following wing failure. Leutnant Theo Osterkamp of the *Marine Jagdgeschwader* won his 25th and 26th victories while flying a Fokker D VIII.

The largest German aeroplane to fly during the First World War was the Aviatik R-Type (*Reisen-flugzeug*) Giant heavy bomber; basically a Zeppelin Staaken R VI built under licence by Automobil und Aviatik A.G., this colossal aeroplane had a wing span of 180 ft. 5½ in. (55·0 m.) and a length of 88 ft. 7 in. (27·0 m.). It was powered by two 250 h.p. Benz IVa and two 500 h.p. Benz VI engines which bestowed a maximum speed of 90 m.p.h. (145 km./hr.). It is believed to have flown bombing missions on the Eastern Front in 1918.

The greatest altitude attained by a German aircraft on test during the First World War was 31,160 ft. (9,500 m.) by the Fokker V 10, which was in effect a Fokker Dr.I triplane powered by a 145 h.p. Oberursel Ur III engine. This flight was probably undertaken early in 1918.

The fastest German aircraft scheduled for combat service during the First World War was the Siemens-Schuckert D VI. Designed and ordered during 1918, this single-seat fighting scout, a parasol monoplane powered by a 160 h.p. Siemens-Halske Sh IIIa engine, was not completed until January 1919, but on test returned a maximum speed of 137·5 m.p.h. (220 km./hr.) during the spring of that year.

The heaviest German aeroplane built during the First World War is believed to have been the Siemens-Schuckert R VIII which, with a wing span of 157 ft. 6 in., weighed 34,980 lb. (15,900 kg.) fully loaded. It was powered by six 300-h.p. Basse und Selve BuS IV engines. It was not completed until 1919 and was damaged before flight; armistice prohibitions prevented its repair.

The largest aeroplane to be powered by a powerplant driving a single propeller was the Linke-Hofman R II of Germany. This aircraft, of which only one example ever flew (shortly after the Armistice of 1918), was designed on the principle of simply scaling up a conventional single-engine biplane. With a span of 138 ft. 4 in. (42·16 m.) and a length of 66 ft. 7⅞ in. (20·32 m.), the R II (R55/17) was powered by four 260 h.p. Mercedes D IVa engines, arranged in pairs in the nose, driving a single airscrew through a central gearbox. **The airscrew was the largest ever used by an aeroplane** and had a diameter of 22 ft. 8 in. (0·61 m.) and was driven at 545 r.p.m. The maximum speed of the aircraft was 81·25 m.p.h. (130 km./hr.).

Maj. W. G. Barker with the Sopwith Camel he flew as commander of No. 28 Squadron, R.F.C., in Italy.
An account of the action in which he won the Victoria Cross may be found on page 32

THE GREAT AIR FIGHTERS OF THE FIRST WORLD WAR

British and Empire pilots credited with 40 or more confirmed victories

Maj. Edward Mannock, V.C., D.S.O.,** M.C.*.	73
Lt. Col. W. A. Bishop, V.C., C.B., D.S.O.,* M.C., D.F.C., E.D.	72
Lt. Col. R. Collishaw, C.B., D.S.O.,* O.B.E., D.S.C., D.F.C.	60
Maj. J. T. B. McCudden, V.C., D.S.O.,* M.C.,* M.M.	57
Capt. A. W. Beauchamp-Proctor, V.C., D.S.O., M.C.,* D.F.C.	54
Maj. D. R. MacLaren, D.S.O., M.C.,* D.F.C.	54
Lt. Col. W. G. Barker, V.C., D.S.O.,* M.C.**	53
Capt. R. A. Little, D.S.O.,* D.S.C.*	47
Capt. P. F. Fullard, C.B.E., D.S.O., M.C.,* A.F.C.	46
Capt. G. E. H. McElroy, M.C.,** D.F.C.*	46
Capt. Albert Ball, V.C., D.S.O.,** M.C.	44
Capt. J. Gillmore, D.S.O., M.C.**	44
Maj. T. F. Hazell, D.S.O., M.C., D.F.C.*.	41
Capt. J. I. T. Jones, D.S.O., M.C., D.F.C.,* M.M.	40

In addition to the above
  11 pilots gained between 30 and 39 victories
  40 pilots gained between 20 and 29 victories
  126 pilots gained between 10 and 19 victories
  341 pilots gained between 5 and 9 victories.
Thus by the "five victory" convention (see below), the British and Empire air
forces of the First World War produced 532 aces.

Albert Ball, Britain's first great fighter ace

Ernst Udet, Germany's second ranking ace, with Fokker D VII

German pilots credited with 40 or more confirmed victories

Rittmeister Manfred, Freiherr von Richthofen	80
Oberleutnant Ernst Udet	62
Oberleutnant Erich Loewenhardt	53
Leutnant Werner Voss	48
Leutnant Fritz Rumey	45
Hauptmann Rudolph Berthold	44
Leutnant Paul Baumer	43
Leutnant Josef Jacobs	41
Hauptmann Bruno Loerzer	41
Hauptmann Oswald Boelcke	40
Leutnant Franz Büchner	40
Oberleutnant Lothar, Freiherr von Richthofen	40

All these pilots were decorated with the *Ordre Pour le Mérite*.

In addition to the above
> 21 pilots gained between 30 and 39 victories
> 38 pilots gained between 20 and 29 victories
> 98 pilots gained between 10 and 19 victories
> 196 pilots gained between 5 and 9 victories.

Thus by the "five victory" convention, the Imperial German air forces of the First World War produced 364 aces.

Werner Voss (see page 34)

French pilots credited with 40 or more confirmed victories

Capitaine René P. Fonck	75
Capitaine Georges M. L. J. Guynemer	54
Lieutenant Charles E. J. M. Nungesser	45
Capitaine Georges F. Madon	41

In addition to the above
> 2 pilots gained between 30 and 39 victories
> 8 pilots gained between 20 and 29 victories
> 39 pilots gained between 10 and 19 victories
> 105 pilots gained between 5 and 9 victories.

Thus the French air forces of the First World War produced 158 aces.

The ten most successful American pilots of the First World War

Capt. Edward V. Rickenbacker (C.M.H.)	26
2nd Lt. Frank Luke, Jr. (C.M.H.)	21
Maj. G. Raoul Lufbery (*Left*)	17
Lt. G. A. Vaughn, Jr.	13
2nd Lt. F. L. Baylies	12
Capt. F. E. Kindley	12
Capt. E. W. Springs	12
Lt. D. E. Putnam	11
Maj. R. G. Landis	10
Capt. J. M. Swaab	10

In addition to the above 78 pilots gained between five and nine victories; thus America produced during the First World War 88 aces. (It should be noted that the above figures include pilots who served with foreign air forces only, pilots who served with the American forces only, and pilots with mixed service, and all victories gained by these pilots irrespective of service.)

The ten most successful Italian pilots of the First World War

Maggiore Francesco Baracca	34
Tenente Silvio Scaroni	26
Tenente-Colonello Pier Ruggiero Piccio	24
Tenente Flavio Torello Baracchini	21
Capitano Fulco Ruffo di Calabria	20
Sergente Marziale Cerutti	17
Tenente Ferruccio Ranza	17
Tenente Luigi Olivari	12
Tenente Giovanni Ancillotto	11
Sergente Antonio Reali	11

In addition to the above 33 pilots gained between five and ten victories; thus Italy produced 43 aces during the First World War.

The five most successful Austro-Hungarian pilots of the First World War

Hauptmann Godwin Brumowski	*c.* 40
Offizierstellvertreter Julius Arigi	*c.* 32
Oberleutnant Frank Linke-Crawford	*c.* 30
Oberleutnant Benno Fiala, Ritter von Fernbrugg . . .	*c.* 29
Leutnant Josef Kiss	19

(It should be noted that Austrian, Hungarian and Italian sources disagree as to the absolute accuracy of four of these pilots' scores.)

In addition to the above approximately 25 pilots apparently gained between five and eighteen victories. Thus it can be stated only with reasonable certainty that the Austro-Hungarian Imperial air forces produced between 25 and 30 aces during the First World War.

The most successful Imperial Russian pilots of the First World War

Staff Capt. A. A. Kazakov D.S.O., M.C., D.F.C. (*Left*) . . .	17
Capt. P. V. d'Argueeff	15
Lt. Commander A. P. Seversky	13
Lt. I. W. Smirnoff	12
Lt. M. Safonov	11
Capt. B. Sergeivsky	11
Ensign E. M. Thomson	11

In addition to the above either 11 or 12 pilots are thought to have gained between five and ten victories; thus the Imperial Russian air forces are believed to have produced either 18 or 19 aces during the First World War.

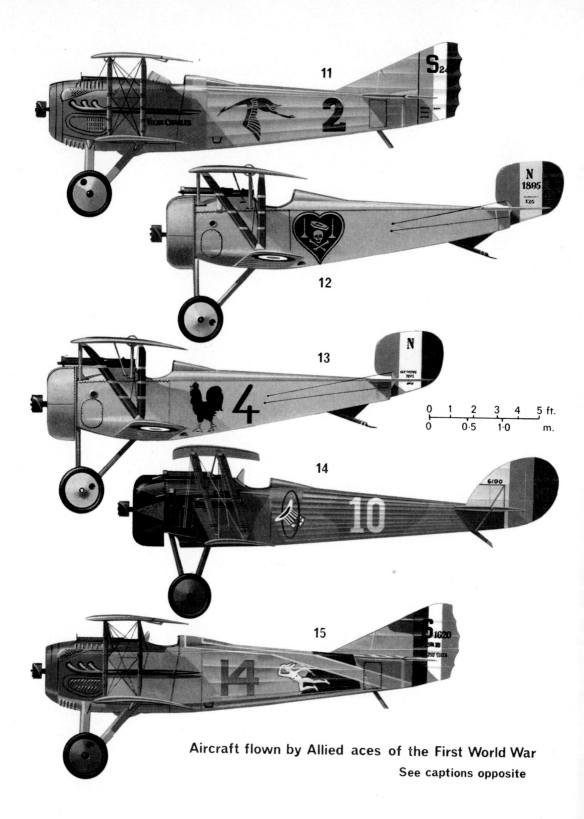

Aircraft flown by Allied aces of the First World War
See captions opposite

11. SPAD VII *245* "*Vieux Charles*", flown by Capitaine Georges Guynemer of *Escadrille SPA.3*, *Groupe de Combat No. 12* "*Les Cigognes*", *Service Aéronautique Française*. Guynemer, whose 54 confirmed victories place him second on France's roll of aces, flew this aircraft early in 1917; full details of his career may be found in the text. The stork insignia was the badge of *SPA.3*.

12. Nieuport 17 *1895*, flown by Lt. Charles Nungesser of *Escadrille N.65* during the summer of 1917. Third among French aces with 45 confirmed victories, Nungesser was a pilot of enormous determination in the face of constant pain; his career is described in the text. He first used his macabre personal marking in November 1915, and from that time onward it was painted on all his aircraft. From May 1917 onwards the wings (and later the fuselage top decking) of his aircraft were painted with broad *tricoleur* stripes as an additional identification; in that month he was forced to shoot down a British aircraft in self-defence.

13. Nieuport 17 flown during the summer of 1917 by Sgt. Marius Ambrogi of *Escadrille N.90*. "Marc" Ambrogi was a specialist in shooting down heavily defended observation balloons; these hazardous targets accounted for ten of his 14 confirmed victories. He survived the war, and later rejoined the colours to fight in the Second World War; in 1940 he was serving as deputy commander of *Groupe de Chasse I/8* when he shot down a Junkers Ju 52/3m.

14. Nieuport 28 flown by Lt. Douglas Campbell of the 94th Aero Squadron, American Expeditionary Force, in March 1918. On 19th March he accompanied Maj. Raoul Lufbery and Lt. Edward Rickenbacker on the first patrol over enemy lines by an American unit; and on 14th April he became the first American-trained pilot to score an aerial victory, his victim being an Albatros shot down near the squadron's base at Toul. His fifth victory on 31st May 1918 made him the first ace who had served exclusively with the American forces. He was to score one further victory before a wound put him out of the war on 6th June 1918; he was eventually discharged in 1919 with the rank of Captain.

15. SPAD XIII *1620*, flown by Lt. David E. Putnam of the 139th Aero Squadron, American Expeditionary Force, in the summer of 1918. Putnam was officially credited with 11 victories, but unofficial estimates indicate a considerably higher total. He flew with various French units between December 1917 and July 1918 (though not, as is sometimes claimed, with the *Escadrille Lafayette*), and gained his first victory on 19th January 1918. On 5th June he fought an epic battle against ten enemy aircraft, sending five down destroyed or damaged. He was transferred in July to the 139th Squadron, in which he served as a Flight Commander until his death in action on 12th September 1918.

16. SPAD XIII *1719*, flown by Lt. Gervais Raoul Lufbery of *Escadrille SPA.124*—the *Escadrille Lafayette*—during the winter of 1917–18. With 17 confirmed victories Lufbery was third in the roll of American aces. Born in France of French parents who later emigrated to America, Lufbery travelled widely as a young man; when war broke out he joined the French Foreign Legion and obtained a quick transfer to the *Service Aéronautique*. In December 1914 Lufbery successfully applied for pilot training, and was posted to *Escadrille VB.106*. In May 1916 he was transferred to the *Escadrille Lafayette*, and had scored five victories by early October. His subsequent career brought him promotion and many decorations, including the first award of the British Military Cross to an American. With America's entry into the war Lufbery was transferred, with the rank of Major, to the U.S. Air Service, and was subsequently given command of the famous 94th Aero Squadron. He was killed on 19th May 1918; flying a Nieuport 28, he was attacking an Albatros two-seater reconnaissance aircraft over the 94th Squadron's base at Toul when his machine burst into flames. Lufbery fell from the

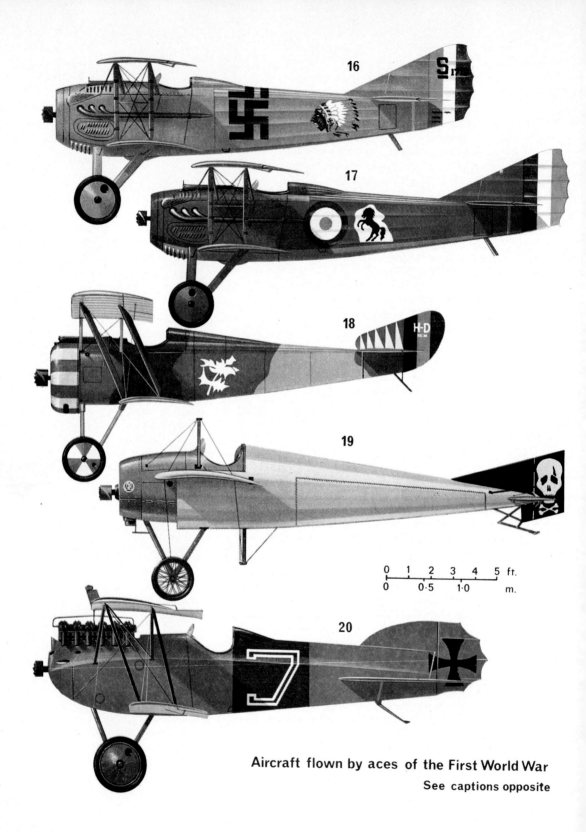

Aircraft flown by aces of the First World War
See captions opposite

(continued from p. 43)

burning aircraft at an altitude of 6,000 ft.—whether deliberately or accidentally will never be known. The Sioux Indian head insignia was the badge of *SPA.124*; the swastika was Lufbery's personal good luck symbol. At this early date it was naturally innocent of any political significance, and was used widely by pilots on both sides.

17. SPAD XIII flown by Maggiore Francesco Baracca as commanding officer of the *91ᵃ Squadriglia* of the Italian *Aeronautica del Regio Esercito* during the winter of 1917–18. Italy's leading ace with 34 confirmed victories, Baracca had qualified as a pilot in 1912, and had flying experience with many types of Italian, French and Belgian aircraft by the time Italy declared war on Austria in May 1915. His first victory was gained on 7th April 1916; leading a dawn patrol of Nieuport 11 scouts from the *70ᵃ Squadriglia*, he shot down an Aviatik two-seater near Medea. His fifth victory came on 25th November 1916, and from this date onwards he had his famous prancing horse insignia painted on all his aircraft. He continued to score steadily, including two "doubles"—on 21st and 26th October 1917—and was heavily decorated. He failed to return from a ground-strafing mission near Montello on 19th June 1918, and his body and burned-out aircraft were not located until after the Austrian retreat; various theories about his death gained currency, but it seems most probable that, like so many other great air fighters of the First World War, he was killed by ground fire from some nameless infantryman crouching in a trench.

18. Hanriot HD-1 flown by Lt. Jan Olieslagers of the *1ᵉʳᵉ Escadrille de Chasse, Aviation Belge Militaire*. A pre-war motor-cycle racing star and a pilot since 1909, Olieslagers became one of the great names of Belgian aviation. He served with distinction in Belgium's first all-fighter squadron alongside such aces as Willy Coppens and André de Meulemeester; although his official score was six victories, his contemporaries in the *1ᵉʳᵉ Escadrille* maintained that he scored many more kills behind the German lines, where ground confirmation was seldom possible. Olieslagers died in Antwerp in 1942; the thistle insignia on his aircraft was the badge of the *1ᵉʳᵉ Escadrille*.

19. Morane Saulnier MS 5 scout flown during 1915 by Staff Captain Alexander Alexandrovitch Kazakov as commander of the XIX Corps Air Squadron, Russian Imperial Air Service. Kazakov is acknowledged as Russia's leading First World War ace with 17 confirmed victories, but unofficial estimates put his true score at 32. He conceived the idea of fixing a steel grapnel on a length of cable to his unarmed Morane scout, and flying low over enemy aircraft to tear away wings, control surfaces or flying wires. He scored his first victory on 18th March 1915, when he brought down an Albatros two-seater near Gusov partly by means of his grapnel, partly by ramming it with his undercarriage. A quiet and deeply religious man, Kazakov went on to command the 1st Fighter Group comprising four squadrons, and to receive 16 decorations including the British D.S.O., M.C., and D.F.C. During the British intervention in the Russian Civil War he was attached to the R.A.F., flying Sopwith Camels. Shortly after the announcement that British forces were to be withdrawn from the campaign, Kazakov died in a rather ambiguous and inexplicable flying accident on 3rd August 1919.

20. Phönix D I flown by Oberleutnant Frank Linke-Crawford as commander of *Fliegerkompagnie 60J*, Austro-Hungarian Imperial *Luftfahrtruppen*; this squadron was based at Feltre on the Piave front during the winter of 1917–18. With an official score of 30, Linke-Crawford stands third in the roll of Austro-Hungarian aces; little is known of his personal life, beyond the fact that he was a rather earnest and reserved young man who earned promotion at a rate considered phenomenal in the ultra-conservative Imperial forces. He fell in action on 31st July 1918 near Montello; various Italian and British pilots have been credited with his death, including Maj. W. G. Barker, V.C., but the truth will probably never be known.

The five Belgian aces of the First World War

2nd Lt. Willy Coppens, D.S.O.	37
Adjutant André de Meulemeester	11
2nd Lt. Edmond Thieffry	10
Capt. Fernand Jacquet, D.F.C.	7
Lt. Jan Olieslagers	6

The confirmation of aerial victories during the First World War was subject to the most stringent regulations, and this has led to confusion over the actual number of victories scored by various pilots. The figures quoted above are, with certain indicated exceptions, those officially accepted as accurate in the countries of origin, and refer only to confirmed victories within the letter of the regulations. They are thus more liable to err on the side of under- rather than over-statement. Where certain notable pilots are generally considered to have destroyed significantly more enemy aircraft than are allowed in their official totals, such unconfirmed figures are quoted below in the sections dealing with the pilots by name, or in the captions to the accompanying colour paintings.

Manfred von Richthofen in cockpit of Albatros, with pilots of his Jagdstaffel. Sitting in foreground in pale coat is his brother Lothar.

The "ace" system, and the policy of public recognition of particularly successful fighter pilots originated in France and was subsequently copied by many nations. Under the French system a pilot who scored five confirmed aerial victories was named in an official communiqué, and thereafter his career was subject of wide publicity. Successful pilots were, as a matter of policy, concentrated in certain units which enjoyed an enormous reputation, for example, the five Escadrilles (*3, 26, 73, 103* and briefly *167*) which made up the famous "Stork" group, *Groupe de Combat No. 12 "Les Cigognes"*. This latter step might be thought to have had a poor effect on the morale of less prominent units, and was peculiar to the French Air Service. The United States adopted the five-victory rule when their squadrons entered the War, and has applied it ever since. The ace system has never been followed by Great Britain however; while successful pilots naturally tended to become household names through service "grapevines" and normal journalistic activity, it has always been the official view that to single out individuals for massive publicity in this way would be harmful to the morale of the thousands of anonymous servicemen whose contribution to the war effort was just as great, if less glamorous. In Britain the term "ace" passed into everyday language, but did not and does not depend on any specific number of aerial victories. In Germany the leading fighter pilots were the subjects of considerable publicity, and it became normal practice for certain decorations to be awarded to them on the achievement of a certain number of victories, but no rigid mathematical formula was followed. (The German equivalent to the term "ace" was *Oberkanone*—loosely "top gun".)

The greatest ace of the First World War, in terms of confirmed aerial victories, was Rittmeister (Cavalry Captain) Manfred, Freiherr von Richthofen—the so-called "Red Baron". The eldest son of an aristocratic Silesian family, he was born on 2nd May 1882 and was killed in action on 21st April 1918, by which time he had been credited with 80 victories, had been awarded his country's highest decoration, commanded the élite unit of the Imperial German Air Service (*Luftstreitkräfte*), and was the object of universal adulation in his homeland and an ungrudging respect among his enemies. Early in the War Richthofen served on the Eastern Front as an officer in *Uhlan Regiment Nr. 1 "Kaiser Alexander III"*, and transferred to the Air Service in May 1915. His first operational posting was to *Feldfliegerabteilung Nr. 69*; with this unit he flew two-seater reconnaissance machines in the East—without apparently any unusual skill—and he continued to serve in general purpose units until September 1916 when he was lucky enough to be selected for *Jagdstaffel 2*, the single-seater scout squadron trained and led by the brilliant Oswald Boelcke (*q.v.*). By this time it was probable that Richthofen had already gained two victories, a Maurice Farman S.11 over Champagne in September 1915, and a Nieuport 11 near Douaumont on 25th April 1916—but for lack of ground confirmation these were not included in his official list of victories. His first officially recognised victory was over an F.E.2b, number *7018* of No. 11 Squadron, R.F.C.; Richthofen, flying an Albatros D II scout, shot this aircraft down on 17th September 1916, and the crew, 2nd Lt. L. B. F. Morris and Lt. T. Rees, both lost their lives. Richthofen continued to score steadily, and in January 1917 was awarded the coveted "Blue Max", the *Ordre pour le Mérite*. He was given command of *Jagdstaffel 11*, and began to enjoy considerable fame. A cold and calculating fighter, he brought to air combat the attitudes of the aristocratic huntsman; he maintained a collection of silver cups, each engraved with the particulars of a victim. His silversmith's most lucrative month was the "Bloody April" of 1917, when he shot down 21 aircraft. The most famous pilot to fall to his guns was Maj. Lanoe G. Hawker, V.C., D.S.O., commanding officer of No. 24 Squadron, R.F.C., who has been called "the English Boelcke" for his skill, vision and

von Richthofen flying a Fokker Dr I triplane

organising ability. Maj. Hawker, flying D.H.2 number *5964*, had himself gained nine victories when he was shot down after a prolonged and unequal

dogfight with Richthofen on 23rd November 1916, to become the "Red Baron's" eleventh victim. Late in June 1917 Richthofen was given command of a new formation, *Jagdgeschwader Nr. 1*, comprising *Jastas 4, 6, 10* and *11*; this group of squadrons became known to the Allies as "Richthofen's Flying Circus", partly on account of the bright colours used by various pilots to decorate and identify their aircraft. Contrary to popular legend Richthofen did not invariably fly a personal aircraft painted blood red overall; he flew several aircraft, Albatros D IIIs and Fokker Dr Is, and one of each type is thought to have been painted red overall; but he also used several which were only partially finished in red, an example of one such machine being illustrated in the accompanying colour pages. Richthofen's death on 21st April 1918 has been the subject of controversy ever since. He was flying Fokker Dr I number *425/17* when he became engaged in a low-level combat with two Sopwith Camels of No. 209 Squadron, R.A.F., over Sailly-le-Sec. At one point the aircraft of 2nd Lt. W. R. May was flying at low altitude with Richthofen in pursuit, and the aircraft of Capt. A. Roy Brown, D.F.C., behind the German; Brown opened fire in an attempt to save the inexperienced May from the enemy ace, and Richthofen's triplane was then seen to break away and crash-land. The exact relative timing of these events has never been established; but

Capt. A. Roy Brown, D.F.C.

whatever the details, Richthofen was found dead in his cockpit with a bullet wound in the chest. Brown was officially credited with his death, but prolonged, not to say hysterical research by many amateur and professional historians has failed to settle with any certainty whether the fatal shot was fired by Brown or by a member of an Australian Field Artillery battery which was putting up a considerable volume of small-arms fire at the time. Richthofen's last victim was 2nd Lt. D. G. Lewis, a Camel pilot of No. 3 Squadron, R.A.F., who was shot down, wounded and taken prisoner near Villers-Bretonneux the day before Richthofen's death.

The first true fighter leader of the First World War was Hauptmann Oswald Boelcke, whose name, with those of Richthofen and Immelmann, is still commemorated today in the honour title of a German Air Force combat unit. Boelcke was born in 1891 and was commissioned in a communications unit in 1912. He became interested in aviation during army manoeuvres, and gained his pilot's certificate at the Halberstadt Flying School on 15th August 1914. He was posted to La Ferte to join *Feldfliegerabteilung 13* in September, and, with his brother Wilhelm as observer, soon amassed a considerable number of sorties in army co-operation Albatros B II biplanes. By early 1915 he had 42 missions in his log-book, and had been awarded the Iron Cross, 2nd Class. The visit of Leutnant Parschau to his unit to demonstrate the Fokker M.8 monoplane scout fired him with enthusiam; and in April, having received the Iron Cross, 1st Class, he secured a posting to Hauptmann Kastner's *Feldfliegerabteilung 62*, where he flew an armed machine for the first time—an Albatros C I, number *162/15*. He displayed great spirit, and enabled his observer to shoot down a Morane by his skillful and aggressive flying. His greatest stroke of fortune came when he was selected to fly early examples of Fokker's E-series armed monoplane scouts; few were available, and Boelcke, Kastner and Leutnant Max Immelmann at first took turns to fly them. His success as a combat pilot was matched by his grasp of technical matters and his organising ability. His ideas for the use of squadrons composed entirely of fighting scouts commanded attention in high places; until mid-1916 most units operated mixed equipment, and the concept of an offensive force of single-seater scouts carrying the war directly to the enemy's air forces was entirely new. After a tour of other fronts early in 1916, Boelcke returned to the West and was given command of the new *Jagdstaffel Nr. 2* (contracted to *Jasta 2*). He trained his pilots personally, and revealed a

Oswald Boelcke

great gift for patient and inspiring instruction, so that his hand-picked group of pilots, flying the sleek new Albatros D I and D II scouts, became the scourge of the Western Front. Many of the greatest aces of the *Luftstreitkräfte* served their apprenticeship in *Jasta 2*, and Boelcke commanded great respect and affection among his young subordinates. He was killed on 28th October 1916; in the course of an engagement a colleague's undercarriage struck the wing of his Albatros, and the aircraft broke up before he could land it. He was 25 years old, young for his rank, a holder of the *Ordre Pour le Mérite* and numerous other decorations, the victor of 40 aerial combats, and the idol of his country. Since his death he has remained the father-figure of German fighter aviation.

Leutnant Max Immelmann, "The Eagle of Lille", was Germany's first great fighter ace. As mentioned above, he was serving with *Fl. Abt. 62* at Douai when the first Fokker monoplane scouts became available. Hauptmann Kastner instructed Boelcke in the subtleties of the new machine, and Boelcke taught Immelmann. On 1st August 1915 Immelmann scored his first victory while flying an E I (believed to have been one of Boelcke's two machines), when his comrade was forced to drop out of the fight with a defective machine gun. Thereafter he and Boelcke ranged over their sector of the front, sometimes together, sometimes alone, hunting the enemy from the sky. Even a year later only a comparative handful of German pilots were operating the Fokker scouts; yet so great was the superiority of the agile single-seater, with its synchronised forward-firing machine gun, that the "Fokker Scourge" became a major disaster for Allied arms. Immelmann and his colleagues were regarded with an almost spectral awe by their enemies (who claimed with straight faces that his aircraft could remain in the air for a week at a time) and was idolised at home. He finally met his death, after shooting down 15 Allied aircraft, on 18th June 1916; flying near Lens, Immelmann attacked an F.E.2b of No. 25 Squadron R.F.C. flown by 2nd Lt. G. R. McCubbin, with Cpl. J. H. Waller as gunner. The Fokker made an attacking pass, then went into a dive and broke up in mid-air. Some sources claim that his death was caused by technical failure, but the R.F.C. credited Cpl. Waller with the victory. As a measure of the recognition accorded to Immelmann by a grateful nation, we quote his full style of address and decorations:

The Royal Saxon Reserve-Lieutenant Herr Max Immelmann, Commander of the Order of St. Heinrich, Knight of the Ordre Pour le Mérite, Knight of the Iron Cross, First and Second Class, Knight of the Military Order of St. Heinrich, Knight of the Albrecht Order with Swords, Knight of the Hohenzollern House Order with Swords, Knight of the Bavarian Order of Military Merit with Swords, Holder of the Iron Crescent, Holder of the Imbias Medal in Silver, Holder of the Friedrich August Medal in Silver and Holder of the Hamburg Hanseatic Cross.

Capt. Albert Ball, the first great British ace, occupied a place in the affections of the British public and armed forces analogous to that held by Max Immelmann on the other side. He was the first high-scoring fighter pilot whose exploits became widely known on the home front, and his fighting philosophy—usually involving an unhesitating charge straight at the enemy, whether equally matched or outnumbered six or seven to one—had a unique appeal for his civilian contemporaries, whose grasp of the more sophisticated methods adopted by some other pilots was regrettably weak. Born in Nottingham in 1896, and a good shot while still a boy, Albert Ball joined the Sherwood Foresters on the outbreak of war. During a visit to Hendon he became fired with enthusiasm for flying, and secured a transfer to the R.F.C. He joined No. 13 Squadron in France on 15th February 1916, and flew B.E.2C's on artillery-spotting flights. In May he was posted to No. 11 Squadron, which had on charge a Nieuport scout; he immediately fell in love with the little machine, and was to fly Nieuports by preference throughout his career. His first two successes came on 22nd May; he shot down (but could not get confirmed) an Albatros D I, and forced a two-seater to land. On 1st June he flew over the German airfield at Douai; a Fokker and an Albatros rose to challenge him, and though he did not destroy them he completely outflew them, and returned safely. On 25th June he shot down a balloon, and his M.C. was gazetted two days later. He shot down a Roland C II, later to become his favourite prey, on 2nd July, and while on a brief "rest" with No. 8 Squadron he forced an enemy balloon observer to take to his parachute while on an artillery-spotting flight. Given a new Nieuport on his return to No. 11 on 10th August, Ball resumed his private war against the Rolands. When homogeneous fighting squadrons were formed he took his Nieuport to No. 60 and was given a roving commission, which suited his style admirably. Uncaring of odds, he would charge at enemy formations and deliver a devastating fire at close range, generally from a position immediately below the belly of the enemy machine, with his wing-mounted Lewis gun pulled down and back to fire almost vertically upwards. His D.S.O. and Bar were gazetted simultaneously on 26th September, and a second Bar on 25th November; the record which won him these decorations was impressive enough by any standards. On 15th September he shot down two Rolands; on the 19th he forced down an Albatros; on the 21st, shot down two Rolands and forced a third to land; on the 23rd, destroyed an Albatros; on the 28th, destroyed an Albatros and forced down two more. By the time he left France on 4th October Ball was credited with the destruction of ten enemy aircraft

Capt. Albert Ball in the cockpit of an S.E.5. Many of this ace's victories were achieved by firing straight upwards into the belly of an enemy aircraft at short range

and with forcing down 20 more. On 7th April 1917, after a period spent instructing pupil pilots in England, he returned to the front as a Flight Commander in No. 56 Squadron. This unit flew the new S.E.5 scout, and Ball did not at first view the change of equipment with enthusiasm. He acquired a Nieuport for his personal use, but as he continued to increase his score while using both types of aircraft he became reconciled to the S.E.5. His forty-fourth and last victory, on 6th May 1917, was nevertheless gained in the classic Ball manner; flying close beneath an Albatros scout of *Jasta 20* in his beloved Nieuport, he hauled the gun back and shot it out of the sky near Sancourt. Late the following evening Ball, flying his S.E.5, dived into dense cloud while chasing a German single-seater near Lens; the enemy later discovered his wrecked aircraft and his body. His death remains a mystery. Lothar von Richthofen was officially credited with the victory, but himself denied it, maintaining that the aircraft he shot down was a triplane—an opinion confirmed by other witnesses. Ball's body bore no wound, and what caused his aircraft to crash has never been established. He was twenty years and nine months old when he died; his Victoria Cross was gazetted on 3rd June 1917.

The greatest Allied ace of the First World War was Capitaine René Paul Fonck, who served with *Escadrille SPA.103*, one of the units of the famous *Groupe de Combat No. 12 "Les Cigognes"*. Officially Fonck is credited with 75 victories; his own personal estimate, including aircraft destroyed but not confirmed by Allied ground observers, was 127. Born in the Vosges in 1894, Fonck died peacefully in his sleep at his Paris home on June 18th 1953. A keen aviation enthusiast in his boyhood, Fonck was disgusted to find himself posted to the 11th Engineer Regiment on mobilisation in 1914. After unhappy months digging trenches, he finally reported to St. Cyr for aviation training in February 1915; and in June, having received his brevet, he joined *Escadrille C.47*. He flew Caudron G.IVs on reconnaissance duties and low-level bombing missions, and distinguished himself by his courage. On several occasions he nursed home damaged aircraft, and it is thought that he destroyed a Fokker on 1st March 1916, although this could not be confirmed. In July 1916 he fitted a machine gun to his aircraft; and on 6th August he forced down a Rumpler, whose crew surrendered. On 14th October 1916 he shot down an Aviatik two-seater, but again failed to secure confirmation. On 17th March 1917 he fought off five Albatroses, destroying one; and this second confirmed victory led to his transfer to the *Cigognes* group a month later. He gained an unconfirmed victory on 3rd May, and a "definite" on 5th May, a Fokker shot down over Laon. His first "double" came on 12th June 1917, when he attacked and destroyed a pair of Albatroses. He repeated this feat on numerous occasions, and on 9th May 1918 he achieved no less than six confirmed "kills"—including three two-seaters destroyed in a total of 45 seconds, the three wrecks being found in a radius of 400 yards. On 26th September he again shot down six aircraft, comprising a two-seater, four Fokker D VIIs, and an Albatros D V. Fonck's last victory was over a leaflet-dropping two-seater on 1st November 1918. He was a thoughtful and analytical pilot, a master of deflection shooting, and his economy of ammunition bordered on the uncanny; he frequently sent an aircraft down for the expenditure of only five or six rounds, placed, in his own words, "*comme avec la main*"—"as if by hand". His many decorations included the Belgian Croix de Guerre, the French Croix de Guerre with 28 palms, the British Military Cross and Bar, and the British Military Medal; his first sextuple victory also brought him the Croix d'Officier de la Legion d'Honneur. There is little doubt that he was in fact the most successful fighter pilot of any combatant nation in the First World War.

René Fonck, the deadly marksman, who was credited with 75 victories but may have achieved fifty more which could not be confirmed

Britain's most successful fighter pilot in the First World War was Major Edward "Mick" Mannock of Nos. 40, 74, and 85 Squadrons, R.F.C. His official score of enemy aircraft destroyed stands at 73, but he is known to have insisted that several additional victories, justly attributable to him, should be credited to other pilots in various engagements; his actual total is unknown. The son of a soldier, Mannock was working in Constantinople when the war broke out, and was interned by the Turks. He was repatriated in April 1915 on health grounds; rejoined the Territorial Army medical unit to which he had belonged before leaving the country; was commissioned in the Royal Engineers in April 1916; and finally transferred to the Royal Flying Corps in August 1916. His acceptance for flying duties is remarkable; he suffered from astigmatism in the left eye, and must have passed his medical by a ruse. He was posted to France, and joined No. 40 Squadron on 6th April 1917, the unit being equipped at that time with Nieuport scouts. He shot down a balloon on 7th May, and on 7th June scored his first victory over an aeroplane. Returning from leave in July he shot down two-seaters on the 12th and 13th of that month; and his Military Cross was gazetted on 17th September. He was promoted Captain, and took command of a flight. His score grew rapidly; he was possessed by a bitter and ruthless hatred of the enemy uncommon among his contemporaries, and showed no mercy to any German airman. His care of the pilots under his command, however, was irreproachable, and he has been judged the greatest patrol leader of any combatant air force. He took the greatest pains to plan every sortie in detail, and shepherded less experienced pilots until they gained skill and confidence, often insisting on crediting them with victories to which he was rightfully entitled. His patrols were never on any occasion attacked by surprise. In January 1918 he returned to England to take enforced leave; by that time his score stood at 23. His squadron had recently been equipped with the excellent S.E.5A, an aircraft he exploited to the full. He returned to France late in March as a Flight Commander in the newly-formed No. 74—"Tiger"—Squadron, also flying the S.E.5A, and in his three months with the unit added 36 to his score. He was promoted Major in mid-June, and was sent on leave before taking command of No. 85 Squadron. With No. 85 he raised his score to 73 by 26th July; on that day his petrol tank was hit by a random shot from the German trenches, fired by some nameless infantryman. His grave has never been found. It was nearly a year later that he was awarded a posthumous Victoria Cross, and his career attracted no great public attention until long after his death.

France's second most successful fighter pilot was Capitaine Georges Marie Ludovic Jules Guynemer, who served in the *Cigognes* group with *Escadrille N.3/SPA.3*; although, with a score of 54 confirmed victories, he was second to René Fonck in achievement, Guynemer occupied an unrivalled place in the hearts of the French public. He was born on Christmas Eve 1894; a frail and delicate youth, he was twice rejected for military service before finally securing a posting to Pau airfield as a pupil-mechanic in November 1914. A transfer to flying training followed, and on 8th June 1915 he joined *Escadrille MS.3*, then flying Morane Bullet monoplanes. (In the French manner, the unit was later designated *N.3* and *SPA.3* on re-equipment with Nieuport and SPAD scouts respectively.) Guynemer's first victory came on 19th July; by July the following year he had eight victories to his name, and was flying Nieuports. During the latter half of 1916 his score mounted at ever-increasing speed, bringing decorations and swift promotion; and by the end of January 1917 he was credited with 30 kills. A quadruple victory (two within the space of one minute) on 25th May brought his score to 45. His prowess, his pale good looks and dark eyes, his youth and

general air of tortured romanticism, all made him a hero the French people could take to their hearts. He continued to fly combat sorties despite attempts to ground him; he was shot down seven times, and his health, never robust, was failing. He finally failed to return from a flight over Poelcapelle on 11th September 1917, and was mourned by his whole nation. No trace of his aircraft or his body has ever been found; no German pilot put in an immediate claim, and it is possible that he fell to ground fire. A certain Leutnant Wisseman was rather belatedly credited with his death by the German authorities, but the claim is open to question. Wisseman was killed by René Fonck three weeks later.

The third of France's great trio of First World War aces was Lt. Charles Eugène Jules Marie Nungesser of *Escadrilles VB.106* and *N.65*. He scored 45 confirmed victories, and survived the war to die in a record attempt in May 1927. A brilliant athlete and promising scholar, Nungesser left France as a teenage boy and sailed to South America to find an uncle who was reputed to live in Rio de Janeiro. Failing to locate him, the boy found work and stayed in South America for several years, winning a name as a racing motorist and teaching himself to fly. He took part in his first flying display two weeks after climbing into an aeroplane for the first time. He returned to France in 1914, joined a Hussar regiment, and distinguished himself in a lone battle against a squad of enemy infantry and a car full of German officers during the Battle of the Marne. He transferred to the *Service Aéronautique*, and reported to the Voisin reconnaissance and bombing unit *VB.106* on 8th April 1915. On 26th April he was shot down, and for the next two months devoted himself to vain attempts to lure enemy scouts within range of his lumbering Voisin—usually by imitating a crippled aircraft—in the hope of exacting revenge. He finally scored his first victory late in 1915, on an unauthorised night sortie; and in November he joined *Escadrille N.65*. His career with *N.65* opened with a victory on 28th November, and continued in a series of brilliant successes punctuated by frequent spells in hospital. Nungesser suffered numerous wounds and injuries, and was particularly dogged by the aftermath of a serious crash in January 1916; he sustained multiple fractures which failed to knit satisfactorily, and for the rest of the war was obliged to make periodic trips to hospital to have the bones re-broken and re-set. Despite the appalling pain from which he was seldom free Nungesser continued to fly and to add to his score; many of his total of 45 kills were gained during a period when he was unable to walk, and had to be carried to and from his aircraft for every flight. After the war he quickly bored of life as an idol of Paris society, and turned first to running a flying school, and later to barnstorming in the United States. Finally he became absorbed in the idea of an East-West Atlantic attempt, and the Levasseur company prepared a special aircraft designated the P.L.8. The machine was named "*Le Oiseau Blanc*"— "The White Bird"—and bore on the fuselage the macabre insignia which Nungesser had made famous in the skies over the Western Front: a black heart charged with a skull and crossbones, two candles, and a coffin. With Capitaine Coli as navigator, Nungesser flew the White Bird out over Le Havre at 06.48 on the morning of 8th May 1927, and was never seen again.

The second most successful British and Empire pilot of the War was the Canadian, William Avery Bishop. In England as a cavalry subaltern in the Canadian Mounted Rifles in 1915, Bishop decided he would see more action as a pilot, and transferred to the Royal Flying Corps in July of that year. He flew in France as an observer with No. 21 Squadron for several months, and was hospitalised as the result of a crash-landing and frostbite. He subsequently trained as a pilot and joined

William Avery Bishop, who shot down twelve aircraft in three days

No. 60 Squadron in March 1917. The squadron was at that time equipped with Nieuport 17 scouts, an aircraft which Bishop was to handle brilliantly. On 25th March he scored his first victory over an Albatros, and repeated the feat on 31st March. During the following week he shot down three more enemy aircraft, and on 7th April destroyed one aircraft and one observation balloon. His M.C. was awarded for this exploit. His score continued to mount at a phenomenal rate; he frequently flew for seven hours a day, and by early May he had destroyed 20 enemy machines. His D.S.O. was awarded for his actions on 2nd May, during the course of which day he attacked a total of 19 enemy aircraft in nine separate engagements, shooting down two. The Nieuport which he usually flew at this time, *B1566*, is illustrated on the accompanying colour page. On 2nd June he won the Victoria Cross in an engagement which was typical of his style. Flying alone over an enemy airfield at dawn, he shot down three of the aircraft which took off to intercept him, damaged others on the ground, and returned safely to his home base for a late breakfast. When his score reached 45 Bishop was promoted Major and awarded a Bar to his D.S.O. Late in 1917 and early in 1918 he carried out a number of non-combat duties, including recruiting drives in Canada and instructing at an aerial gunnery school. He was subsequently given command of No. 85 Squadron, flying S.E.5A's, and led them back to France on 22nd May 1918. Despite orders to avoid risking his life in combat he returned to the fray with characteristic enthusiasm, shooting down 25 enemy aircraft in a period of twelve days, twelve of them in the last three days, and all within a total of $36\frac{1}{2}$ hours flying time. He was then recalled to England, and never flew operationally again; his D.F.C. was gazetted on 2nd July. Bishop remained in the service, rising to the rank of Honorary Air Marshal in the Royal Canadian Air Force. He died in Florida, U.S.A., in September 1956.

The most successful fighter pilot of the Royal Naval Air Service during the First World War, and, with 60 confirmed victories, third in the overall aces' list, was Raymond Collishaw, born in November 1893 at Nanaimo, British Columbia. He went to sea at the age of 17 and served as second mate on a merchant ship, and later on fishery protection vessels. He transferred to the R.N.A.S. in January 1916, joining No. 3 Wing in August, and scored his first victory on 12th October. While flying a Sopwith $1\frac{1}{2}$ Strutter with the escort for a Franco-British bombing force, he shot down an enemy scout over Oberndorf. His second and third victories came on 25th October, in the course of a ferry flight; and in February 1917 he joined a scout unit, No. 3 (Naval) Squadron. He scored one more victory while flying Sopwith Pups with this squadron, and in April was posted to No. 10 (Naval) Squadron as commander of "B" Flight. Equipped with Sopwith

Raymond Collishaw, brilliant exponent of the Sopwith Triplane and leader of the formidable "Black Flight", who achieved sixty confirmed victories

Triplanes, the "Black Flight" of "Naval Ten" earned a reputation as one of the most formidable Allied units of the war. The Flight was composed entirely of Canadians; their aircraft were decorated with black paint, and named "Black Maria" (Collishaw), "Black Prince", "Black Sheep", "Black Roger", and "Black Death". Between May and July 1917 the Flight destroyed 87 enemy aircraft, and during June Collishaw himself shot down 16 in 27 days. On 6th June he shot down three Albatroses in a single engagement, for which feat he was awarded the D.S.C. On 15th June he scored four victories, and ten days later shot down Leutnant Karl Allmenröder, a 30-victory ace who flew with von Richthofen in *Jasta 11*. On 3rd July, his score standing at 27, Collishaw gained the D.S.O. He shot down ten more victims before the end of the month and was shot down himself, for the second time. For the second time, he escaped without significant injury. After home leave Collishaw returned to France on 24th November 1917, taking command of No. 13 (Naval) Squadron, a Sopwith Camel unit. He was posted back to No. 3 (Naval) Squadron as commander in January 1918, by which time his score was 40 confirmed victories. He saw no action until June, but between 8th and 30th of that month added six to his score, and continued to fly and fight brilliantly until reaching his final total of 60. He was back in England on administrative duties in October, but commanded No. 47 Squadron in the Russian campaign of 1919/20. He remained in the Royal Air Force, serving in the Second World War and reaching the rank of Air Vice Marshal, C.B., with the D.S.O. and Bar, D.S.C., D.F.C., and Croix de Guerre, as well as both military and civil grades of the O.B.E.

Major James Thomas Byford McCudden is officially placed fourth in the roll of British and Empire aces of the First World War, with 57 confirmed victories; recent research indicates that the actual number may have been higher. McCudden joined the Royal Engineers as a bugler in 1910, transferring to the Royal Flying Corps, Military Wing, in 1913. He arrived in France on 13th August 1914 as a First Class Air Mechanic with No. 3 Squadron. By the summer of 1915 he had reached the rank of Sergeant, had made a few flights as an observer, and was gaining some piloting experience by strictly unofficial flights in a Morane Parasol. His first combat, as an observer, took place on 19th December 1915, and he was awarded the Croix de Guerre the following month. Late in January 1916 he was promoted Flight Sergeant and posted home for flying training. In July he returned to France and joined No. 20 Squadron, flying reconnaissance and escort missions in F.E.2d aircraft. In August he was posted to a scout squadron, No. 29, equipped with D.H.2s; and his first victory, over a two-seater, came on 6th September 1916. He was awarded the Military Medal on October 1st, and was commissioned on 1st January 1917. He shot down an Albatros C-type on 6th February, and a Roland C II on the 15th. His Military Cross was awarded the following day, and late in the month he was posted home. During the first half of 1917 he served with various training establishments and did a short "refresher course" with No. 66 Squadron, and managed to make a patrol with No. 56 Squadron in July, flying the S.E.5 for the first time. In mid-August he joined No. 56 as a Flight Commander, with seven victories to his name. In the six months which he spent with the squadron, he raised that total to at least 57. Many of his victims fell after a long "stalk"; he was an instinctive lone hunter, and would wait patiently for the right moment to attack. He was also a sound patrol leader, and his technical background led him to make a thorough study of his engine and guns, and of the potentialities of enemy machines. By 23rd November 1917 he had earned a Bar to his M.C., and his score stood at 20. Between that date and 31st December he destroyed at least a further 17 aircraft, four of them falling on 23rd December.

...mes T. B. McCudden, whose ...illiance in combat was founded on ...deep technical knowledge of air-...ft and guns

He repeated this quadruple victory on 16th February 1918, bringing his score to 51. On 25th February he destroyed his last victim, a Hannover CL III. He returned to England for an instructional tour, and on 6th April was decorated with the Victoria Cross, the D.S.O. and Bar, and the Bar to his M.C. Five months later, now a Major and commanding officer designate of No. 60 Squadron, he crashed and was killed at Auxi-le-Chateau shortly after taking off to fly to his new command. His engine failed, and he made the mistake—inexplicable for such a brilliant and experienced pilot—of trying to turn back towards the airfield.

The most successful American pilot of the First World War was Capt. Edward Vernon Rickenbacker, whose score totalled 26 confirmed aerial victories. Born in 1890 in Columbus, Ohio, Rickenbacker made a considerable name for himself between 1910 and 1917 as one of America's leading racing motorists. In England to negotiate the establishment of a Sunbeam racing team in 1917, he became interested in flying; and when America's entry into the war sent him back to the United States, he advanced the idea of a squadron composed entirely of racing drivers. The idea did not arouse official interest, but a meeting with General Pershing in Washington led to Rickenbacker's enlistment and sent him to France as the General's chauffeur. In August 1917 he transferred to the Aviation Section, and his mechanical expertise led to a posting to the 3rd Aviation Instruction Centre at Issoudun as Chief Engineering Officer—a post he filled with great competence, but much impatience. In his own time he completed advanced flying and gunnery courses, and in March 1918 he finally secured a transfer to the 94th Aero Squadron—the "Hat-in-the-Ring" squadron commanded by Raoul Lufbery, the *Escadrille Lafayette* ace. With Lufbery and Douglas Campbell (q.v.), Rickenbacker flew the first American patrol over enemy lines on 19th March; and on 29th April he shot down his first victim, an Albatros scout. On 30th May his fifth victory qualified him as an ace, but it was to be his last for four months. An ear infection put him in hospital and convalescence until mid-September, when he returned to the squadron as a Captain and Flight Commander. On 14th September he shot down a Fokker, and by the end of the month had sent three more Fokkers, a Halberstadt and a balloon to join it. He took over command of the 94th on 25th September, and continued to score heavily until the Armistice. Capt. Rickenbacker was active in the automobile and airline industries between the wars, and was largely responsible for building up Eastern Airlines, of which corporation he became Chairman in 1953. During the Second World War he toured widely, visiting Air Force units abroad and undertaking various missions for his government. In the course of a flight over the Pacific his aircraft was forced to ditch, and Rickenbacker and the crew survived 21 days on a life-raft before being picked up. At the time of writing he is still alive and still active in various public fields at 80 years of age. His many American and foreign decorations include his country's highest award for gallantry, the Congressional Medal of Honor.

America's second ranking ace in the First World War was Lt. Frank Luke, Jr., who between 16th August and 28th September 1918 scored 21 victories and earned immortality as a "balloon buster". Luke was born in Phoenix, Arizona in 1897; as a boy he was an excellent athlete, and he is reputed to have been a considerable shot with both rifle and pistol. His early life around the copper mines of Arizona was not easy, and he acquired a tough reputation. He enlisted in the Signal Corps in September 1917 and was commissioned in January 1918, sailing for France in March. His first duty was ferrying aircraft at Orly, a task which improved his flying skill but frustrated his aggressive spirit. He obtained a posting to the

27th Aero Squadron in late July; and on 16th August broke formation against orders and scored his first victory. This was to be the first of many brushes with authority; Luke was impatient of discipline, and was constantly in trouble with his superiors. He was not a good mixer, and his tough self-confidence did not endear him to his fellow pilots, who considered him a conceited braggart. He was, however, a born combat pilot, whose marksmanship and flying skill were equalled by his aggressive spirit. He became an embittered "loner", and formed a close friendship with only one other pilot, Lt. Wehner. Luke shot down his first balloon on 12th September, and landed his SPAD so badly damaged that it was written off—the first of five aircraft which he "used up" in his meteoric career. On 14th September Luke and Wehner began their short but brilliant partnership; Luke shot down two balloons while Wehner fought off the protective patrol of eight Fokkers. The next day Luke destroyed two more balloons, only to be attacked by seven Fokkers. Wehner, who had shot down a balloon himself, then arrived and shot two of the Fokkers off Luke's tail. The same afternoon Luke accounted for another balloon, and the following evening three more fell to the teamwork of Luke and Wehner. On 18th September Luke dived to destroy two balloons near Labeuville while Wehner remained above. On regaining altitude Luke found his comrade engaged with six Fokkers, two of which he promptly shot down. He lost contact with the other pilot, and on his way back to base alone he shot down a Halberstadt two-seater in flames. His elation was short-lived, however; on landing he found that Wehner had been killed. He took a short leave in Paris, but soon returned; and on 26th September he scored again, but again lost his wingman, Lt. Roberts. Deeply depressed, Luke went A.W.O.L. for a day. He destroyed another balloon on an unauthorised flight, and then spent the night at a French airfield. His persistent flouting of orders had become a disgrace, and a grounding and arrest order was issued; but it was destined never to be served. Just before sunset, having fuelled his SPAD at a forward airfield, he flew over the American balloon headquarters in Souilly and dropped a note reading "Watch three Hun balloons on the Meuse, Luke." He shot down the first balloon at Dun-sur-Meuse, and a second at Briere Farm; badly wounded in the second action, he nevertheless flew on to Milly and shot the third down in flames. He dived to strafe German troops in the streets of Murvaux, eventually crash-landing on the outskirts of the village. He was surrounded by German troops and called upon to surrender, but preferred to fight it out with his .45 service pistol. Inevitably he was riddled with rifle bullets and died instantly. It was not until 1919 that his grave was located, and the story of his last fight pieced together from eyewitness accounts. He was awarded a posthumous Congressional Medal of Honor. His habit of making unauthorised sorties has led to some confusion over his actual score, recorded accounts varying between 17 and 21. The higher score is, however, the more generally accepted, and thus is quoted here.

BETWEEN THE WARS

The first six-engined American aeroplane was the Barling XNBL-1. Powered by six 420-h.p. Liberty 12A engines, this large experimental "long-range" night bomber triplane had a span of 120 ft. (36·5 m.) and a maximum loaded weight of 42,569 lb. (19,325 kg.). First flown on 22nd August 1923, it was found to possess a range of only 170 miles (275 km.) with a bomb-load, or 335 miles (540 km.) without, and therefore, hardly surprisingly, it was abandoned. The development had cost $350,000.

The Barling XNBL-1

The Hawker Fury I

The first fighter to enter service with the Royal Air Force capable of a maximum level speed
of more than 200 m.p.h. (322 km./hr.) was the Hawker Fury I biplane.
Powered by a 525-h.p. Rolls-Royce Kestrel II liquid-cooled engine and armed
with two synchronised Vickers machine guns, the Fury had a top speed of
207 m.p.h. at 14,000 ft. (4,270 m.). Designed by the late Sir Sydney Camm,
it entered service in May 1931.

**The first monoplane fighter with a fully enclosed cockpit and a fully retractable undercarriage
to enter squadron service anywhere in the world** was the Polikarpov I-16
Ishak ("Little Donkey"). The prototype first flew on 31st December 1933,
and deliveries of the Type 1 production fighter to Soviet squadrons commenced
during the autumn of 1934. The I-16 Type 1 was powered by a 480 h.p. M22
engine, had a top speed of 224 m.p.h. (360 km./hr.) at sea level, and was
armed with two 7·62-mm. *Shkas* machine guns.

The first German monoplane fighter with a fully enclosed cockpit and a fully retractable undercarriage
to enter squadron service was the Messerschmitt Bf 109B-1. The prototype
Bf 109V-1 first flew during September 1935, and the first production Bf 109B-1
fighters commenced deliveries to *Jagdgeschwader 2 "Richthofen"* in the spring
of 1937. The B-1 model was powered by a 635 h.p. Junkers Jumo 210D engine,
had a top speed of 292 m.p.h. (470 km./hr.) at 13,000 ft. (3,960 m.), and was
armed with three 7·92-mm. MG 17 machine guns.

The first American monoplane fighter with a fully enclosed cockpit and a retractable, though exposed,
undercarriage to enter squadron service was the Seversky P-35. The production
model commenced deliveries in July 1937; powered by a 950 h.p. Pratt &
Whitney R-1830-9 engine, it had a top speed of 281 m.p.h. (452 km./hr.) at
10,000 ft. (3,050 m.), and was armed with one 0·5-in. and one 0·3-in. machine
gun.

The first British monoplane fighter with a fully enclosed cockpit and a fully retractable undercarriage
to enter squadron service was the Hawker Hurricane. The prototype first flew
on 6th November 1935, and deliveries to No. 111 (Fighter) Squadron, R.A.F.,
commenced during November 1937. The Hurricane I was powered by a
1,030 h.p. Rolls-Royce Merlin II engine, had a top speed of 322 m.p.h.
(515 km./hr.) at 20,000 ft. (6,100 m.), and was armed with eight 0·303-in.
Browning machine guns.

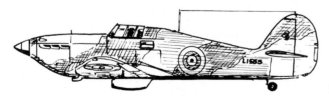

The Hawker Hurricane I

The first French monoplane fighter with a fully enclosed cockpit and a fully retractable undercarriage to enter squadron service was the Morane Saulnier M.S.406. The experimental M.S.405 aircraft from which the series was derived first flew on 8th August 1935, and deliveries of the production fighter to the 6th *Escadre de Chasse* commenced in December 1938. The M.S.406 was powered by an 860 h.p. Hispano–Suiza HS 12Y 31 engine, had a top speed of 304 m.p.h. (490 km./hr.) at 14,700 ft. (4,500 m.), and was armed with one 20 mm. HS 59 cannon and two 7.5-mm. MAC machine guns.

The Morane-Saulnier M.S.406

The first Italian monoplane fighter with a fully enclosed cockpit and a fully retractable undercarriage to enter squadron service was the Macchi C.200 *Saetta* ("Lightning"). The prototype first flew on 24th December 1937, and deliveries to the *4° Stormo C.T.* commenced during 1939. The C.200 Series 1 was powered by an 870 h.p. Fiat A.74.RC38 engine, had a top speed of 313 m.p.h. (504 km./hr.) at 14,700 ft. (4,500 m.), and was armed with two 0·5-in. SAFAT machine guns.

The Macchi C.200

The first Japanese monoplane fighter with a fully enclosed cockpit and a fully retractable undercarriage to enter squadron service was the Mitsubishi A6M2, popularly known as the *Zero-Sen*. The prototype first flew on 1st April 1939, and deliveries to the Imperial Japanese Navy's 12th *Rengo Kokutai* were authorised on 21st July 1940. The A6M2 was powered by a 950 h.p. Nakajima NK1C *Sakae* 12 engine, had a top speed of 331 m.p.h. (533 km./hr.) at 14,930 ft. (4,550 m.), and was armed with two 20-mm. Type 99 cannon and two 7·7-mm. Type 97 machine guns.

The Mitsubishi Zero-Sen

Junkers Ju 87A, first production model of the immortal Stuka, *which made its combat debut in Spain with the* Jolanthe Kette.

The Spanish Civil War (*1936–39*) provided the setting for many significant advances in military aviation. The political background—a rebellion by right-wing elements of the armed forces and population against an extreme left-wing government and popular movement—was such that massive aid was dispatched to the opposing forces by two major international camps. Italy and Germany supported General Francisco Franco y Bahamonde's Nationalists, and the Soviet Union supported the Republican Government, which also drew aid from various other countries and from many volunteer organisations more dedicated in their resistance to Fascism than their outright support of Communism.

German aid, in the form of twenty Junkers Ju 52/3m transport aircraft, six Heinkel He 51b fighter biplanes and eighty-five volunteer air and ground crews, arrived in August 1936, less than a month after the outbreak of war. These aircraft were at once employed in ferrying 10,000 Moorish troops across the Straits of Gibraltar from Tetuan. From this small beginning grew the *Legion Cóndor*—a balanced force of between forty and fifty fighters, about the same number of multi-engined bombers, and about 100 miscellaneous ground-attack, reconnaissance, and liaison aircraft. Volunteers from the ranks of the *Luftwaffe* served in rotation, to ensure the maximum dissemination of combat experience. Many of the major combat designs upon which Germany was to rely in the first half of the Second World War were first evaluated under combat conditions in Spain; the Heinkel He III bomber, the Dornier Do 17 reconnaissance-bomber, the Messerschmitt Bf 109 fighter, and the Henschel Hs 123 and Junkers Ju 87 ground-attack aircraft were prominent. The contribution of the *Legion Cóndor* to the eventual Nationalist victory was considerable, but more important still were the inferences drawn by *Luftwaffe* staff planners. Valid lessons learned in Spain included the value of the dive-bomber in hampering enemy communications, and the effects of ground-strafing by fighters in the exploitation of a breakthrough by land forces. Less realistic was the impression gained of the relative invulnerability of unescorted bombers and dive-bombers —an impression based on the lack of sophisticated fighter resistance. In the field of fighter tactics, and in terms of combat experience by her fighter pilots, the Spanish Civil War put Germany at least a year ahead of her international rivals.

Italy's intervention in the Spanish Civil War commenced in August 1936, with the arrival by sea at Melilla of twelve Fiat CR. 32 biplane fighters. The eventual strength of the Italian *Aviacion del Tercio* in Spain was some 730 aircraft (total supplied) including Fiat CR. 32s, SM. 81s, SM. 79s, BR. 20s, Ro. 37s, Ba. 65s, and a squadron of Fiat G. 50s. Of these, 86 aircraft were lost on operations and 100 from other causes, and 175 flying personnel were killed. A total of 903 enemy aircraft were claimed destroyed in aerial combat, and a further 40 on the ground. Total sorties flown were 86,420, and bombing sorties totalled 5,318.

The Spanish Republican air force mustered 214 obsolete aircraft at the outbreak of the Civil War. Additionally, the Government had at its disposal 40 civil types of various designs; and between 1937 and 1939, 55 aircraft were built in the Republican zone. Foreign aircraft dispatched to Spain by various friendly nations totalled 1,947, of which 1,409 were sent from Russia. The others included 70 Dewoitine D. 371, D. 500 and D. 510 fighters, 20 Loire-Nieuport 46s and 15 S. 510 fighters from France; 72 aircraft—but no fighters—from the U.S.A.; 72 aircraft from the Netherlands; 57 from Britain; and 47 from Czechoslovakia. Of these some 400 are thought to have been destroyed other than in aerial combat, and 1,520 were claimed shot down by Nationalist, German and Italian pilots.

The first Russian aircraft to enter combat in Spain were the Polikarpov I-16 Type 6 fighters of General Kamanin's expeditionary command, based at Santander. By September 1936 105 of these aircraft had arrived in Spain—by sea to Cartagena— and had been assembled; some 200 pilots and 2,000 other personnel had also arrived from the Soviet Union. The I-16—known in Spain as the *Rata* (Rat) and the *Mosca* (Fly) to Nationalists and Republicans respectively—first entered combat on 5th November 1936. Eventually a total of 475 I-16s were supplied; and from March 1937 they were gathered in one formation designated Fighter Group 31, comprising seven squadrons of fifteen aircraft each. More numerous but inevitably less successful was the I-15 biplane fighter, of which some 550 were supplied. The I-15 was inferior to both the Fiat CR. 32 and the Messerschmitt Bf 109, and no less than 415 are believed to have been lost either in combat or on the ground. The most numerous Republican bomber type, the Soviet Tupolev SB-2, also fared badly; of 210 supplied, 178 were lost.

The Polikarpov I-16

Messerschmitt Bf 109B fighter in the insignia of the Legion Cóndor. *The first Messerschmitts arrived in Spain in March 1937, and were flown by the 2nd* Staffel *of the Legion's fighter component* J.88. *Many famous Luftwaffe aces of the Second World War won their spurs with J.88, including Werner Mölders, Günther Lützow, and Adolf Galland.*

The first maliciously-motivated bombs to fall on the U.S.A. were dropped on 12th November 1926 from an aeroplane on a farmhouse in Williamson County, Ill., during a Prohibition gang feud. They were of crude manufacture and failed to explode.

The largest British landplane built prior to the Second World War was the Beardmore Inflexible three-engined monoplane, designed principally by Dr. Adolf Rohrbach at the invitation of the Air Ministry during 1923; built by William Beardmore & Co.; and assembled at the R.A.F. Flight Test establishment at Martlesham Heath, Suffolk, during the early months of 1928. It was flown for the first time on 5th March that year by Sqdn. Ldr. J. Noakes, M.M. (later Gp. Capt., A.F.C., M.M.) who reported that the huge monoplane handled extremely well. With a wing span of 157 ft. 6 in. (48·0 m.) and a loaded weight of 37,000 lb. (16,780 kg.), the Inflexible was somewhat underpowered with three 650 h.p. Rolls-Royce Condor engines which bestowed a maximum speed of 109 m.p.h. (175 km./hr.).

The last biplane heavy bomber to serve as such with the Royal Air Force was the Handley Page Heyford which first flew in June 1930 at Radlett, Hertfordshire, entered service with No. 99 (Bomber) Squadron at Upper Heyford, Oxfordshire, on 14th November 1933, and was withdrawn from front line service in March 1939. The last Heyford was struck off R.A.F. charge in May 1941. Powered by two 575 h.p. Rolls-Royce Kestrel engines the Heyford I had a top speed of 142 m.p.h. at 12,500 ft. (228 km./hr. at 4,000 m.) and could carry a maximum bomb-load of 2,616 lb. (1,190 kg.).

THE SECOND WORLD WAR

The Polish fighter most widely used at the time of the German invasion in September 1939 was the P.Z.L. P-11, of which 128 were on strength on 1st September 1939. They equipped Nos. 111, 112, 113 and 114 Squadrons of the 1st Air Regiment based on Warsaw, Nos. 121 and 122 Squadrons of the 2nd Air Regiment based at Krakow, Nos. 131 and 132 Squadrons of the 3rd Air Regiment at Poznan, Nos. 141 and 142 Squadrons of the 4th Air Regiment at Torun, No. 152 Squadron of the 5th Air Regiment in the Wilno/Lida area, and No. 161 Squadron of the 6th Air Regiment based at Lwow. Armed with two or four 7·7-mm. machine guns, the P-11 had a top speed of 242 m.p.h. (390 km./hr.) and had first flown in September 1931.

The greatest losses suffered by the Luftwaffe during the Polish campaign in a single day were those of 3rd September 1939 when 22 German aircraft were destroyed (four Dornier Do 17, three Messerschmitt Bf 110, two Heinkel He 111, three Junkers Ju 87, two Messerschmitt Bf 109s, three Henschel Hs 126, two Fieseler Fi 156, one Henschel Hs 123, one Junkers Ju 52 and one Heinkel He 59). One of the Messerschmitt Bf 110s was accidentally shot down by German troops near Ostrolenka. *Luftwaffe* personnel casualties on this day amounted to 34 killed, one wounded and 17 missing.

The first occasion on which a British aircraft crossed the German frontier during the Second World War was on 3rd September 1939 when Blenheim IV, *N6215*, of No. 139 Squadron, flown by Fg. Off. A. McPherson, and carrying Cdr. Thompson, R.N., and Cpl. V. Arrowsmith, photographed German naval units leaving Wilhelmshaven.

The first British aircraft to drop bombs on enemy targets during the Second World War was Blenheim IV, *N6204*, flown by Flt. Lt. K. C. Doran, leading a formation of five aircraft from No. 110 (Hyderabad) Squadron in a raid on German shipping off Wilhelmshaven on 4th September 1939; a formation of five Blenheims from No. 107 Squadron also took part in the attack.

The first British gallantry decorations to be gazetted during Second World War were two Distinguished Flying Crosses on 10th September 1939 to Fg. Off. McPherson and Flt. Lt. Doran (see above).

The first German aircraft shot down by British forces during the Second World War was a Dornier Do 18 (Wrk.Nr. 731) of *2 Staffel, Küstenfliergergruppe 506* on 26th September 1939 in German Grid Square 3440 (North Sea). The crew of four was rescued and made prisoner aboard H.M.S. *Somali*, 1,870 tons. (H.M.S. *Somali* foundered in tow three days after being torpedoed in North Russian convoy action, September 1942.)

The first German aircraft shot down by British forces to land on British soil during the Second World War was a Heinkel He 111H-1 (1H+JA) of *Stabsstaffel, Kampfgeschwader 26*, shot down by British fighters and crashed on Dalkeith Hills, six miles south of Haddington near the Firth of Forth on 28th October 1939. Two of the crew were killed, one wounded (Leutnant Rolf Niehoff, the commander) and one unwounded.

The first loss suffered by the Finnish Air Force during the "Winter War" with Russia in 1939–40 was Sgt. Kukkonen who, flying a Fokker D.XXI of Fighter Squadron HLeLv.24 near Viipuri, was shot down by his own anti-aircraft guns on 1st December 1939.

Fokker D.XXI

The first aerial victory claimed during the "Winter War" between Finland and Russia was claimed by Lt. Eino Luukkanen on 1st December 1939; flying a Fokker D.XXI *(FR-104)* of Fighter Squadron HLeLv.24, he destroyed a Russian SB-2 bomber.

The first Royal Air Force aircraft to drop bombs deliberately on German soil is believed to have been an Armstrong-Whitworth Whitley, *N1380*, DY-R of No. 102 Squadron. Based at Driffield, Yorkshire, the squadron raided Hornum on the night of 19th/20th March 1940.

Armstrong-Whitworth Whitley bombers of No. 102 Squadron, R.A.F. (see above)

The worst losses in aircraft destroyed as the result of air combat and anti-aircraft gunfire suffered by a single air force on a single day are believed to have been those of the *Luftwaffe* on 10th May 1940. On this day Germany invaded the Netherlands and Belgium and was opposed simultaneously by the air forces of Holland, Belgium, France and Great Britain. The Norwegian campaign, by then nearing its end, also claimed a small number of German victims. On this day the *Luftwaffe*, according to its own records, lost:

Junkers Ju 52 transports	157 destroyed
Heinkel He 111 bombers	51 destroyed, 21 damaged
Dornier Do 17 bombers	26 destroyed, 7 damaged
Fieseler Fi 156 artillery support	22 destroyed
Junkers Ju 88 bombers	18 destroyed, 2 damaged
Junkers Ju 87 dive-bombers	9 destroyed
Messerschmitt Bf 109 fighters	6 destroyed, 11 damaged
Dornier Do 215 reconnaissance	2 destroyed
Henschel Hs 126 reconnaissance	1 destroyed, 3 damaged
Messerschmitt Bf 110 fighters	1 destroyed, 3 damaged
Dornier Do 18 flying boat	1 destroyed
Henschel Hs 123 dive-bomber	1 damaged
Other types	10 destroyed, 3 damaged

Total 304 destroyed, 51 damaged

Aircrew casualties amounted to 267 killed, 133 wounded and 340 missing; other *Luftwaffe* personnel (Flak, engineers, etc.) casualties amounted to 326 killed or missing.

Apart from the purely academic significance of these figures (not previously published), they indicate conclusively that the operations undertaken by the *Luftwaffe* on this day represented the true commencement of *blitzkrieg* against substantial opposition. On this day Germany suffered losses in excess of all previous cumulative losses since 1st September 1939, including the Polish campaign. Losses suffered by the *Luftwaffe* during the invasion of Poland may be summarized as follows:

1st–8th September 1939:
   116 aircraft destroyed, 128 aircrew killed, 68 wounded, and 137 missing.
9th–13th September 1939:
   34 aircraft destroyed, 15 aircrew killed, 15 wounded and 63 missing.
14th–18th September 1939:
   23 aircraft destroyed, 24 aircrew killed, 32 wounded and 14 missing.
19th–27th September 1939:
   30 aircraft destroyed, 54 aircrew killed, 18 wounded and 4 missing.

The first German aircraft to be destroyed in the air by the Royal Netherlands Air Force during the German invasion of the Low Countries was a Junkers Ju 88A-2 of *Kampfgeschwader 30* which was shot down off the Dutch coast by a pilot of *1e Ja.V.A.* fighter squadron (the famous "three white mice" unit) on 10th May 1940. On this day KG 30 was briefed to attack targets at Nijmegen, Rotterdam, Utrecht and Waalhaven.

The greatest single victory achieved by the Royal Netherlands Air Force during the German invasion of the Low Countries was gained at 06.45 hrs. on 10th May 1940 when a force of Fokker D.XXIs intercepted fifty-five Junkers Ju 52/3m transport aircraft of KGzbV 9. The Dutch pilots claimed to have shot down 37 of the formation, but German records indicate a total loss of 39 aircraft, 6 occupants killed, 41 presumed dead, 15 wounded and 79 missing.

The most numerous French military aeroplane in service at the commencement of the Battle of France on 10th May 1940 was the Potez 63, which existed in five main variants: a 2/3-seat day and night fighter, a 2-seat light bomber, a 3-seat reconnaissance version and a 3-seat army co-operation aircraft. Up to that time 1,115 aircraft had been delivered and approximately 300 more were delivered before France capitulated. About 400 were lost during the Battle of France.

THE BATTLE OF BRITAIN

The highest-scoring Allied pilot during the Battle of Britain was Sgt. Josef František, a Czech pilot who served with No. 303 (Polish) Squadron, R.A.F. His confirmed score of 17 enemy aircraft shot down was achieved entirely during September 1940; he was killed on 9th October 1940. The only British gallantry decoration awarded to František was the Distinguished Flying Medal, but he had previously been awarded the Czech War Cross and the Polish *Virtuti Militari*.

The Allied pilots who scored ten or more confirmed victories during the Battle of Britain:

†Sgt. J. František, D.F.M.	17	Hurricanes	(303 Sqdn.)	Czech. Top-scoring Czech and Allied pilot.
†Plt. Off. E. S. Lock, D.S.O., D.F.C.*	16 + 1 shared	Spitfires	(41 Sqdn.)	Top-scoring British pilot.
Fg. Off. B. J. G. Carbury, D.F.C.*	15 + 1 shared	Spitfires	(603 Sqdn.)	Top-scoring New Zealander.
Sgt. J. H. Lacey, D.F.M.*	15 + 1 shared	Hurricanes	(501 Sqdn.)	Top-scoring Auxiliary pilot.
Plt. Off. R. F. T. Doe, D.S.O., D.F.C.*	15	{Hurricanes Spitfires	(238 Sqdn.) (234 Sqdn.)	British.
†Flt. Lt. P. C. Hughes, D.F.C.	14 + 3 shared	Spitfires	(234 Sqdn.)	Top-scoring Australian pilot.
Plt. Off. C. F. Gray, D.S.O., D.F.C.**	14 + 2 shared	Spitfires	(54 Sqdn.)	New Zealander.
†Flt. Lt. A. A. McKellar, D.S.O., D.F.C.*	14 + 1 shared	Hurricanes	(605 Sqdn.)	British.
Fg. Off. W. Urbanowicz, D.F.C.	14	{Hurricanes Hurricanes	(303 Sqdn.) (601 Sqdn.)	Top-scoring Polish pilot.
†Fg. Off. C. R. Davis, D.F.C.	11 + 1 shared	Hurricanes	(601 Sqdn.)	Top-scoring South African pilot.
Flt. Lt. R. F. Boyd, D.S.O., D.F.C.*	11 + 1 shared	Hurricanes	(601 Sqdn.)	British.
Sgt. A. McDowall, D.S.O., A.F.C., D.F.M.*	11	Spitfires	(602 Sqdn.)	British.
Fg. Off. J. W. Villa, D.F.C.*	10 + 4 shared	{Spitfires Spitfires	(72 Sqdn.) (92 Sqdn.)	British.
Fg. Off. D. A. P. McMullen, D.F.C.**	10 + 3 shared	{Spitfires Spitfires	(54 Sqdn.) (222 Sqdn.)	British.
Flt. Lt. R. S. S. Tuck, D.S.O., D.F.C.**	10 + 1 shared	{Spitfires Hurricanes	(92 Sqdn.) (257 Sqdn.)	British.
Plt. Off. H. C. Upton, D.F.C.	10 + 1 shared	{Spitfires Spitfires	(43 Sqdn.) (607 Sqdn.)	Top-scoring Canadian pilot.
Flt. Sgt. G. C. Unwin, D.S.O., D.F.M.*	10	Spitfires	(19 Sqdn.)	British.

(† = deceased. The ranks shown are those held during the Battle of Britain. The decorations are shown to include *all* gallantry awards won by these pilots before, during and after the Battle.)

The first Victoria Cross to be won during the Battle of Britain was awarded posthumously to Acting Seaman J. F. (Jack) Mantle, R.N., who was operating an anti-aircraft gun aboard H.M.S. *Foyle Bank* in Portsmouth Harbour on 4th July 1940. The ship, the only one in the port with an anti-aircraft gun, became the focus of an enemy raid and was hit by a bomb which cut the power supply. Jack Mantle, though severely wounded, continued to fire the gun, operating it manually; despite another direct hit upon the ship, which severed his left leg, he remained at his post until the end of the raid but succumbed to his terrible wounds almost immediately afterwards. His Victoria Cross was only the second to be awarded for an action in or over Great Britain, the first having been awarded to Lt. W. Leefe Robinson of No. 39 (Home Defence) Squadron, R.F.C., for his destruction of a Schutte-Lanz airship on the night of 2nd/3rd September 1916 at Cuffley, Hertfordshire.

The only Victoria Cross ever to be awarded to a member of R.A.F. Fighter Command was that won by Flt. Lt. James Brindley Nicolson, R.A.F., on 16th August 1940. A Flight Commander of No. 249 Hurricane Squadron, Nicolson was leading a section of three fighters on patrol near Southampton, Hants, when he sighted enemy aircraft ahead. Before he could complete the attack his section was "bounced" from above and behind by German fighters which shot down one Hurricane and set Nicolson's aircraft ablaze. With flames sweeping up through his cockpit, the British pilot remained at his controls long enough to complete an attack on an enemy aircraft which had flown into his sights, and then baled out. Meanwhile on the ground a detachment of soldiers, seeing Nicolson and his wingman descending on parachutes and believing them to be enemy para-troops, opened fire with rifles. Nicolson was hit but survived his wounds and burns, but his colleague was dead when he reached the ground (whether or not he was killed by rifle fire has never been established).

The first member of the Royal Air Force to be awarded the George Cross (and indeed among the first group of any to be awarded) was Aircraftman Vivian ("Bob") Holloway who, in July 1940, at Cranfield, Bedfordshire, entered a crashed and blazing bomber and extricated the pilot, and in so doing suffered severe burns to his hands. One month later, at the moment of returning from hospital, he again dashed into a blazing aircraft *three times* amidst exploding ammunition, and brought out three crew members. He survived his near-fatal burns despite having been on the danger list for 27 days.

The first regular-serving American pilot to die in action during the Second World War was Plt. Off. William M. L. Fiske, R.A.F., who on 17th August 1940 died of wounds suffered in action at Tangmere, England, during the Battle of Britain against the *Luftwaffe* on 16th August 1940.

The first air victory scored in the Greek-Italian campaign of 1940–41 was achieved by a Greek pilot of No. 21 Squadron of the Royal Hellenic Air Force, flying a Polish P.Z.L. P.24, when he destroyed an Italian aircraft north of Yannina on 1st November 1940.

The world's first twin-engined jet fighter was the German Heinkel He 280 whose first prototype, the He 280V-1, first flew on 5th April 1941 powered by two 1,320-lb. (600 kg.) thrust Heinkel-Hirth HeS 8A turbojets. Maximum speed was estimated to be more than 550 m.p.h. (884 km./hr.), though subsequently it has become obvi-ous that the aircraft would have been unable to exceed 400 m.p.h. (645 km./hr.). It did not achieve production status.

The largest airborne assault mounted by the Luftwaffe during the Second World War was
Operation "Mercury", the landing of 22,750 men on the island of Crete
commencing at 07.00 hrs. on 20th May 1941. The *Luftwaffe* used 493 Junkers
Ju 52/3m aircraft and about 80 DFS 230 gliders. The assault was made by
10,000 parachutists, 750 troops landed by glider, 5,000 landed by Ju 52/3ms
and 7,000 by sea. The operation, although regarded as a brilliant success, cost
Germany about 4,500 men killed and some 150 transport aircraft destroyed or
badly damaged, and effectively brought *Luftwaffe* paratrooping operations to
an end.

The first combat mission ever flown by the Boeing B-17 Flying Fortress was a raid flown at 30,000
feet (10,000 m.) by aircraft of No. 90 (Bomber) Squadron, R.A.F. on Wilhelmshaven on 8th July 1941. The aircraft, Fortress Is, were the equivalent in
the R.A.F. of the B-17C.

R.A.F. Fortress I (Boeing B-17C)

The first aerial victories claimed during the "Continuation War" between Finland and Russia,
which broke out in June 1941, were two Russian DB-3 bombers shot down by
six Fokker D.XXIs over the Riihimäki railway junction in the first air battle
which probably took place on 25th June.

The first combat operation carried out by Avro Lancaster heavy bombers was a mining sortie
flown by No. 44 (Bomber) Squadron, based at Waddington, Lincolnshire, over
the Heligoland Bight on 2nd March 1942. **Their first bombing raid** was
over Essen on 10th March 1942.

The only fighter of Australian design to fire its guns in anger during the Second World War was
the Commonwealth Boomerang of which a total of 250 were built between
May 1942 and January 1945. The first aircraft *A46-1*, was first flown by
Ken Frewin at Fisherman's Bend, Victoria, on 29th May 1942. Powered by
an Australian-built Pratt & Whitney R-1830 engine, which bestowed a top
speed of 305 m.p.h. at 15,500 ft. (490 km./hr. at 5,500 m.), the Boomerang
eventually served on Nos. 4, 5, 83, 84 and 85 Squadrons, Royal Australian Air
Force. Although it is true that the Boomerang was used principally as a ground
attack fighter, it is perhaps surprising to record that, frequently in action
against Japanese aircraft, it never destroyed an enemy aeroplane in the air.

Commonwealth Boomerang

The largest-calibre multi-barrelled weapon fired by an aircraft was the six-barrelled 77-mm.
Sondergeräte 113A Forstersonde rocket mortar fitted in three Henschel Hs 129
ground attack aircraft to fire Sabot-type shells vertically downwards. The
weapon was triggered by a photo-electric cell actuated by the shadow of a tank
beneath the aircraft.

The most successful Russian woman fighter pilot of the Second World War, and thus presumably the most successful woman fighter pilot in the world, served with the mixed-sex 73rd Guards Fighter Air Regiment. She was Junior Lieutenant Lydia Litvak, and she was killed in action on 1st August 1943 at the age of 22 with a total of 12 confirmed victories to her name. She flew Yak fighters.

Lydia Litvak, leading woman fighter pilot with twelve confirmed victories

(*During the Second World War, most Russian women combat pilots served with the 122nd Air Group of the Soviet Air Force. This all-female unit comprised the 586th Fighter Air Regiment, the 587th Bomber Air Regiment and the 588th Night Bomber Air Regiment. The 586th I.A.P. (Istebitelnyi aviatsionnyi polk = fighter air regiment) was formed at Engels, on the Volga River, in October 1941; it was commanded by Major Tamara Aleksandrovna Kazarinova. The pilots of this unit flew a total of 4,419 operational sorties, took part in 125 air combats, and were credited with 38 confirmed victories. The unit flew Yak-1, -7B and -9 fighters. During the Second World War, 30 Russian airwomen received the gold star of a Hero of the Soviet Union. It is believed that 22 of them served with the 588th/46th Guards Night Bomber Air Regiment, which was equipped with PO-2 biplanes.*)

The Royal Air Force bomber with the greatest number of operational missions to its credit was the AVRO Lancaster B. Mark III, *ED888*, PM-M, of No. 102 (Bomber) Squadron. "Mike Squared", alternatively known as "The Mother of Them All", made its first operational sortie in a raid on Dortmund on the night of 4th/5th May 1943. By the time the aircraft was retired in December 1944 it had logged 140 missions—the first 66 with 102 Squadron, then 65 with No. 576 Squadron, and 9 more with No. 102 Squadron—totalling 974 operational hours. Both squadrons were based at R.A.F. Elsham Wolds, Lincolnshire.

The only known pilot who has been both gaoled and awarded his country's highest gallantry decoration for the same exploit was Lt. Michael Devyatayev, a Soviet fighter pilot shot down by the *Luftwaffe* over Lvov on 13th July 1944. Taken prisoner by the Germans, Devyatayev escaped and seized a Heinkel He 111 bomber and flew nine other escapees back to Russian-held territory. On regaining his freedom the 23-year-old pilot was gaoled under the U.S.S.R. criminal code which labelled him a traitor for having been taken prisoner. Nine years later, in 1953, he was freed under an amnesty prevailing at the time, and in 1958 was made Hero of the Soviet Union and awarded the Order of Lenin and Gold Star Medal.

The first jet aircraft to enter operational service with any air force was the Messerschmitt Me 262A-1a twin turbojet fighter, powered by two Junkers Jumo 109-004B-1 engines with eight-stage axial-flow compressor, six combustion chambers and single-stage turbine. The swept-wing fighter was armed with four 30-mm. MK 108 automatic cannon grouped in the nose; a frequent addition to the armament was a rack of twelve unguided 55-mm. R4M rocket projectiles under each wing. These rockets were aimed through the standard gunsight, fired electrically at a range of about 650 yards (250 m.) from the target, and proved most effective against bomber formations. The Me 262A-1a entered operational service on 3rd October 1944; a test unit was expanded and re-named *Kommando Nowotny*—under the command of the Austrian ace, Maj. Walter Nowotny—and became operational on that date. One of the two *Staffeln* of the

Messerschimitt Me 262A-2a, fighter-bomber version of the world's first operational jet, and Walter Nowotny, the Austrian ace who commanded the world's first jet fighter squadron

unit was based at Achmer, the other at Hesepe. At approximately the same time the Me 262A-2a fighter-bomber variant entered operational service with *Kommando Schenk*, a unit commanded by Maj. Wolfgang Schenk and largely drawn from former personnel of *Kampfgeschwader 51 "Edelweiss"*.

The first jet bomber to enter operational service with any air force—apart from the Me 262A-2a (see above), which was merely a fighter with two bomb pylons fitted beneath the nose—was the Arado Ar 234B, powered by two Jumo 004B series turbojets. Issued in small numbers to various *Luftwaffe* reconnaissance units during the summer of 1944, the AR 234B entered true bomber squadron service in October 1944 when deliveries of the type commenced to *Kampfgeschwader 76*, then based at Achmer and commanded by Oberstleutnant Robert Kowalewski.

The first aerial victory to be gained by the pilot of a jet aircraft has never been positively identified, but was certainly achieved in the first week of October 1944 by a pilot of *Kommando Nowotny*, the target being a Boeing B-17 Flying Fortress of the U.S. 8th Air Force.

The first loss of a jet aircraft in aerial combat is thought to have taken place on or about 10th October 1944, when two Me 262A-1a fighters were shot down by North American P-51D Mustang escort fighters of the 361st Fighter Group, U.S. 8th Air Force.

North American P-51D Mustang, the outstanding long range escort fighter of the Second World War

The first major operational success by a guided free-falling (i.e. un-powered) bomb was the sinking of the Italian battleship *Roma* by Dornier Do 217s of III *Gruppe*, *Kampfgeschwader 100*, commanded by Maj. Bernhard Jope, west of Corsica on 9th September 1943, using Ruhrstahl Fritz-X 3,100-lb. (1,406 kg.) bombs. The *Roma* was hit by two bombs, the second of which started a disastrous fire which reached the magazine and caused the battleship to blow up, break in two and sink with most of her crew. In this Italian fleet, which was *en route* to surrender to the Allies at Malta, the *Roma*'s sister ship, the *Italia*, received a direct hit on the bows and took on about 800 tons of water before reaching Malta under her own steam. Fritz-X bombs later scored hits on the battleship H.M.S. *Warspite*, the British cruisers H.M.S. *Uganda* and *Spartan* (sunk), and the American cruiser U.S.S. *Savanna*.

The first jet fighter ace in the world has not been positively identified, but it is thought that he was one of the pilots of *Kommando Nowotny*. The unit was withdrawn from operations following the death in action of Maj. Walter Nowotny on 8th November 1944, and later provided the nucleus for the new fighter Wing, *Jagdgeschwader 7 "Nowotny"*; III *Gruppe*, *JG 7* became operational during December 1944. Hauptmann Franz Schall is known to have scored three aerial victories on the day of Nowotny's death, and subsequently served with *10 Staffel*, *JG 7*; it is therefore entirely possible that he was the first pilot in the world to have achieved five confirmed aerial victories while flying jet aircraft. Other known jet aces of the Second World War are listed below. The fragmentary records which survived the final immolation of the *Luftwaffe* in 1945 prevent the preparation of a complete list, and the following should therefore be regarded simply as a confirmed framework for future research:

Oberstleutnant Heinz Bär (JV 44)	16
Hauptmann Franz Schall (10./JG 7)	14
Major Erich Rudorffer (II/JG 7)	12
Oberfeldwebel Hermann Buchner (III/JG 7)	12
Leutnant Karl Schnörrer (11./JG 7)	9
Leutnant Rudolf Rademacher (11./JG 7) . . . . Not less than 8
Major Theodor Weissenberger (Staff/JG 7)	8
Oberleutnant Walter Schuck (3./JG 7)	8
Oberst Johannes Steinhoff (Staff/JG 7, JV 44)	6
Major Wolfgang Späte (Staff/JG 7)	5
Leutnant Klaus Neumann (JV 44)	5

The first, and only, rocket-powered aeroplane to enter operational squadron service with any air force was the Messerschmitt Me 163B-1 *Komet* interceptor fighter, powered by a Walter HWK 109-509A-2 bi-fuel liquid rocket motor. The swept-wing, tailless Me 163B-1 was armed with two 30-mm. MK 108 cannon; some machines are known to have carried various experimental armament systems in addition. The *Komet* equipped only one combat unit, *Jagdgeschwader 400*; *1 Staffel*, *JG 400*, was established at Wittmundhafen in March 1944, and *2 Staffel* at Venlo in May. The whole unit was concentrated on Brandis in July 1944, and operations commenced shortly afterwards; Allied reports mention encounters for the first time on 16th August. The unit's aircraft are thought to have destroyed about a dozen Allied aircraft in all; the only pilot known to have gained two confirmed solo victories was Oberleutnant August Hachtel. The last combat sortie by a *Komet* was carried out by Oberleutnant Fritz Kelb who took off from Husum on 7th May 1945 and did not return.

The first operational Allied jet fighter was the Gloster Meteor I, of which sixteen (*EE213* to *EE222*, and *EE224* to *EE229*) were delivered to No. 616 Squadron. The first two aircraft were delivered on 12th July 1944 to the Squadron, based at Culmhead, Somerset, under the command of Wg. Cdr. A. McDowall, D.S.O., A.F.C. D.F.M.* (see page 65 for top scoring Battle of Britain pilots). **The first combat sortie** was flown from Manston by the Squadron on 27th July 1944 against V-1 flying bombs but was unsuccessful owing to gun-firing difficulties. **The first combat success** was scored by Fg. Off. Dean on 4th August 1944 who, after his guns had jammed, flew alongside the enemy bomb and, by tipping it with his wing, forced the missile into the ground. The aircraft was *EE216*.

The shortest elapsed time for the development of an entirely new jet fighter (which achieved combat status) was sixty-nine days for the Heinkel He 162. Conceived in an R.L.M. specification issued to the German aircraft industry on 8th September 1944, the He 162 was made subject of a contract issued on 29th September 1944 for an aircraft capable of being mass-produced by semi-skilled labour using non-strategic materials. Sixty-nine days later, on 6th December 1944, the first prototype He 162V-1 was flown by Heinkel's chief test pilot, Kapitan Peter, at Vienna-Schwechat. On 10th December the prototype broke up in the air and crashed before a large gathering of officials, and Peter was killed. Notwithstanding this setback, the aircraft entered production and joined *I* and *II Gruppen* of *Jagdgeschwader 1* at Leck/Holstein during April 1945. *III Gruppe* of this *Geschwader* was under orders to receive the new fighter but was forestalled by the end of the War and there is no record of the aircraft ever being used in combat. It has been said on doubtful authority that about 116 He 162s had been completed by VE-day.

The first 22,000-pound (9,988 kg.) bomb, the "Grand Slam" to be dropped was test-dropped by an Avro Lancaster on 13th March 1945. **The first operational drop of this bomb** was made by Sqdn. Ldr. C. C. Calder of No. 617 (Bomber) Squadron flying Lancaster B.1 (Special), *PD112*, on the Bielefeld viaduct on 14th March 1945, smashing two of its spans.

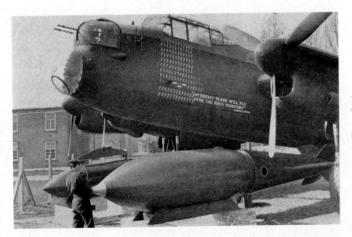

Avro Lancaster, Britain's outstanding heavy bomber of the Second World War. This machine is "S-Sugar" of No. 467 Sqdn. R.A.A.F. (ex-"Q-Queenie" of No. 83 Sqdn. R.A.F.), which survived 137 bombing missions; it bears Göring's boast that no enemy aircraft would ever fly over the Reich painted on the nose. The bomb is a 22,000 lb. Tallboy.

The last known enemy piloted aircraft to fall on British soil is believed to have been a Junkers Ju 88G-6 (D5+AX) of *13 Staffel, Nachtjagdgeschwader 3*, which had been on intruder operations and crashed at 01.51 hrs. on 4th March 1945 at Elvington, near Pocklington airfield, Yorkshire. All the crew members perished.

(*Left*) "*Johnnie*" *Johnson, 38 victories over German fighters and England's leading ace of the Second World War*

(*Right*) *Clive Caldwell, 28 victories in North Africa and the Pacific, and Australia's leading ace*

"Screwball" Beurling, leading Canadian ace, and "Bob" Braham, 29 confirmed victories and only man ever to win seven British gallantry decorations.

The most successful fighter pilots of the Second World War, by nationality, are listed below: all scores are levelled down to the nearest unit: British gallantry decorations are quoted:

Country of origin		*Aircraft destroyed in combat*
Australia	Gp. Capt. Clive R. Caldwell, D.S.O., D.F.C.*	28
Austria	Maj. Walter Nowotny	258
Belgium	Flt. Lt. Vicki Ortmans, D.F.C.	11
Canada	Sqdn. Ldr. George F. Beurling, D.S.O., D.F.C., D.F.M.*	31
Czechoslovakia	Sgt. Josef František, D.F.M.	28
Denmark	Gp. Capt. Kaj Birksted	either 8 or 10
Finland	F/Mstr. E. I. Juutualainen	94
France	Sqdn. Ldr. Pierre H. Clostermann, D.F.C.*	33
Germany	Maj. Erich Hartmann	352
Hungary	2nd Lt. Dezjö Szentgyörgyi	43
Ireland	Wg. Cdr. Brendan E. Finucane, D.S.O., D.F.C.**	32
Italy	Maj. Adriano Visconti	26
Japan	Sub-Officer Hiroyoshi Nishizawa	103
Netherlands	Lt. Col. van Arkel	12 V-1s, and 5
New Zealand	Wg. Cdr. Colin F. Gray, D.S.O., D.F.C.**	27
Norway	Flt. Lt. Svein Heglund	either 14 or 16
Poland	Jan Poniatowski (rank unknown)	36
Rumania	Capt. Prince Constantine Cantacuzino	60
South Africa	Sqdn. Ldr. M. T. St. J. Pattle, D.F.C.*	41
United Kingdom	Gp. Capt. James E. Johnson, D.S.O.**, D.F.C.*	38
United States	Maj. Richard I. Bong.	40
U.S.S.R.	Guards Col. Ivan N. Kozhedub	62

The most successful destroyer of flying bombs (V-1s) in flight was Sqdn. Ldr. Joseph Berry, D.F.C.**, who shot down 60 during 1944.

*Sqdn. Ldr. Joseph Berry, D.F.C.***

Fighter pilots serving with the Royal Air Force during the Second World War who achieved 25 or more confirmed aerial victories (countries of origin indicated in parentheses):

Sqdn. Ldr. M. T. St. J. Pattle, D.F.C.* . . . . 41 (SA)
Gp. Capt. J. E. Johnson, D.S.O.**, D.F.C.* . . . . 38 (UK)
Gp. Capt. A. G. Malan, D.S.O.*, D.F.C.* . . . . 35 (SA)
Sqdn. Ldr. P. H. Closterman, D.F.C.* . . . . . 33 (Fr)
Wg. Cdr. B. E. Finucane, D.S.O., D.F.C.** . . . . 32 (Ir)
Sqdn. Ldr. G. F. Beurling, D.S.O., D.F.C., D.F.M.* . 31 (Ca)
Wg. Cdr. J. R. D. Braham, D.S.O.**, D.F.C.**, A.F.C. . . 29 (UK)
Wg. Cdr. R. R. S. Tuck, D.S.O., D.F.C.** . . . . 29 (UK)
Sqdn. Ldr. N. F. Duke, D.S.O., D.F.C.**, A.F.C. . . . 28 (UK)
Gp. Capt. C. R. Caldwell, D.S.O., D.F.C.* . . . . 28 (Au)
Gp. Capt. F. H. R. Carey, D.F.C.**, A.F.C., D.F.M. . . 28 (UK)
Sqdn. Ldr. J. H. Lacey, D.F.M.* . . . . . 28 (UK)
Wg. Cdr. C. F. Gray, D.S.O., D.F.C.**. . . . . 27 (NZ)
Flt. Lt. E. S. Lock, D.S.O., D.F.C.* . . . . 26 (UK)
Wg. Cdr. L. C. Wade, D.S.O., D.F.C.** . . . . 25 (US)

"Sailor" Malan

Fighter pilots serving with the United States air forces during the Second World War who achieved 25 or more confirmed aerial victories:

U.S.A.A.F.
Maj. Richard I. Bong (C.M.H.) 40
Maj. T. B. McGuire (C.M.H.) 38
Col. F. S. Gabreski 31
Lt. Col. R. S. Johnson 28
Col. C. H. MacDonald 27
Maj. G. E. Preddy 26

U.S.N.
Capt. D. McCampbell 34

U.S.M.C.
Maj. J. J. Foss 26
Lt. R. M. Hanson 25
Lt. Col. G. Boyington 22
(Lt. Col. Boyington is known to have destroyed an additional six enemy aircraft while serving with the Air Volunteer Group under Chinese command.)

Robert S. Johnson, 28 confirmed victories over Europe

Lt. Col. Francis Gabreski, leading American fighter pilot in Europe with 31 confirmed victories

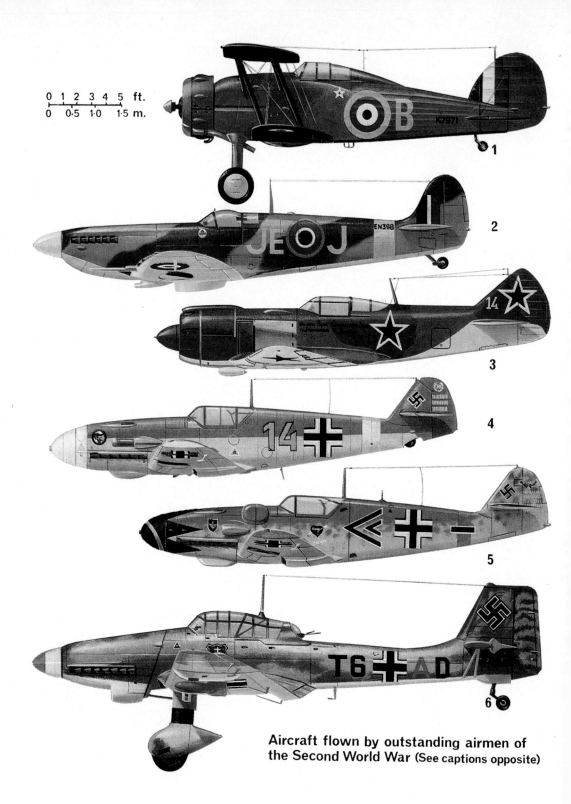

Aircraft flown by outstanding airmen of
the Second World War (See captions opposite)

AIRCRAFT FLOWN BY OUTSTANDING AIRMEN OF THE SECOND WORLD WAR

1. Gloster Gladiator II flown late in 1940 by Flt. Lt. M. T. St.J. Pattle, D.F.C., as commander of "B" Flight, No. 80 (Fighter) Squadron R.A.F.; the serial of this aircraft is believed to have been *K7971*. Flying from various bases in Greece, Pattle is known to have shot down at least 24 enemy aircraft by the end of 1940. Converting on to Hawker Hurricane aircraft early in 1941, he went on to shoot down an estimated total of 41 enemy aircraft before his death in action over the Piraeus on 20th April 1941. The South African-born Pattle was thus the most successful fighter pilot to serve with the British air forces during the Second World War.

2. Supermarine Spitfire IX, serial *EN398*, flown by Wing Cdr. James E. ("Johnnie") Johnson, D.F.C., in April 1943 as Wing Leader of the Kenley Wing—later No. 127 Wing, R.A.F. When Johnson took command of the Wing in March 1943 his score of confirmed victories was six; by the time he relinquished command in September 1943, it stood at 25. Johnson went on to achieve 38 confirmed aerial victories, all single-engined German fighters, and was thus the most successful English fighter pilot of the Second World War, the second most successful R.A.F. fighter pilot, and the most successful Allied fighter pilot in terms of single-engined enemy fighters destroyed in aerial combat.

3. Lavochkin La 5FN flown between May and mid-July 1944 by Capt. Ivan N. Kozhedub, Hero of the Soviet Union; he is believed to have been operating in the Ukraine during this period. By the close of hostilities Kozhedub had attained the rank of Guards Lt.-Col., and had been awarded the Gold Star of a Hero of the Soviet Union three times. His final score of aerial victories is stated to be 62, which qualifies him as the most successful Allied fighter pilot of the Second World War.

4. Messerschmitt Bf 109F-4/Trop, *5237*, flown during June 1942 by Oberleutnant Hans-Joachim Marseille, *Staffelkapitän* of *3 Staffel, Jagdgeschwader 27*. Based at Ain-El Gazala in Libya, Marseille scored his 101st confirmed aerial victory on 18th June 1942, and was subsequently awarded the Swords for this feat. His final score of 158 victories qualifies him as the most successful German fighter pilot to see combat exclusively against the British and Commonwealth air forces during the Second World War.

5. Messerschmitt Bf 109G-14 flown in February 1945 by Maj. Erich Hartmann as commanding officer of *II Gruppe, Jagdgeschwader 52*. During his service on the Russian Front Hartmann achieved a total of 352 confirmed aerial victories, and is thus the most successful fighter pilot the world has ever known. Fuller biographical details may be found in the body of the text.

6. Junkers Ju 87D-5 flown during the winter of 1943/44 by Maj. Hans-Ulrich Rudel as commanding officer of *III Gruppe, Schlachtgeschwader 2 "Immelmann"* in Russia. The most successful of Germany's *Stuka* pilots, and probably the greatest ground attack pilot of that or any other war, Rudel flew a total of 2,530 combat sorties, destroyed 519 Soviet armoured vehicles, and was the only man ever awarded (on 1st January 1945) the Golden Oakleaves to the Knight's Cross.

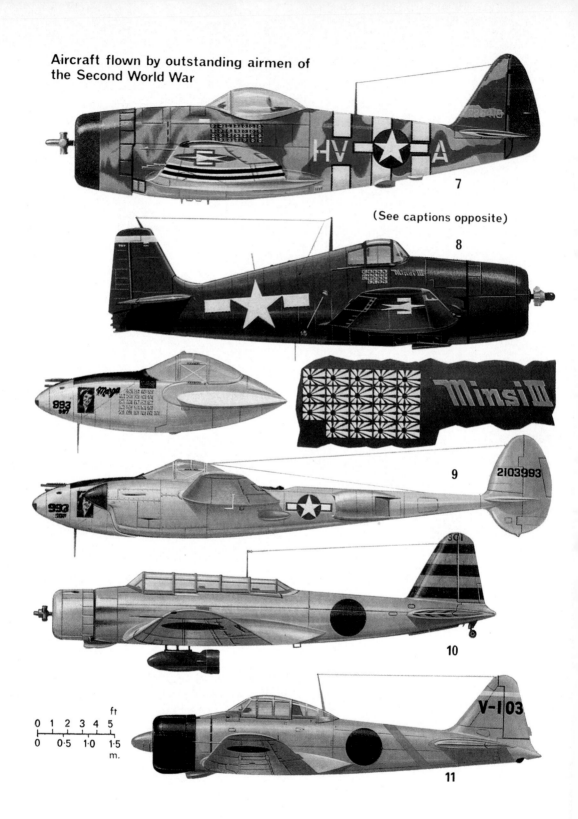

Aircraft flown by outstanding airmen of
the Second World War

(See captions opposite)

7. Republic P-47D Thunderbolt, *42-26418*, flown from Boxted, England, during the summer of 1944 by Lt. Col. Francis S. Gabreski, commanding officer of the 61st Fighter Squadron, 56th Fighter Group, United States 8th Air Force. Gabreski's final score of 31 confirmed aerial victories qualifies him as America's leading ace in the European theatre of operations.

8. Grumman F6F-5 Hellcat "*Minsi III*", flown from the carrier USS *Essex* during the summer of 1944 by Cdr. David McCampbell of Fighter Squadron VF-15. McCampbell's final score of 34 confirmed aerial victories qualifies him as the U.S. Navy's leading ace of the Second World War.

9. Lockheed P-38J Lightning, *42-103993* "*Marge*", flown between October 1943 and March 1944 by Capt. Richard I. Bong, at that time an assistant operations officer at the headquarters of the U.S. 5th Fighter Command in New Guinea. Bong's final score of 40 confirmed aerial victories qualifies him as America's leading ace of the Second World War.

10. Nakajima B5N2 "Kate" in which Cdr. Mitsuo Fuchida, General Commander (Air) of the Imperial Japanese Navy 1st Carrier Division, led the first wave of the attack on Pearl Harbour on 7th December 1941, and from the cockpit of which he transmitted the order to attack at 07.49 hours that morning.

11. Mitsubishi A6M2 *Reisen* ("Zero-Sen") flown in July 1942 from Lae, New Guinea by Petty Officer First Class Saburo Sakai of the *Tainan Kokutai*, Imperial Japanese Navy Air Force. Sakai, who scored 60 confirmed aerial victories in China and the Pacific before being seriously wounded over Guadalcanal in August 1942, finished the war as Japan's third ranking, and senior surviving, fighter pilot.

The first operational military use of composite combat aeroplanes was by the German *Luftwaffe*, probably during June–July 1944. Using explosive-filled Junkers Ju 88A bombers as lower components "carrying" piloted Messerschmitt Bf 109 fighters above, the German *Mistel* (Mistletoe) weapon was first issued to the 2nd *Staffel* of *Kampfgeschwader 101*, commanded by Hauptmann Horst Rudat, during May–June 1944; and it is thought likely that one or two such weapons struck the old French battleship *Courbet* which was used as a blockship for the British artificial Mulberry harbour at Courseulles. More than one hundred Mistletoe weapons are known to have been completed before the end of the War for it is known that on 26th March 1945 eighty-two weapons were available for the proposed German attack (Operation Iron Hammer) upon the Vistula bridges, over which the Russian armies were pouring in their advance to the west.

The most successful fighter pilot in the world, and Germany's leading ace in the Second World War, was Maj. Erich Hartmann of *Jagdgeschwader 52*. He was born in Weissach, Württemberg, in 1922, and was still a 17-year-old schoolboy when war broke out. It was October 1942 before he was posted to his first combat unit, the 9th *Staffel* of JG 52, which was operating in the Ukraine. This unit had earned the reputation of being one of the most formidable *Staffeln* in the *Luftwaffe*; in the spring of 1942 its pilots, led by the ace Oberleutnant Hermann Graf, had been credited with 47 victories in 17 days. Among the most successful members of the *Staffel* were Oberfeldwebel Leopold Steinbatz, Graf's wingman, who gained 35 victories during the month of May 1942, and was the first N.C.O. to be awarded the Swords and Oak Leaves to the Knight's Cross; Oberfeld-webeln Füllgrabe and Süss, both of whom were to score between 60 and 70 victories; and Feldwebel Alfred Grislawski, who was to score 133 kills. In this rarified atmosphere the slim, classically handsome Hartmann, just 20 years old, did not give any immediate signs of future promise. He gained his first victory on 5th November, but by April 1943, when he had amassed 100 missions in his log-book, his score stood at seven victories only. Like Johnson and many other leading aces, he had a lengthy "running-in" period during which he perfected his technique. His eyesight and co-ordination were excellent, his flying was cool and calculated, and he was economical with his ammunition, usually closing to very short range before opening fire with short bursts. He did not strive for high scores on each sortie, preferring to gain one good, clean text-book kill and then concentrate on his flying and his rear-view mirror. Nevertheless, he was to gain multiple victories on many occasions, his first major success being achieved on 7th July 1943; JG 52 was one of the units involved in covering the great *Zitadelle* tank offensive in the Kursk-Orel-Bielgorod area, and on that day Hartmann led the 7th *Staffel's* Messerschmitt Bf 109G fighters from their base at Ugrim, to score seven personal victories on three sorties—three Ilyushin Il-2 ground attack aircraft, and four Lavochkin LaGG 3 fighters. These were his 22nd to 28th victories; by 20th September his score had risen to no less than 100; he had been shot down, captured, and escaped four hours later; and he was clearly emerging as something special, even among the veterans of JG 52. His Knight's Cross came with his 148th victory on 29th October 1943, the Oak Leaves on 2nd March 1944 with his 200th, and the Swords on 4th July 1944, with his 239th. The summer of 1944 saw another period of multiple successes; in four weeks he destroyed 78 enemy aircraft, including eight on 23rd August, and 11 on the following day, bringing his score to 301—and making him the first of the only two fighter pilots in the world who ever scored 300 victories. This feat brought him into the select band of men—numbering 27 only—who wore the Diamonds to the Knight's Cross. In October 1944 he became *Staffelkapitän* of 4./JG 52, and took over command of *II Gruppe*, JG 52 on 1st February 1945. His unit retreated steadily westwards as the Red Army swept across central Europe in the final great offensive, and Hartmann eventually surrendered to American forces in Czecho-slovakia in May 1945; by this time he had scored 352 victories, including 260 fighter aircraft, of which five were American P-51 Mustangs shot down during a brief posting to Rumania. In accordance with a prior political commitment, the American authorities handed him over to the Russians; he was made to stand trial as a criminal, and sentenced to ten years' imprisonment. The fact that he survived this sentence and returned home in 1955 is a considerable testimony to his character and determination. He rejoined the *Luftwaffe*, and rose to high rank during the 1960s; at the time of writing he is still in uniform.

The most successful German fighter pilot in combat against the Western Allies during the Second World War was Hauptmann Hans-Joachim Marseille, who was born in Berlin-Charlottenburg in December 1919. As an N.C.O./officer candidate he saw action on the Channel Coast in 1940, flying with *Lehrgeschwader 2* and 4./JG 52 during the closing stages of the Battle of Britain. In this campaign he scored his first seven victories, all R.A.F. fighters, but was himself shot down four times in the process; he was awarded the Iron Cross 1st Class in September 1940. In April of 1941 he was posted to *I Gruppe, Jagdgeschwader 27* in Libya, and it was in desert warfare that he excelled. He worked with great perseverance to master his trade, and in the blinding skies of North Africa his superb depth vision and marksmanship became a legend. He was credited with many multiple victories, including the astounding total of 17 aircraft destroyed on 1st September 1942. He was awarded the Knight's Cross on 22nd February 1942 for his 50th victory; the Oak Leaves on 6th June, for his 75th; and the Swords only 12 days later, by which time his score stood at 101. On 8th June he had become *Staffelkapitän* of 3./JG 27. On 2nd September 1942 he received the Diamonds, then his country's highest award; he was only the fourth man to receive the award, the others being Werner Mölders, Adolf Galland, and Gordon Gollob—the first 150-victory ace. On 30th September the "Star of Africa" died; returning from an uneventful mission over the Alamein line, he was forced to bale out when the engine of his Bf 109G began to smoke for no apparent reason. He is thought to have been struck by the tail of his aircraft as he jumped, and his parachute was not seen to open. He was 22 years old, and had been credited with 158 victories, all of them gained in combat against the R.A.F. and Commonwealth air forces.

The most successful English fighter pilot of the Second World War was Gp. Capt. James Edgar "Johnnie" Johnson, credited with 38 confirmed aerial victories over German aircraft. Johnson was born in Loughborough, Leicestershire in 1915; in 1937, a qualified civil engineer, he applied to join the Royal Air Force, but was rejected. In 1939, when the need for aircrew was receiving priority, he was invited to apply once more, and two days later was a Flight Sergeant in the Royal Air Force Volunteer Reserve. He attended flying school at Stapleford Tawney in Essex; with the outbreak of war and the mobilization of the R.A.F.V.R. he was posted to various flying schools, was granted a commission as Pilot Officer, and began training on the Spitfire. Towards the end of August 1940 he was posted to No. 19 Squadron, then based at Duxford, the famous fighter station near Cambridge. He had just 23 hours flying time on Spitfires, and had never fired his guns; and even under the desperate conditions of the Battle of Britain, the squadron was unwilling to send him and the other young replacement pilots into action against the veterans of the *Luftwaffe*, especially as No. 19 was then experiencing great difficulties with the 20 mm. cannon on their aircraft, and losses were high. There was no time to train tyro pilots at Duxford, and Johnson was transferred to No. 616 Squadron, then going through a rest and reorganisation period at Coltishall after being withdrawn from combat. Yet again he was thwarted in his ambition to get into action; an old shoulder fracture began giving trouble, and Johnson was forced to undergo an operation. It was not until January of 1941 that he returned to No. 616 and operational flying. He shared a victory over a Dornier Do 17 with a fellow pilot, and in June 1941 scored his first solo victory—a Messerschmitt Bf 109, shot down over Gravelines. During this period Johnson was flying in the leading section of the three-squadron Tangmere Wing, under the leadership and tutelage of the legless Douglas Bader. His score rose steadily but not spectacularly ($6\frac{1}{2}$ victories by the end of the summer of 1941); he was awarded the D.F.C., and given command of No. 610 Squadron in July 1942. It was

Gabreski's Republic P-47D Thunderbolt; the mighty "Jug" was noted for its weight—just short of 20,000 lb.—and consequently spectacular diving performance

while leading this mixed-nationality unit that he began to emerge as one of the brightest stars of Fighter Command. In March 1943 he was given command of the Kenley Wing, flying Spitfires, a formation which included two Canadian squadrons; during the summer of that year the Wing was heavily engaged in daylight operations in support of American bombing raids, and Johnson's personal score between March and September rose by 19. An enforced period of non-combat duty followed this successful tour, and it was March of 1944 before Johnson returned to operational flying; he was given command of No. 144 Canadian Wing, and in his last air battle—a sortie over Arnhem on 27th September 1944—he scored his 38th kill. This was, incidentally, the only occasion during his 515 combat missions when his aircraft was hit by enemy fire. All his solo victories had been won in combat with single-engined fighters—Messerschmitt Bf 109s and Focke-Wulf Fw 190s—and the majority of them during a period of *Luftwaffe* air superiority over the Channel Coast. Johnson remained in the Royal Air Force, finally retiring with the rank of Air Vice Marshal in 1966; during the Korean War he secured an exchange posting to the U.S.A.A.F. and flew several combat missions. His decorations include the D.S.O. and two Bars, the D.F.C. and Bar, the American D.F.C., Air Medal and Legion of Merit, the C.B. and the C.B.E. From an international point of view, Johnson certainly destroyed the **greatest number of German fighters** of any Allied pilot.

The most successful American fighter pilot of the Second World War was Maj. Richard Ira Bong, whose 40 confirmed aerial victories are unsurpassed by any American military pilot of any war. Born at Superior, Wisconsin, on 24th September 1920, Bong enlisted as a flying cadet on 29th May 1941. After flying training at Tulare and Gardner Fields, California, and Luke Field, Arizona, he received his "wings" and a commission (all American military pilots were automatically commissioned) on 9th January 1942. In May he was posted to Hamilton Field, California, for combat training on the Lockheed P-38 Lightning twin-engined fighter, and subsequently joined the 9th Fighter Squadron of the 49th Fighter Group, then based in Australia. In November 1942 Bong transferred to the 39th Fighter Squadron of the 35th Fighter Group; in January 1943 he returned to the 9th, having shot down five Japanese aircraft in the meantime. He remained with the 9th until November 1943, being promoted 1st Lieutenant in April and Captain in August. On 11th November he was posted to the Headquarters of V Fighter Command (New Guinea), as assistant operations officer in charge of replacement aircraft; nevertheless, he continued to fly combat missions in P-38s, and by the time he was promoted Major and posted home to instruct in air superiority techniques, in April 1944, his score had risen to 28 confirmed kills. He returned to the Pacific as gunnery training officer of V Fighter Command in September 1944; although not required to continue combat flying, he voluntarily put in 30 further combat missions over Borneo and the Philippines and was credited with a further 12 victories. General George C. Kenney, his commanding officer, ordered him back to the United States in December of 1944, with a recommendation for the Congressional Medal of Honor—which award was subsequently granted. Bong became a test pilot for Lockheed at Burbank, California; and on August 6th 1945, the day the world's first atomic bomb was dropped on Hiroshima, he died when the engine of his P-80 jet failed. Apart from his Medal of Honor, Richard Bong was awarded the D.S.C., two Silver Stars, seven D.F.C.s, and 15 Air Medals. His score of 40 kills was achieved during more than 200 combat missions, totalling over 500 flying hours; many of these victories were gained while flying the P-38J "*Marge*", named after his fiancée, which is illustrated in the accompanying colour pages.

The numbers of aircraft shot down by fighter pilots of the Second World War varied much more widely than was the case in the First World War, due to the enormous differences in conditions and standards of equipment in the various combat areas. Comparison of the list of national top-scoring fighter pilots will immediately reveal the almost incredible superiority of German pilots in terms of confirmed victories—i.e., Major Erich Hartmann, the *Luftwaffe*'s leading ace, is credited with nearly nine times as many victories as the leading British and American pilots, and 35 Germans are credited with scores in excess of 150.

Since the end of the War there have been persistent attempts to discredit these scores; but by any reasonable criterion, the figures must now be accepted as accurate. The *Luftwaffe*'s confirmation procedure was just as rigorous as that followed by Allied air forces, and the quoted figures are those prepared at unit level and were not subject to manipulation by the Propaganda Ministry. The phenomenon becomes less astonishing if studied in context. The main reasons for the gulf between German and Allied scores were the different conditions of service and the special circumstances which existed on the Russian Front in 1941 and 1942. In Allied air forces an operational tour by a fighter pilot was almost invariably followed by a posting to a second-line establishment for several months. This process of rotating pilots to areas where they could recover from the strain of prolonged combat operations was unknown in the *Luftwaffe*; apart from very short periods of leave, a German fighter pilot was effectively on combat operations from the day of his first posting until the day his career ended—in death, serious injury, or capture. The *Luftwaffe* fighter pilot's career was thus, in real terms, about twice as long as his R.A.F. or U.S.A.A.F. counterpart; many of the leading German pilots recorded well over 1,000 combat sorties in their log books, roughly twice the British average.

When Germany invaded the Soviet Union in June 1941, the Russian air forces were equipped with very large numbers of obsolescent aircraft. They had no fighter whose speed and armament approached the performance of the Messerschmitt Bf 109E and Bf 109F, and their bombers in squadron service were markedly inferior to contemporary European designs. The enormous advances achieved by the German army in the early months of the campaign were accompanied by close air support, and from the first day of the invasion the *Luftwaffe* enjoyed a measure of air superiority which was quite unprecedented. Operating from forward airfields and keeping up with the advancing tank armies, the German fighters frequently flew five or six sorties every day, and individual scores of four, five or six victories on a single sortie were not uncommon. The *Luftwaffe* was presented with large numbers of easy targets— the perfect environment for the development of a fighter pilot's skill and

Werner Mölders, first great German ace of the Second World War, who had achieved 115 confirmed victories at the time of his death on 22nd November 1941.

confidence. The situation did not become significantly more challenging for
many months by which time many of the *Jagdflieger* had learned their trade so
well that they were equal to the challenge.

It should be noted, however, that Maj. Hartmann did not start his combat
career until the end of 1942, and that his most consistently successful period
of operations fell between August and November 1943, when Russian designs
of comparable quality to Western equipment were coming into service in
large numbers. It is true that the training of Russian aircrew was still markedly
inferior to that of *Luftwaffe* pilots; but there must come a point at which the
search for "special factors" becomes mere rationalisation, and one is left with
the inescapable conclusion that Germany simply produced a group of officers
who were fighter pilots of a skill and determination unequalled by any other
nation.

This conclusion is borne out by a study of the records of fighter units
which were based on the Western Front or in the Mediterranean area throughout the war. While the accompanying table reveals that the vast majority of
the most successful pilots saw combat exclusively (or almost exclusively) in
Russia, there remain many who spent the whole war in action against the
Western Allies, and achieved scores two or three times as great as the leading
Allied pilots. After the end of 1942 German and Allied fighter designs were
roughly comparable in quality; the explanation must therefore lie in the unbroken combat careers of the *Luftwaffe* pilots, and in sheer ability. The pilots
who scored **100 or more victories against the Western Allies** in Northern
Europe, Southern Europe, the Mediterranean area and North Africa were as
follows (Western victories only, in cases of mixed service):—

*Gerhard Barkhorn, 301
confirmed victories*

Hauptmann Hans-Joachim Marseille	.	.	.	.	.	.	158
Oberstleutnant Heinz Bär	.	.	.	.	.	.	124
Oberstleutnant Kurt Bühligen	.	.	.	.	.	.	112
Generalleutnant Adolf Galland	.	.	.	.	.	.	104
Major Joachim Müncheberg .	.	.	.	.	.	.	102
Oberstleutnant Egon Mayer .	.	.	.	.	.	.	102
Major Werner Schroer .	.	.	.	.	.	.	102
Oberst Josef Priller	.	.	.	.	.	.	101

These figures become even more impressive if one reflects on the fact that
Marseille achieved 151 of his victories between April 1941 and September
1942; that Galland did virtually no combat flying between November 1941
and the end of 1944, while he occupied the post of General of Fighters; and
that Müncheberg was killed in March 1943.

Two categories of victories in Northern Europe are worthy of special
attention; those scored over heavy bombers, and those scored while flying jet

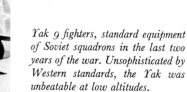

*Yak 9 fighters, standard equipment
of Soviet squadrons in the last two
years of the war. Unsophisticated by
Western standards, the Yak was
unbeatable at low altitudes.*

aircraft. The achievements of the world's first generation of jet combat pilots are described elsewhere in this chapter. The *Luftwaffe* placed great value on the destruction of the very heavily armed four-engined Boeing Fortress and Consolidated Liberator bombers which formed the United States 8th Air Force's main equipment in the massive daylight bombing offensive of 1943–45. Usually flying in dense formations protected by an enormous combined fire-power—and, in the later months, by superb escort fighters—these large aircraft were obviously far more difficult to destroy than smaller aircraft. The leading "heavy baby specialists" among Germany's home defence pilots included:—

Oberleutnant Herbert Rollwage	44
Oberst Walther Dahl	36
Major Werner Schroer	26
Hauptmann Hugo Frey	26
Oberstleutnant Egon Mayer	25
Oberstleutnant Kurt Bühligen	24
Oberstleutnant Heinz Bär	21
Hauptmann Hans-Heinrich König	20
Hauptmann Heinz Knoke	19

Hans-Ulrich Rudel, the greatest of all ground-attack pilots and only man ever awarded the Golden Oak-leaves to the Knight's Cross

Supermarine Spitfire, best known British fighter of the war and held by many to be the most beautiful air-craft ever built; in all 22,759 Spitfires and Seafires were produced.

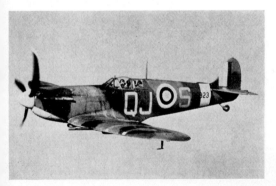

Boeing B-29 Superfortresses on a fire raid over Japan. The B-29's of the U.S. 20th Bomber Command, based on the Marianas, played a decisive part in the Pacific victory.

The last Victoria Cross won during the Second World War was awarded to Lt. Robert Hampton Gray, D.S.C., Royal Canadian Navy Volunteer Reserve (attached to the Fleet Air Arm), and pilot of a Corsair fighter-bomber, who was killed in an attack on a Japanese destroyer in the Bay of Onagawa Wan on 9th August 1945—after both atomic bombs had been dropped upon Japan and only a few days before the Japanese surrender. Gray's V.C. was the only such award to a member of the Royal Canadian Navy during the Second World War.

(It was said (presumably by the then Air Ministry) in 1960 that during World War II a total of 19,244 Distinguished Flying Crosses were awarded, as well as 1,576 Bars to the D.F.C. Subsequent research however has demonstrated that both these figures are somewhat lower than the actual number of these decorations awarded as they do not include all those awarded to non-British subjects which were not gazetted in the London Gazette.)

Above: *The Hawker Hurricane (background) was R.A.F. Fighter Command's first monoplane fighter; the aircraft shown here was the last of 14,533 built. The Supermarine Spitfire, of which 22,759 were built, was probably the best-known British fighter of all time.* **Below**: *The Gloster Gladiator was the R.A.F.'s last biplane fighter.*

LUFTWAFFE FIGHTER PILOTS WITH 100 OR MORE CONFIRMED VICTORIES DURING THE SECOND WORLD WAR AND THE SPANISH CIVIL WAR

E. = Eastern Front; W = Europe; Afr. = North Africa; Gr. = Greece; * = at least
✠ ⚜ ⚔ ◆ = Knight's Cross with Oakleaves, Swords and Diamonds
✠ ⚜ ⚔ = Knight's Cross with Oakleaves and Swords
✠ ⚜ = Knight's Cross with Oakleaves
✠ = Knight's Cross of the Iron Cross

Name, rank, decorations	Units	Total score	Day/ Night	Fronts	4-engined	With jet a/c
Major Erich Hartmann ✠⚜⚔◆	JG 52	352	352/0	352 E.	0	0
Major Gerhard Barkhorn ✠⚜⚔	JG 52, 6, JV 44	301	301/1	301 E.	0	?
Major Günther Rall ✠⚜⚔	JG 52, 11, 300	275	275/0	3 W., 272 E.	?	0
Oberleutnant Otto Kittel ✠⚜⚔	JG 54	*267	267/0	267 E.	0	0
Major Walter Nowotny ✠⚜⚔◆	JG 54, Kdo. Nowotny	258	258/0	255 E., 3 W.	*1	3
Major Wilhelm Batz ✠⚜⚔	JG 52	237	237/0	232 E., 5 W.	2	0
Major Erich Rudorffer ✠⚜⚔	JG 2, 54, 7	222	222/0	136 E., 60 W., 26 Afr.	10	12
Oberstleutnant Heinz Bär ✠⚜⚔	JG 51, 77, 1, 3, JV 44	220	220/0	96 E., 79 W., 45 Afr.	*21	16
Oberst Hermann Graf ✠⚜⚔◆	JG 51, 52, 50, 11, 52	212	212/0	202 E., 10 W.	10	0
Major Theodor Weissenberger ✠⚜	JG 77, 5, 7	208	208/0	175 E., 33 W.	?	8
Oberstleutnant Hans Philipp ✠⚜⚔	JG 76, 54, 1	206	206/0	177 E., 29 W.	1	0
Oberleutnant Walter Schuck ✠⚜	JG 5, 7	206	206/0	198 E., 8 W.	4	8
Major Heinrich Ehrler ✠⚜	JG 5, 7	*204	204/0	204 E.?	?	?
Oberleutnant Anton Hafner ✠⚜	JG 51	204	204/0	184 E., 20 Afr.	5	0
Hauptmann Helmut Lipfert ✠⚜	JG 52, 53	203	203/0	Majority E., *4 W.	2	0
Major Walter Krupinski ✠⚜	JG 52, 5, 11, 26, JV 44	197	197/0	177 E., 20 W.	1	?
Major Anton Hackl ✠⚜⚔	JG 77, 11, 26, 300, 11	192	192/0	105 E., 87 W.	32	0
Hauptmann Joachim Brendel ✠⚜	JG 51	189	189/0	189 E.	0	0
Hauptmann Max Stotz ✠⚜	JG 54	189	189/0	173 E., 16 W.	0	0
Hauptmann Joachim Kirschner ✠⚜	JG 3, 27	188	188/0	167 E., 13 Gr., 6 W., 2 Malta	*2	0
Major Kurt Brändle ✠⚜	JG 53, 3	180	180/0	160 E., 20 W.	0	0
Oberleutnant Günther Josten ✠⚜	JG 51	178	178/0	Majority E.	1	0
Oberst Johannes Steinhoff ✠⚜⚔	JG 26, 52, 77, 7, JV 44	176	176/0	148 E., 28 W. & Afr.	4	6
Oberleutnant Ernst-Wilhelm Reinert ✠⚜⚔	JG 77, 27	174	174/0	103 E., 51 Afr., 20 W.	2	0
Hauptmann Günther Schack ✠⚜	JG 51, 3	174	174/0	174 E.	0	0
Hauptmann Emil Lang ✠⚜	JG 54, 26	173	173/0	148 E., 25 W.	?	0
Hauptmann Heinz Schmidt ✠⚜	JG 52	173	173/0	173 E.	0	0
Major Horst Ademeit ✠⚜	JG 54	166	166/0	165 E., 1 W.	0	0
Oberst Wolf-Dietrich Wilcke ✠⚜⚔	JG 53, 3	162	162/0	137 E., 21 W., 4 Malta	4	0
Hauptmann Hans-Joachim Marseille ✠⚜⚔◆	JG 52, 27	158	158/0	151 Afr., 7 W.	0	0

Name, rank, decorations	Units	Total score	Day/ Night	Fronts	4-engined	With jet a/c
Hauptmann Heinrich Sturm✠	JG 52	**157**	157/0	157 E.	0	0
Oberleutnant Gerhard Thyben✠	JG 3, 54	**157**	157/0	152 E., 5 W.	?	0
Oberleutnant Hans Beisswenger✠	JG 54	**152**	152/0	152 E.	0	0
Leutnant Peter Düttmann✠	JG 52	**150**	150/0	150 E.	0	0
Oberst Gordon Gollob✠◆	ZG 76, JG 3, 77	**150**	150/0	144 E., 6 W.	0	0
Leutnant Fritz Tegtmeier✠	JG 54, 7	**146**	146/0	146 E.	0	0
Oberleutnant Albin Wolf✠	JG 54	**144**	144/0	144 E.	0	0
Leutnant Kurt Tanzer✠	JG 51	**143**	143/0	126 E., 17 W.	4	0
Oberstleutnant Friedrich-Karl Müller✠	JG 53, 3	**140**	140/0	100 E., rest W. and Afr.	*2	0
Leutnant Karl Gratz✠	JG 52, 2	**138**	138/0	121 E., 17 W.	0	0
Major Heinrich Setz✠	JG 77, 27	**138**	138/0	132 E., 6 W.	0	0
Hauptmann Rudolf Trenkel✠	JG 77, 52	**138**	138/0	Majority E., *1 W.	1	0
Oberleutnant Walter Wolfrum✠	JG 52	**137**	137/0	137 E.	0	0
Hauptmann Franz Schall✠	JG 52, Kdo. Nowotny, JG 7	**137**	137/0	123 E., 14 W.	?	14
Oberst Adolf Dickfeld✠	JG 52, 2, 11	**136**	136/0	115 E., 21 W. and Afr.	11	0
Hauptmann Horst-Günther von Fassong✠	JG 51, 11	**136**	136/0	90 E., 46 W.	4	0
Oberleutnant Otto Fönnekold✠	JG 52	**136**	136/0	Majority E.	0	0
Hauptmann Karl-Heinz Weber✠	JG 51, 1	**136**	136/0	136 E.	0	0
Major Joachim Müncheberg✠	JG 26, 51, 77	**135**	135/0	102 W. and Afr., 33 E.	0	0
Oberleutnant Hans Waldmann✠	JG 52, 3, 7	**134**	134/0	121 E., 13 W.	?	2
Major Johannes Wiese	JG 52, 77	**133**	133/0	133 E.	0	0
Hauptmann Alfred Grislawski✠	JG 52, 50, 1, 53	**133**	133/0	109 E., 24 W.	18	0
Major Adolf Borchers✠	JG 51, 52	**132**	132/0	127 E., 5 W.	0	0
Major Erwin Clausen✠	JG 77, 11	**132**	132/0	114 E., 18 W.	14	0
Hauptmann Wilhelm Lemke✠	JG 3	**131**	131/0	125 E., 6 W.	0	0
Oberst Herbert Ihlefeld✠	JG 77, 52, 25, 11, 1	**130**	130/0	67 E., 56 W., 7 Sp.	15	0
Oberleutnant Heinrich Sterr✠	JG 54	**130**	130/1	127 E., 3 W.	?	0
Major Franz Eisenach✠	ZG 76, JG 1, 54	**129**	129/0	129 E.	0	0
Oberst Walther Dahl✠	JG 3, 300	**128**	128/0	77 E., 51 W.	36	0
Hauptmann Franz Dörr✠	E. JG 3, JG 5	**128**	128/0	122 E., 6 W.	0	0
Oberleutnant Josef Zwernemann✠	JG 52, 77, 11	**126**	126/0	106 E., 20 W.	?	0
Leutnant Rudolf Rademacher✠	JG 54, 7	**126**	126/0	90 E., 36 W.	*10	*8, possibly 25
Leutnant Gerhard Hoffmann✠	JG 52	**125**	125/0	125 E.	0	0
Oberst Dietrich Hrabak✠	JG 54, 52, 54	**125**	125/0	109 E., 16 W.	0	0
Oberst Walter Oesau✠	JG 51, 3, 2, 1	**125**	125/0	73 W., 44 E., 8 Sp.	10	0
Oberlautnant Wolf Ettel✠	JG 3, 27	**124**	124/0	Majority E., *4 W.	2	0
Hauptmann Robert Weiss✠	JG 26, 54	**121**	121/0	Majority E., 31 W.?	0	0
Major Heinz-Wolfgang Schnaufer✠◆	NJG 1, 4	**121**	0/121	121 W.	Majority	0

Name, rank, decorations	Units	Total score	Day/ Night	Fronts	4-engined	With jet a/c
Oberfeldwebel Heinz Marquardt✠	JG 51	**121**	121/0	Majority E.	o	o
Oberleutnant Friedrich Obleser✠	JG 52	**120**	120/0	111 E., 9 W.	2	o
Oberstleutnant Erich Leie✠	JG 2, 51, 77	**118**	118/0	75 E., 43 W.	1	o
Leutnant Heinz Wernicke✠	JG 54	**117**	117/0	117 E.	o	o
Leutnant Jakob Norz✠	JG 5	**117**?	117/0	117 E.	o	o
Leutnant Hans-Joachim Birkner✠	JG 52, 51	**117**	117/0	Probably 116 E., W.	o	o
Leutnant Franz-Josef Beerenbrock✠	JG 51	**117**	117/0	117 E.	o	o
Oberleutnant August Lambert✠	SG 2, 151, 77	**116**	116/0	116 E.	o	o
Oberst Werner Mölders✠◆	JG 53, 51	**115**	115/0	68 W., 33 E., 14 Sp.	o	o
Major Werner Schroer✠	JG 27, 54, 3	**114**	114/0	102 W., 12 E.	26	o
Leutnant Wilhelm Crinius✠	JG 53	**114**	114/0	100 E., 14 W.	1	o
Leutnant Hans Dammers✠	JG 52	**113**	113/0	113 E.	o	o
Leutnant Berthold Korts✠	JG 52	**113**	113/0	113 E.	o	o
Oberstleutnant Kurt Bühligen✠	JG 2	**112**	112/0	112 W. and Afr.	24	o
Oberst Helmut Lent✠◆	ZG 76, NJG 1, 2, 3	**110**	8/102	110 W.	Majority	o
Major Kurt Ubben✠	JG 77, 2	**110**	110/0	90 E., 20 W. and Afr.	o	o
Oberleutnant Franz Woidich✠	JG 27, 52, 400	**110**	110/0	108 E., 2 Afr.	o	o
Major Reinhard Seiler	JG 54	**109**	93/16	96 E., 4 W., 9 Sp.	1	o
Hauptmann Emil Bitsch✠	JG 3	**108**	108/0	104 E., 4 W.	o	o
Major Hans "Assi" Hahn✠	JG 2, 54	**108**	108/0	68 W., 40 E.	4	o
Oberst Günther Lützow✠	JG 3, JV 44	**108**	108/0	85 E., 18 W., 5 Sp.	o	o
Oberleutnant Bernhard Vechtel✠	JG 51	**108**	108/0	108 E.	o	o
Hauptmann Werner Lucas✠	JG 3	**106**	106/0	Probably 100 E., 6 W.	1	o
Oberst Victor Bauer✠	JG 2, 3	**106**	106/0	102 E., 4 W.	o	o
Generalleutnant Adolf Galland✠◆	JG 27, 26, JV 44	**104**	104/0	104 W.	4	?
Leutnant Heinz Sachsenberg✠	JG 52, JV 44	**104**	104/0	103 E., 1 W.	1?	1?
Major Hartmann Grasser✠	ZG 2, JG 51, 1, 210	**103**	103/0	86 E., 17 W.	2	o
Major Siegfried Freytag✠	JG 77, 7	**102**	102/0	Probably 70 E., 32 W. and Afr.	o	o
Hauptmann Friedrich Geisshardt✠	LG 2, JG 77, 26	**102**	102/0	75 E., 27 W. and Afr.	?	o
Oberstleutnant Egon Mayer✠	JG 2	**102**	102/0	102 W.	25	o
Oberleutnant Max-Hellmuth Ostermann✠	ZG 1, JG 54	**102**	102/0	93 E., 9 W.	o	o
Oberleutnant Herbert Rollwage✠	JG 53	**102**	102/0	91 W. and Afr., 11 E.	44	o
Major Josef Wurmheller✠	JG 53, 2	**102**	102/0	93 W., 9 E.	*13	o
Oberst Josef Priller✠	JG 26	**101**	101/0	101 W.	11	o
Hauptmann Rudolf Miethig✠	JG 52	**101**	101/0	101 E.	o	o
Leutnant Ulrich Wernitz✠	JG 54	**101**	101/0	101 E.	o	o

AFTER THE SECOND WORLD WAR

The fastest twin piston-engined combat aircraft in the world to reach operational status was the de Havilland Hornet fighter which possessed a maximum speed of 485 m.p.h. (780 km./hr.) in "clean" combat configuration. Powered by two 2,070 h.p. Rolls-Royce Merlin 130 engines, the Hornet was armed with four 20-mm. guns and had a maximum range of more than 2,500 miles (3,050 km.). It was first flown by Geoffrey de Havilland, Jr., on 28th July 1944 but did not reach the first R.A.F. squadron (No. 64 (Fighter) Squadron at Horsham St. Faith, Norfolk) until after the end of hostilities in Europe.

The de Havilland Hornet

The first two post-war world absolute air speed records were established by Gloster Meteor IV fighters. On 7th November 1945 Gp. Capt. H. J. Wilson established a record speed of 606 m.p.h. (974 km./hr.) at Herne Bay, Kent, and on 7th September 1946 Gp. Capt. E. M. Donaldson raised the record to 616 m.p.h. (990 km./hr.) near Tangmere, West Sussex. The Meteors featured in the latter speed record had had their wings clipped, and in this configuration entered squadron service with the R.A.F. whose principal day fighter equipment they represented until in 1950 they were replaced by the Meteor 8 version. Both the Mark IV and 8 Meteors were powered by 3,500-lb. (1,590 kg.) thrust Rolls-Royce Derwent V turbojets.

The first Russian jet bomber to achieve production status was the Tupolev Tu-12, which was a direct development of the Tu-2 piston-engined bomber re-engined with RD-10 turbojets of 2,000-lb. (908 kg.) thrust and which first flew in 1946.

The first Russian jet fighter to enter squadron service with the Soviet Air Forces was the Yak-15, designed by Alexander S. Yakovlev, entering service with the IA-PVO early in 1947, powered by a single RD-10 turbojet (a Russian adaptation of the German Jumo 004B engine), developing 1,980-lb. (900 kg.) thrust. Armed with two 23-mm. Nudelman-Suranov NS-23 guns, the Yak-15 possessed a top speed of approximately 495 m.p.h. (800 km./hr.).

The first European swept-wing jet fighter to enter operational service after the Second World War was the Swedish SAAB J-29 (first flight, 1st September 1948) which joined the Day Fighter Wing F.13 of the *Flygvapnet* near Norrkoping in May 1951. Nicknamed *Tunnan* (=Barrel) and powered by a British de Havilland Ghost turbojet, the J-29B possessed a top speed of 658 m.p.h. at 5,000 ft. (1,064 km./hr. at 1,500 m.) or Mach 0·90 at the tropopause.

A miscellany of famous aircraft. Top is a racing version of the famous P-51 Mustang escort fighter; many of these aircraft remain operational in private hands in the United States. Centre left is the best two-seat fighter of the First World War, the Bristol Fighter F.2B; one specimen is maintained in flying condition by the Shuttleworth Trust in England. Centre right is a Hawker Siddeley Kestrel—now known, in its operational configuration, as the Harrier. This photograph of the world's first operational vertical take-off fighter was taken during the evaluation programme by a tripartite squadron of R.A.F., American and German personnel. Bottom is a prototype view of the General Dynamics F-111 variable geometry multi-rôle aircraft, since dogged by delays in its development and service acceptance programme, which have led to cancellations at home and abroad.

The first aerial victory to be gained by the pilot of one jet aircraft over another was achieved on 8th November 1950, when Lt. Russell J. Brown, Jr., of the 51st Fighter–Interceptor Wing, U.S.A.F., flying a Lockheed F-80C, shot down a MiG-15 jet fighter of the Chinese People's Republic Air Force over Sinuiju on the Yalu River, the border between North Korea and China.

The first jet pilot to achieve five confirmed aerial victories over jet aircraft was Capt. James Jabara, an F-86 Sabre pilot of the 4th Fighter-Interceptor Wing, U.S.A.F., who shot down his fifth MiG-15 on 20th May 1951. Capt., later Maj. Jabara went on to destroy a total of 15 MiG-15s, thereby becoming the second most successful Allied pilot of the Korean War.

The most successful Allied fighter pilot of the Korean War was Capt. Joseph McConnell, Jr., of the 16th Fighter Squadron, 51st Fighter-Interceptor Wing, U.S.A.F.; an F-86 Sabre pilot, McConnell scored his 16th and last victory on 18th May 1953, a day on which he destroyed a total of three MiG-15s. He was subsequently killed testing a North-American F-86H on 25th August 1954.

Capt. Joseph McConnell, Jr., and North American F-86 Sabre

The most successful jet fighter pilot in the world cannot be identified. The record set by Oberstleutnant Bär in 1945 stood, as stated above, until it was equalled by Capt. McConnell in 1953. It is thought unlikely that any Communist pilot equalled or surpassed this figure during the Korean War; in general the standard of MiG-15 pilots encountered was not high, though there were some notable exceptions who were assumed to be Russian "advisers". The loss ratio of American jet fighters to MiGs throughout the war was 111 to 807, so it is possible but unlikely that one of the Communist "honchos" surpassed McConnell's achievement. Since the close of hostilities in Korea, encounters between jet combat aircraft have been few and limited in scope; no ace is thought to have emerged from either the India-Pakistan confrontation or the Vietnam War. However, although security considerations have prevented the release of details, it is thought likely by informed opinion that at least one jet fighter pilot of the Israeli Defence Force/Air Force has achieved approximately 20 aerial victories over jet aircraft of the Arab air forces during and since the June 1967 War.

The first jet aircraft to fly the Atlantic non-stop and un-refuelled, was an English Electric Canberra B.Mk.2 on 21st February 1951 which was flown from Britain to Baltimore and was later purchased by the U.S.A.F. to become the first Canberra to carry American markings. It later entered service with that Air Force as the B-57.

The first British delta-wing interceptor fighter was the Gloster Javelin. First flown in prototype form (*WD804*) by Sqdn. Ldr. W. A. Waterton on 26th November 1951, the Javelin was also **the R.A.F.'s first purpose-built all-weather interceptor fighter**. Flying characteristics of the prototype left much to be desired and when it crashed in July 1952, following the loss of both elevators in flight, Waterton was awarded the George Medal for recovering the auto-observer recordings from the wreck.

The first British V-Bomber (so-called from the wing leading edge plan-form) was the Vickers Valiant, whose prototype first flew on 18th May 1951. Two Mark 1 and one Mark 2 prototypes were built, and were followed by 104 production aircraft, the first of which flew on 21st December 1953. They were powered by various versions of the Rolls-Royce Avon axial-flow turbojet, four such engines being located in the wing roots. The Valiant entered R.A.F. service with No. 138 Squadron at Gaydon, Warwickshire, early in 1955 and afterwards equipped Nos. 7, 49, 90, 148, 207, 214 and 543 Squadrons. The production also included versions for photo-reconnaissance (the B. (P.R.) Mark 1) and tankers (B. (P.R.) K. Mark 1 and B.K. Mark 1). Its maximum speed was 567 m.p.h. at 36,000 ft. (Mach 0·84). Normal loaded weight with a 10,000 lb. (4,540 kg.) bomb-load was 140,000 lb. (63,560 kg.). Range without external fuel tanks was 3,450 miles (5,564 km.).

Vickers Valiant

The world's first high performance variable-geometry military aircraft was the Grumman XF10F-1 Jaguar experimental single-seat carrier-borne fighter which first flew on 19th May 1953. With wings that could be swept back 40° in flight, the Jaguar had a designed top speed of 722 m.p.h. (1,164 km./hr.) and was powered by an afterburning Westinghouse J-40 turbojet. Although a pre-production batch of thirty aircraft was ordered, the project was abandoned after two prototypes had been completed, owing to the enormous complexity of the problems associated with variable geometry.

The heaviest bomb-load carried by an operational bomber was that of the Boeing B-52 Stratofortress at 75,000 lb. (34,050 kg.); with this warload on board, the B-52B possessed a range of approximately 3,000 miles (4,840 km.). Dubbed "the big stick", the B-52 bomber first flew on 5th August 1954 and subsequently became the main flying deterrent of the U.S. Strategic Air Command for a dozen years.

The last British heavy bomber powered by piston engines was the Avro Lincoln four-engine aircraft ultimately powered by 1,760 h.p. Packard-built Rolls-Royce Merlin 68, 85 or 300 engines. With a wing span of 120 ft. 0 in. (36·58 m.) and a maximum loaded weight of 82,000 lb. (37,195 kg.) the last Lincoln was retired from Bomber Command in December 1955, when that R.A.F. Command became an all-jet force. It was capable of carrying a 22,000-lb. (9,980 kg.) high-explosive bomb, the largest used by the R.A.F.

The first British atomic bomb was dropped by a Vickers Valiant, *WZ366*, of No. 49 (Bomber) Squadron, captained by Sqdn. Ldr. E. J. G. Flavell, A.F.C., over Maralinga, Australia, on 11th October 1956.

The first British hydrogen bomb was dropped by a Vickers Valiant of No. 49 (Bomber) Squadron, captained by Wg. Cdr. K. G. Hubbard, O.B.E., D.F.C., A.F.C., on 15th May 1957. The bomb was detonated at medium altitude over the Pacific in the Christmas Island area.

The greatest measure of air superiority ever gained by one air force over another, with rough parity of equipment, is undoubtedly attributable to the Israeli Defence Forces/Air Force. During the Six Day War of June 1967 the following results were achieved (figures confirmed by subsequent analysis of camera-gun film).

Egyptian Air Force:	338 aircraft destroyed
Syrian Air Force:	61 aircraft destroyed
Royal Jordanian Air Force:	29 aircraft destroyed
Iraqi Air Force:	23 aircraft destroyed
Lebanese Air Force:	1 aircraft destroyed
Total:	452 aircraft destroyed

(Of this total, 79 aircraft were destroyed in air combat, the remainder on the ground.)

Israeli Defence Forces/Air Force losses during the Six Day War totalled 40 aircraft, the majority of these losses being attributable to ground fire.

Between the close of the Six Day War, and April 30th 1970, the following losses and victories have been recorded:

Egyptian Air Force:	85 aircraft destroyed
Syrian Air Force:	15 aircraft destroyed

In addition to these combat losses, two Syrian MiG-17 ground-attack fighters landed by mistake inside Israeli territory, bringing **total losses by the Arab air forces to 102**, of which 100 were destroyed in air combat. In the same period the Israeli Defence Forces/Air Force has suffered the following losses:

Over Egypt:	11 aircraft
Over Jordan:	7 aircraft
Over Syria:	1 aircraft
Total:	19 aircraft

Of this total, it is believed that two were Douglas A-4 Skyhawk ground attack fighters, lost in air combat; 16 were fighters and ground attack fighters of various types destroyed by ground fire during low-level missions, the majority to radar-predicted anti-aircraft artillery; and one was a Piper light reconnaissance/liaison aircraft brought down over Egypt by a SAM-2 ground-to-air missile. The comparative figures for **Arab/Israeli losses in air combat between 10th June 1967 and 30th April 1970 are thus 100/2.** The majority of the Arab aircraft in this total were MiG-21 fighters, although single figures of Sukhoi-7 and Ilyushin Il-28 aircraft are also believed to figure in the score.

The Egyptian air defence system based on Russian SAM-2 missile sites, at the time of writing virtually destroyed by Israeli air strikes during 1969, is thought to have accounted for the following targets during its operational period:

1 Israeli Defence Forces/Air Force Piper liaison aircraft
1 Egyptian Air Force MiG-21 fighter
1 Ethiopian Air Lines airliner.

ORIGINS OF THE WORLD'S AIR FORCES

Afghanistan   The Royal Afghan Air Force was formed in 1924 by King Amanullah with an initial equipment of two Bristol F.2B Fighters flown by two German pilots.

Albania   The Albanian Air Force was established in 1947 under Soviet sponsorship with initial equipment of twelve YAK-3 fighters. (An original attempt to form an air force in 1914 had proved abortive.)

Argentine   The Argentine Air Force was formed on 8th September 1912 with the establishment of the *Escuela de Aviacón Militar* at El Palomar. The Argentine Naval Aviation Service was formed on 17th October 1919 with the presentation by the Italian Government of facilities established by an Italian mission at San Fernando.

Austria   Formation of the *Deutschösterreichische Fliegertruppe* (Austro-German Flying Troop) took place on 6th December 1918. The current Austrian Air Force (*Österreichischen Luftstreitkräfte*) was founded in 1955 with four Yak-11 and four Yak-18 trainers.

Belgium   *La Force Aérienne Belge* came into effective being on 5th March 1911 with the inauguration of its first airfield at Brasschaet, Antwerp.

Bolivia   The *Cuerpo de Aviación* was founded in August 1924, although a Flying School had been established at Alto Laz Pa as early as 1915.

Brazil   The Brazilian Naval Air Force was founded with the establishment of a seaplane school in 1913 at Rio de Janeiro with an Italian Bossi seaplane. The Army Air Service was founded under French training supervision in October 1918 at Rio de Janeiro.

Bulgaria   A Bulgarian Army Aviation Corps was originally formed in 1912 with Blériot and Bristol monoplanes and fought in the Balkan War of 1912–13. It was resurrected shortly after 12th October 1915 when Bulgaria entered the War as one of the Central Powers.

Cambodia   The Royal Khmer Aviation was formed in 1954.

Ceylon   The Royal Ceylon Air Force was formed on 10th October 1950 with de Havilland Vampire trainers.

Chile   The Chilean Air Force was formed with the establishment of a flying school at Lo Espejo on 11th February 1913.

China   The Chinese Army Air Arm came into being with the establishment in January 1914 of a flying school at Nan Yuan at which members of the Chinese Army commenced flying instruction under an American, Art Lym.

Colombia   The *Fuerza Aérea Colombiana* originated in the *Escuela de Avación* (flying school) which was founded at Flandes with a Caudron G.IIIA-2 aircraft on 4th April 1922, on the authority of the Colombian Minister of War, Dr. Aristóbulo Archila.

Czechoslovakia The Czechoslovak Army Air Force was formed early in 1919 from air components previously serving with the Czech Legions in Russia and France.

Denmark   The Danish Army Air Corps was established on 2nd July 1912 with the formation of a flying school.

Ecuador   The *Cuerpo de Aviadores Militares* commenced formation in 1920 under the supervision of an Italian Aviation Mission.

Egypt   The Egyptian Army Air Force was originally planned in 1930 under British influence, but its official foundation was not effected until May 1932 with the arrival of its first five aircraft (Gipsy Moths) from Britain.

Ethiopia   The Imperial Ethiopian Air Force commenced formation in 1924 with the procurement of French and German aircraft by Ras Tafari (later Emperor Haile Selassie).

France   The French Army Air Force (originally the *Service Aéronautique,* and later *l'Armée de l'Air*) was founded as a separate command in April 1910. By this time several army pilots had learned to fly and the new command had been issued with a Blériot, two Wrights and two Farmans.

Germany   The German Military Air Force owes its origins to the purchase by the Army of its first Zeppelin dirigible in 1907 and its first eleven aeroplanes in 1910. The Military Aviation Service was formally established on 1st October 1912.

Great Britain	The Royal Air Force owes its origins to the balloon experiments by the Royal Engineers at Woolwich which commenced in 1878. The Air Battalion of the R.E. was established in February 1911, and the Royal Flying Corps in May 1912 with Military and Naval Wings. In November 1913 the Admiralty announced the formation of the Royal Naval Air Service. The R.F.C. and R.N.A.S. continued as separate services until amalgamated to form the Royal Air Force on 1st April 1918. The Fleet Air Arm came into being in 1924.
Greece	The Royal Hellenic Army formed its first military squadron of four Farman biplanes in September 1912 at Larissa, its pilots being trained in France. In February 1914 the Naval Air Service was established under the guidance of a British Naval Mission.
Guatemala	Military aeroplanes were first flown by the Guatemalan Army shortly after the First World War, but it was not until 1929 that the *Cuerpo de Aeronautica Militar* was established as an echelon of the Army.
Haiti	The Haitian *Corps d'Aviation* was formed in 1943 primarily as a national mail carrying organisation but in the late nineteen-forties air patrols were added to its duties.
Hungary	Forbidden under the terms of the Treaty of Versailles, Hungary as a separate Republic did not make provision for a small air service until 1936 when it made limited purchases of German and Italian aircraft.
India	Scene of many years of British aviation influence, India established its own air force on 1st April 1933 with one squadron of Westland Wapiti general purpose aircraft.
Indonesia	After transfer of sovereignty from the Dutch to the United States of Indonesia on 27th December 1949, the Netherlands continued to influence aviation in the area and assisted in the establishment of the Indonesian Air Force (*Angkatan Udara Republik Indonesia*) which, in the following year, took over from the Netherlands Indies Air Force, which was disbanded.
Iran (Persia)	Aviation in Iran originated in the Air Department of the Army Headquarters established in 1922 by the Prime Minister, Reza Khan. The first military aircraft was a Junkers F-13 transport based at Galeh-Morghi.
Iraq	The Royal Iraqi Air Force was formed in 1931 with five de Havilland D.H.60T Gipsy Moths flown by Cranwell-trained Iraqi pilots.
Ireland	The Irish Air Corps was formed in 1922 after the completion of the Anglo-Irish Treaty of December 1921. Its first aeroplane was a Martinsyde Type A Mark II which had been purchased during the truce period to assist General Michael Collins to escape from England had the London talks failed.
Israel	The Israel Defence Force/Air Force owes its origin to the *Sherut Avir*, a military air service planned in 1947 at the time of Israel's emergence as a sovereign state. The *Sherut Avir* gave way to the Israeli Air Force (*Chel Ha'avir*) in March 1948, and this in turn was integrated with the Army and Navy as the IDF/AF in 1951.
Italy	Fairly extensive and successful use of aircraft by the Italian Army in the Italo-Turkish War of 1911 led to the formal establishment of the Air Battalion (*Battaglione Aviatori*) under the *Ufficio d'Ispezione Servizi Aeronautici* on 27th June 1912. A fully-fledged Military Aviation Service followed on 28th November 1912.
Japan	Origins of military aviation in Japan date back to July 1909 with the formation of the Temporary Military Balloon Research Committee. In 1911 the Army and Navy formed separate air services, the Japanese Army Air Force and the Imperial Japanese Naval Air Force. The current Japanese Air Self Defence Force was formed on 1st July 1954.
Jordan	The Royal Air Force was formed in 1949 as the Arab Legion Air Force after the Arab-Israeli war of that year. Equipment was initially one de Havilland Rapide.
Korea (North)	Under Russian influence the Korean People's Armed Forces Air Corps (KPAFAC) was formed in October 1948 to absorb the North Korean Army's Aviation Division which, using a small number of ex-Japanese World War II aircraft had in turn originated in the Soviet-styled North Korean Aviation Society in 1946.
Korea (South)	The Republic of Korea Air Force was established on a limited basis in 1949, the year before North Korean forces crossed the 38th Parallel. The three year war resulted in rapid expansion by means of massive assistance from the U.S. Air Force.
Lebanon	The Lebanese Air Force was established in 1949 under R.A.F. influence and supervision, being equipped initially with two Percival Prentice trainers.

Malaya	Origins of indigenous military aviation in the Federated Malay States date from the Straits Settlements Volunteer Air Force which was born in 1936. Although the R.A.F. assumed the major share of operations against the Communist terrorists, the Malayan Auxiliary Air Force was brought into being in 1950.
Mexico	After operations against rebel forces in 1911 by an American mercenary pilot, Hector Worden, the Mexican Government was encouraged to lay the seeds of a small air force which became the Mexican Aviation Corps in 1915, later to be enlarged into the Mexican Air Force (*Fuerza Aérea Mexicana*).
Morocco	Following the emergence of Morocco as an independent state in 1956, the Royal Moroccan Air Force was established on 19th November that year with a variety of light aircraft and a small number of personnel trained in France and Spain.
Netherlands	Origins of the Royal Netherlands Air Force date back to the last century when, in 1886, the Dutch Army formed a balloon unit for artillery observation duties. Aircraft were first used experimentally during military manoeuvres in September 1911, and on 1st July 1913 an Aviation Division of the Royal Netherlands Army was established by Royal Warrant, to be based at Soesterburg. The Naval Aviation Arm (*Marine Luchtvaartdienst*) was formed on 18th August 1917.
New Zealand	Although originally conceived in 1909, no formal military aviation corps existed in New Zealand during the First World War, pilots serving instead with the R.F.C. and R.N.A.S. Continuing efforts to pursue military aviation during the 'twenties led to the formation of the New Zealand Permanent Air Force and Territorial Air Force in June 1923. The Royal New Zealand Air Force was constituted on 1st April 1937.
Nicaragua	In about 1923 the Nicaraguan Army was provided with a small number of Curtiss JN-4s and DH-4s by the U.S.A., but little was done to form a regular air arm until 9th June 1938 when, under American guidance, the Nicaraguan Air Force (*Fuerza Aerea de la Guardia Nacional*) formally came into being.
Norway	In mid-1912 a German Taube (named *Start*) was purchased by five Norwegian naval officers who presented it to the Royal Norwegian Navy. Almost simultaneously a Maurice Farman (named *Ganger Rolf*) was presented to the Royal Norwegian Army by Norwegians resident in France. Army and Navy flying schools were founded in 1914 and in the following year the Army Air Service (Haerens Flyvåpen) and Naval Air Service (*Marinens Flyvevaesen*) were formed.
Pakistan	The emergence of Pakistan as a dominion in July 1947 was accompanied by the formation of the Royal Pakistan Air Force. Two squadrons were established with former members of the Royal Indian Air Force.
Paraguay	The Paraguayan-Bolivian War of 1932 encouraged the Paraguayan Army to acquire some Potez XXV biplanes and, under the guidance of an Italian Air Mission, these were operated by mercenary pilots; by the end of the war in 1935 a regular Air Force, *Fuerzas Aereas Nacionales*, had been formed.
Peru	Although financial appropriations were provided for the training of military pilots as early as 1912 it was not until late in 1919 that under the aegis of a French Air Mission and with twenty-four British and French aeroplanes that a military air corps was formed. The Peruvian Naval Air Service followed in 1924, but on 20th May 1929 the two were combined to form the *Cuerpo de Aeronatica del Perú*.
Philippines	The Air Corps of the Philippine Army was formed on 2nd May 1935 as a branch of the Philippine Constabulary. The Philippine Air Force came into being on 3rd July 1947, exactly one year after the inauguration of the Philippine Republic.
Poland	A Polish squadron was incorporated in the Polish Army Corps in 1917, but a fully integrated Air Force was not formed until 29th September 1919 when, under Brig. Gen. Macewicz, the new force operated against the U.S.S.R.
Portugal	The Portuguese Air Force (*Forca Aérea Portuguesa*) owes its origins to funds publicly subscribed in 1912 which were used to purchase a small number of British and French aircraft, and a school was established at Villa Nova da Rainha. In 1917 army and naval air arms (*Arma da Aeronáutica* and *Aviação Maritima*) came into being.

Rhodesia	In 1936 Southern Rhodesia organised the basis of an Air Section of the Permanent Staff Corps at Salisbury. This administered substantial contributions to the R.A.F. during the Second World War. The Southern Rhodesian Air Force changed its title to the Royal Rhodesian Air Force in October 1954.
Romania	Romania was one of the first countries in the world to form a regular air force using aeroplanes, its army having established a Flying Corps late in 1910.
Saudi Arabia	The establishment of a small air force was proposed by Ibn Saud in 1923 and this was equipped by Britain with a small number of D.H.9s under an agreement for collaboration which terminated in 1933.
South Africa	After six officers of the Union Defence Forces, who had received flying training at a flying school at Kimberley, had been sent to join the R.F.C. on the outbreak of the First World War, the South African Aviation Corps was formed under Maj. Van der Spuy early in 1915.
Spain	Spain formed its first military aviation force in 1896 with the establishment of the *Servicio Militar de Aerostacion*, a captive balloon section. Later in 1910 plans were laid for the formation of the *Aeronáutica Militar Española* and in March the following year four French aeroplanes formed the new air force's initial equipment.
Sudan	After the proclamation confirming Sudan as a Republic on 1st January 1956 steps were taken to form an air force. Four light aircraft were presented by Egypt in the following year with the founding of the Sudanese Air Force.
Sweden	Although the *Flygvapnet* of today came into being on 1st July 1926, military and naval aviation in Sweden started in 1911 with the presentation of single military and naval aircraft to the nation. Flying schools were formed at Axvall and Oscar Fredriksborg. In 1914 a military flying echelon, the *Fälttelegrafkårens Flygkompani* (Field Telegraph Aviation Company) was formed.
Switzerland	The Swiss *Fliegertruppe* was established on 31st July 1914 at Buedenfeld. Initial equipment comprised one indigenous and three French monoplanes.
Thailand	The Royal Siamese Flying Corps was formed on 23rd March 1914 after three officers of the Royal Siamese Engineers, who had received their flying training in France, returned home. Eight French aircraft provided its initial equipment.
Turkey	Foreign pilots flew the small number of aeroplanes operated during the Balkan Wars of 1912–13. The Turkish Flying Corps came into formal being early in 1915, almost exclusively manned by German crews in German aircraft.
United States of America	Balloons were used by both sides in the American Civil War between 1861 and 1863. An Aeronautical Division of the Signal Corps (with a personnel strength of three) was formed in August 1907, and the first aeroplane, a Wright biplane, was accepted by the Army on 2nd August 1909. A Signal Corps Aviation Section was authorised on 18th July 1914, and, following outstanding pioneering maritime flying, a Naval Office of Aeronautics was established on 1st July 1914.
Uruguay	A Department of Military Aviation was created on 20th November 1916 as well as a School of Military Aeronautics at San Fernando.
U.S.S.R.	The Imperial Russian Flying Corps was formed in 1910 together with an Army Central Flying School at Gatchina and a Naval Flying School at Sevastopol. This Flying Corps disintegrated soon after the outbreak of the Revolution in November 1917. In two orders issued on 20th November 1917 and 24th May 1918 the Chief Administration of the Workers' and Peasants' Red Air Fleet (*Glavnoe Upravlenie Raboche-Krestyanskogo Krasnogo Vozdushnogo Flota*, GU-RKKVF) was formed.
Venezuela	The Venezuelan Military Air Service was established on 17th April 1920 and a flying school set up at Maracay; the first pilots underwent training in 1921 under French supervision.
Vietnam	The Vietnam Air Force owes its origins to the setting up under French supervision of flying training facilities at the *Armée de l'Air* base at Nha Trang in 1951. Observation squadrons were brought into being and these participated with the French against Vietminh forces between 1952 and 1955.
Yugoslavia	Although Yugoslvia as a sovereign state only emerged in 1918, its aviation origins lay in the Serbian Military Air Service formed in 1913 with the return home of six Serbian army officers from France where they had received their flying training.

Above: *The Lockheed SR-71A strategic reconnaissance aircraft, of which an interceptor fighter version, the YF-12A currently holds three world records for speed and altitude.* **Below**: *The General Dynamics F-111A variable-geometry fighter of the USAF Tactical Air Command, the first high-performance "swing-wing" aircraft in the world to achieve combat status. Although at one time more than 500 F111s were on order, cancellations, including fifty ordered by the R.A.F., have considerably reduced the number likely to be built, following difficulties encountered during the working-up stages of development.*

CHAPTER 3 MARITIME AVIATION

The use of aircraft over water stemmed directly from the "purest" application of military aviation—the employment of flying observation platforms. The first generation of ship-borne aircraft were intended purely as a means of pushing back the naval commander's horizon, and it was to be many years before the vulnerability of surface vessels to aerial attack—although repeatedly demonstrated by such lonely prophets as "Billy" Mitchell—was recognized by the naval Establishment. It is ironic that America's admirals, the most sceptic of the theory during the inter-War years, should emerge a decade later as commanders of the great carrier task forces which brought Japan to her knees. Imperial Japan's brief but shattering tide of victory swept over the Pacific in the wake of her highly mobile carrier strike aircraft; and it was in the clash of carrier aircraft, whose parent vessels never came within sight or gun-range of one another, that the fate of Japan was sealed. Today the pundits of naval warfare are divided; some say that the future lies with the nuclear-missile-armed submarine, others that nuclear weapons delivered by carrier aircraft offer a greater flexibility of response. Whatever the eventual outcome, those powers which have the means and the will to support carrier strike forces seem certain to dictate events during the predictable conventional outbreaks of the 1970s.

The world's first aircraft carrier (defined as a water-borne craft used to tether, transport or launch an aircraft) was the *G. W. Parke Curtis*, a coal barge converted during the American Civil War in 1861 under the direction of Thadeus S. C. Lowe for the transport and towing of observation balloons. The *G. W. Parke Curtis* entered service with General McClellan's Army of the Potomac in November 1861, frequently towing balloons on the Potomac River for the observation of the opposing Confederate forces.

The first take-off in the world from the water by an aeroplane was made by Henri Fabre, a Frenchman, in his Gnôme-powered monoplane floatplane at Martigues, near Marseilles, in March 1910.

The first active interest in marine air warfare was displayed by the New York newspaper *World* which established a bombing range on Lake Keuka, near Hammondsport, New York, simulating a battleship target in 1910. Glenn O. Curtiss carried out a demonstration flight "bombing" this target with lengths of lead pipe.

The first naval officer in the world to learn to fly was Lt. G. C. Colmore, R.N., who took flying lessons in a Short biplane at Eastchurch, England, at his own expense and was awarded British pilot's Certificate No. 15 on 21st June 1910.

The first aeroplane to take off from a ship was a Curtiss biplane flown by Eugene B. Ely from an 83-ft. (30-m.) platform built over the bows of the American light cruiser U.S.S. *Birmingham*, 3,750 tons, on 14th November 1910. It has often been averred that the vessel was anchored at the time of take-off; this is not correct as it had been proposed to take off as the ship steamed at 20 knots into wind. In the event, the *Birmingham* had weighed anchor in Hampton Roads, Virginia, but, impatient to take off, Ely gave the signal to release his aircraft at 3·16 p.m. before the ship was underway. With only 57 ft. (17 m.) of platform ahead of the Curtiss, the aircraft flew off but touched the water and damaged its propeller; the pilot managed to maintain control and landed at Willoughby Spit, two-and-a-half miles distant. As Ely became airborne from the cruiser, the *Birmingham* sent an historic radio message "Ely's just gone".

The first naval officer to commence flying instruction was Lt. Theodore G. Ellyson, U.S. Navy, who was ordered to report to Glenn Curtiss in December 1910 at North Island, San Diego, Calif.* Seven weeks later, on 1st March 1911, three officers of the Royal Navy, Lts. R. Gregory, C. R. Samson and A. M. Longmore, together with Lt. G. V. W. Lushington of the Royal Marine Artillery, commenced instruction at Eastchurch, England.

The first aeroplane to land on a ship was a Curtiss biplane flown by Eugene B. Ely on 18th January 1911 when he landed on a 119 ft. 4 in. (40 m.) long platform constructed over the stern of the American armoured cruiser, U.S.S. *Pennsylvania*, 13,680 tons, anchored in San Francisco bay. It had been intended that the vessel would be underway during the landing, but the Captain considered that there was insufficient sea space to manoeuvre and the *Pennsylvania* remained at anchor. Despite landing downwind the Curtiss rolled to a stop at 11·01 a.m. after a run of only 30 ft. (10 m.). Capt. C. F. Pond is reputed to have remarked that "this is the most important landing of a bird since the dove flew back to the Ark". After lunch Ely successfully took off again from the *Pennsylvania* at 11.58 a.m. and returned to his airfield near San Francisco.

The first aeroplane to perform a premeditated landing on water, taxy and then take off was a Curtiss "hydroaeroplane" flown by Glenn Curtiss during February 1911. He landed beside U.S.S. *Pennsylvania* (see above), anchored in San Diego harbour, was hoisted aboard, put back on the water and took off again.

The U.S. Navy's first aeroplane, a Curtiss A-1 "hydroaeroplane" or seaplane was first flown on 1st July 1911. This of course was not the same aircraft as that flown by Curtiss for his sea landing flight earlier in the year.

The first gallantry decoration to be "earned" by a marine aviator was the Distinguished Flying Cross awarded posthumously to Eugene B. Ely, who was killed while flying towards the end of 1911. The award of the D.F.C. was made 25 years later in recognition of his outstanding contributions to marine aviation during 1910 and 1911. His sole reward during his life was an award of $500 made by the U.S. Aeronautical Reserve during 1911.

---

* Ellyson reported to Curtiss on or about 26th January 1911, and was subsequently awarded American Naval Aviator's Certificate No. 1 on 1st July 1911.

The first officer of the Royal Navy to negotiate successfully a water take-off in an aeroplane was Cdr. O. Schwann, R.N., who took off on 18th November 1911, but crashed on landing.

The first officer of the Royal Navy to land successfully on the water in an aeroplane was Lt. Arthur Longmore, R.N. (later Air Chief Marshal Sir Arthur Longmore, G.C.B., D.S.O., R.A.F. (Retd.)), who landed a Short S.27 seaplane on the Medway River on 1st December 1911.

The first officer of the Royal Navy to take off from a ship in an aeroplane was Lt. Charles Rumney Samson who is said to have made a secret flight in a Short S.27 from a platform on the bows of the British battleship, H.M.S. *Africa*, 17,500 tons, moored in Sheerness harbour during December 1911. His first officially recorded take-off was from H.M.S. *Africa* at 2.20 p.m. on 10th January 1912. Cdr. Samson was appointed Officer Commanding, the Naval Wing of the Royal Flying Corps in October 1912.

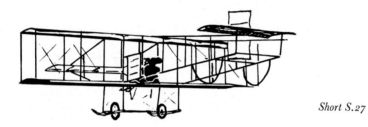

Short S.27

The first pilot in the world to take off in an aeroplane from a ship underway was Cdr. Samson, who took off in a Short pusher biplane amphibian from the forecastle of the battleship H.M.S. *Hibernia* while it steamed at 10½ knots off Portland during the Naval Review of May 1912. At the conclusion of the Review, Cdr. Samson was one of the Officers commanded to dine with H.M. King George V aboard the *Victoria and Albert*.

The first U.S. Marine pilot was Lt. Alfred A. Cunningham, U.S. Marine Corps, who qualified for his pilot's badge during 1912.

The first Japanese naval pilots began flying instruction during 1912. Three such men were ordered to France and two to America to receive their instruction.

The first naval aeroplanes acquired by the Japanese Navy were two Short-built Maurice Farmans and a Curtiss hydroaeroplane purchased during 1912.

The first naval aeroplane acquired by the French Navy was a Maurice Farman biplane purchased on 12th September 1912, equipped with pontoons. In the same year the French torpedo boat carrier, *Foudre*, 6,090 tons, was converted to accommodate two seaplanes. Later a platform was added over the ship's bows and from this René Caudron took off on 8th May 1914 while the *Foudre* was anchored in St. Raphaël harbour.

The first naval aviator to gain a pilot's certificate in the Argentine was Teniente de Navio Melchor Z. Escola who obtained his flying certificate on 23rd October 1912 with the Argentine Aero Club.

The first naval vessel in the world to be commissioned for service as a parent ship for aircraft was H.M.S. *Hermes*, an old light cruiser which was converted to accommodate two seaplanes late in 1912. At the instigation of Winston Churchill, Cdr. Charles Rumney Samson carried out trials with **the world's first seaplanes with folding wings** for service with the *Hermes*. This ship was followed by the *Empress*, *Engadine* and *Riviera* which were commandeered ex-cross Channel steamers adapted to carry seaplanes immediately after the outbreak of the First World War in 1914.

The first Japanese naval vessel converted to support seaplanes was the *Wakamiya*, 7,600 tons, converted from a naval transport in 1913. The *Wakamiya* commenced operations against German forces at Kiaochow Bay, China, on 1st September 1914, using Farman seaplanes. Dropping improvised bombs made from naval shells, the pilots of these Farmans succeeded in sinking a German minelayer before the *Wakamiya* struck a mine herself and was damaged.

The first torpedo dropped by an aeroplane was a dummy weapon dropped by a twin-engined Italian monoplane designed by Pateras Pescara in 1914. The pilot, Capitano Alessandro Guidoni, did not record the exact date but claimed it to be "the first torpedo drop ever attempted and accomplished". His torpedo weighed 825 lb. (375 kg.).

The first standard naval torpedo dropped by a naval airman in a standard naval aircraft was a naval 14-in. (35·6 cm.) torpedo weighing 905 lb. (411 kg.), dropped by a Short seaplane flown by Sqdn. Cdr. Arthur Longmore, R.N., (R.Ae.C. Pilot's Certificate No. 72) on 28th July 1914.

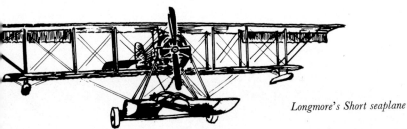

Longmore's Short seaplane

The first occasion on which naval aeroplanes and aviators participated in combat was the Vera Cruz incident of April 1914 when five Curtiss A-1s were flown on reconnaissance flights over the Mexican port from the battleship U.S.S. *Mississippi* and cruiser U.S.S. *Birmingham* and came under rifle fire which caused damage but no loss to aircraft or pilots.

THE FIRST WORLD WAR

The first air operations undertaken by airmen of the Royal Navy during the First World War were reconnaissance flights by a naval squadron commanded by Sqdn. Cdr. Charles Samson in support of a Brigade of Royal Marines on the Belgian coast in August 1914.

The first active combat sortie by naval airmen against German territory was a raid undertaken by four aeroplanes of Sqdn. Cdr. Samson's naval squadron against German airship sheds at Cologne and Düsseldorf on 22nd September 1914. Only one of the aircraft reached its target at Düsseldorf and its bombs did little damage; all four aircraft returned safely. (See Military Aviation, p. 31.)

(Among the most distinguished of British airmen (and almost certainly the most distinguished British naval pilot) was Air Commodore Charles Rumney Samson, C.M.G., D.S.O., A.F.C., who was born in Manchester in 1883 and died on 5th February 1931. He entered the Royal Navy in 1898. He served aboard H.M.S. Pomone *(Somaliland, 1903–04, Medal and Clasp), and as First Lieutenant aboard H.M.S.* Philomel *(Persian Gulf, 1909–10, Medal and Clasp). He qualified for and was awarded R.Ae.C. Pilot's Certificate No. 71 on a Short biplane at the Naval School, Eastchurch, on 25th April 1911. He was the first British pilot to take off in an aeroplane from a ship (H.M.S.* Africa, *Sheerness, December 1911) and was the first pilot in the world to take off in an aeroplane from a ship underway (H.M.S.* Hibernia, *Royal Naval Review, Portland, May 1912). He commanded the first Naval Wing, R.F.C. in October 1912, and the first Naval Squadron, R.N.A.S., to be used on operations during the First World War (Belgian coast, August 1914: 1914 Star). He formed and commanded the first Royal Naval Armoured Car Force, September 1914, and commanded the first naval squadron to bomb targets in Germany (see above). Was among the first batch of seven naval officers to be awarded the D.S.O. in World War I on 23rd October 1914. Served on the Western Front, 1915; Siege of Antwerp; First Battle of Ypres; commanded Brigade of French Territorials at the Battle of Orchies (awarded* Chevalier Legion d'Honneur *and* Croix de Guerre, *14th January 1916); Mentioned in Despatches, October 1914 (Admiralty) and February 1915 (France).*

Also during 1915 Samson commanded a squadron of aircraft on the island of Tenedos operating against the Turks early in the Dardenelles campaign and in the same area was later Mentioned in Despatches twice, March 1916 and July 1916 (both Admiralty, Gallipoli). While on a "search-and-bomb" sortie Samson attacked and damaged a staff car carrying Mustafa Kemâl Pasha, the famous Atatürk (1881–1938); he also dropped a 500-lb. (227-kg.) bomb, the largest bomb hitherto used by an aeroplane. Samson then became the first commander of a "carrier task force" when, as captain of H.M. Seaplane Carrier Ben-My-Chree, *he led two other seaplane carriers (Anne and Raven II) on air operations against Turkish forces in Sinai, Palestine and Arabia. After* Ben-My-Chree *was sunk by Turkish gunfire off the coast of Turkey, Samson took* Raven *into the Indian Ocean to search for the German raider* Wolf *(awarded a bar to the D.S.O., 23rd January 1917, East Indies). By 1918 Samson was back in home waters and on 1st January that year was promoted to Wing-Captain, R.N.A.S., transferring as Lieutenant-Colonel, temporary Colonel, R.A.F., on 1st April 1918. He proposed a scheme for launching a Sopwith Camel from a towed barge, and attempted the first take-off in July 1918; this failed and the barge rammed the ditched Camel but Samson escaped unhurt. This system was used with success when Lieutenant Stuart Culley took off from the barge on 12th August 1918 and shot down Zeppelin L.53 off the Dutch coast. Promoted Group Captain in 1919, Samson was appointed C.M.G. on 3rd June 1919, and awarded the A.F.C. on 1st January 1919.)*

Charles Rumney Samson

The first significant damage inflicted in a raid by naval aircraft was that caused by bombs dropped by an aircraft flown by Flt. Lt. R. L. G. Marix on 8th October 1914 in a raid on the airship base at Düsseldorf. His two 20-lb. (9-kg.) bombs were released from about 600 ft. (200 m.) and destroyed the Zeppelin Z.IX. (See also Military Aviation, page 31.) *See also page 101 for action by Japanese aircraft.*

The first operational seaplane unit of the Imperial German Navy was formed on 4th December 1914, moving to its base at Zeebrugge two days later.

The first naval vessel fully converted for aircraft duties while still under construction was H.M.S. *Ark Royal*, and as such was the first ship in the world to be completed as an aircraft (seaplane) carrier. Launched in 1914 *Ark Royal* became the first aircraft carrier to operate aeroplanes against the enemy in Europe (the *Wakamiya* had launched seaplanes against the Germans in the Far East by this time) when, arriving at the entrance to the Dardanelles on 17th February 1915, one of her seaplanes was sent on reconnaissance against the Turks.

The first air attack using a torpedo dropped by an aeroplane was carried out by Flt. Cdr. C. H. Edmonds flying a Short 184 seaplane from H.M.S. *Ben-My-Chree* on 12th August 1915 against a 5,000-ton Turkish supply ship in the Sea of Marmara. Although the enemy ship was hit and sunk, the captain of a British submarine claimed to have fired a torpedo simultaneously and sunk the ship. It was further stated that the British submarine *E.14* had attacked and immobilised the ship four days earlier. However on 17th August 1915 another Turkish ship was sunk by a torpedo of whose origin there can be no doubt. On this occasion Flt. Cdr. C. H. Edmonds, flying a Short 184, torpedoed a Turkish steamer a few miles north of the Dardanelles. His formation colleague, Flt. Lt. G. B. Dacre, was forced to land on the water owing to engine trouble but, seeing an enemy tug close by, taxied up to it and released his torpedo. The tug blew up and sank. Thereafter Dacre was able to take off and return to the *Ben-My-Chree*.

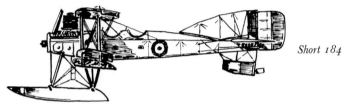

Short 184

The first launching of an aeroplane by catapult aboard ship took place on 5th November 1915 when an AB-2 flying boat was catapulted from the stern of the American battleship, U.S.S. *North Carolina*, anchored in Pensacola Bay, Florida.

The first major fleet battle in which an aeroplane was used was the Battle of Jutland on 31st May 1916 when Flt. Lt. F. J. Rutland (accompanied by his observer, Assistant Paymaster G. S. Trewin) spotted and shadowed a force of German light cruisers and destroyers. Taking off from alongside H.M. Seaplane Carrier *Engadine* at about 3.10 p.m. Rutland sighted the enemy ships and continued to radio position reports to the *Engadine* until a broken fuel pipe forced the seaplane down on to the sea. Having repaired the damage, Rutland took off and returned to his ship. (The following day Rutland performed an act of supreme gallantry, not associated with aviation, which brought him the award of the Albert Medal in Gold, an award so rare that his was one of only three ever made. As the *Engadine* withdrew from the battle she went to the assistance of the crippled armoured cruiser, H.M.S. *Warrior*, and on the next morning went alongside to take off her crew. During this operation a wounded man fell into the sea between the two ships and, despite the great danger of being crushed, Rutland entered the water and rescued the seaman, who was however found to have died from exposure.)

(Thereafter Rutland pursued an outstanding, but ultimately tragic career. After the Battle of Jutland, and promoted Flight Commander, Rutland conducted a series of experiments flying Sopwith Pups off short platforms and the decks of H.M. seaplane carriers Manxman and Campania. These led to the decision to build a platform for the purpose on the light cruiser, H.M.S. Yarmouth. However while this construction work was being carried out during the summer and autumn of 1916, Rutland was forced to land near the Danish coast while engaged on an anti-Zeppelin sweep. Having travelled through Denmark, Sweden and Norway, he managed to return to England in 1917 in time to carry out the tests aboard the Yarmouth. After further wide-ranging trials (which included flying a Pup from a platform on top of the forward 15-in. gun turret of the battlecruiser H.M.S. Repulse, on 1st October 1917), Commander Rutland was appointed senior flying officer aboard H.M.S. Furious, the first aircraft carrier (as distinct from a seaplane or balloon carrier). See below. He was awarded the Distinguished Service Cross and Bar, in addition to the Albert Medal, before the end of the War. Subsequently he went to Japan to advise that nation on naval aviation matters, only to be brought back to the United Kingdom during the Second World War where he committed suicide shortly after.)

The first vessel in the world to be defined as an aircraft carrier (in the modern sense, i.e. equipped with a flying deck for operations of landplanes) was the light battlecruiser, H.M.S. *Furious*. This ship commenced construction shortly after the outbreak of the First World War, it being intended to arm her with a pair of 18-in. guns. In March 1917 authority to alter her design was issued, and at the expense of one of these huge guns she was completed with a hangar and flight deck on her forecastle. With a displacement of 22,000 tons and a speed of $31\frac{1}{2}$ knots, she carried six Sopwith Pups in addition to four seaplanes. Her first senior flying officer was Sqdn. Ldr. E. H. Dunning.

The first landing in the world by an aeroplane upon a ship underway was carried out by Sqdn. Ldr. E. H. Dunning who flew a Sopwith Pup on to the deck of H.M.S. *Furious* on 2nd August 1917. Steaming at 26 knots into a wind of 21 knots, *Furious* thus provided a 47-knot headwind for Dunning who flew his Pup for'ard along the starboard side of the ship before sideslipping towards the deck located on the forecastle. Men then grabbed straps on the aircraft and brought it to a standstill. On 7th August Dunning attempted to repeat the operation in an even greater headwind but stalled as he attempted to overshoot and was killed when his aircraft was blown over the side of the ship.

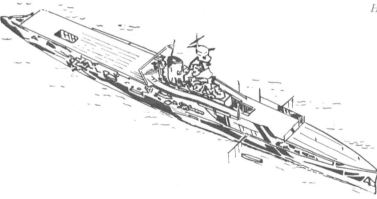

H.M.S. Furious, late 1917

(*H.M.S.* Furious *became the longest-lived active carrier in the world. Launched in 1916 she featured a flying deck on her forecastle until mid-1917 when another deck was added aft with interconnecting trackways abaft the superstructure. Between 1921 and 1925 the midships superstructure was eliminated and she emerged as a flush-deck carrier displacing 22,450 tons, with two aircraft lifts and an aircraft capacity of 33. Her overall length was 786 ft. (239 m.). After an extraordinarily active and exciting career in the Second World War (and a near head-on collision at night in the Atlantic with a troopship which passed so close as to carry away some of the carrier's radio masts), she was finally scrapped in 1949.*

The first enemy airship to be shot down by a landplane launched from a ship was the Zeppelin L.23 which was shot down by Flt. Sub-Lt. B. A. Smart flying a Sopwith Pup which had taken off from a platform aboard the light cruiser H.M.S. *Yarmouth* on 21st August 1917 off the Danish coast.

The first flush-deck aircraft carrier in the world was H.M.S. *Argus*, 15,775 tons. Originally laid down in 1914 as the Italian liner *Conte Rosso*, she was purchased by Great Britain and launched in 1917, and completed in 1918. She featured an unrestricted flight deck of 565 ft. length (172 m.) and could accommodate 20 aircraft. She was ultimately scrapped in 1947. She was **the first carrier in the world to embark a full squadron of torpedo-carrier landplanes**, when in October 1918 a squadron of Sopwith Cuckoos was activated. They did not however see action.

H.M.S. Argus

The first aeroplane in the world designed from the outset as a torpedo-bomber for operation from an aircraft carrier was the Sopwith Cuckoo. First flown in June 1917 and powered by an Hispano-Suiza engine, the single-seat Cuckoo could carry an 18-in. (45·7 cm.) torpedo and entered service when a squadron embarked in H.M.S. *Argus* in October 1918 (see above).

Sopwith Cuckoo

The first pilot to attempt to take off from a towed barge in an aeroplane was Col. Samson who, as pilot of a Sopwith Camel, attempted in July 1918 to take off from a 40-ft. (12 m.) barge being towed at 31 knots behind a destroyer. The Camel evidently fouled part of the barge and fell into the water, Samson being fortunate to escape with his life. **The first pilot to perform this feat successfully** was the American-born Flt. Sub-Lt. Stuart Culley, R.N., who on 1st August 1918 rose from the barge as it was being towed at 35 knots. At 8.41 a.m. on 11th August 1918 Culley took off from the barge being towed off the Dutch coast and climbed to 18,000 ft. (6,000 m.) to shoot down the German Zeppelin L.53 using incendiary ammunition. He was thus **the first (and probably the only) pilot to shoot down an enemy aircraft having taken off from a towed vessel.** Landing in the sea alongside his towing destroyer, H.M.S. *Redoubt*, he was rescued—and later awarded the D.S.O. for his feat—and his Camel was salvaged by a derrick (invented by Col. Samson). The only survivor of the Zeppelin baled out from 19,000 ft. (6,500 m.)—almost certainly a record at that time.

The largest British aircraft constructed and flown during the First World War was the Porte/Felixstowe Fury triplane flying boat, with a span of 123 ft. (37·5 m.), a maximum loaded weight of 33,000 lb. (15,000 kg.) and powered by five 334 h.p. Rolls-Royce Eagle VII engines. Flown by John Cyril Porte from Harwich harbour in 1918, the Fury never entered service and continued on test until in 1919 it crashed and was almost totally destroyed. On one occasion it was flown with twenty-four passengers, sufficient fuel for seven hours' flying and 5,000 lb. (2,270 kg.) of ballast.

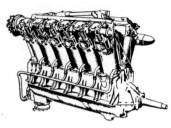

The first flight of America's famous Liberty 12-cylinder engine took place on 21st October 1917, installed in the Curtiss HS-1 flying boat. The Liberty engine, whose power rose from 375 to 420 h.p. during development, came to be used by more American aeroplanes than any other prior to 1926, and was one of the world's outstanding aeroplane engines.

Liberty engine

The only American naval pilot to shoot down five enemy aircraft during the First World War is believed to have been Lt. David S. Ingalls, U.S. Navy, who, while serving with No. 213 Squadron, R.A.F., in 1918 was credited with the destruction of four enemy aeroplanes and one balloon. He was awarded the British D.F.C. (citation dated 25th October 1918) and the U.S. Distinguished Service Medal (citation dated 11th November 1920). He later served as Assistant Secretary of the Navy for Aeronautics from 1929 until 1932.

BETWEEN THE WORLD WARS

The first American naval pilot to take off from a platform aboard an American warship was Lt. Cdr. Edward O. McDonnell who flew a Sopwith Camel from a turret platform on the U.S. battleship *Texas* on 9th March 1919 anchored in Guantánamo Bay, Cuba. All told, eight American battleships were fitted with aircraft platforms during the 1919–20 period and various aeroplanes, including Camels, Nieuport 28s, Hanriot HD-1s and Vought VE-7s, were flown from them.

The first aircraft carrier in the world to introduce the offset "island" superstructure and split-level aircraft hangar was H.M.S. *Eagle*. Originally laid down as the battleship *Almirante Cochrane* (intended for Chile) in 1913, she was purchased and completed as a carrier in 1920, serving with the Royal Navy until in 1942 she was sunk by a German submarine.

The first American aircraft carrier was the U.S.S. *Jupiter*, an ex-collier of 11,050 tons, which was converted to feature a stem-to-stern flight deck of 534 ft. length (163 m.) in 1920.

The first capital warship sunk by bombs dropped by American aeroplanes was the ex-German battleship *Ostfriesland*, 22,800 tons, during a demonstration of bombing by U.S. Army MB-2 bombers commanded by Brigadier General William Mitchell on 21st July 1921. During these trials, prior to the sinking of the *Ostfriesland*, U.S. Navy flying boats had sunk the submarine *U-117*, and U.S. Army bombers had sunk the ex-German destroyer *G-102* and the cruiser *Frankfurt*, 5,100 tons. Subsequently Army bombers sank the battleships *Alabama*, *New Jersey* and *Virginia*. The *Washington*, an unfinished battleship of 32,500 tons, was attacked with and hit by all manner of weapons and was finally sunk by naval gunfire.

The first American carrier-based fighter to be designed specifically as such was the Naval Aircraft Factory TS-1, the first of which appeared in May 1922, two months after the first U.S. aircraft carrier, the *Langley*, had been commissioned. Designed by the U.S. Bureau of Aeronautics, the TS-1 was built by the Curtiss Aeroplane and Motor Company and first joined the *Langley* in December 1922. It had a top speed of 123 m.p.h. (198 km./hr.).

Brig.-Gen. William Mitchell

(The aircraft carrier limitations imposed by the Washington Treaty (signed on 6th February 1922) per-mitted the United States and Great Britain to build aircraft carriers up to a total tonnage of 135,000 tons per country; Japan, 81,000 tons, and France and Italy, 60,000 tons each. Aircraft carriers were not per-mitted to carry guns of greater calibre than eight inches. Moreover, carriers already under construction at the time of the signing of the Treaty were exempt from its provisions. A limit of 27,000 tons was placed on each ship, but each nation might possess up to two vessels each of 33,000 tons. The U.S.S. Saratoga *and* Lexington *each displaced approximately 33,000 tons, but at full load the figure was nearer 40,000. When no longer considered to be bound by the provisions of the Treaty, Japan rebuilt several of her carriers during the nineteen-thirties to displace more than 33,000 tons. Of all the signatory nations (as major sea powers) of the Washington Treaty, only Italy chose to ignore the significance of the aircraft carrier, and constructed no such ship between the two World Wars.*

The first American aircraft carrier to be commissioned for fleet service was the U.S.S. *Langley*, 11,050 tons, a converted ex-collier (the *Jupiter*), which was completed in September 1922. **The first pilot to take off from her deck** was Cdr. Virgil C. Griffin on 17th October that year, and on 26th October Lt. Cdr. Chevalier carried out **the first landing.**

The first Japanese aircraft carrier to be laid down as such (and second in the world only to H.M.S. *Hermes*) was the *Hosho*, 7,474 tons, laid down in December 1919 and completed in December 1922. Her aircraft complement was up to 21 and she was not scrapped until 1947.

The first ship in the world to be laid down as an aircraft carrier (but not the first to be completed as such) was H.M.S. *Hermes*, 12,900 tons at full load. Laid down in 1918 and completed in 1923, she could accommodate 25 aircraft and served with the Royal Navy until 1942 when she was sunk by Japanese aircraft off the coast of Ceylon. **She was the first carrier in the world to be sunk by aircraft from another carrier.**

H.M.S. Hermes

The first squadron of regular U.S. Navy aircraft to embark on an American carrier went aboard U.S.S. *Langley* in January 1925.

U.S.S. Langley

One of the most remarkable feats of seamanship by the crew of a flying boat must be that of the crew of the NAF PN-9 flying boat who, on 1st September 1925, set off from San Francisco Bay to fly to Hawaii, a distance of 2,400 miles (3,860 km.) in an attempt to establish a new world seaplane distance record. When 559 miles (964 km.) from their destination they were forced to alight on the sea, but completed the voyage by *sailing* the flying boat after stripping the fabric from the lower wings and making sails. They were sighted by a submarine off Honolulu on 10th September. Nevertheless their flight of 1,841 miles (2,958 km.) was recognised as a world seaplane record.

PN-9 flying boat

The last occasion on which American pilots flew aircraft designed during the First World War under combat conditions was during the action by the U.S. Marine Corps against the Nicaraguan bandits during 1927. Their aircraft were Naval Aircraft Factory-built de Havilland DH-4Bs and Boeing-rebuilt DH-4Ms.

The first French aircraft carrier was the *Béarn*, 21,800 tons, converted from a *Normandie*-class battleship originally laid down in 1914. She was not completed until May 1927 and, although **the longest-lived carrier in the world**, she spent the greater part of the Second World War out of commission and was subsequently converted for use as an aircraft transport. She was ultimately scrapped in 1968.

The first U.S. Marine Corps squadron to serve aboard an aircraft carrier was Marine Scouting Squadron VS-14M which embarked in U.S.S. *Saratoga* on 2nd November 1931. Simultaneously VS-15M embarked in U.S.S. *Lexington*.

The first and only American operational fighters to serve aboard airships were naval Curtiss F9C Sparrowhawk biplanes which served on board the U.S. airships *Akron* and *Macon* between 1932 and 1935. The prototype Sparrowhawk (XF9C-1) achieved the first "hook-on" on the airship *Los Angeles* on 27th October 1931, and the first production aircraft hooked-on to *Akron* on 29th June 1932.

F9C Sparrowhawk

The last operational American biplane to remain in production was the Curtiss SBC Helldiver, whose first flight as the parasol monoplane XF12C-1 was in 1933 (and was almost immediately redesigned as a biplane), and remained in production in the United States until 1941. At the time of the Japanese attack on Pearl Harbour in December 1941 the U.S. Navy still retained 186 Helldiver biplanes on strength.

SBC Helldiver

Grumman FF-1

The first aeroplane flown by the U.S. Navy to feature a retractable undercarriage was the Grumman XFF-1 fighter, and as the FF-1 entered service with Navy Squadron VF-5B on 21st June 1933 attached to the U.S.S. *Lexington*.

The flying-boat produced in the greatest numbers anywhere in the world was the Consolidated PBY Catalina. Excluding production in Russia, 1,196 Catalina flying boats and 944 amphibians were built and these served with the air forces and airlines of more than twenty-five nations. Widely regarded as one of Aviation's classic designs, the PBY in 1970 still continues to give yeoman service in several parts of the world—thirty-five years after the prototype's first flight.

PBY Catalina

The world's first carrier-based monoplane fighter to achieve operational status was Japan's Mitsubishi A5M "Claude" which entered service with the carrier *Kaga* in 1937 during air operations against the Chinese.

A5M "Claude"

At the outbreak of the Second World War there were nineteen aircraft carriers in commission and eleven under construction by the world's major naval powers:

	Under construction	Completed
Great Britain	6	7
Japan	2	6
United States of America	2	5
France	1	1

AIRCRAFT CARRIERS COMPLETED BETWEEN THE WORLD WARS

Name	Displacement at full load tons	Length ft.	m.	Speed kt.	Aircraft accommodation	Completed	Ultimate fate	Remarks
GREAT BRITAIN								
Furious	22,450	786	(239·6)	32·5	33	Re-commissioned 1925	Scrapped in 1945	Converted from light battlecruiser during construction. Originally completed in 1917.
Argus	15,775	565	(172·2)	20·76	20	1918	Scrapped in 1947	Converted from liner *Conte Rosso* during construction.
Eagle	26,400	667	(203·3)	24	21	1920	Sunk by U-Boat, 1942	Converted from battleship *Almirante Cochrane* during construction.
Hermes	12,900	598	(182·3)	25	25	1923	Sunk by Jap. a/c, 1942	World's first carrier designed as such.
Courageous	26,500	786	(239·6)	32	48	1928	Sunk by U-Boat, 1939	Converted from light battlecruiser.
Glorious	26,500	786	(239·6)	32	48	1930	Sunk by German warships, 1940	Converted from light battlecruiser.
Ark Royal	27,000	800	(243·8)	31·5	60	1938	Sunk by U-Boat, 1941	Max. accommodation, 72 aircraft.
UNITED STATES OF AMERICA								
Langley	11,050	542	(165·2)	15	34	1922	Sunk by Jap. a/c, 1942	Converted from collier *Jupiter*, 1920–21.
Lexington	40,000	888	(270·7)	34	80	1927	Sunk by Jap. a/c, 1942	Converted from battlecruiser during construction. Max. accommodation, 120 aircraft.
Saratoga	40,000	888	(270·7)	34	80	1927	Destroyed in A-Bomb test, Bikini 1946 Scrapped later	Remarks as for *Lexington*.
Ranger	14,500	769	(234·4)	29·5	80	1934	Sunk by Jap. a/c, 1942	
Yorktown	19,900	741	(225·9)	29·5	80	1937	Scrapped in 1958	
Enterprise	19,900	741	(225·9)	29·5	80	1938		
JAPAN								
Hosho	7,470	551	(167·9)	21	21	1922	Scrapped in 1947	Converted from battlecruiser during construction. Accommodation increased to 90 aircraft in 1938 on re-building.
Akagi	36,500	855	(260·6)	32	60	1927	Sunk by U.S. a/c, 1942	
Kaga	38,200	812	(247·5)	28	60	1930	Sunk by U.S. a/c, 1942	Converted from battleship during construction. Aircraft accommodation increased to 90 in 1936.
Ryujo	10,600	590	(179·8)	29	48 (max.)	1933	Sunk by U.S. a/c, 1942	
Soryu	15,900	746	(227·4)	34·5	73 (max.)	1937	Sunk by U.S. a/c, 1942	
Hiryu	17,300	746	(227·4)	34	73 (max.)	1939	Sunk by U.S. a/c, 1942	
FRANCE								
Béarn	25,000	599	(182·6)	21·5	40	1927	Scrapped in 1968	Converted from battleship during construction. Was not used as aircraft carrier (*sic*) after Second

THE SECOND WORLD WAR

The first German aircraft to be shot down by British aircraft during the Second World War
was claimed by naval aircraft. Three Dornier Do 18s of *Küstenfliegergruppe 506*
were sighted by a patrol of Swordfish aircraft flying from H.M.S. *Ark Royal*
over the North Sea on 26th September 1939. Nine Skuas were forthwith
launched from the carrier and these succeeded in forcing one of the Dorniers
(Werke Nr. 731, of *2 Staffel*, Kü. Fl. Gr. 506) down on to the sea in German
Grid Square 3440. The German four-man crew was later rescued and made
prisoner aboard a British destroyer.

Blackburn Skua

The American fighter of the Second World War to remain in production longest was the Vought
F4U Corsair which first flew on 29th May 1940, commenced delivery to VF-12
(U.S. Navy Fighter Squadron Twelve) on 3rd October 1942, and remained in
production until the last aircraft was completed at Dallas, Texas, in December
1952. It was thus **the last piston-engined American fighter to remain in
production.**

The first American naval pilot to destroy five enemy aircraft in the Second World War was Lt.
Edward Henry O'Hare, U.S. Navy, who, on 20th February 1942, attacked
single-handed a formation of nine Japanese bombers in the South-West Pacific
area and shot down five and damaged a sixth.

The first naval battle in which the participating warships relied entirely upon aeroplanes was
the Battle of Coral Sea, fought on 7th–9th May 1942, between U.S. Navy Task
Force 17 and Vice-Admiral Takeo Takagi's Carrier Striking Force (part of
Vice-Admiral Shigeyoshi Inouye's Task Force MO). The battle was fought to
prevent Japanese support of an invasion of Port Moresby and disrupt Japanese
plans to launch air strikes against the Australian mainland. In this respect the
battle must be considered to have been an American victory, although the
large American carrier U.S.S. *Lexington* was sunk (**the first American carrier
to be lost in the Second World War**). The opposing carrier forces were as
follows:

U.S. Navy:
U.S.S. *Lexington*   23 F4F Wildcat fighters, 36 SBD Dauntless dive-bombers and 12 TBD
Devastator torpedo-bombers.
U.S.S. *Yorktown*   21 F4F Wildcat fighters, 38 SBD Dauntless dive-bombers and 13 TBD
Devastator torpedo-bombers.
Imperial Japanese Navy:
Shoho   12 A6M Zero fighters, 9 B5N Kate torpedo-bombers.
Shokaku 21 A6M Zero fighters, 21 D3A Val dive-bombers and 21 B5N torpedo-bombers.
Zuikaku 21 A6M Zero fighters, 21 D3A Val dive-bombers and 21 B5N torpedo-bombers.

The Japanese carrier *Shoho* was attacked and sunk by Dauntlesses and Devastators from the *Lexington* and *Yorktown* (giving rise to the famous radio call from
Lt. Cdr. Robert Dixon "Scratch one flat-top"). A total of 69 American naval
aircraft were lost during the battle while the Japanese losses amounted to about
85 as well as around 400 naval airmen (many of whom went down with the
Shoho); it was the loss of these experienced airmen that was critically to weaken
the Japanese naval air forces in the vital Battle of Midway of 1st–7th June
1942, for the *Shokaku* was forced to return to Japan for repairs and to re-equip.

The first operational American naval aircraft to feature hydraulically-operated folding wings was the Douglas TBD Devastator. It is perhaps interesting to record that of the total number of 75 Devastators on strength with the U.S. Navy on 4th June 1942—the day of the Battle of Midway—37 were lost during the course of this battle.

The first operational carrier-based fighter in the world with a tricycle undercarriage was the Grumman F7F-1 Tigercat which first flew in December 1943, but was too late to give combat service during the Second World War. Powered by two 2,100 h.p. Pratt & Whitney R-2800-34W engines, the Tigercat had a top speed of 435 m.p.h. at 22,200 ft. (699 km./hr. at 6,770 m.), was armed with four 20-mm. and four 0·50-in. guns and up to 1,000 lb. (454 kg.) of bombs under each wing, and could carry a torpedo under the fuselage. A two-seat night fighter variant (the F7F-2N) was also produced.

Grumman F7F Tigercat

The largest military flying boat built by Great Britain was the Short Shetland which first flew on 14th December 1944, and of which only two prototypes were completed. Designed for long-range maritime reconnaissance, the Shetland was powered by four 2,500 h.p. Bristol Centaurus radial engines and had an endurance of 23·6 hours; its span was 150 ft. 4 in. (45·72 m.) and fully loaded it weighed 125,000 lb. (56,750 kg.). The end of the Second World War and the loss of the first prototype (which caught fire at its moorings on 28th January 1946) brought interest in the project to an end.

The first aviation unit specifically formed for suicide operations was the *Shimpu* Special Attack Corps, a group of 24 volunteer pilots commanded by Lt. Yukio Seki, formed within the 201st (Fighter) Air Group, Imperial Japanese Navy, during the third week of October 1944; the unit, equipped with Mitsubishi A6M Zero-Sen single-seat fighters, was formed for the task of diving into the flight decks of American aircraft carriers in the Philippines area, with 250 kg. bombs beneath the fuselages of the fighters (*Shimpu* is an alternative pronunciation of the Japanese ideographs which also represent *kamikaze*, Divine Wind, the name more generally applied to Japanese suicide operations.) **The first successful suicide attack was carried out** by Lt. Seki on 25th October 1944; flying from Mabalacat, he and another pilot crashed into the American escort carrier *St. Lo*, which sank as a result of the damage inflicted.

The first successful use of a purpose-built suicide aircraft is thought to have taken place on 1st April 1945, when three *Ohka* (=Cherry Blossom) piloted rocket-powered bombs of the 721st Air Group, Imperial Japanese Navy, were released over an American naval force near Okinawa (approximate position 26° 15′ N, 127° 43′ E). Damage was inflicted on the battleship U.S.S. *West Virginia*, the attack cargo ships *Achernar* and *Tyrell*, and the attack transport *Alpine*. **The first ship to be sunk by a purpose-built suicide aircraft** was the destroyer *Mannert L. Abele*, on 12th April 1945, near Okinawa (approximate position 27° 25′ N, 126° 59′ E).

Ohka *suicide aircraft, nicknamed* Baka (=*Fool*) *by Allies. The first successful use of this weapon was on 1st April 1945.*

The last sortie by suicide aircraft, according to Japanese accounts, was flown on 15th August 1945 by seven aircraft of the Oita Detachment, 701st Air Group, Imperial Japanese Navy, led in person by Admiral Matome Ugaki, commander of the 5th Air Fleet. United States records fail to confirm any *kamikaze* attacks on this date however.

The total number of suicide aircraft expended, and the results of these attacks, are believed to be as follows:

	Sorties	Aircraft returned	Expended
Philippines area	421	43	378
Formosa area	27	14	13
Okinawa area*	1,809	879	930
Total	2,257	936	1,321

The total number of American naval vessels sunk by suicide attacks from the air was 34, and 288 damaged. Those which were sunk comprised three escort aircraft carriers, 13 destroyers, one destroyer escort, two high-speed minelayers, one submarine chaser, one minesweeper, five tank landing ships, one ocean tug, one auxiliary vessel, one patrol craft, two motor torpedo boats and three other vessels.

AFTER THE SECOND WORLD WAR

The first American aeroplane to land under jet power on a ship was a Ryan FR-1 Fireball compound fighter, powered both by a piston engine and turbojet, flown by Ensign Jake C. West on to the escort carrier *Wake Island* on 6th November 1945. It had been intended to fly on using the reciprocating engine, but this failed on the approach and West landed under jet power.

---

* It has not proved possible to distinguish between actual suicide aircraft and escort fighters in the Okinawa operations and this must necessarily invalidate the total figures to some extent. A rough estimate would show that the usual ratio of escort fighters to suicide aircraft on most sorties was about three to two, although late in the campaign many sorties were flown entirely without escort.

The world's first pure-jet aircraft to operate from an aircraft carrier was the de Havilland Vampire, the third prototype of which, *LZ551*, was flown off H.M.S. *Ocean* by Lt. Cdr. E. M. Brown on 3rd December 1945. For the purpose of these trials the aircraft was designated the Sea Vampire Mk. 10 (not to be confused with the Vampire N.F. Mk. 10 two-seat night fighter).

The first American pure-jet aeroplane to land on a ship was the McDonnell FH-1 Phantom, the prototype of which (the XFD-1) landed for the first time on board the carrier U.S.S. *Franklin D. Roosevelt* on 21st July 1946.

The first post-War world long distance record for aeroplanes was set up by a modified Lockheed P2V-1 Neptune (maritime reconnaissance aircraft), the "*Truculent Turtle*", in September 1946 which flew a distance of 11,236 miles (18,064 km.).

The last operational fighter aircraft of the U.S. Navy to use 0·50-in. (50 calibre) machine guns as standard was the North American FJ-1 Fury naval jet fighter which first flew on 27th November 1946.

The greatest utilitarian range of duties ever applied to a *bona fide* combat aeroplane was probably that applied to the Douglas Skyraider, which was fundamentally an "attack bomber" of the U.S. Navy. To this was added the following scope and range of duties: Night attack, airborne early warning, reconnaissance, electronic counter-measures, target-towing, drone control, specialist anti-submarine attack, submarine search, torpedo-bomber, freighter, 12-seat transport and ambulance. The first aircraft were delivered to the U.S. Navy in December 1946, and the last withdrawn in April 1968. The aircraft is still in service with other forces, and at the time of writing is on active service in the Republics of Chad and Vietnam.

The first pure-jet fighter to serve with the U.S. Navy and the U.S. Marine Corps was the McDonnell FH-1 Phantom which commenced delivery to VF-17A (U.S. Navy Fighter Squadron Seventeen) in July 1947.

The largest flying boat in the world, and the aircraft with the greatest wingspan ever built, was the Hughes H.2 *Hercules*. The 190-ton eight-engined aircraft was 219 ft. long and had a wingspan of 320 ft. It only flew on one occasion; piloted by Howard Hughes, it was raised 70 ft. into the air during a 1,000 yard test run (*below*) off Long Beach Harbor, California, on 2nd November 1947.

The first flying boat in the world capable of a maximum level speed of over 500 m.p.h. (804 km./hr.) was the Saunders-Roe SR.A/1 jet fighter flying boat of Great Britain which first flew on 16th July 1947. Powered by two Metrovick Beryl axial-flow turbojets, the SR.A/1 had a top speed of 512 m.p.h. (821 km./hr.) and an armament of four 20-mm. guns. Three prototypes were built but the project was abandoned when interest waned in the flying boat at the end of the nineteen-forties.

Saunders-Roe SR.A/1

The first U.S. Navy jet fighter squadron to go to sea under operational conditions was VF-5A (U.S. Navy Fighter Squadron Five), equipped with North American FJ-1 Fury fighters, aboard U.S.S. *Boxer*, on which the aircraft were first landed on 10th March 1948.

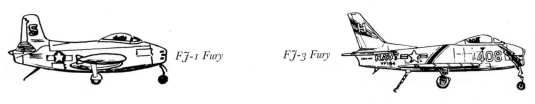

FJ-1 Fury   *FJ-3 Fury*

The first U.S. Navy jet fighter to take part in air combat was the Grumman F9F-2 Panther, several of which took off from the carrier U.S.S. *Valley Forge* off Korea on 3rd July 1950 and went into action against North Korean forces. A U.S. Navy pilot of a Grumman Panther shot down a MiG-15 on 9th November 1950 and thus became **the first U.S. Navy jet pilot to shoot down another jet aircraft.**

The first jet aircraft in the world to destroy another jet aircraft at night was a U.S. Marine Douglas F3D-2 Skyknight which destroyed a night-flying MiG-15 over Korea on 2nd November 1952.

Douglas F3D-2 Skyknight

The first American naval pilot to achieve five air victories over Korea was Lt. Guy Bordelon who, flying a piston-engined F-4U Corsair, shot down his fifth victim on 17th July 1953.

The first supersonic operational carrier-borne naval interceptor in the world was the Grumman F11F-1 Tiger of the U.S. Navy. Capable of supersonic speed in level flight, the Tiger was first flown on 7th July 1954, was powered by an afterburning Wright J-67 turbojet and carried an armament of four 20-mm. guns.

The first variable-incidence jet fighter in the world was the Chance-Vought (LTV, or Ling-Temco-Vought) XF8U-1 Crusader naval interceptor of the U.S. Navy which first flew on 25th March 1955. Later designated the LTV F-8A, the Crusader was powered by a single 10,700 lb. (4,860 kg.) thrust Pratt & Whitney J-57-P-12 or P-14 engine with afterburning, was armed with four 20-mm. guns and 32 air-to-air rockets, and had a top speed of 1,120 m.p.h. (Mach $1.7 = 1,780$ km./hr.). The purpose of the wing's variable incidence was to eliminate an exaggerated nose-up tendency during landing.

The heaviest aeroplane ever to serve as standardised equipment aboard aircraft carriers was the Douglas A3D Skywarrior. First delivered to VAH-1 (U.S. Navy Heavy Attack Squadron One) on 31st March 1956, Skywarriors later served aboard carriers of the *Essex* and *Midway* classes. With a span of 72 ft. 6 in. (22·6 m.) and a loaded weight of 82,000 lb. (37,230 kg.), they were powered by two 12,400 lb. thrust (5,630 kg.) Pratt & Whitney J57-P-10 turbojet which bestowed a top speed of 610 m.p.h. (980 km./hr.).

Douglas A3D Skywarrior

The fastest strategic reconnaissance/attack aircraft to serve with the U.S. Navy was the North American A-5/RA-5C Vigilante which first flew on 31st August 1958 and entered service with VAH-9 in June 1961. The Vigilante's performance was impressive for, powered by two afterburning General Electric J79-GE-8 turbojets, it had a top speed of 1,385 m.p.h. at 40,000 ft. (2,258 km./hr. at 12,200 m.), or Mach 2·1, a range of 3,000 miles (4,820 km.) and a service ceiling of 64,000 ft. (19,500 m.). Originally designed to launch a nuclear weapon from a unique linear bomb-bay which extended through the tail, the Vigilante later was used as a high-speed strategic reconnaissance aircraft. It was the second largest aircraft (after the Douglas Skywarrior) to be accepted for operational service aboard an aircraft carrier, with a gross weight of 61,730 lb. (28,025 kg.).

The last biplanes in U.S. military or naval service were a small number of NAF N3N-3 primary trainers of the U.S. Navy which were retired from service in 1961.

NAF N3N-3

FIRST FLIGHT DATES OF THE WORLD'S PRINCIPAL MARITIME AEROPLANES

1918

Supermarine Baby flying boat (U.K.)	February
Navy/Curtiss NC-1 flying boat (U.S.)	4th October

Supermarine Baby

1926

Blackburn Iris flying boat (U.K.)	June
Short Singapore flying boat (U.K.)	August
Boeing Model 69 fighter (U.S.)	3rd November

1928

Boeing F4B-1 fighter (U.S.)	25th June

1930

Short Rangoon flying boat (U.K.)	August

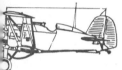

Boeing F4B

1932

Short Sarafand flying boat (U.K.)	30th June

1933

Grumman XJF-1 Duck (U.S.)	4th May
Grumman XF2F-1 fighter (U.S.)	18th October
Supermarine Seagull V/Walrus (U.K.)	21st June

1934

Mitsubishi G3M (Nell) bomber (Jap.)	April

Grumman F2F

1935

Mitsubishi A5M (Claude)fighter (Jap.) . . .	4th February
Consolidated PBY Catalina flying boat (U.S.) . . .	28th March
Douglas XTBD-1 Devastator (U.S.)	15th April
NAF XN3N-1 naval trainer (U.S.)	August

1936

Vought XSB2U-1 Vindicator/Chesapeake (U.S.) . . .	1st January

Devastator

1937

Nakajima B5N (Kate) bomber (Jap.)	January
Grumman XF4F-2 Wildcat fighter (U.S.) . . .	2nd September
Short Sunderland flying boat (U.K.)	October
Brewster XF2A-1 Buffalo fighter (U.S.)	December

1938

Wildcat

Aichi D3A (Val) bomber (Jap.)	January
Vought XOS2U-1 Kingfisher (U.S.)	20th July
Supermarine Sea Otter amphibian (U.K.) . . .	August
Fairey Albacore torpedo bomber (U.K.) . . .	12th December
Blackburn Roc fighter (U.K.)	23rd December

1939

Martin XPBM-1 Mariner flying boat (U.S.) . . .	18th February
Mitsubishi A6M Zero-Sen fighter (Jap.) . . .	1st April
Mitsubishi G4M (Betty) bomber (Jap.) . . .	22rd October

Buffalo

1940
Fairey Fulmar fighter (U.K.)   .   .   .   .   .   .   4th January
Curtiss XSB2C-1 Helldiver (U.S.).   .   .   .   .   .   12th December
Yokosuka D4Y dive bomber (Jap.)   .   .   .   .   .   December

1941
Brewster XSB2A-1 Buccaneer (U.S.)   .   .   .   .   17th June
Lockheed PV Ventura bomber (U.S.)   .   .   .   .   31st July
Grumman Avenger torpedo-bomber (U.S.)   .   .   .   .   1st August
Fairey Firefly fighter (U.K.)   .   .   .   .   .   22nd December

1942
Blackburn Firebrand fighter (U.K.)   .   .   .   .   27th February
Mitsubishi J2M (Jack) fighter (Jap.)   .   .   .   .   20th March
Grumman XF6F Hellcat fighter (U.S.).   .   .   .   26th June
Kawanishi N1K1-J (George) seaplane fighter (Jap.)   .   27th December

1943
Grumman Tigercat fighter (U.S.).   .   .   .   .   .   December

1944
Curtiss XSC-1 Seahawk (U.S.)   .   .   .   .   .   16th February
Grumman XF8F-1 Bearcat fighter (U.S.)   .   .   .   .   21st August
Martin XBTM-1 Mauler (U.S.)   .   .   .   .   .   26th August
Hawker Fury/Sea Fury fighter (U.K.)   .   .   .   .   1st September
Yokosuka MXY7 Ohka suicide aircraft (Jap.)   .   .   .   October
Short Shetland flying boat (U.K.).   .   .   .   .   14th December

1945
McDonnell XFD-1 Phantom fighter (U.S.)   .   .   .   .   26th January
Douglas XBT2D-1 Skyraider (U.S.)   .   .   .   .   18th March
de Havilland Sea Hornet fighter (U.K.)   .   .   .   19th April
Short Seaford flying boat (U.K.)   .   .   .   .   .   April
Lockheed Neptune patrol bomber (U.S.)   .   .   .   .   17th May
Grumman XTB3F-1 Guardian (U.S.)   .   .   .   .   19th December

1946
Supermarine Attacker fighter (U.K.)   .   .   .   .   27th July
North American FJ-1 Fury fighter (U.S.)   .   .   .   27th December

1947
McDonnell Banshee fighter (U.S.)   .   .   .   .   11th January
Saunders-Roe SR.A/1 flying boat fighter (U.K.)   .   .   .   16th July
Hawker P.1040 (Sea Hawk) fighter (U.K.)   .   .   .   2nd September
Grumman Panther fighter (U.S.)   .   .   .   .   24th November
Grumman Albatross amphibian (U.S.)   .   .   .   .   24th October

1948
Douglas Skyknight fighter (U.S.)   .   .   .   .   .   23rd March
Martin Marlin flying boat (U.S.)   .   .   .   .   .   30th May
Vought Cutlass fighter (U.S.)   .   .   .   .   29th September

1949
North American T-28 Trojan trainer (U.S.)   .   .   .   26th September

Top, *the North American OV-10 Bronco, the only purpose-designed counter-insurgency aircraft in the world, produced in response to U.S. experience in S.E. Asia. Powered by two AiResearch T76 turboprops, the Bronco has a two-man crew and accommodates either five paratroopers or two stretcher-cases and an attendant. Fixed armament includes two M60 guns in each sponson and provision for two Sidewinders; wing and belly points accommodate up to 3,600 lb. of warload. The North American Vigilante (bottom) is the second heaviest aircraft ever accepted for carrier operations, and, with a top speed in excess of Mach 2, the fastest in its class* (see p. 116).

1951
Douglas Skyray fighter (U.S.)   .   .   .   .   .   23rd January
McDonnell Demon fighter (U.S.) .   .   .   .   .   7th August
Grumman Cougar fighter (U.S.) .   .   .   .   .   . 20th September
de Havilland Sea Vixen (D.H.110) fighter (U.K.) .   .   . 26th September
North American FJ-2 fighter (U.S.)   .   .   .   . 27th December

1952
Douglas XA3D-1 Skywarrior (U.S.)   .   .   .   .   .   28th October
Grumman XS2F-1 Tracker (U.S.)   .   .   .   .   . 4th December

1954
Douglas A-4 Skyhawk fighter (U.S.)   .   .   .   .   22nd June
Grumman Tiger fighter (U.S.)   .   .   .   .   .   30th July
North American FJ-4 Fury fighter (U.S.)   .   .   .   . 28th October

1955
Chance Vought (LTV) F8U Crusader fighter (U.S.)   .   .   25th March

1956
Supermarine Scimitar fighter (U.K.)   .   .   .   .   20th January

1958
North American Buckeye trainer (U.S.) .   .   .   .   . 7th February
McDonnell F4H Phantom II fighter (U.S.)   .   .   .   .   27th May
North American A-5 Vigilante (U.S.)   .   .   .   .   31st August

1960
Grumman Intruder (U.S.) .   .   .   .   9th April
Grumman Hawkeye (U.S.) .   .   .   . 21st October

1965
LTV A-7A Corsair II (U.S.)   .   .   .   .   .   . 27th September

CHAPTER 4:
ROUTE-PROVING AND
COMMERCIAL AVIATION

A Tupolev TU-104 of Aeroflot

The first recorded carriage of freight by air was a box of Osram lamps carried on 4th July 1911 by a Valkyrie monoplane flown by Horatio Barber from Shoreham to Hove in Sussex, England, on behalf of the General Electric Company who paid £100 ($240) for the flight.

The first official carriage of mail by air in the U.S.A. was carried by Earl L. Ovington on 23rd September 1911 in a Blériot monoplane from Garden City, N.Y., to Mineola, L.I., a distance of six miles.

The first air crossing of the Mediterranean was achieved on 23rd September 1913 by a Morane-Saulnier monoplane flown by Roland Garros who flew 453 miles (700 km.) from Saint-Raphaël to Bizerte in 7 hrs. 53 min.

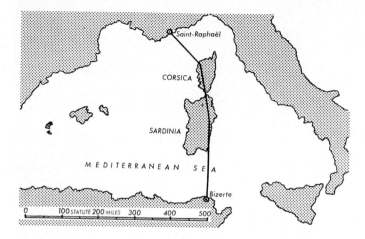

The first flight from France to Egypt was accomplished by Jules Védrines in a Blériot powered by an 80 h.p. Gnôme engine, between 29th November and 29th December 1913. Setting out from Nancy, France, his route was *via* Wurtzburg, Prague, Vienna, Belgrade, Sofia, Constantinople, Tripoli (Syria), Jaffa and Cairo.

The first passenger to be carried from one city to another in Canada by air was flown in the Curtiss flying-boat *Sunfish* from Toronto to Hamilton and back by Theodore Macaulay on 15th May 1914.

The first flight across the North Sea by an aeroplane was achieved by the Norwegian pilot Tryggve Gran flying a Blériot monoplane on 30th July 1914.

The world's first all-metal aeroplane was the Junkers J.1 (the "tin donkey"), initiated as a private venture by the *Forschungsansalt Professor Junkers* and flown (on a short "hop") for the first time on 12th December 1915 at Dessau, Germany. Designed by Hugo Junkers, Dr. Mader and Otto Reuter, the J.1 (of which only one was built) had a top speed of 105·5 m.p.h. (170 km./hr.).

Junkers J.1

The first British airline company to be registered was Aircraft and Travel Ltd. It was registered in London in October 1916 by George Holt Thomas.

The first scheduled regular international air mail service in the world was inaugurated between Vienna and Kiev, *via* Kraków, Lwów and Proskurov on 20th March 1918. The service was principally for military mails and was operated with Hansa-Brandenburg C I biplanes, continuing until November 1918.

The first air crossing of the Andes was achieved by the Argentine army pilot Teniente Luis C. Candelaria flying a Morane-Saulnier parasol monoplane on 13th April 1918 from Zapala, Argentina, to Cunco, Chile, a distance of approximately 200 km. (124 miles). The maximum altitude achieved was about 4,000 m. (13,000 ft.). Candelaria had attended the fifth military flying course at El Palomar which commenced in September 1916.

The first experimental air mail service in the U.S.A. was flown by War Department Curtiss JN-4 aircraft on 15th May 1918 between Washington, D.C., Philadelphia, Pa., and New York City. Lieutenant Torrey H. Webb was the first pilot.

Curtiss JN-4 "Jenny"

The first official air mail flight in Canada was flown on 24th June 1918 in a Curtiss JN-4 from Montreal to Toronto by Captain Brian A. Peck, R.A.F., accompanied by Corporal Mathers.

The first regular air mail service in the U.S.A. was established on 12th August 1918 by the U.S. Post Office Department between New York City and Washington, D.C. Edward V. Gardner, Max Miller, Maurice Newton and Robert F. Shank were the pilots.

The first West-East crossing of the Andes was reputedly achieved by the Chilean Army pilot Teniente Dn. Dagoberto Godoy of the Chilean Military School of Aviation who flew a Bristol M.1C monoplane fighter from Santiago de Chile to Mendoza in Argentina on 12th December 1918. (For the first-ever crossing of the Andes, see above. There is no record of the Argentinian pilot returning by air, and it is therefore assumed that Teniente Godoy's flight was the first eastward crossing.)

The first flight from Egypt to India was made by Capt. Ross M. Smith, D.F.C., A.F.C., Maj.-Gen. W. G. H. Salmond, D.S.O., Brig.-Gen. A. E. Borton, and two mechanics between 29th November and 12th December 1918, in a Handley Page 0/400 from Heliopolis to Karachi *via* Damascus, Baghdad, Bushire, Bandar Abbas and Chahbar. The same aircraft had made **the first flight from England to Egypt** between 28th July and 8th August 1918.

Handley Page 0/400

The first American international air mail was inaugurated between Seattle, Wash., and Victoria, British Columbia, Canada, by the Hubbard Air Service on 3rd March 1919 using a Boeing Type C aircraft. The service was regularised by contract on 14th October 1920.

The first British aeroplane to carry civil markings (*K-100*) was a de Havilland D.H.6 in 1919. It was sold to the Marconi Wireless Telegraph Co., Ltd., and used for radio trials; it became the second aircraft entered on the British Civil Register (as *G-EAAB*; see below).

The first British civil aeroplane (i.e. the first on the British Civil Register proper) was the de Havilland D.H.9 (*G-EAAA*, previously *C6054*), operated as a mailplane by Air Transport and Travel Ltd., in mid-1919 between London and Paris.

The first British Certificate of Airworthiness was issued on 1st May 1919 to the Handley Page 0/400 (*F5414*) which thereafter became registered as *G-EAAF*, owned by Handley Page Air Transport Ltd.

The first trans-Atlantic crossing by air was achieved by the American Navy/Curtiss NC-4 flying boat commanded by Lt. Cdr. A. C. Read between 8th May and 31st May 1919. Three flying boats, the NC-1, NC-3 and NC-4, under the command of Cdr. John H. Towers, set out from Rockaway, N.Y., on 8th May, but only NC-4 completed the crossing, arriving at Plymouth, England, on 31st May, having landed at Chatham, Mass.; Halifax, Nova Scotia; Trepassy Bay, Newfoundland; Horta, Azores; Ponta Delgada, Azores; Lisbon, Portugal; Ferrol del Caudillo, Spain. Total distance flown was 3,925 miles (6,310 km.) in 57 flying hours, 16 minutes, at a speed of 68·4 knots. Both NC-1 and NC-3 were forced down on the sea short of the Azores, and NC-1 sank—its crew being rescued. NC-3, with Cdr. Towers aboard, taxied the remaining 200 miles to the Azores. The crews of the three NC boats were:

NC-1: Lt. Cdr. P. N. L. Bellinger, Commander
Lt. Cdr. M. A. Mitscher, pilot
Lt. L. T. Barin, pilot
Lt. Harry Sadenwater, radio operator
Chief Machinist's Mate C. I. Kesler, engineer

NC-3: Cdr. John H. Towers, Flight Commander
Cdr. H. C. Richardson, pilot
Lt. David H. McCullough, pilot
Lt. Cdr. R. A. Lavender, radio operator
Machinist L. R. Moore, engineer

NC-4: Lt. Cdr. A. C. Read, Commander
Lt. E. F. Stone, pilot
Lt. Walter Hinton, pilot
Ensign H. C. Rodd, radio operator
Chief Machinist's Mate E. S. Rhoades, engineer

The Curtiss NC-4

The first non-stop air crossing of the Atlantic was achieved on 14th–15th June 1919 by Capt. John Alcock and Lt. Arthur Whitten Brown who flew in a Vickers Vimy bomber from St. John's, Newfoundland, to Clifden, Co. Galway, Ireland. Powered by two Rolls-Royce engines, the Vimy was fitted with long-range fuel tanks and achieved a coast-to-coast time of 15 hr. 57 min. Total flying time was 16 hr. 12 min. Both Alcock and Brown were knighted in recognition of this achievement; Sir John Alcock, as Chief Test Pilot of Vickers, was however killed on 18th December 1919 in a flying accident in bad weather near Rouen, France.

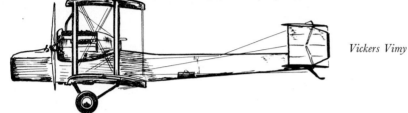

Vickers Vimy

The first airport at which Customs clearance could be obtained for outward-bound flights from London was Hounslow, Middlesex. It was also the only such aerodrome in operation from July 1919 until March 1920.

The first flight across the Canadian Rocky Mountains was made on 7th August 1919 by a Curtiss Jenny flown by Capt. Ernest C. Hoy who flew from Vancouver to Calgary *via* Lethbridge in 16 hr. 42 min. This was also **the first air mail flight across the Rockies.**

The first scheduled commercial airline flight anywhere in the world was flown from London to Paris on 25th August 1919. On that day a de Havilland D.H.4A, flown by Lt. E. H. "Bill" Lawford of Air Transport and Travel Ltd., took off from Hounslow with one passenger and a small quantity of freight at 9.10 a.m. Despite bad weather Lawford landed at Le Bourget, Paris, two and a half hours later. On the same day Handley Page Air Transport Ltd. flew a Handley Page o/7 with a number of Press correspondents from Cricklewood, London, to Le Bourget, and although the aircraft took off at 8.20 a.m. it did not reach Paris until 1.15 p.m., and it was not a scheduled flight. The pilot was Maj. E. L. Foot.

de Havilland D.H.4A

The first Dutch national airline, K.L.M. (Royal Dutch Airlines), was founded on 7th October 1919.

The first flight from Britain to Australia was completed between 12th November and 10th December 1919 by two Australian brothers, Capt. Ross Smith and Lt. Keith Smith, in a Vickers Vimy bomber powered by two Rolls-Royce Eagle engines. They set out from Hounslow, Middlesex, England, and flew to Darwin, Australia, a distance of 11,294 miles (18,157 km.) in under 28 days. Their feat earned them the Australian Government's prize of £10,000 ($24,000) and knighthoods. Sir Ross Smith was killed in a flying accident near Brooklands aerodrome, England, on 13th April 1922. By tragic coincidence, both Sir Ross and Sir John Alcock (famous for his Atlantic crossing, see above) were killed in Vickers Viking amphibians.

The first flight from Britain to Cape Town, South Africa, was made between 4th February and 20th March 1920 by Col. Pierre van Ryneveld, D.S.O., M.C., and Capt. Christopher Quintin Brand, D.S.O., M.C., D.F.C. They set out from Brooklands, England, in a Vickers Vimy bomber, but on 11th March they crashed at Koroto, Uganda. Returning to Cairo, Egypt, they set off again in another aircraft but crashed again, this time at Bulawayo on 6th March. Finally, in a de Havilland D.H.9 provided by the Union Government, they set out from Bulawayo and reached the Cape on 20th March. They received the Union Government's prize of £5,000 ($12,000) and were knighted by H.M. King George V.

The first regular use of Croydon as London's air terminal was on 29th March 1920. On that day the main airport facilities were moved from Hounslow (see above) to Croydon —or Waddon, as the airport was originally known. It was officially opened on 31st March 1921.

Croydon Airport

The first automatic pilot to be fitted in a British commercial aircraft was the Aveline Stabiliser fitted in a Handley Page 0/10 during 1920.

The first regular air services in equatorial Africa were flown from Kinshasha (later re-named Léopoldville) to N'Gombé, inaugurated by the Belgian airline SNETA on 1st July 1920 with a Lévy-Lepen flying boat; the N'Gombé to Lisala route opened on 3rd March 1921, and the Kinshasha to Stanleyville route opened on 1st July 1921.

The first American international scheduled passenger air service was inaugurated on 1st November 1920 by Aeromarine West Indies Airways between Key West, Florida, and Havana, Cuba.

The first Australian commercial airline, QANTAS (Queensland and Northern Territory Aerial Service) was formed on 16th November 1920 for air taxi and regular air services in Australia. The Company's first Chairman was Sir Fergus McMaster (1879–1950), and its first scheduled service commenced on 2nd November 1922 with flights between Charleville and Cloncurry, Queensland.

The first fatal accident to a scheduled British commercial flight occurred on 14th December 1920 when a Handley Page 0/400 crashed soon after take off in fog at Cricklewood, London. The pilot, R. Bager, his engineer and two passengers were killed, but four other passengers escaped.

The first regular scheduled air services in Australia commenced being operated by West Australian Airways on 4th December 1921.

The first Coast-to-Coast flight in the United States of America was achieved between 21st and 24th February 1921 by Lt. William D. Coney of the Air Service, who flew from Rockwell Field, San Diego, Calif., to Jacksonville, Florida, in a flying time of 22 hr. 27 min.

The first Coast-to-Coast air mail flight in the United States of America was made by E. M. Allison and Jack Knight who left San Francisco at 4.30 a.m. on 22nd February 1921 and arrived at Mineola, Long Island, New York, at 4.50 p.m. the following day.

The first air collision between airliners on scheduled flights occurred on 7th April 1922 between a Daimler Airways de Havilland D.H.18 (*G-EAWO*) flown by Robin Duke from Croydon, and a Farman Goliath of *Grands Express Aèriens* flown by M. Mier from Le Bourget. The two aircraft, which were following a road on a reciprocal course, collided over Thieuloy-St. Antoine eighteen miles north of Beauvais. All seven occupants were killed.

D.H.18 and Farman Goliath

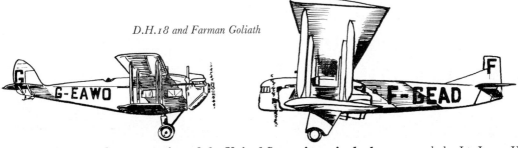

The first Coast-to-Coast crossing of the United States in a single day was made by Lt. James H. Doolittle who flew a modified de Havilland D.H.4B from Pablo Beach, Florida, to Rockwell Field, San Diego, Calif., on 4th September 1922. Actual flying time to cover the 2,163 miles (3,477 km.) 21 hr. 20 min.; elapsed time, with a refuelling stop at Kelly Field, Texas, was 22 hr. 35 min.

The first aeroplane to take off from the Hooghly River, West Bengal, India, was a Fairey IIIC (*G-EBDI*), flown by Capt. Norman Macmillan on 19th August 1922.

The first Czechoslovak-designed commercial aeroplane was the Aero A-10, whose construction commenced in 1921 at Prague, was completed in 1922 and entered service with *Československé Státní Aerolinie* (ČSA), flying the Prague-Brno-Bratislava route in 1924. Powered by a single 260 h.p. Maybach Mb IVa engine, the A-10 carried up to five passengers.

Aero A-10

The first Czechoslovak national airline was *Československé Státní Aerolinie* (ČSA) which commenced operations between Prague and Brastislava on 1st March 1923 with Aero A-14 aircraft.

The first successful in-flight re-fuelling of an aeroplane was accomplished by Capt. L. H. Smith and Lt. J. P. Richter in a de Havilland D.H.4B on 27th June 1923 at San Diego, California, U.S.A. The following month Smith and Richter established a world's endurance record by remaining aloft for 37 hr. 15 min. 43·8 sec. during 27th–28th August 1923 covering a distance of 3,293·26 miles (5,299·9 km.) over a measured 50-km. course at San Diego, California. Their DH-4B was flight-refuelled fifteen times.

The first scheduled air service between London and Berlin was inaugurated by Daimler Airways on 10th April 1923, with intermediate landings at Bremen and Hamburg.

The first non-stop air crossing of the United States of America by an aeroplane was achieved on 2nd–3rd May 1923 by Lt. O. G. Kelly and Lt. J. A. Macready of the U.S. Air Service in a Fokker T-2 aeroplane. Taking off from Roosevelt Field, Long Island, at 12.36 p.m. (Eastern Time) on 2nd May, they arrived at Rockwell Field, San Diego, Calif. at 12.26 p.m. (Pacific Time) on 3rd May. They overflew Dayton, Ohio; Indianapolis, Ind.; St. Louis, Mo.; Kansas City, Mo.; Tucumcari, New Mexico; and Wickenburg, Ariz. The distance flown, 2,520 miles (4,051 km.) was covered in 26 hr. 50 min. 38·4 sec. Kelly and Macready also established a new world's endurance record for aeroplanes on 16th–17th April 1923 in the Fokker T-2 flying a distance of 2,518 miles (4,048 km.) over a measured course in 36 hr. 5 min.

The first British national airline, Imperial Airways, was formed on 1st April 1924. This was the manifestation of the British Government's determination to develop air transport, and the company was to receive preferential air subsidies, having acquired the businesses of the British Marine Air Navigation Co., Daimler Airways, Handley Page Transport and Instone Air Lines.

The first recorded flight of a bull was that of the champion animal *Nico V* carried in a Fokker F.III of K.L.M. from Rotterdam, Holland, to Paris, France, on 9th July 1924. **The first recorded flight by a cow** was that by a Guernsey, *Elm Farm Ollie* which was taken aloft over St. Louis, Missouri, on 18th February 1930 during a publicity stunt. She was milked in the air and her milk despatched to the ground by parachute in sealed paper cartons.

The first successful round-the-world flight was accomplished by Douglas DWC (Douglas World Cruisers) between 6th April and 28th September 1924. Four such aeroplanes set out from Seattle, Washington, and two of these circumnavigated the world. The flagplane (named *Seattle*) only reached Alaska where it crashed on a mountain and the crew returned to the U.S.A.; another (the *Boston*) was forced to give up the flight near the Faroes and was replaced by a fifth Douglas. The aircraft and crews were as follows:

Douglas World Cruiser

Flagplane *Seattle*:	Maj. Frederick Martin, flight commander and pilot Sgt. Alva L. Harvey,
(Aircraft No. 1)	mechanic
Chicago:	Lt. Lowell H. Smith, deputy flight commander and pilot
(Aircraft No. 2)	Lt. Leslie P. Arnold, mechanic and alternate pilot

Boston: Lt. Leight Wade, pilot
(Aircraft No. 3)   S. Sergeant Henry H. Ogden, mechanic

New Orleans: Lt. Erik Nelson, pilot and engineer officer
(Aircraft No. 4)   Lt. John Harding, Jr., mechanic and maintenance officer.

The route flown was as follows:

Seattle, Washington	Haiphong, Indo-China	Budapest, Hungary
Prince Rupert,	Tourane, Indo-China	Vienna, Austria
British Columbia	Saigon, Indo-China	Strasbourg, France
Sitka, Alaska	Kawrong Island	Paris, France
Seward, Alaska	Bangkok, Siam	London, England
Chignic, Aleutian	Tavoy, Malaya	Brough, England
Peninsula	Rangoon, Burma	Kirkwall, Orkneys
Dutch Harbour,	Akyab, Burma	Hornafjord, Iceland
Aleutians	Chittagong, India	Reykjavik, Iceland
Atka, Aleutians	Allahabad, India	Frederiksdal, Greenland
Attu Island	Umballa, India	Ivigtut, Greenland
Komandorski, Kamchatka	Multan, W. Pakistan	Indian Harbour, Labrador
Paramashiru, Kuriles	Karachi, Pakistan	Hawkes Bay, Newfoundland
Hittokapu, Yetorofu	Chabar, Persia	Pictou, Nova Scotia
Minato, Japan	Bandar Abbas, Persia	Casco Bay, Maine
Kasumiga Ura, Japan	Bushire, Persia	Boston, Massachusetts
Kushimoto, Japan	Bagdhad, Mesopotamia	New York
Kagoshima, Japan	Aleppo, Turkey	Washington, D.C.
Shanghai, China	Constantinople,	Eugene, Oregon
Amoy, China	Turkey	Seattle, Washington
Hong Kong	Bucharest, Rumania	

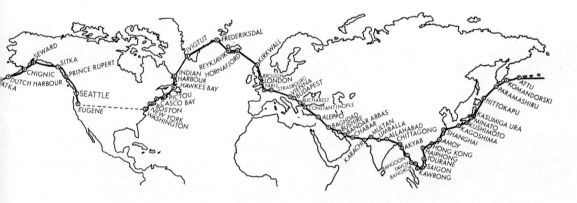

The total mileage flown by the two aeroplanes (Nos. 2 and 4) which completed the historic flight was 27,553 (44,298 km.) and the elapsed time 175 days. The flying time was given as 365 hours.

(Note on the Douglas DWC amphibians. These aircraft were specially commissioned by the U.S. Army as adaptations of the Douglas DT Navy torpedo bombers. Powered by a single in-line engine, the twin-float biplanes had a span of 50 ft. (15·24 m.) and a fuel capacity of 600 U.S. gallons. Two of the World Cruisers are preserved to this day, one being maintained at the Smithsonian Institution at Washington, the other in the Air Force Museum at Wright-Paterson Air Force Base.)

The first regular American trans-continental air mail service, which was flown daily with fourteen intermediate stops, was inaugurated on 1st July 1924. The pilot of the first westward flight was Wesley L. Smith, who took off from New York; the first eastbound pilot was Claire K. Vance who took off from San Francisco, Calif.

The first three-engined all-metal monoplane transport in the world to enter commercial airline service was the Junkers G 23, four of which served with Swedish Air Lines (*AB Aerotransport*) on the Malmö-Hamburg-Amsterdam route, commencing on 15th May 1925. There is no doubt that this aircraft built in Germany and Sweden, provided the basis for the Junkers Ju 52/3m, and certainly set the pattern for low-wing multi-engined monoplanes thereafter.

The only commercial transport aeroplane designed and built in Belgium was the SABCA S-2 (*Société Anonyme Belge de Constructions Aéronautiques*) four-passenger high-wing monoplane powered by a single 240-h.p. Armstrong Siddeley Puma engine. It was delivered to SABENA in December 1926.

The first attempt to fly from Great Britain to India non-stop was made on 20th May 1927 by Flt. Lt. C. R. Carr, D.F.C. (later Air Marshal Sir Roderick Carr, K.B.E., C.B., D.F.C., A.F.C., R.A.F.(Retd.)) accompanied by Flt. Lt. L. E. M. Gillman as navigator. Flying a Hawker Horsley bomber, *J8607*, they took off from Cranwell, Lincolnshire, but were forced down in the Persian Gulf after flying 3,420 miles (5,504 km.) in just over thirty-four hours.

The first light aeroplane flight from London to Karachi, India, was flown by T. Neville Stack in the de Havilland D.H.60 Moth (Cirrus II engine), *G-EBMO*, accompanied by B. S. Leete in a similar aircraft, *G-EBKU*, from Croydon to Karachi between 16th November 1926 and 8th January 1927.

The first non-stop solo air crossing of the Atlantic was made by Captain Charles Lindbergh during 20th-21st May 1927 in a single-engine Ryan high-wing monoplane, *Spirit of St. Louis*, from Long Island, New York, to Paris, France. (It is perhaps worth emphasising that this crossing was being made at the same time as Carr was attempting to fly non-stop from England to India, and there is little doubt that had the latter not been forced to alight in the Persian Gulf, Lindbergh's epic flight might well have been eclipsed to some extent.)

The first non-stop aeroplane flight between the United States mainland and Hawaii was achieved by Lt. Albert F. Hegenberger and Lt. Lester J. Maitland during 28th-29th June 1927 flying an Army Fokker C-2 three-engine monoplane *Bird of Paradise*. They flew the 2,407 miles (3,874 km.) from Oakland, California, to Honolulu, Hawaii, in 25 hours 50 minutes.

The first intercontinental charter flight in the world was made by the Fokker F.VIIa *H-NADP*. Chartered by the American W. van Lear Black, the aircraft was flown from Amsterdam to Jakarta and return between 15th June and 23rd July 1927. The crew comprised Capt. G. J. Geysendorffer, First Officer J. B. Scholte and Flt. Eng. K. A. O. Weber. The outward journey took 13 days, a flying time of 86 hrs. 27 min., to cover 9,120 miles (14,677 km.) and the return journey, 14 days, a flying time of 97 hours to cover 9,590 miles (15,433 km.).

Fokker F.VIIa

The first flight by a light aircraft from London to Cape Town, South Africa, was made between 1st and 28th September 1927 by Flt. Lt. R. R. Bentley flying a de Havilland D.H.60X Moth, *Dorys*. Bentley made two return flights during the next two years between these points, totalling 51,652 miles (83,126 km.)

The first non-stop air crossing of the South Atlantic by an aeroplane was made on 14th–15th October 1927 when Dieudonné Costes and Lt. Joseph Le Brix flew a Breguet aircraft, *Nungesser-Coli*, from St. Louis, Senegal, to Port Natal, Brazil, a distance of 2,150 miles (3,460 km.) in 19 hours 5 minutes.

The first air service operated by Pan American Airways was inaugurated on 19th October 1927 on the 90-mile (145-km.) route between Key West, Florida, and Havana, Cuba.

The first solo flight from Great Britain to Australia was made by Sqdn. Ldr. H. J. L. ("Bert") Hinkler in the Avro 581 Avian prototype light aircraft, *G-EBOV*, flying from Croydon, London, to Darwin, Australia, between 7th and 22nd February 1928. His 11,005 mile (17,711 km.) route was via Rome, Malta, Tobruk, Ramleh, Basra, Jask, Karachi, Cawnpore, Calcutta, Rangoon, Victoria Point, Singapore, Bandoeng and Bima. His aircraft was placed on permanent exhibition in the Brisbane Museum.

The first solo flight by a woman from South Africa to London was accomplished by Lady Heath (previously Mrs. Elliott-Lynn) flying an Avro Avian III, *G-EBUG*, from the Cape to Croydon between 12th February and 17th May 1928. She later sold her aircraft to the famous American woman pilot, Miss Amelia Earhart.

The first solo return flight between London and South Africa by a woman was achieved by Lady Bailey who, in a de Havilland Moth (Cirrus II) *G-EBSF*, left London on 9th March 1928. This aircraft was virtually destroyed at Tabora a month later, but the pilot completed the flight to the Cape in a replacement Moth, *G-EBTG*, subsequently flying round Africa and returning to London on 16th January 1929. Her outward flight occupied the period 9th March to 30th April, and her return flight 21st September 1928 to 16th January 1929.

The Australian Flying Doctor Service was inaugurated on 15th May 1928 using the joint services of the Australian Inland Mission and QANTAS at Cloncurry. The first aircraft was a de Havilland D.H. 50 *Victory*, modified to accommodate two stretchers; its first pilot was A. Affleck and the first flying doctor was Dr. K. H. Vincent Welsh.

The first trans-Pacific flight was made between 31st May and 9th June 1928 by the Fokker F.VIIb-3m *Southern Cross* flown by Capt. Charles Kingsford Smith and C. T. P. Ulm (pilots), accompanied by Harry Lyon (navigator) and James Warner (radio operator), from Oakland, California, to Eagle Farm, Brisbane, via Honolulu, Hawaii, and Suva, Fiji. The *Southern Cross* has been preserved and is displayed at Eagle Farm Airport. It was **the first aircraft ever to land in Fiji.**

The first crossing of the Tasman Sea by air was made on 10th-11th September 1928 by the *Southern Cross* (see above), flown from Richmond Aerodrome, Sydney, to Wigram, Christchurch, New Zealand, in 14 hours 25 minutes, by Charles Kingsford Smith and C. T. P. Ulm, accompanied by H. A. Litchfield (navigator) and T. H. McWilliam (radio operator).

The first largescale airlift evacuation of civilians in the world was undertaken by transport aircraft of the Royal Air Force between 23rd December 1928 and 25th February 1929 from the town of Kabul, Afghanistan, during inter-tribal disturbances. 586 people were evacuated over treacherous country using eight Vickers Victoria transports of No. 70 Squadron, R.A.F., and a Handley Page Hinaidi.

The first commercial air route between London and India was opened by Imperial Airways on 30th March 1929. The route was from London to Basle, Switzerland, by air (Armstrong Whitworth Argosy aircraft); Basle to Genoa, Italy, by train; Genoa to Alexandria, Egypt, by air (Short Calcutta flying boats); Alexandria to Karachi, India, by air (de Havilland D.H.66 Hercules aircraft). The total journey from Croydon to Karachi occupied seven days, for which the single fare was £130. The stage travelled by train was necessary as Italy forbade the air entry of British aircraft, an embargo which lasted several years and substantially frustrated Imperial Airways' efforts to develop the Far East route.

The first non-stop flight from Great Britain to India was accomplished by Sqdn. Ldr. A. G. Jones Williams, M.C., and Flt. Lt.N. H. Jenkins, O.B.E., D.F.C., D.S.M. (pilot and navigator respectively) between 24th and 26th April 1929. Flying from Cranwell, Lincolnshire, to Karachi, India, in a Fairey Long-range Monoplane, *J9479*, powered by a 530 h.p. Napier Lion engine, they covered the 4,130 miles (6,647 km.) in 50 hours 37 minutes. It had been intended to fly to Bangalore to establish a world distance record but the attempt was abandoned owing to headwinds.

The first airship flight around the world was accomplished by the German *Graf Zeppelin* between 8th and 29th August 1929. Captained by Dr. Hugo Eckener, the craft set out from Lakehurst, New Jersey, and flew via Friedrichshafen, Germany, Tokyo, Japan, and Los Angeles, California, returning to Lakehurst 21 days, 7 hours 34 minutes later.

The two large British commercial airships, R-100 and R-101, were completed at the end of 1929, the R-101 (G-FAAW) flying first at Cardington, Bedford, on 14th October, and the R-100 (G-FAAV) on 16th December, flying from Howden, Yorkshire, to the Royal Airship Works, Cardington. The R-100 made a trans-Atlantic flight from Britain to Canada between 29th July and 1st August 1930, returning between 13th and 16th August. The R-101 was destroyed on 5th October 1930 when it struck a hill near Beauvais, France, during a flight from Cardington to India, via Egypt. Commanded by Flt. Lt. H. C. Irwin, A.F.C., the R-101 was carrying 54 people, of whom 48 were killed or died later, including Lord Thompson, Secretary of State for Air, and Major General Sir Sefton Brancker, Director of Civil Aviation. This tragedy ended British efforts to develop airships for commercial use.

The first American air stewardess was Ellen Church who, with United Air Lines, made her first flight between San Francisco, California, and Cheyenne, Wyoming, on 15th May 1930.

Ellen Church (top left)

The de Havilland Comet 4 (top) was the first pure-jet airliner to enter regular service on the transatlantic run. The first service in each direction was flown on 4th October 1958; two B.O.A.C. aircraft, G-APDC (Capt. R. E. Millichap) and G-APBD (Capt. T. B. Stoney) made the East–West and West–East runs respectively, the latter flight setting a record time of 6 hours 11 minutes. The Boeing 707 (bottom) is the world's most widely used four-jet commercial aircraft; up to April 1970 no less than 679 had been supplied to the world's carriers.

The first flight of the Handley Page 42 Hannibal four-engine biplane airliner, G-AAGX, was made on 14th November 1930 from Radlett, Hertfordshire. These stately aeroplanes brought new standards of luxury and reliability to air travel besides providing the backbone of Imperial Airways' routes during the nineteen-thirties.

The first Coast-to-Coast all-air commercial passenger service in America was opened simultaneously by Transcontinental and Western Air Inc. between New York and Los Angeles, California, on 25th October 1930.

The first commercial air route between London and Central Africa was opened on 28th February 1931 by Imperial Airways. The route lay from Croydon to Alexandria (using Argosy aircraft from Croydon to Athens, and Calcutta flying boats from Athens to Alexandria via Crete), and from Cairo to Mwanza, on Lake Victoria (using Argosy aircraft). Passengers were only carried as far as Khartoum, mail being carried over the remainder of the route.

The first non-stop flight from Japan to the United States was made by Clyde Pangborn and Hugh Herndon between 3rd and 5th October 1931 flying from Tokyo, to Wenatchee, Washington, in a Bellanca aircraft.

The first solo flight from New York to London in a light aircraft was made by Sqdn. Ldr. H. J. L. Hinkler between 27th October and 7th December 1931 in a de Havilland Puss Moth, *CF-APK*. His flight was via Jamaica (representing the first British crossing of the Caribbean), Jamaica to Venezuela, Venezuela to Port Natal, and across the South Atlantic to Bathurst, thence to Hanworth, England, via Madrid, Spain. (Hinkler was killed on 7th January 1933 when his Puss Moth crashed in the Alps.)

The first regular commercial air route from London to Cape Town was inaugurated by Imperial Airways on 20th January 1932 by the extension of the England to Central Africa route. The total scheduled time was eleven days and the first service arrived at Cape Town on 2nd February. Imperial Airways also inaugurated the first air mail service from Cape Town to London on 27th January 1932, but the first mail flight encountered a series of misfortunes including accidents to two airliners (*City of Basra* and *City of Delhi*, both de Havilland D.H. 66 Hercules aircraft), from which the mail was salvaged on both occasions, to be delivered in London on 16th February. (It is worth recording that between 24th and 28th March 1932, J. A. Mollison flew solo from Lympne, Kent, to Cape Town, South Africa, in 4 days, 17 hours 50 minutes—compared with the eleven days for the scheduled Imperial Airways London-to-Cape route.)

The first flight by an aeroplane over the South Pole was made by Cdr. R. E. Byrd, U.S. Navy, during 28th-29th November 1929, flying a Ford monoplane.

The first solo flight from Great Britain to Australia by a woman was achieved by Miss Amy Johnson between 5th and 24th May 1930, flying a de Havilland D.H. 60G Gipsy Moth *Jason*, (*G-AAAH*) from Croydon to Darwin.

(Top) *The de Havilland D.H.125, the most successful British-built jet executive aircraft, which has achieved wide military and commercial sales.* (Bottom) *The Model 24B Learjet, one of the world's most exotic jet executive aircraft, which has a maximum speed of 545 m.p.h. (877 km./hr.) at 31,000 ft. (9,450 m.)*

The first solo crossing of the North Atlantic by a woman was made by the American pilot Miss Amelia Earhart (Mrs. Putnam) during 20th-21st May 1932 when she flew a Lockheed Vega aircraft from Harbour Grace, Newfoundland, to Londonderry, Northern Ireland.

The first solo east-west crossing of the Atlantic was made by J. A. Mollison during 18th-19th August 1932 flying a special long-range de Havilland Puss Moth, *G-ABXY*, from Portmarnock, near Dublin, to Pennfield, New Brunswick. Mollison, flying *G-ABXY*, also became **the first man to fly from England to South America, the first man to fly solo across the South Atlantic from east to west, and the first man to cross both the North and South Atlantic,** when he landed at Natal, Brazil, on 9th February 1933 having flown from Lympne, England, in 3 days 10 hours 8 minutes.

The first non-stop flight from England to South Africa was made by the Fairey Long-range Monoplane, *K1991*, between 6th and 8th February 1933, flown by Sqdn. Ldr. O. R. Gayford and Flt. Lt. G. E. Nicholetts. The flight of 5,431 miles (8,595 km.) from Cranwell, Lincolnshire, to Walvis Bay, South-West Africa, was completed in 57 hours 25 minutes and established a world long distance record.

The first ten million miles of flying was completed by Imperial Airways on 18th February 1933. Less than a month later the accident insurance premium rate for air travel was reduced from twelve shillings to one shilling per one thousand pounds for passengers travelling with Imperial Airways, bringing air insurance into line with that for surface travel for the first time.

The first solo flight round the world was achieved by Wiley Post between 15th and 22nd July 1933 when he flew a Lockheed monoplane from New York for a distance of 15,596 miles (25,099 km.) in 7 days 18 hours 49 minutes. His route was via Berlin, Moscow, Irkutsk and Alaska.

Internal air mail services in the United States were first flown by pilots of the U.S. Army Air Corps on 19th February 1934, but after nine fatalities the service was suspended on 10th March, only to be started again on the 19th March, finally ending on 1st June.

The first regular internal air mail in Great Britain was carried by Highland Airways on 29th May 1934. The de Havilland Dragon *G-ACCE*, flown by E. E. Fresson, carried 2,000 letters from Inverness to Kirkwall, and the service operated thereafter on every weekday.

The first non-stop aeroplane flight from the Canadian mainland to Britain was made during 8th-9th August 1934 by the de Havilland D.H.84 Dragon *Trail of the Caribou* flown by J. R. Ayling and Capt. L. Reid. The crew took off from Georgian Bay, Ontario, for an attempt at a long-distance record flight to Baghdad, but owing to excessive fuel consumption were forced to land at Heston, London, after a flight of 30 hours 50 minutes.

The first flight by an aeroplane from Australia to the United States was made by a Lockheed aircraft flown by Sir Charles Kingsford Smith accompanied by Capt. Taylor from Brisbane to Oakland, California, *via* Fiji and Hawaii, between 22nd October and 4th November 1934.

The first regular weekly air mail service between Britain and Australia commenced on 8th December 1934 from London to Brisbane *via* Karachi and Singapore. The airlines participating were Imperial Airways, Indian Trans-Continental Airways and Qantas Empire Airways. Mail which left London on this day reached Brisbane on 21st December.

The first solo flight from Honolulu, Hawaii, to the American mainland by a woman was made by Miss Amelia Earhart on 11th-12th January 1935 in a Lockheed Vega, flying from Honolulu to Oakland, California. Her time was 18 hours 16 minutes.

The first through passenger air service between London and Brisbane, Australia, was inaugurated on 13th April 1935 by Imperial Airways and Qantas Empire Airways. The single fare for the 12,754-mile (20,525 km.) route was £195. Owing to heavy stage bookings no through passengers were however carried on the inaugural flight. The journey took twelve and a half days.

The first airline flight from the American mainland to Hawaii was made by a flying boat of Pan American World Airways from Alameda, California, to Honolulu on 16th-17th April 1935. The flight, which was part of a Company proving flight, occupied 18 hours 37 minutes.

The first non-stop flight from Mexico City to Newark, New Jersey, was made by the American woman pilot, Miss Amelia Earhart, on 19th-20th April 1935; her elapsed time was 14 hours 19 minutes.

The first scheduled air mail flight across the Pacific was flown by Capt. Edwin C. Musick in a Pan American Airways Martin M-130 flying boat on 22nd November 1935 from San Francisco, California, to Honolulu, and afterwards to Midway, Wake Island, Guam and Manila.

The first Douglas DC-3 made its first flight at 3 p.m. on 17th December 1935 flown by Carl A. Cover at Clover Field (near Santa Monica), California. The **first customer** for the famous aircraft was American Airlines, its first aircraft entering service on 7th June 1936, flying non-stop from New York to Chicago, Illinois. The first European operator was K.L.M. (1936) followed by the Swedish A.B.A. (1937).

The first Douglas DC-2 to be introduced into Australia for commercial operation was the aircraft *VH-USY Bungana* owned by Holyman's Airways and flown between Melbourne and Hobart, Tasmania, in June 1936. The **first Douglas DC-3** was *VH-UZK Kurana* operated by Australian National Airways in December 1937.

The first direct, solo east-to-west crossing of the North Atlantic was made by Mrs. Beryl Markham during 4th-5th September 1936, flying from Abingdon, England, to Baleine, Nova Scotia, where she crashed after a flight of 24 hours 40 minutes. She was not hurt.

The first Short C-Type Empire flying boat *Canopus* (*G-ADHL*) made her first flight on 4th July 1936 with John Lankester Parker, Shorts' Chief Test Pilot, at the controls. Her first flight with Imperial Airways was made on 17th September 1936. The Empire boats represented the last word in luxury travel before the Second World War and, as their name implied, were flown on the Empire routes to Africa and the Far East.

The first commercial survey flights over the North Atlantic were carried out simultaneously by Imperial Airways and Pan American Airways during 5th-6th July 1937. The former flew the long-range C-Class flying boat *Caledonia G-ADHM* westwards from Foynes to Botwood, while the latter flew the Sikorsky S-42 *Clipper III* eastwards.

(Top) *The Boeing 747, currently the largest commercial aircraft in the world: see "Two Outstanding Aircraft", Appendices.* (Bottom) *The Lockheed C-5A Galaxy, long-range military heavy transport, and currently the largest aircraft in the world with a wing span of 222 ft. 8½ in. (67·88 m.). Current production plans cover the manufacture of 115 aircraft of this type.*

The first jet-powered airliner in the world to receive an airworthiness certificate was the Vickers Viscount 630 four-turboprop aircraft which was awarded Certificate No. A907 on July 1950. The following day British European Airways commenced the **first jet airliner service in the world** with *G-AHRF* flown by Capt. Richard Rymer from London to Le Bourget, Paris, in 57 minutes. The Viscount was powered by four Rolls-Royce Dart turboprop engines.

The world's first pure-jet airliner to enter airline service was the de Havilland D.H. 106 Comet 1 powered by four de Havilland Ghost 50 turbojet engines. **The world's first regular passenger service to be flown by pure-jet aircraft** was inaugurated by British Overseas Airways Corporation on 2nd May 1952 using the de Havilland Comet 1 *G-ALYP* between London and Johannesburg, South Africa. Its route was *via* Rome, Beirut, Khartoum, Entebbe and Livingstone, and the aircraft was captained in turn by Capts. A. M. Majendie, J. T. A. Marsden and R. C. Alabaster. It carried 36 passengers and the total elapsed time for the 6,724 miles (10,810 km.) was 23 hours 34 minutes.

The world's first fatal accident involving a pure-jet airliner occurred on 3rd March 1953 when *Empress of Hawaii*, a de Havilland Comet 1, *CF-CUN*, of Canadian Pacific Air Lines crashed on take-off at Karachi, Pakistan, killing all eleven occupants. The accident was stated to have been caused by the pilot lifting the nose too high during take-off, thereby preventing the aircraft from accelerating sufficiently quickly to achieve flying speed.

The first trans-Atlantic passenger service to be flown by jet powered airliners was inaugurated by B.O.A.C. on 19th December 1957 flying Bristol Britannia 312 propjet aircraft. The first flight from London to New York was by *G-AOVC* captained by Capt. A. Meagher. The **first trans-Atlantic service by pure-jet airliners** was started by B.O.A.C. with de Havilland Comet 4s between London and New York (in both directions simultaneously) on 4th October 1958.

The first round-the-world passenger service by jet airliners was established by Pan American World Airways during October 1959. The first aircraft flown on this service was a Boeing 707-321, *Jet Clipper Windward*.

CRIME IN THE SKY

Disasters in the Air
The two worst known disasters resulting from criminal violence in aircraft while in flight both involved the **loss of forty-four lives.**

On 1st November 1955 a Douglas DC-6B, operated by United Air Lines, exploded in the air and crashed near Longmont, Colorado, U.S.A., killing all forty-four occupants. It was later established that John G. Graham had introduced a bomb aboard in an insurance plot to murder his mother who was a passenger.

On 7th May 1964 a Fairchild F-27, operated by Pacific Airlines, crashed near Doublin, California, U.S.A., and all forty-four occupants were killed. A tape recording indicated that the pilot was shot by an intruder in the airliner's cockpit.

The first known use of aircraft for violence in civil crime was the dropping of three small bombs on 26th November 1926 by an aeroplane on a farmhouse in Williamson County, Illinois; the raid was carried out by a member of the Shelton gang against members of the rival Birger gang in a Prohibition feud involving illicit supply of beer and rum. The bombs however failed to detonate.

The first supersonic airliner in the world to fly was the Tupolev Tu-144 (above), which made its maiden flight on 31st December 1968. It flew at supersonic speed for the first time on 5th June 1969.
Of extraordinarily similar configuration and dimensions is the BAC/Sud-Aviation Concorde, whose French prototype made its maiden flight on 2nd March 1969, followed by the first British aircraft on 9th April 1969. Sales options had been granted for 74 Concordes at the time of writing (April 1970).

Skyjacking

Described as "the most serious problem (commercial aviation) has ever been confronted with" by the President of *Lufthansa*, Herr Gerhard Holtje, and by President Nixon as "morally, politically and legally indefensible", the skyjacking of commercial airliners has been increasing rapidly over the past year or so, to the extent that no fewer than 77 instances were reported during the year of 1969; seen as a proportion of the 178 total skyjacking figure for the last forty years, the extent of the problem may be judged.

Although aircraft of the United States have featured in eighty skyjacking attempts since 1930 (of which fifty-eight were successful), the majority of attempts to divert aircraft have been made on those of other nations; these include, Argentina, Australia, Brazil, Bulgaria, Canada, Colombia, Cuba, Czecho-slovakia, Ecuador, Egypt, Ethiopia, France, Great Britain, Greece, Haiti, Holland, Honduras, Israel, Mexico, Nigeria, Nicaragua, Peru, Poland, Philippines, Rumania, Russia, Turkey, Venezuela and Yugo-slavia.

The longest distance flown by a skyjacked airliner was the 6,900 miles (11,095 km.) travelled by the Trans-World Airlines Boeing 707 skyjacked by U.S. Marine Lance Corporal Raphael Minichiello of Seattle, Washington at gunpoint on 31st October 1969. The 19-year-old Marine ordered the airliner's pilot, Donald Cook, at 4.42 a.m. to fly to Denver, Colorado, and thence to Kennedy Airport, New York. Here FBI agents attempted to board the aircraft but were persuaded from doing so when Minichiello threatened spectators with his carbine. After permitting two overseas pilots to board, the aircraft was flown to Leonardo da Vinci Airport, Rome, but the Marine was captured shortly afterwards. He was indicted by a New York court for piracy and kidnapping, but continued to be held in Rome's Queen of Heaven gaol.

WORLD POINT-TO-POINT SPEED RECORDS

From	To	Date	Pilot	Nationality	Aircraft	Time	Speed (m.p.h./km./hr.)
Amsterdam	Brussels	25th June 1961	Robert W. Fero, Jr.	U.S.A.	North American Sabreliner	9 min. 45 sec.	529·27/850·50
Anchorage	Chicago	16th October 1963	Lt. Col. G. A. Andrews	U.S.A.	B-58A Hustler	5 hr. 36 min. 34·8 sec.	524·90/843·49
Anchorage	London	16th October 1963	Maj. S. J. Kubesch	U.S.A.	B-58A Hustler	5 hr. 24 min. 54 sec.	828·16/1,330·80
Atlanta	Paris	31st May 1963	Vern F. Peterson	U.S.A.	Lockheed Hercules	12 hr. 43 min. 48·5 sec.	344·23/553·15
Baltimore	Moscow	19th May 1963	Col. J. B. Swindal	U.S.A.	Boeing VC-137 (707)	8 hr. 33 min. 45·4 sec.	564·20/906·64
Baltimore	Oslo	19th May 1963	Col. J. B. Swindal	U.S.A.	Boeing VC-137 (707)	6 hr. 29 min. 47·2 sec.	592·00/951·31
Baltimore	Stockholm	19th May 1963	Col. J. B. Swindal	U.S.A.	Boeing VC-137 (707)	6 hr. 58 min. 27·1 sec.	587·64/944·30
Belfast	Gander	31st August 1951	Roland Beamont	G.B.	English Electric Canberra	4 hr. 18 min. 24·4 sec.	418·82/774·255
Berlin	Hanoi	28th–30th Nov. 1938	A. Henke	Germany	Fw 200 Kondor	34 hr. 17 min. 27 sec.	151·23/243·011
Berlin	New York	10th–11th Aug. 1938	A. Henke	Germany	Fw 200 Kondor	24 hr. 56 min. 12 sec.	159·00/255·499
Berlin	Tokyo	28th–30th Nov. 1938	A. Henke	Germany	Fw 200 Kondor	46 hr. 18 min. 19 sec.	119·67/192·308
Bermuda	London	6th May 1962	M. Gudmundsson	G.B.	Boeing 707-465	6 hr. 2 min. 16 sec.	572·99/920·763
Bierut	Karachi	2nd January 1962	A. Baig	Pakistan	Boeing 720B	3 hr. 8 min. 27·6 sec.	634·94/1,020·311
Boston	Bonn	22nd April 1962	Miss Jacqueline Cochrane	U.S.A.	Lockheed Jetstar	10 hr. 15 min. 56 sec.	350·08/562·56
Boston	London	22nd April 1962	Miss Jacqueline Cochrane	U.S.A.	Lockheed-Jetstar	9 hr. 25 min. 54·3 sec.	347·55/558·50
Boston	Moscow	19th May 1963	Col. J. B. Swindal	U.S.A.	Boeing VC-137 (707)	7 hr. 58 min. 15·7 sec.	563·44/905·42
Boston	Oslo	19th May 1963	Col. J. B. Swindal	U.S.A.	Boeing VC-137 (707)	5 hr. 54 min. 14·7 sec.	592·82/952·63
Boston	Paris	22nd April 1962	Miss Jacqueline Cochrane	U.S.A.	Lockheed Jetstar	9 hr. 47 min. 31 sec.	351·52/564·88
Boston	Shannon	22nd April 1962	Miss Jacqueline Cochrane	U.S.A.	Lockheed Jetstar	8 hr. 13 min. 38 sec.	351·88/565·45
Boston	Stockholm	19th May 1963	Col. J. B. Swindal	U.S.A.	Boeing VC-137 (707)	6 hr. 22 min. 54·1 sec.	587·99/944·87
Brussels	Amsterdam	25th June 1961	Robert W. Fero, Jr.	U.S.A.	North American Sabreliner	9 min. 33 sec.	537·92/864·41
Brussels	Paris	6th June 1961	B. A. Neefs	Belgium	Lockheed F104G Starfighter	10 min. 3·9 sec.	981·02/1,576·435
Buenos Aires	Washington	13th Nov. 1957	Gen. Curtiss E. Le May	U.S.A.	Boeing KC-135	11 hr. 5 min. 0·8 sec.	472·16/758·728
Buenos Aires	Christchurch	16th–17th Nov. 1965	J. L. Martin et al.	U.S.A.	Boeing 707-320	14 hr. 18 min. 37·7 sec.	431·16/692·85
Christchurch	Honolulu	17th November 1965	J. L. Martin et al.	U.S.A.	Boeing 707-320	9 hr. 1 min. 32·9 sec.	551·91/886·88
Copenhagen	London	4th April 1950	Janusz Zurakowski	G.B.	Gloster Meteor	1 hr. 11 min. 17 sec.	501·42/805·752
Fort Worth	Madrid	11th January 1962	Maj. Clyde P. Evely	U.S.A.	Boeing B-52H	8 hr. 35 min. 24·4 sec.	578·30/929·30
Fort Worth	Saint Louis	21st June 1963	M. E. Payne	U.S.A.	Republic F-47 Thunderbolt	2 hr. 17 min. 37·9 sec.	248·95/400·05
Fort Worth	Washington	11th January 1962	Maj. Clyde P. Evely	U.S.A.	Boeing B-52H	2 hr. 0 min. 22·66 sec.	605·34/972·75
Gander	Belfast	26th August 1952	Roland Beamont	G.B.	English Electric Canberra	3 hr. 25 min. 18·13 sec.	606·43/974·503
Gander	Bonn	22nd April 1962	Miss Jacqueline Cochrane	U.S.A.	Lockheed Jetstar	5 hr. 54 min. 17·6 sec.	453·20/728·26
Gander	London	22nd April 1962	Miss Jacqueline Cochrane	U.S.A.	Lockheed Jetstar	5 hr. 3 min. 50·5 sec.	466·17/749·11
Gander	Paris	22nd April 1962	Miss Jacqueline Cochrane	U.S.A.	Lockheed Jetstar	5 hr. 26 min. 6·9 sec.	464·37/746·22
Gander	Shannon	22nd April 1962	Miss Jacqueline Cochrane	U.S.A.	Lockheed Jetstar	3 hr. 52 min. 4 sec.	511·96/822·69
Gibraltar	London	19th September 1949	A. C. P. Carver	G.B.	de Havilland Hornet	2 hr. 30 min. 31 sec.	436·54/701·492
Honolulu	London	15th November 1965	J. L. Martin et al.	U.S.A.	Boeing 707-320	13 hr. 54 min. 3·3 sec.	521·27/837·58
Havana	Washington	27th November 1947	Woodrow W. Edmondson	U.S.A.	North American P-51	3 hr. 15 min. 13 sec.	350·85/563·800
Cairo	London	11th May 1950	John Cunningham	G.B.	de Havilland Comet I	5 hr. 39 min. 21·7 sec.	386·46/621·026
Cape of Good Hope	London	19th December 1953	A. H. Humphrey	G.B.	English Electric Canberra	13 hr. 16 min. 25·2 sec.	453·44/728·648
Lisbon	Buenos Aires	16th November 1965	J. L. Martin et al.	U.S.A.	Boeing 707-320	11 hr. 54 min. 8·4 sec.	502·44/807·39
Lisbon	Frankfurt	27th October 1963	G. P. Eremea	U.S.A.	North American Sabreliner	2 hr. 24 min. 46·1 sec.	488·57/785·11
London	Aden	30th March 1962	John R. Ward	G.B.	Avro Vulcan	6 hr. 13 min. 59·9 sec.	590·25/948·495
London	Amsterdam	29th July 1954	R. S. Overbury	G.B.	Hawker Sea Hawk		572·37/919·76
London	Baghdad	31st July 1955	John Finch	G.B.	Vickers Valiant	4 hr. 51 min. 28·8 sec.	524·26/842·463
London	Basra	8th October 1953	L. E. Burton	G.B.	English Electric Canberra	5 hr. 11 min. 5·6 sec.	545·14/876·011
London	Bermuda	5th May 1962	G. N. Henderson	G.B.	Boeing 707-465	6 hr. 53 min. 1 sec.	499·69/802·974
London	Bierut	2nd January 1962	A. Baig	Pakistan	Boeing 720B	3 hr. 35 min. 20·3 sec.	600·22/964·517
London	Bonn	22nd April 1962	Miss Jacqueline Cochrane	U.S.A.	Lockheed Jetstar	49 min. 44·4 sec.	386·13/620·49
London	Brussels	10th July 1952	David Morgan	G.B.	Supermarine Swift	18 min. 3·3 sec.	666·89/1,071·648
London	Buenos Aires	15th–16th Nov. 1965	J. L. Martin et al.	U.S.A.	Boeing 707-320	16 hr. 40 min. 2·2 sec.	415·95/668·40
London	Christchurch	8th–9th Oct. 1953	L. E. Burton	G.B.	English Electric Canberra	23 hr. 50 min. 42 sec.	495·28/795·887

From	To	Date	Pilot	Nationality	Aircraft	Time	Speed (m.p.h./km./hr.)
London	Colombo	8th–9th Oct. 1953	L. M. Hodges	G.B.	English Electric Canberra	10 hr. 23 min. 21·5 sec.	520·25 / 836·004
London	Copenhagen	4th April 1950	Janusz Zurakowski	G.B.	Gloster Meteor	1 hr. 5 min. 5 sec.	524·24 / 871·344
London	Darwin	27th–28th Jan. 1953	L. M. Whittingham	G.B.	English Electric Canberra	22 hr. 0 min. 21·8 sec.	391·77 / 629·553
London	Johannesburg	23rd–24th Oct. 1957	John Cunningham	G.B.	de Havilland Comet 4	12 hr. 59 min. 7·3 sec.	434·56 / 668·309
London	Karachi	2nd January 1962	A. Baig	Pakistan	Boeing 720B	6 hr. 43 min. 51 sec.	584·21 / 938·786
London	Khartoum	16th October 1957	John Cunningham	G.B.	de Havilland Comet 4	5 hr. 51 min. 14·8 sec.	524·20 / 842·354
London	Kuwait	2nd February 1964	A. W. Hebbron	G.B.	de Havilland Comet	6 hr. 0 min. 25 sec.	481·58 / 773·87
London	Valetta	25th April 1961	Harry Bennett	G.B.	Hawker Hunter	2 hr. 3 min. 8 sec.	634·27 / 1,019·24
London	Cairo	13th April 1965	John Cunningham	G.B.	de Havilland Trident	3 hr. 37 min. 44 sec.	603·00 / 968·993
London	Cape Town	17th December 1953	G. G. Petty	G.B.	English Electric Canberra	12 hr. 21 min. 3·8 sec.	487·31 / 783·078
London	Lisbon	15th–16th Nov. 1965	J. L. Martin et al.	U.S.A.	Boeing 707-320	2 hr. 21 min. 12·4 sec.	421·38 / 677·14
London	Melbourne	8th–10th Oct. 1953	W. Baillie	G.B.	Vickers Viscount	35 hr. 46 min. 47·6 sec.	294·05 / 472·517
London	Nairobi	28th Sept. 1952	H. P. Conolly	G.B.	English Electric Canberra	9 hr. 55 min. 16·7 sec.	427·90 / 687·611
London	New York	27th June 1958	Burl B. Davenport	U.S.A.	Boeing KC-135	5 hr. 53 min. 12·77 sec.	588·34 / 945·423
London	Paris	5th July 1953	M. J. Lithgow	G.B.	Supermarine Swift	19 min. 5·6 sec.	670·48 / 1,077·417
London	Reykjavik	31st July–1st Aug. 1964	Lord Trefgarne et al.	G.B.	de Havilland Dragonfly	32 hr. 36 min. 36 sec.	36·07 / 57·906
London	Rome	20th Oct. 1956	A. W. Bedford	G.B.	Hawker Hunter	1 hr. 34 min. 28·5 sec.	566·92 / 911·01
London	Sydney	15th–19th Mar. 1938	A. E. Clouston	G.B.	de Havilland 88 Comet	80 hr. 56 min.	130·50 / 209·712
London	Tripoli	18th February 1952	L. C. E. de Vigne	G.B.	English Electric Canberra	2 hr. 41 min. 49·5 sec.	538·92 / 866·021
London	Wellington	21st–24th Aug. 1946	N. H. d'Aeth	G.B.	Avro Lancaster Aries	59 hr. 50 min.	194·95 / 313·270
Los Angeles	New York	5th March 1962	Robert G. Sowers	U.S.A.	B-58A Hustler	2 hr. 0 min. 58·71 sec.	1,216·47 / 1,954·79
Los Angeles	Paris	28th–29th May 1953	Ch. Billet	France	Douglas DC-6	20 hr. 26 min.	276·72 / 444·681
Los Angeles	Stockholm	15th–16th Nov. 1956	Jackson J. Armstrong	U.S.A.	Douglas DC-7C	21 hr. 39 min. 11.88 sec.	255·23 / 410·143
Los Angeles	Tokyo	15th–16th Aug. 1966	A. G. Heimerdinger	U.S.A.	Douglas DC-8-61	11 hr. 30 min. 2·4 sec.	477·33 / 767·04
Madrid	New York	7th July 1961	Robert W. Fero, Jr.	U.S.A.	North American Sabreliner		372·43 / 598·48
Moscow	Baltimore	20th–21st May 1963	Col. J. B. Swindal	U.S.A.	Boeing VC-137 (707)	9 hr. 47 min. 53·2 sec.	493·04 / 792·28
Moscow	Boston	20th–21st May 1963	Col. J. B. Swindal	U.S.A.	Boeing VC-137 (707)	9 hr. 1 min. 7·8 sec.	497·97 / 800·21
Moscow	New York	20th–21st May 1963	Col. J. B. Swindal	U.S.A.	Boeing VC-137 (707)	9 hr. 24 min. 48 sec.	496·06 / 797·14
Moscow	Philadelphia	20th–21st May 1963	Col. J. B. Swindal	U.S.A.	Boeing VC-137 (707)	9 hr. 35 min. 54·9 sec.	494·87 / 795·32
Moscow	Washington	20th–21st May 1963	Col. J. B. Swindal	U.S.A.	Boeing VC-137 (707)	9 hr. 54 min. 48·5 sec.	490·79 / 788·67
New Orleans	Bonn	22nd April 1962	Miss Jacqueline Cochrane	U.S.A.	Lockheed Jetstar	13 hr. 10 min. 31 sec.	375·68 / 603·69
New Orleans	Boston	22nd April 1962	Miss Jacqueline Cochrane	U.S.A.	Lockheed Jetstar	2 hr. 54 min. 33·6 sec.	467·98 / 752·01
New Orleans	Gander	22nd April 1962	Miss Jacqueline Cochrane	U.S.A.	Lockheed Jetstar	4 hr. 42 min. 52·9 sec.	483·12 / 776·34
New Orleans	London	22nd April 1962	Miss Jacqueline Cochrane	U.S.A.	Lockheed Jetstar	12 hr. 20 min. 14·9 sec.	375·68 / 603·69
New Orleans	New York	22nd April 1962	Miss Jacqueline Cochrane	U.S.A.	Lockheed Jetstar	2 hr. 31 min. 8·5 sec.	465·81 / 748·53
New Orleans	Paris	22nd April 1962	Miss Jacqueline Cochrane	U.S.A.	Lockheed Jetstar	12 hr. 42 min. 3·9 sec.	378·20 / 607·75
New Orleans	Shannon	22nd April 1962	Miss Jacqueline Cochrane	U.S.A.	Lockheed Jetstar	11 hr. 8 min. 7 sec.	382·17 / 614·12
New Orleans	Washington	22nd April 1962	Miss Jacqueline Cochrane	U.S.A.	Lockheed Jetstar	2 hr. 5 min. 2·4 sec.	464·37 / 746·22
New York	Berlin	13th–14th April 1938	A. Henke	Germany	Fw 200 Kondor	19 hr. 55 min. 1 sec.	199·71 / 320·919
New York	Bonn	22nd April 1962	Miss Jacqueline Cochrane	U.S.A.	Lockheed Jetstar	10 hr. 39 min. 12·5 sec.	354·77 / 570·09
New York	London	11th May 1969	Lt. Cdr. Brian Davies	G.B.	McDonnell F-4K Phantom	4 hr. 36 min. 30·4 sec.	724·90 / 1,164·865
New York	Los Angeles	5th March 1962	Robert G. Sowers	U.S.A.	B-58A Hustler	2 hr. 15 min. 50·08 sec.	1,083·42 / 1,741·00
New York	Moscow	19th May 1963	Col. J. B. Swindal	U.S.A.	Boeing VC-137 (707)	8 hr. 15 min. 54·1 sec.	564·96 / 907·86
New York	Oslo	19th May 1963	Col. J. B. Swindal	U.S.A.	Boeing VC-137 (707)	6 hr. 11 min. 58·8 sec.	594·02 / 954·56
New York	Paris	26th May 1961	William R. Payne	U.S.A.	B-58A Hustler	3 hr. 19 min. 44·53 sec.	1,090·93 / 1,753·068
New York	Shannon	22nd April 1962	Miss Jacqueline Cochrane	U.S.A.	Lockheed Jetstar	8 hr. 36 min. 57·5 sec.	358·01 / 575·30
New York	Stockholm	19th May 1963	Col. J. B. Swindal	U.S.A.	Boeing VC-137 (707)	6 hr. 40 min. 36 sec.	589·19 / 946·79
Oslo	Baltimore	20th–21st May 1963	Col. J. B. Swindal	U.S.A.	Boeing VC-137 (707)	7 hr. 39 min. 20·9 sec.	502·64 / 807·71
Oslo	Boston	20th–21st May 1963	Col. J. B. Swindal	U.S.A.	Boeing VC-137 (707)	6 hr. 52 min. 34·9 sec.	509·05 / 818·01
Oslo	New York	20th–21st May 1963	Col. J. B. Swindal	U.S.A.	Boeing VC-137 (707)	7 hr. 16 min. 21 sec.	506·37 / 813·71
Oslo	Philadelphia	20th–21st May 1963	Col. J. B. Swindal	U.S.A.	Boeing VC-137 (707)	7 hr. 27 min. 19 sec.	504·93 / 811·40
Oslo	Washington	20th–21st May 1963	Col. J. B. Swindal	U.S.A.	Boeing VC-137 (707)	7 hr. 46 min. 18·7 sec.	499·55 / 802·75
Ottawa	London	27th–28th June 1955	I. G. Broom	G.B.	English Electric Canberra	6 hr. 42 min. 12 sec.	497·57 / 799·563
Paris	Bonn	22nd April 1962	Miss Jacqueline Cochrane	U.S.A.	Lockheed Jetstar	26 min. 5·5 sec.	576·86 / 926·98
Paris	Frankfurt	27th Oct. 1963	G. P. Eremea	U.S.A.	North American Sabreliner	35 min. 51·4 sec.	500·71 / 804·61
Paris	Hanoi	15th–18th Nov. 1936	André Japy	France	Caudron Simoun	50 hr. 59 min. 49 sec.	112·14 / 180·208

From	To	Date	Pilot	Nationality	Aircraft	Time	Speed (m.p.h./k.m./hr.)
Paris	London	9th July 1953	M. J. Lithgow	G.B.	Supermarine Swift	19 min. 14·3 sec.	665·42/1,069·291
Paris	Nice	18th June 1955	Gérard Muselli	France	Mystère IV-N	41 min. 55·8 sec.	611·37/982·433
Paris	Saigon	19th–23rd Dec. 1937	Mlle. Maryse Hilsz	France	Caudron Simoun	92 hr. 36 min.	68·03/109·316
Paris	Tananarive	21st December 1935	Génin and Robert	France	Caudron Simoun	57 hr. 35 min. 21 sec.	94·53/151·908
Philadelphia	Moscow	19th May 1963	Col. J. B. Swindal	U.S.A.	Boeing VC-137 (707)	8 hr. 24 min. 36·2 sec.	564·81/907·62
Philadelphia	Oslo	19th May 1963	Col. J. B. Swindal	U.S.A.	Boeing VC-137 (707)	6 hr. 20 min. 31 sec.	593·55/953·80
Philadelphia	Stockholm	19th May 1963	Col. J. B. Swindal	U.S.A.	Boeing VC-137 (707)	6 hr. 49 min. 11·6 sec.	588·76/946·10
North Pole	Portland, Mn.	15th–17th Nov. 1965	J. L. Martin et al.	U.S.A.	Boeing 707-320	35 hr. 46 min. 20 sec.	348·56/560·11
Portland, Or.	South Pole	30th July 1967	James F. Nields	G.B.	Beech Baron	11 hr. 40 min. 10 sec.	217·25/349·11
Reykjavik	New York	2nd–5th August 1964	Lord Trefgarne et al.	G.B.	de Havilland Dragonfly	77 hr. 13 min. 30 sec.	33·87/54·426
Rome	Addis Ababa	6th–7th March 1939	M. Lualdi	Italy	Fiat BR.20L	11 hr. 25 min.	243·30/390·971
Rome	London	25th October 1956	A. W. Bedford	G.B.	Hawker Hunter	1 hr. 40 min. 7 sec.	534·74/859·29
Seattle	Rio de Janeiro	24th–25th Jan. 1938	Attileo Biseo	Italy	Savoia Marchetti SM.79	41 hr. 32 min.	138·15/221·996
Seattle	Fort Worth	11th January 1962	Maj. Clyde P. Evely	U.S.A.	Boeing B-52H	3 hr. 0 min. 24·62 sec.	553·32/889·16
Shannon	Madrid	11th January 1962	Maj. Clyde P. Evely	U.S.A.	Lockheed Jetstar	11 hr. 34 min. 9·22 sec.	457·37/735·97
Shannon	Bonn	22nd April 1962	Miss Jacqueline Cochrane	U.S.A.	Lockheed Jetstar	1 hr. 38 min. 15·8 sec.	426·87/685·96
Shannon	London	22nd April 1962	Miss Jacqueline Cochrane	U.S.A.	Lockheed Jetstar	47 min. 36·5 sec.	477·35/767·07
Singapore	Paris	7th–8th August 1955	John Finch	G.B.	Vickers Valiant	1 hr. 10 min. 10·8 sec.	476·63/765·91
Stockholm	Darwin	20th–21st May 1963	Col. J. B. Swindal	U.S.A.	Boeing VC-137 (707)	4 hr. 0 min. 50·1 sec.	519·13/834·218
Stockholm	Baltimore	20th–21st May 1963	Col. J. B. Swindal	U.S.A.	Boeing VC-137 (707)	8 hr. 11 min. 33·3 sec.	500·24/803·86
Stockholm	Boston	20th–21st May 1963	Col. J. B. Swindal	U.S.A.	Boeing VC-137 (707)	7 hr. 24 min. 45·6 sec.	506·19/813·42
Stockholm	New York	20th–21st May 1963	Col. J. B. Swindal	U.S.A.	Boeing VC-137 (707)	7 hr. 48 min. 31·1 sec.	503·77/809·53
Sydney	Philadelphia	21st–26th March 1938	A. E. Clouston	G.B.	de Havilland 88 Comet	7 hr. 59 min. 31·8 sec.	502·41/807·34
Tokyo	Washington	16th October 1963	Maj. S. J. Kubesch	U.S.A.	B-58A Hustler	8 hr. 18 min. 30·8 sec.	497·40/799·29
Tokyo	London	16th October 1963	G. A. Andrews	U.S.A.	B-58A Hustler	130 hr. 3 min.	81·38/130·777
Tokyo	Anchorage	10th–11th Jan. 1962	Maj. S. J. Kubesch	U.S.A.	Boeing B-52H	3 hr. 9 min. 41·8 sec.	1,095·08/1,759·73
Tokyo	Chicago	16th October 1963	Maj. Clyde P. Evely	U.S.A.	B-58A-Hustler	8 hr. 38 min. 42 sec.	730·34/1,173·61
Tokyo	Fort Worth	10th–11th Jan. 1962	Maj. Clyde P. Evely	U.S.A.	Boeing B-52H	11 hr. 41 min. 24·69 sec.	550·90/885·26
Tokyo	London	7th–8th April 1958	William E. Eubank	U.S.A.	Boeing B-52H	8 hr. 35 min. 204 sec.	693·75/1,114·81
Washington	Madrid	18th August 1966	A. G. Heimerdinger	U.S.A.	Boeing C-135	20 hr. 22 min. 12 sec.	329·27/529·12
Washington	Seattle	22nd April 1962	Miss Jacqueline Cochrane	U.S.A.	Douglas DC-8-61	8 hr. 43 min. 40·83 sec.	550·18/884·11
Washington	Washington	22nd April 1962	Miss Jacqueline Cochrane	U.S.A.	Lockheed Jetstar	13 hr. 45 min. 45·5 sec.	493·00/792·219
Washington	Winnipeg	22nd April 1962	Miss Jacqueline Cochrane	U.S.A.	Lockheed Jetstar	10 hr. 57 min. 23·9 sec.	510·88/820·95
Washington	Bonn	22nd February 1958	John W. Hackett	G.B.	English Electric Canberra	11 hr. 5 min. 12·1 sec.	359·45/577·62
Washington	Boston	22nd April 1962	Miss Jacqueline Cochrane	U.S.A.	Lockheed Jetstar	49 min. 29·7 sec.	477·35/767·07
Washington	Caracas	25th November 1947	Woodrow W. Edmondson	U.S.A.	North American P-51	4 hr. 10 min. 59·75 sec.	492·67/791·697
Washington	Gander	22nd April 1962	Miss Jacqueline Cochrane	U.S.A.	Lockheed Jetstar	2 hr. 37 min. 48·4 sec.	498·26/800·68
Washington	Havana	22nd April 1962	Miss Jacqueline Cochrane	U.S.A.	Lockheed Jetstar	3 hr. 37 min. 28·6 sec.	314·94/506·092
Washington	London	22nd April 1962	Miss Jacqueline Cochrane	U.S.A.	Lockheed Jetstar	10 hr. 15 min. 5 sec.	358·01/575·30
Washington	New York	22nd April 1962	Miss Jacqueline Cochrane	U.S.A.	Lockheed Jetstar	26 min. 9·6 sec.	471·58/757·80
Washington	Moscow	19th May 1963	Col. J. B. Swindal	U.S.A.	Boeing VC-137 (707)	8 hr. 39 min. 2·2 sec.	562·43/903·80
Washington	Oslo	19th May 1963	Col. J. B. Swindal	U.S.A.	Boeing VC-137 (707)	6 hr. 34 min. 49·9 sec.	590·02/948·13
Washington	Stockholm	19th May 1963	Col. J. B. Swindal	U.S.A.	Boeing VC-137 (707)	7 hr. 3 min. 33·4 sec.	585·44/940·77
Washington	Paris	26th May 1961	William R. Payne	U.S.A.	B-58A Hustler	3 hr. 39 min. 19·08 sec.	1,050·25/1,687·69
Washington	Shannon	22nd April 1962	Miss Jacqueline Cochrane	U.S.A.	Lockheed Jetstar	9 hr. 2 min. 53·6 sec.	363·42/583·99
Wellington	London	20th–26th March 1938	A. E. Clouston	G.B.	de Havilland 88 Comet	140 hr. 12 min.	83·58/134·306

CHAPTER 5

LIGHTER-THAN-AIR

In all mankind's modern preoccupation with wing-borne and rocket flight, one perhaps tends to forget that "exploration" of the air had commenced more than one hundred years before the Wright brothers successfully achieved manned, powered flight in their aeroplane; that the advance of science towards the end of the eighteenth century had enabled men (and women) to be carried aloft and float fairly peacefully across country—albeit at the mercy of the elements. For some years after the advent of the Montgolfier hot-air balloons in Paris, opinions were divided on the relative merits of heated air and of hydrogen as the best lifting agent, but inevitably the inherent dangers of carrying a bonfire suspended under the envelope decided early pioneers to resort to the more expensive process of chemical reaction for the generation of hydrogen. It was not until well into the twentieth century that the inert helium gas gained preference over hydrogen (whose use had caused countless aerial tragedies down the years), but was then too late to preserve lighter-than-air travel in the age of the passenger aeroplane.

Nevertheless ballooning during the nineteenth century was undertaken on a far greater scale than is perhaps realised today. Not only were the aeronauts the daring sportsmen of their age, but they were frequently called upon to demonstrate the practical uses to which their craft could be put. Balloons were used in wartime—even on the battlefield—and for the carriage of mail and military despatches; even the English Channel was crossed by air 124 years before Louis Blériot made his perilous flight.

In describing the achievements of those early pioneers it is necessary to remember that the almost total lack of scientific education among the great majority of "civilised" populations allowed an almost mediaeval fear of the sky to persist, and a man who allowed himself to be carried aloft (as if by magic) would certainly face unknown terrors. Moreover the unheralded arrival of a balloon from the sky might engender widespread hysteria among the local populace. One can learn of similar attitudes of mind towards the aeroplane among primitive tribes in the modern age.

It was the helplessness of those early balloonists, drifting at the whim of the wind, that determined the more constructive and adventurous to seek propulsion and directional control; their success led to the airship or "dirigible", which was at one time regarded as the most destructive harbinger of war as well as the ultimate in safety and comfort in air travel.

Today the balloon and the airship are the playthings of a diminutive band of diehards, swept aside as the chaff of jet and rocket blast.

The first identification of hydrogen was made by the English scientist Henry Cavendish in 1766 who referred to it as "inflammable air" or Phlogiston. It was first named hydrogen by the French chemist Lavoisier in 1790.

The first identification of oxygen was made by Dr. Joseph Priestly of Birmingham, England, in 1774, reference being made to "dephlogisticated air". It was later named oxygen by Lavoisier.

The first balloon to leave the ground capable of sustaining a weight equivalent to that of a man was a hot-air balloon made by the brothers Joseph and Etienne Montgolfier (1740–1810 and 1745–1799 respectively). This balloon, calculated as being able to lift 450 lb. (205 kg.), was released on 25th April 1783, probably at Annonay, France, rose to about 1,000 ft. (300 m.) and landed about 1,000 yards from the point of lift-off. The balloon had a diameter of about 35 ft. (12 m.) and achieved its lift using hot air provided by combustion of solid waste (probably paper, straw and wood) below the neck of the envelope.

The first ascent of a hydrogen-filled balloon (**unmanned**) was made on 25th August 1783 in Paris when Jacques Alexandre César Charles (1746–1823) launched a 12-ft. (3·5 m.) balloon. Capable of lifting about 20 lb. (9 kg.), the balloon was filled with hydrogen generated by the action of 498 lb. (225 kg.) of sulphuric acid upon 1,000 lb. (454 kg.) of iron scrap. The balloon was tethered and on the following day was permitted to rise to 100 ft. (30 m.). **The first free ascent of the balloon** (christened the *Globe*) was made from the Champ de Mars, Paris, on 27th August 1783, when it rose to about 3,000 ft. (1,000 m.), drifted for 45 minutes and came to earth at Gonesse, 15 miles (25 km.) from Paris, where it was promptly attacked by a frenzied mob of panic-stricken peasants.

Jacques Charles

The first living occupants of a balloon to ascend were a sheep, a duck and a cock which rode aloft under a 41 ft. (13 m.) diameter hot-air Montgolfier balloon at the Court of Versailles on 19th September 1783 before King Louis XVI, Marie Antoinette and their Court. The balloon achieved an altitude of 1,700 ft. (550 m.) before descending in the forest of Vaucresson 8 minutes later, having travelled about two miles. The occupants were scarcely affected by their flight nor by their landing.

The first man carried aloft in a balloon was François Pilâtre de Rozier (30.3.1757–15.6.1785) who on 15th October 1783 ascended in a tethered 49-ft. (15 m.) diameter Montgolfier hot-air balloon to 84 ft. (27 m.)—the limit of the restraining rope. The hot air was provided by a straw-fed fire below the fabric envelope.

François Pilâtre de Rozier

The first men carried aloft in free flight by a balloon were de Rozier (see above) and the Marquis d'Arlandes who rose in the 49-ft. (15 m.) diameter Montgolfier balloon at 1.54 p.m. on 21st November 1783 from the gardens of the Chateau La Muette in the Bois de Boulogne. These first aeronauts were airborne for twenty-five minutes and landed on the Butte-aux-Cailles, about 5½ miles (8·5 km.) from their point of departure, having drifted to and fro across Paris. Their maximum altitude is unlikely to have been above 1,500 feet (about 500 m.).

The first men to be carried aloft in free flight by a hydrogen-filled balloon were Jacques Charles and Ainé Robert who ascended from the gardens of the Tuileries, Paris, at 1.45 p.m. on 1st December 1783, in a balloon 27 ft. 6 in. (8·6 m.) in diameter before a crowd estimated at 400,000. The craft landed twenty-seven miles distant, near the town of Nesles.

The first women to ascend in a balloon (**tethered**) were the Marchioness de Montalembert, the Countess de Montalembert, the Countess de Podenas and Mademoiselle de Lagarde who rose aloft in a Montgolfier hot-air balloon on 20th May 1784 from the Faubourg St. Antoine, Paris.

(Top left) *The stone erected near North Mimms, Hertfordshire, marking the spot at which Vincenzo Lunardi first descended in his balloon on 15th September 1784.* (Top right) *The stone at Standon, north of Ware, Hertfordshire, which marks the point at which Lunardi finally alighted.* (Bottom left) *The memorial stone at Godstow, Oxford, commemorating the deaths of Lts. C. A. Bettington and E. Hotchkiss on 10th September 1912.* (Bottom right) *The memorial obelisk at Cuffley, Hertfordshire, recording the destruction by Capt. William Leefe Robinson, V.C., of L. 21, the first German airship to be shot down on British soil, on 3rd September 1916.*

ERECTED BY READERS OF
"The Daily Express"
TO THE MEMORY OF
CAPTAIN WILLIAM LEEFE ROBINSON, V.C.
WORCS. REGT AND R.F.C.
WHO ON SEPTEMBER 3, 1916
ABOVE THIS SPOT BROUGHT DOWN
L 21, THE FIRST GERMAN AIRSHIP
DESTROYED ON BRITISH SOIL.

The first woman to be carried in free flight in a balloon was Madame Thible who ascended in a Montgolfière with a Monsieur Fleurant on 4th June 1784 from Lyons, France. The balloon, named *Le Gustav*, reached an altitude of 8,500 ft. (2,600 m.) and was watched by the King of Sweden.

The first balloon ascent in Italy was made on 25th February 1784 by a Montgolfière carrying Chevalier Paul Andreani and the brothers Augustin and Charles Gerli at Moncuco, near Milan, Italy.

The first British aeronaut is claimed to have been James Tytler, a Scotsman, who on 25th August 1784 made a short ascent in a Montgolfier-type balloon, probably from Heriot's Garden, Edinburgh. His maximum altitude is believed not to have exceeded 500 ft. (150 m.).

The first aerial voyage by a hydrogen balloon made in Great Britain was that of Vincenzo Lunardi, an employee of the Italian Embassy in London, who on 15th September 1784 ascended in a Charlière from the Honourable Artillery Company's training ground at Moorfields, London. His flight was northwards to the parish of North Mimms (today the site of the village of Welhamgreen), Hertfordshire. Here Lunardi landed his cat and jettisoned his ballast and in so doing ascended again and finally landed at Standon Green End near Ware, Hertfordshire. On the spot where he landed stands a rough stone monument on which a tablet proclaims:

Let Posterity know
And knowing be astonished!
That
On the 15th day of September, 1784
Vincent Lunardi
of
Lucca in Tuscany
The First Aerial Traveller in Britain
Mounting from the Artillery Ground
in London
And traversing the Regions of the Air
For two Hours and fifteen Minutes
in this Spot
Revisited the Earth.
On this rude Monument
For ages be recorded
That wonderous enterprize, successfully
achieved
By the powers of Chymistry
And the fortitude of man
That improvement in Science
Which
The Great Author of all Knowledge
Patronising by his Providence
The Inventions of Mankind
Hath generously permitted
To their benefit
And
His own Eternal Glory

Vincenzo Lunardi

The first woman to be carried aloft in a balloon in Britain was Mrs. Letitia Ann Sage who rose aloft in Lunardi's hydrogen balloon from St. George's Fields, London, on 29th June 1785. Lunardi, who had proclaimed that he would be accompanied by three passengers (Mrs. Sage, a Colonel Hastings and George Biggin), discovered that his balloon's lifting power was not equal to the task and, rather than draw attention to the lady's weight (by her own admission, she weighed more than 200 pounds), stepped down from the basket with Colonel Hastings. The balloon eventually came to earth near Harrow, Middlesex, where the two occupants were rescued from an irate farmer by the boys from that famous school.

The first aeronaut in the world to be killed while ballooning was François Pilâtre de Rozier who was killed when attempting to fly the English Channel from Boulogne on 15th June 1785. It is believed that when venting hydrogen from the envelope, escaping gas was ignited by a discharge of static and the balloon fell at Huitmile Warren, near Boulogne. Also killed was Jules Romain, Pilâtre's companion.

The first aerial crossing of the English Channel was achieved by the Frenchman, Jean-Pierre Blanchard, accompanied by the American, Dr. John Jeffries, who on 7th January 1785 rose from Dover at 1 p.m. and landed in the Forêt de Felmores, France, at approximately 3.30 p.m., having discarded almost all their clothes to lighten the craft *en route*. Their balloon was hydrogen-filled.

Dr. John Jeffries

The first free flight by a balloon in the United States of America was made on 9th January 1793 by the Frenchman, Jean-Pierre Blanchard, who ascended in a hydrogen balloon from Philadelphia and landed in Gloucester County, New Jersey, after a flight of 46 minutes.

The first military use of a man-carrying balloon was that by the French republican army at the Battle of Fleurus on 26th June 1794. Capitaine Coutelle was the aeronaut and observer.

The first long-distance voyage by air from England was made during 7th–8th November 1836 by the hydrogen balloon—*The Royal Vauxhall Balloon*—manned by Charles Green (English, aeronaut) accompanied by Robert Holland, M.P., and Monck Mason, who ascended from Vauxhall Gardens, London, and travelled 480 miles (770 km.) to land near Weilberg in the Duchy of Nassau. The balloon was subsequently named the *Great Balloon of Nassau*.

The first American Army Balloon Corps was formed on 1st October 1861 with five balloons and fifty men under the command of Thaddeus Sobieski Coulincourt Lowe, Chief Aeronaut of the Army of the Potomac. They were used for reconnaissance and artillery direction.

The first military use of a man-carrying balloon in America was that by the Federal Army during the crossing of the Rappahannock River on 11th December 1862 in the American Civil War. Balloons were also used by the Federal Army during the Battle of Chancellorsville (30th April–5th May 1863).

The first balloon ascent in Australia was made on 29th March 1858 by two men named Brown and Dean in a hydrogen balloon, the *Australasian*, from Cremorne Gardens, Melbourne. (In 1851 a Dr. William Bland, 27 years after he had been transported from India to Australia for killing a ship's purser in a duel, attempted to produce a powered balloon, but there is no evidence that this ever flew.)

The first military use of balloons in an international war outside Europe was by the Brazilian Marquis de Caxias during the Paraguayan War of 1864–1870. (This atrocious conflict, which committed the combined forces of Brazil, Argentina and Uruguay against landlocked Paraguay, brought total disaster to the latter nation whose dictator, Francisco Solano López, ordered mass killings among his own people in a savage attempt to compel them towards victory. In the event Brazil occupied Paraguay until 1876; of about 250,000 Paraguayan male nationals before the war, only 28,000 survived in 1871.)

The first practical development of balloons in the British Army dates from 1878 when the **first "air estimates"** by the War Office allowed the sum of £150 grant for the construction of a balloon. Capt. J. L. B. Templer of the Middlesex Militia (later K.R.R.C.(M)) and Capt. H. P. Lee, R.E., were appointed to carry out the necessary development work. Although Capt. Templer was thus the **first British Air Commander** and an aeronaut in his own right (and the owner of the balloon *Crusader*, which became the **first balloon used by the British Army** in 1879), the **first two aeronauts in the British Army** were Lt. (later Captain) G. E. Grover, R.E., and Capt. F. Beaumont, R.E., who were attached as aeronauts to the Federal Army during the American Civil War from 1862. The **first British Army balloon**, a coal-gas balloon named *Pioneer*, was made during 1879, costing £71 from the £150 appropriation, and had a capacity of 10,000 cu. ft. (283·2 m³.).

Capt. J. L. B. Templer

The first balloon ascent in Canada was made on 31st July 1879 by a hydrogen balloon manned by Richard Cowan, Charles Grimley and Charles Page at Montreal.

The first military use of a man-carrying balloon in Britain was that by a balloon detachment during military manoeuvres at Aldershot, Hants., on 24th June 1880. A balloon detachment accompanied the British military expedition to Bechuanaland, arriving at Cape Town on 19th December 1884, and another accompanied the expeditionary force to the Sudan, departing from Britain on 15th February 1885.

British Army balloon detachment, 1884

The first air crossing of the North Sea was made during 12th–13th October 1907 by the hydrogen balloon *Mammoth* manned by Monsieur A. F. Gaudron (French aeronaut) accompanied by two others. They ascended from Crystal Palace, London, and landed at Brackan on the shore of Lake Vänern in Sweden. The straight-line distance flown was about 720 miles (1,160 km.).

The period 1895–1914 has been termed " the golden age " of ballooning. The science and craft of ballooning, for such it had become with the formation of military balloon units in many parts of the world, was now to be joined by ballooning as a respectable sport and recreation. The showmen–aeronauts began to disappear; stunt flights gave way to organised competition. This was becoming the age of the motor car and the aeroplane. International sport blossomed under the watchful eye of respected clubs and societies. Undoubtedly the greatest and longest-lived international ballooning contest was the James Gordon Bennett Trophy, a competition which continued to be held almost every year from 1906 until the Second World War. (See pages 154–7.)

While ballooning as a sport continued to attract the diehards between the World Wars, it was not unnatural that science would soon take a hand and, while altitude record-breaking provided something of a spur for human achievement, scientific research of the atmosphere provided the necessary finance.

The first ratified altitude record for balloons in the world was that achieved on 31st June 1901 by Professors Berson and Suring of the *Berliner Verein fur Luftschiffarht* who attained a height of 10,800 m. (35,435 ft.). At the time of this record's ratification there was much controversy with those who still firmly believed that James Glaisher had achieved a height of 37,000 ft. on 5th September 1862; as instrumentation to confirm this altitude with any chance of accuracy did not exist at the time ratification of the Berson and Suring record remained; this record remained unbroken for thirty years (although exceeded on a number of occasions by aeroplanes), and on 11th November 1935 Captain Orvil Anderson and Captain Albert Stevens of the U.S.A. attained an altitude of 72,395 ft. (22,066 m.) in a balloon in which they ascended from a point eleven miles south-west of Rapid City, South Dakota, and landed twelve miles south of White Lake, South Dakota.

The first ratified altitude record for a manned balloon of over 100,000 ft. (30,480 m.) was achieved by Maj. David G. Simons, a medical officer of the U.S. Air Force, who reached an altitude of 101,516 ft. (30,942 m.) on 19th–20th August 1957 in a 3,000,000 cu. ft. (84,950 m.³) balloon *AF-WRI-1*. He took off from Crosby, Minnesota, on 19th August to gather scientific data in the Stratosphere and landed at Frederick, South Dakota, the following day.

The current world altitude record for manned free balloons is held by Commander Malcolm D. Ross of the United States Navy Reserve who, on 4th May 1961, ascended over the Gulf of Mexico to an altitude of 113,739·9 feet (34,668 m.) in the Lee Lewis Memorial Winzen Research balloon.

DIRIGIBLES (NAVIGABLE AIRSHIPS)

To many of the adventurous the arrival of the free balloon in 1783 represented the final culmination of man's attempts to fly, albeit without a reliable means of navigation. Of course to others the scarcely-predictable nature of this means of travel was something of a frustration and not many years passed before efforts were made to steer and ultimately to propel balloons at speeds greater and in directions other than that of the wind. Although the first elongated and theoretically steerable balloon was attributed to the Frenchman, Lt. Jean Baptiste Marie Meusnier (1754–93), who published a design of such a craft in 1784, it was not until 1852 that a powered dirigible first carried man into the air.

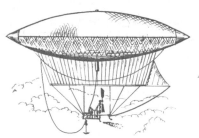

Henri Giffard's steam-powered dirigible

The world's first powered, manned dirigible made its first flight on 24th September 1852 when the Frenchman, Henri Giffard, rose in a steam-powered balloon from the Paris Hippodrome and travelled approximately 17 miles (27 km.) to Trappes, at an average speed of 5 m.p.h. (9 km./hr.). The envelope was 144 ft. (43·89 m.) in length and had a capacity of 88,000 cubic ft. (2,492 m.^{3}); his steam engine developed about 3 h.p. and drove an 11 ft. (3·35 m.) diameter 3-blade propeller.

The world's first fully-controllable powered dirigible was La France, an electric-powered craft which, flown by Capt. Charles Renard and Lt. Arthur Krebs of the French Corps of Engineers, took off on 9th August 1884 from Chalais-Meudon, France, flew a circular course of about 5 miles (9 km.), returned to their point of departure and landed safely. The $7\frac{1}{2}$-h.p. multi-polar electric motor drove a 23-ft. (7·01 m.) four-blade wooden tractor propeller.

The first successful use of a petrol engine in a dirigible was by the German Dr. Karl Wölfert who designed and built a small balloon to which he fitted a 2-h.p. single-cylinder Daimler engine in 1888. Its **first flight** was carried out at Seelberg, Germany, on Sunday 12th August that year, probably flown by a young mechanic named Michaël.

The first flight of a Zeppelin dirigible was made by Count Ferdinand von Zeppelin's LZ 1 on 2nd July 1900 carrying five people from its floating hangar on Lake Constance near Friedrichshafen. The flight lasted about twenty minutes.

The first British Army airship, Dirigible No. 1 (popularly known as *Nulli Secundus*), was first flown on 10th September 1907 with three occupants: Col. John Capper, R.E., pilot; Capt. W. A. de C. King, Adjutant of the British Army Balloon School; Mr. Samuel Cody, "in charge of the engine". The engine in this instance was a 50-h.p. Antoinette. The second and third Army airships were *Beta* (35-h.p. Green engine) and *Gamma* (80-h.p. Green engine) respectively.

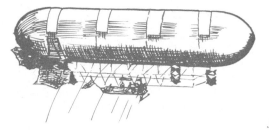

Nulli Secundus

The first dirigible of the U.S. Navy to fly was the DN-1 which was acquired under contract on 1st June 1915. As originally built with two engines it was too heavy to leave the ground; however after redesign with only one engine it made its first of three flights in April 1917 at Pensacola, Florida. It was subsequently damaged and not repaired.

The first successful dirigible of the U.S. Navy was the Goodyear F-1 acquired under contract on 14th March 1917 and first flown from Chicago, Illinois, to Wingfoot Lake, near Akron, Ohio, on 30th May 1917.

The first airship crossing, and double-crossing of the Atlantic was achieved by the British airship R-34 between 2nd–6th July (westward) and 9th–13th July (eastward), 1919. Commanded by Sqdn. Ldr. G. H. Scott, with a crew of thirty, the R-34 set out from East Fortune, Scotland, and flew to New York, returning afterwards to Pulham, Norfolk, England. At the time the R-34 was the largest airship in the world, and the total distance covered, 6,330 miles (10,187 km.) in 183 hr. 8 min., constituted a world record for airships. (The R-34 was destroyed when it broke up over Hull, England, on 24th August 1921. It was to have been sold to the United States and at the time of the disaster there were seventeen Americans aboard in addition to the crew of thirty-two. All the Americans and twenty-seven of the British lost their lives.)

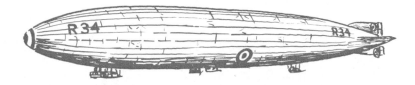

The first helium-filled American rigid airship was the Zeppelin-type ZR-1 *Shenandoah*, which first flew on 4th September 1923 at Lakehurst, New Jersey, U.S.A. On 3rd September 1925 it was destroyed in a storm over Caldwell, Ohio, with heavy loss of life.

The last commercial airship to be developed by Great Britain was the *R-101* which crashed on 4th October 1930 at Beauvais, France, on a flight from Cardington, Bedfordshire, England, to Egypt and India. The accident, which destroyed the airship and killed 47 of the 54 occupants (including Lord Thompson, Secretary of State for Air, and Maj. Gen. Sir Sefton Brancker, Director of Civil Aviation), brought to an end the development of passenger-carrying airships in Great Britain.

The last major airship disaster involved the destruction of the German *Hindenburg*, then the world's largest airship, on 6th May 1937. It was destroyed by fire when approaching its moorings at Lakehurst, New Jersey, U.S.A., after a flight from Frankfurt, Germany. 33 of the 97 occupants were killed in the fire which engulfed the huge craft and which was attributed to the use of hydrogen—the only gas available to Germany owing to the United States' refusal to supply commercial quantities of helium.

THE JAMES GORDON BENNETT INTERNATIONAL BALLOON RACE TROPHY

Without doubt the most famous international balloon contest was the Gordon Bennett contest for a trophy and an annual prize of 12,500 francs presented by the ex-patriate American newspaper magnate, James Gordon Bennett, in 1905 and first contested in 1906. Principal results were as follows:

Date	Starting Point and number of Starters	Winners (Nationality, balloon, qualifying destination and distance)	Remarks
30.9.06	Tuileries, Paris, France (16)	1. Lt. Frank P. Lahm, U.S. Army; *United States*; Fylingdales, Yorkshire, England; 402 miles (647 km.) 2. Alfredo Vanwiller, Italy; *L'Elfe*; New Holland, Hull, England; 362 miles (583 km.) 3. The Hon. C. S. Rolls, England; *Britannia*; Sandringham, Norfolk, England; 289 miles (465 km.)	Only these three finishers managed to cross the English Channel, although the Count de la Vaulx was provisionally announced as sharing third place.
1907	St. Louis, Missouri, U.S.A.	1. Oscar Erbslön, Germany; *Pommern*; 849 miles (1,367 km.) 2. Leblanc, France; *Île de France*; 848.8 miles (1,366 km.) 3. Von Abercron, Germany;	Leblanc's time to cover 1,366 km. was 44 hours and established a new world endurance record.
12.10.08	Berlin, Germany (23)	1. Col. Schaeck, Switzerland; *Helvetia*; 40 km. n. of Molde, Norway; 753 miles (1,212 km.) 2. John Dunville, Britain; *Banshee*; Huidding, Schleswig-Holstein; 270 miles (435 km.) 3. Geerts, Belgium; *Belgica*; near Huidding, Schleswig-Holstein; 263 miles (423 km.)	Many balloons came down in the North Sea. Schaeck's time of 73 hrs. 41 min. established a new world endurance record although he admitted that during the flight his trail rope was caught by fishermen who towed him ashore. Capt. Messner was Col. Schaeck's crew member during his record-breaking flight of 1908.
3.10.09	Zurich, Switzerland (17)	1. E. W. Mix, U.S.A., *America II*; Ostrolenka, Poland; 2. Alfred Leblanc, France; *Île de France*; Zargriva, Hungary; 3. Capt. Messner, Switzerland; *Azurea*; Thule, Silesia;	590 miles (950 km.) 517 miles (832 km.) 515 miles (828 km.)
17.10.10	St. Louis, Missouri, U.S.A.	1. Allan R. Hawley, U.S.A.; *America II*; Lake Tschotogama, Quebec, Canada; 2. Gericke, Germany; *Dusseldog*; near Quebec, Canada; 3. Von Abercron; Germany; *Germania*; near Quebec, Canada;	1,171.13 miles (1,884.75 km.) 1099 miles (1,769 km.) 1095 miles (1,763 km.) Established a new American distance record.
1911	Kansas City, Kansas, U.S.A.	1. O. Gericke, Germany; Holcombe, Wisconsin, U.S.A. 2. Capt. Frank P. Lahm, U.S.A.; La Cross, Wisconsin, U.S.A. 3. Vogt, Germany; Austin, Minnesota, U.S.A.;	468.2 miles (753.5 km.) 406 miles (653 km.) 348 miles (560 km.)
1912	Stuttgart, Germany	1. A. Bienaimé, France; *Picardi*; Ryasan, near Moscow, U.S.S.R.; 2. Alfred Leblanc, France; *Île de France*; Kaluga, U.S.S.R.; 3. H. E. Honeywell, U.S.A.; *Uncle Sam*; Sapadnaja, U.S.S.R.;	1,361 miles (2,191 km.) 1,243 miles (2,001 km.) 1,118 miles (1,800 km.) One of the longest balloon races in history.

Date	Starting Point and number of Starters	Winners (Nationality, balloon, qualifying destination and distance)		Remarks
1913	Tuileries, Paris, France	1. Ralph Upson, U.S.A.; *Goodyear*; Bempton, Yorkshire, England;	384 miles (618 km.)	The extraordinary difference in routes followed is explained by the prevailing upper winds used by Upson.
		2. H. E. Honeywell, U.S.A.; *Uncle Sam*; Finisterre, Galicia, Spain;	300 miles (483 km.)	
		3. Pastine, Italy; *Roma*; Finisterre, Galicia, Spain.	299 miles (481 km.)	
24.10.20	Birmingham, Alabama, U.S.A. (8)	1. Lt. Ernest E. Demuyter, Belgium; *Belgica*; Lake Champlain, Vermont/N.Y., U.S.A.;	1,094 miles (1,760 km.)	Honeywell's time of 48 hrs. 26 min. established a new American duration record.
		2. H. E. Honeywell, U.S.A.; *Kansas City II*; Lake George, N.Y., U.S.A.;	994 miles (1,600 km.)	
		3. Maj. G. del Valle, Italy; *L'Audiens*; Homer, N.Y., U.S.A.;	890 miles (1,432 km.)	
18.9.21	Brussels, Belgium (14)	1. Capt. Paul Armbruster, Switzerland; Lambay Island, Ireland;	476 miles (766 km.)	Some accounts give Spencer and Upson as tying for second place.
		2. Harry Spencer; Britain; Fishguard, Pembroke, Wales;	419 miles (675 km.)	
		3. Ralph Upson, U.S.A.; Near Barmouth; Merioneth, Wales;	413 miles (664 km.)	
6.8.22	Geneva, Switzerland (18)	1. Lt. Ernest Demuyter, Belgium; *Belgica*; Oknitsa, Romania;	853 miles (1,372 km.)	Honeywell, with a time of 26 hr. 30 min., qualified for the duration prize.
		2. H. E. Honeywell, U.S.A.; Tapio-Szecso, Hungary;	659 miles (1,061 km.)	
		3. A. Bienaimé, France; *Picardi*; Mór, Hungary;	574 miles (923 km.)	
23.9.23	Brussels, Belgium (17)	1. Lt. Ernest Demuyter, Belgium; *Belgica*; Skillingaryd (?), Sweden;	994 miles (1,600 km.)	Race started in thunderstorm, met with disaster, five aeronauts killed, five injured. Collision on start line, two balloons struck by lightning, and one collided with high tension cable.
		2. Lt. Veenstra, Belgium; *Prince Leopold*; Mellerud, Lake Vänern, Sweden;	624 miles (1,005 km.)	
		3. Capt. Paul Armbruster, Switzerland; *Helvetia*; Northern Schleswig;	339 miles (546 km.)	
15.6.24	Brussels, Belgium	1. Lt. Ernest Demuyter, Belgium; *Belgica*; St. Abbs Head, Berwick, Scotland;	466 miles (750 km.)	This, the third consecutive win by Belgium, would have qualified that country to retain the trophy outright. The Belgians, however, sportingly announced its renewal for further competition.
		2. Laporte, France; *Ville de Bordeaux*; Brighton, Sussex, England;	245 miles (395 km.)	
		3. H. E. Honeywell, U.S.A.; *Uncle Sam*; Rouen, France;	199 miles (320 km.)	

SECOND TROPHY SERIES

Date	Starting Point and number of Starters	Winners (Nationality, balloon, qualifying destination and distance)		Remarks
1925	Brussels, Belgium	1. Lt. Veenstra, Belgium; *Prince Leopold*;	841 miles (1,354 km.)	In this race Van Orman (U.S. Balloon *Goodyear III*) performed the singular feat of landing on the bridge of a ship at sea; the American balloon, *Elsie*, was hit by a train at Étaples.
		2. Lt. Ernest Demuyter, Belgium; *Belgica*;	411 miles (661·5 km.)	
		3. Col. G. del Valle, Italy; *Ciampino V*;	370 miles (596 km.)	

Date	Starting Point and number of Starters	Winners (Nationality, balloon, qualifying destination and distance)		Remarks
30.5.26	Antwerp, Belgium	1. W. T. Van Orman, U.S.A.; *Goodyear III*; Sölvesborg, Sweden;	535 miles (861 km.)	Some accounts suggest that Herr Kaulen was disqualified; the results quoted are those ratified by the sponsoring body, and later confirmed.
		2. Capt. H. C. Gray, U.S. Army; *S.16*; Kraków Poland;	370 miles (595 km.)	
		3. Lt. Ernest Demuyter, Belgium; *Belgica*; near Hamburg, Germany;	209 miles (336 km.)	
10.9.27	Dearborn, Michigan, U.S.A. (15)	1. E. J. Hill, U.S.A.; *Detroit*; Baxley, Georgia;	745 miles (1,199 km.)	Herr Kaulen was accompanied by his son, Hugo Kaulen, Jr. Once again the trophy was re-presented for competition, this time by the U.S.A.
		2. Hugo Kaulen, Germany; *Barmen*; Fort Valley, Georgia;	688 miles (1,107 km.)	
		3. W. T. Van Orman, U.S.A.; *Goodyear III*; Adrian, Georgia;	685 miles (1,102 km.)	
30.6.28	Detroit, Michigan, U.S.A. (12)	1. Capt. W. E. Kepner, U.S.A.; *U.S. Army*; Kenbridge, Virginia;	460 miles (740·3 km.)	
		2. Hugo Kaulen, Germany; *Barmen*; Chase City, Virginia;	459·4 miles (739·3 km.)	
		3. Charles Dollfus, France; *Blanchard*; Walnut Cove, North Carolina;	447·9 miles (720·8 km.)	

THIRD TROPHY SERIES

Date	Starting Point and number of Starters	Winners (Nationality, balloon, qualifying destination and distance)		Remarks
1929	St. Louis, Missouri, U.S.A.	1. W. T. Van Orman, U.S.A.; Troy, Ohio;	339 miles (545 km.)	
		2. Capt. W. E. Kepner, U.S.A.; *U.S. Army*; Neptune, Ohio;	336 miles (541 km.)	
		3. Lt. T. G. Settle, U.S. Navy; Eaton, Ohio;	302 miles (486 km.)	
1930	Cleveland, Ohio, U.S.A.	1. W. T. Van Orman, U.S.A.; North Canton, Massachusetts;	539 miles (867 km.)	No Gordon Bennett trophy race was held in 1931 and a fourth series of races was started in 1932.
		2. Capt. Ernest Demuyter, Belgium; *Belgica*; North Canton, Massachusetts;	445·5 miles (717 km.)	
		3. E. J. Hill, U.S.A.;		

FOURTH TROPHY SERIES

Date	Starting Point and number of Starters	Winners (Nationality, balloon, qualifying destination and distance)		Remarks
1932	Basle, Switzerland	1. Lt. Cdr. T. G. Settle, U.S.A.; *U.S. Navy*; Vilna, Lithuania;	954 miles (1,536 km.)	New series established under Swiss administration.
		2. W. T. Van Orman, U.S.A.; *Goodyear VIII*; Kovno, Lithuania;	859 miles (1,383 km.)	
		3. Ravaine-Speiss, France; *Petit Mousse*; Tokary, Poland;	766 miles (1,233 km.)	
1933	Chicago, Illinois, U.S.A.	1. Z. J. Burzynski, Poland; Quebec, Canada;	846 miles (1,361 km.)	
		2. Lt. Cdr. T. G. Settle, U.S.A.; *U.S. Navy*; Grove, Long Island, N.Y.;	775 miles (1,248 km.)	
		3. W. T. Van Orman, U.S.A.; *Goodyear VIII*; Sudbury, Ontario, Canada;	492 miles (792 km.)	

Date	Starting Point and number of Starters	Winners (Nationality, balloon, qualifying destination and distance)	Remarks
1934	Warsaw, Poland	1. Hynek, Poland; *Kosciuszko*; Finland (location not recorded);	827 miles (1,331 km.)	Landing area of first two places probably near Savonlinna, Finland.
		2. Z. J. Burzynski, Poland; *Warszawa*; Finland (location not recorded);	810 miles (1,304 km.)	
		3. Ernest Demuyter, Belgium; *Belgica*;	722 miles (1,162 km.)	
15-9-35	Warsaw, Poland	1. Z. J. Burzynski, Poland; *Polonia II*; near Leningrad, U.S.S.R.;	1,025 miles (1,650 km.)	The leading balloons all landed in a desperately remote area and were not rescued for a fortnight after landing. Burzynski's flight established a world record for balloons of 1,601–2,200 cu. m.
		2. Janusz, Poland; *Warszawa II*; near Leningrad, U.S.S.R.;	971 miles (1,563 km.)	
		3. Ernest Demuyter, Belgium; *Belgica*;	904 miles	
1-9-36	Warsaw, Poland	1. Ernest Demuyter, Belgium; *Belgica*; Miedlesza, U.S.S.R.;	1,066·15 miles (1,715·8 km.)	The veteran Demuyter's flight constituted a world distance record in four balloon categories.
		2. Goetze, Germany;	994 miles (1,600 km.)	
		3. Z. J. Burzynski, Poland; *Polonia II*;	982 miles (1,580 km.)	
1937	Brussels, Belgium	1. Ernest Demuyter, Belgium; *Belgica*; Tukumo Lithuania;	889 milles (1,430 km.)	
		2. Janusz, Poland; *Warszawa II*; Anec, Lithuania;	870 miles (1,400 km.)	
1938	Liége, Belgium	1. Janusz, Poland; *L.O.P.P.*; Trojan, Bulgaria;	1,013 miles (1,630 km.)	
		2. Krzyszkowski, Poland; *Warszawa II*; Catuselle, Romania;	913 miles (1,470 km.)	
		3. Thonar, Belgium; *S. II*; Vidin, Bulgaria;	902 miles (1,451 km.)	

(Above) *The abortive Lockheed Cheyenne all-weather combat helicopter, whose top speed of 253 m.p.h. (408 km./hr.) is among the highest achieved by any rotorcraft. Nose and belly turrets mount grenade launchers, Miniguns and a 30 mm. cannon, and wing strongpoints accept a wide range of stores. The Convair B-58A Hustler (below) was the world's first four-jet supersonic bomber.*

CHAPTER 6

ROTORCRAFT

The first documented reference to the possibility of sustaining or propelling upwards a vehicle by means of rotating surfaces is attributed to Leonardo da Vinci (1452–1519), whose design sketches for such are believed to have originated in about the year 1500. Leonardo was otherwise devoted to the concept of flapping wings (i.e. the ornithopter) to achieve forward flight and he was not aware of the lifting characteristics of aerofoils, nor was he acquainted with the properties of the propeller. As a result his design for a helicopter was based strictly on an "air screw"—literally a rotating helical wing which would "screw" its path upwards through the air.

Numerous attempts to evolve models of helicopters followed during the next four centuries, culminating in the unmanned models of W. H. Phillips who, in 1842, succeeded in launching a steam-driven craft whose rotating *blades* were propelled by tip jets.

It is perhaps useful here to interpose simple definitions of the helicopter and "autogiro". Basically a helicopter achieves vertical flight by means of aerodynamic lift from rotor blades which are rotated under power; to eliminate torque (i.e. to prevent the fuselage of the aircraft from spinning uncontrollably on the axis of the rotor), either coaxial rotors, balanced sets of rotors or small tail-mounted rotors are geared to the powerplant. Forward flight is achieved by varying the incidence of the rotating blades so that their resulting thrust lies fore and aft through the aircraft.

An autogiro, on the other hand, is rather nearer to a conventional aeroplane in that forward motion is achieved by a conventional engine (either jet or piston engine-driven propeller); as forward motion is achieved the freely-rotating rotor blades provide lift as aerofoils, enabling the autogiro to perform short, steep take-offs and landings.

The first helicopter to lift a man from the ground was built by the Breguet brothers of France in 1907. Although the craft lifted off the ground at Douai, France, on 29th September that year, it did not constitute a free flight as four men on the ground steadied the machine with long poles which, while not contributing to the aircraft's lift, constituted a form of control restriction. Power was provided by a 50 h.p. Antoinette engine.

The first true free flight by a man-carrying helicopter was performed by Paul Cornu in his 24-h.p. Antoinette-powered twin-rotor aircraft near Lisieux, France, on 13th November 1907.

Neither of the above helicopters incorporated cyclic pitch control (hence the problem overcome by Breguet in using external control stabilisation) although G. A. Crocco had in 1906 suggested its necessity. It was J. C. H. Ellehammer, the Danish pioneer aviator, who first produced a helicopter (of only limited application) in 1912 which incorporated cyclic pitch control.

The first helicopters to successfully demonstrate cyclic pitch control were those designed and constructed by the Marquis de Pescara, an Argentinian, in France and Spain between 1919 and 1925. While demonstrating this feature successfully these aircraft were directionally unstable as the result of inadequate torque counteraction.

The first successful flights by a gyroplane (commercially named an *autogiro*) were accomplished by the Spaniard Juan de la Cierva at Getafe, Spain, in 1923.

The first two-seater autogiro in the world was the Cierva C.6D which was first flown by F. T. Courtney at Hamble, England, on 29th July 1927. Don Juan de la Cierva, the Spanish inventor, became **the first passenger in the world to ride in a rotating-wing aircraft** when he was taken aloft the following day in this autogiro.

The first rotating-wing aircraft to fly the English Channel was the Cierva C.8L Mark II (*G-EBYY*) flown by Don Juan de la Cierva with a passenger from Croydon to Le Bourget on 18th September 1928.

Cierva C.8L Mark II

The first autogiro flown in America was an aircraft brought to the United States by Harold F. Pitcairn and flown at Willow Grove, Philadelphia, on 19th December 1928.

The first autogiro to be publicly demonstrated in the U.S.A. was the Cierva C.19 Mark II (*G-AAKY*) which was flown at the Cleveland Air Races, Ohio, during August 1929.

Cierva C.19 Mark II

The first entirely successful helicopter in the world was the Focke-Wulf Fw 61 twin-rotor helicopter designed by Professor Heinrich Karl Johann Focke during 1932–34. The first prototype Fw 61V1 (*D-EBVU*) made its first free flight on 26th June 1936 and was powered by a 160-h.p. Bramo Sh 14A engine. This aircraft, flown by Ewald Rohlfs in June 1937, established a world's closed circuit distance record for helicopters of 76·105 miles (122·35 km.) and a helicopter endurance record of 1 hour 20 minutes 49 seconds. On other occasions it set up an altitude record of 11,242 ft. (3,426 m.) and a speed record of 76 m.p.h. (122 km./hr.). It gave a flying demonstration in the Berlin Deutschland-Halle during 1938 in the hands of the famous German woman test pilot Hanna Reitsch.

Focke-Wulf Fw 61

The first helicopter to enter production was the Focke-Achgelis Fa 223. The Focke-Wulf Fw 61 (see above) was not commercially exploited, technically successful though it proved to be. Instead, a commercially-developed derivative, the Fa 223 appeared and was put into limited production during 1940.

The first successful helicopters to be designed outside Germany were those of the Russian-born American Igor Sikorsky, although his first helicopter, the VS-300, was of little practical value. Powered by a 75-h.p. engine, it featured full cyclic pitch control and achieved tethered flight in 1939 in America. (It has been suggested that this aircraft did in fact achieve a single free flight that year.)

Sikorsky VS-300

The first helicopter designed and built for military service was the Sikorsky XR-4 which was delivered to Wright Field, Dayton, Ohio, in 1942 for military evaluation. As a result of these trials, machines of a small development batch were used for limited service and training during 1944 and 1945, YR-4s being the first helicopters to fly in Burma and Alaska, and the first to be flown by the British Fleet Air Arm. A YR-4 was **the first helicopter to be flown from a ship** during trials in Long Island Sound, U.S.A., during May 1943.

The first-ever Type-Approval Certificate awarded for a commercial helicopter was for the Bell Model 47 in March 1946; this helicopter made its first flight on 8th December 1945 and provided the design basis for a family of Bell helicopters which continued in production for more than twenty years.

Bell Model 47G-2

Westland/Sikorsky Dragonfly

The first helicopter built in Great Britain to enter service with the R.A.F. was the Sikorsky-designed Westland-Sikorsky Dragonfly (the S-51 built under licence by Westland Aircraft Ltd., Yeovil, England). The first Westland-built S-51 was for commercial use and flew in 1948. The R.A.F.'s first helicopter, a Dragonfly H.C. Mark 2 (*WF308*) powered by an Alvis Leonides engine, was delivered in 1950, and subsequent aircraft equipped No. 194 (Casualty Evacuation) Squadron, **the R.A.F.'s first helicopter squadron**, on 1st February 1953.

The largest helicopter in the world is currently believed to be the Russian Mil Mi-12 twin-rotor aircraft whose overall span (over the rotor tips) is approximately 240 ft. (73 m.), and length is 200 ft. 6 in. (61 m.). First indication of the existence of this enormous helicopter to reach the West was in 1969 when Russia submitted for ratification the lifting of a payload of 68,410 lb. (31,030 kg.) to an altitude of 9,678 ft. (2,950 m.)—approximately the loaded weight of an Avro Lancaster bomber of World War Two.

CHAPTER 7

FLYING FOR SPORT AND COMPETITION

Ray Stit's Sky Baby, the smallest aeroplane ever flown, built at Riverside, California, in 1952. The wing span was 7 ft. 2 in., the length 9 ft. 10 in.; the 85 h.p. Continental C85 engine gave it a top speed of 185 m.p.h.

In realms of commerce and in times of war it is perhaps often overlooked that flying originally approached maturity before the First World War largely through the enthusiasm and courage of a small band of philanthropic sportsmen who sought satisfaction through a precarious recreation, and the measure of whose success lay in their ability to fly further, faster or higher than their colleagues at home and abroad. The very nature of their sport, eliminating as it did the frontiers that had divided nation from nation, brought airmen of different countries closer together, so that almost at once international competition was keen—yet characterised by something of a universal cameraderie. So powerful was this sense of *entente* between all aerial sportsmen that when, inevitably, the Kaiser's war split nations asunder, they were placed under orders to do battle among one another, there was a reluctance at first to so prostitute their new-found sport by turning their frail craft into machines of destruction. One has only to attend an international flying meeting sixty years later to realise that the old *entente* has not altogether disappeared . . .

This Chapter spans the scope of flying by pilots who, perhaps supported only by limited money, indulged their whims in the private ownership of an aeroplane, and also by pilots who, by their prowess (or perhaps in spite of their lack of it) are encouraged to compete against each other either in organised or in informal sporting events. While of course there have been the classic annual spectacles—the Schneider Trophy, the King's Cup Air Race and the American National Air Races—there have also from time to time been the great competitions, sponsored by big finance, like the Australia Race of 1934 and the Trans-atlantic Race of 1969. All have contributed greatly both to the progress of aviation and to the better understanding of what, after all, aviation has to offer: the drawing together of nation to nation by time, distance and competition.

The first major prize to be offered in Great Britain for a feat performed in an aeroplane was the £1,000 offered by the *Daily Mail* for the first aeroplane flight across the English Channel. This was won by the Frenchman, Louis Blériot, who crossed from France to England on Sunday, 25th July 1909 (see page 19).

The World's first international air meeting was held at Rheims, France, and opened on 22nd August 1909. Among the aeroplanes which assembled were seven Voisins, six Wright biplanes, five Blériot monoplanes, four Henry Farman biplanes, four R.E.P.'s, three Antoinettes, two Curtiss, one Santos Dumont, one Breguet and one Sanchis. Competition during the meeting consisted of a number of speed, duration and distance events and Henry Farman established world records for duration and distance by flying 112·5 miles (180 km.) in a closed circuit in 3 hours 4 minutes 56·4 seconds. His prize money totalled 63,000 francs.

The first major prize to be offered in Great Britain for all-British aviation activity was the £1,000 offered by the *Daily Mail* to the first British pilot to complete a circular flight of one mile (1·6 km.) in an all-British aeroplane. This prize was won by J. T. C. Moore-Brabazon who, at Shellbeach, flew a Short-built Wright-type biplane powered by a 50-60 h.p. Green engine over a mile on Saturday, 30th October 1909. This flight is generally regarded as the inauguration of all-British aviation.

The first prize of £10,000 to be offered in Great Britain for an aeroplane flight was again offered by the *Daily Mail* for the first pilot to fly an aeroplane from a point within five miles of the newspaper's London offices to a point within five miles of its Manchester offices. This prize encouraged Louis Paulhan and Claude Grahame-White to compete in their Henry Farman biplanes, success finally attending the efforts of the former on Thursday, 28th April 1910. The event, which ultimately developed into a race (with Grahame-White resorting to an epic night flight), fired the imagination of the whole country as supporters and officials hired special trains to follow the progress of the aviators, and reports were flashed to H.M. King Edward VII who was abroad at the time.

The first prize won by an Englishman flying in America went to Claude Grahame-White who, between 6th and 12th September 1910, won a £2,000 prize offered by the *Boston Globe* after flying a thirty-three-mile cross country in 40 minutes 1·6 seconds. At the same Boston meeting Grahame-White also achieved four other first prizes and three second, so that his total prize money amounted to £6,420 for the week.

The first Gordon-Bennett international aeroplane race was flown at the end of October 1910 at Belmont Park, New York, and attracted teams from the U.S.A. (Messrs. Brookins, Drexel and Moisant), France (MM. Latham and Leblanc) and Great Britain (Messrs. Grahame-White, Ogilvie and Radley). The race was won by Claude Grahame-White, flying a Blériot monoplane, who completed the 100 km. (62·2 mile) course in 1 hour 1 minute 4·74 seconds. Second place was taken by Moisant, also flying a Blériot.

The emphasis placed upon financial reward for competition in the air during the early years of aviation may, by modern definition, tend to detract from the amateur status of the pilots of that time, yet it was the nature of their sport and the absence of national support which threatened to retard their progress by its very cost. It was the farsighted sponsorship by the Press and by such persons as Archdeacon and the Baron de Forest which not only ensured the survival of competitive aviation, but also spurred European aviation to the efforts which very quickly overhauled those of the pioneering Americans. For example, Claude Grahame-White won in prize money during 1910 a total of £10,280—much of which was applied to the support of the important Grahame-White Flying Schools.

The first truly international air race (point-to-point) held in Europe was the Circuit of Europe which started on 18th June 1911, whose route was Paris-Rheims-Liège-Spa-Liège - Verloo - Utrecht - Breda - Brussels - Roubaix - Calais - Dover - Shoreham - London-Shoreham-Dover-Calais-Amiens-Paris. The field included eight Moranes, seven Deperdussins, six Blériots, three Sommers, three Caudrons, three Henry Farmans, two Maurice Farmans, two Bristols, two Voisins, two Astras, and one each of Antoinette, Barillon, Bonnet-Lab, Danton, Nieuport, Pischoff, R.E.P., Tellier, Train, van Meel and Vinet. The race was won after nineteen days on 7th July by Lt. de Vaisseau Conneau flying a Blériot, followed by Roland Garros also in a Blériot. Prize money totalled £18,300, and only nine aeroplanes completed the course.

The first "Round-Britain" air race was sponsored by the *Daily Mail*, which newspaper presented a £10,000 prize for a race which started from Brooklands on 22nd July 1911. The course, which was flown in five days, followed the route Brooklands-Hendon-Harrogate - Newcastle - Edinburgh - Stirling - Glasgow - Carlisle - Manchester - Bristol-Exeter-Salisbury Plain-Brighton-Brooklands, a distance of 1,010 miles (1,625 km.). Only two French aircraft completed the course in the specified time and the race was won by the French naval officer Lt. de Vaisseau Conneau (in a Blériot) from Jules Vedrines (in a Morane-Borel). Samuel Cody completed the course three days late.

Longevity

Left, *the Avro 504 trainer maintained in flying condition by the Shuttleworth Trust. The Avro 504K, born from a 1913 design, served as a trainer and "joy-rider" between the Wars, in great numbers. Below, a Douglas AC-47 "Dragonship"; with three quick-firing Miniguns mounted in the port fuselage door and windows, this air support version of the DC-3 Dakota went into combat in Vietnam with the U.S.A.F.'s 4th Air Commando Squadron late in 1965, and is still in service, 35 years after the first flight of the DC-3. Bottom, a Hawker Hunter of an export batch in the markings of Abu Dhabi; the Hunter was for fifteen years the backbone of the R.A.F.'s fighter and ground attack capability.*

The first Schneider Trophy (or to give its formal title, the *Jacques Schneider Air Racing Trophy for Hydro-Aeroplanes*) was contested at Monaco on 15th April 1913 over twenty-eight laps of a ten-kilometer course and was organised initially by the Aero Club of France. The first race attracted four starters in the final heat, which was won by Prevost flying a 160-h.p. Gnôme-powered Deperdussin. This pilot was the only one to complete the course and was not judged to have flown across the finishing line correctly. He was accordingly sent off again to complete a further lap which added about another hour to his time, so that his average speed is recorded in the official results as being 45·75 m.p.h. (73·63 km./hr.).

The first major British competition for seaplanes was the *Daily Mail* Hydro-Aeroplane Trial of 16th August 1913, and the regulations stated a specified course round Britain, involving a distance to be flown of 1,540 miles (2,478 km.) by an all-British aircraft before 30th August. Four aircraft were entered but Samuel Cody was killed before he could compete and the engines in two other aircraft proved unsuitable. The only starter was therefore Harry Hawker, accompanied by his mechanic Kauper, flying a Sopwith three-seat tractor biplane. The route was from Southampton *via* Ramsgate, Yarmouth, Scarborough, Aberdeen, Cromarty, Oban, Dublin, Falmouth and back to Southampton. After an abortive attempt which ended at Yarmouth owing to a cracked engine cylinder, Sopwith took off again from Southampton on 25th August and managed to fly round the course as far as Dublin when, just before alighting on the water, Hawker's foot slipped off the rudder bar and the aircraft struck the water and broke up. The *Daily Mail* prize of £5,000 was not awarded, but Hawker received £1,000 as consolation.

The first British aeroplane to beat all comers in a major international competitive event was the Sopwith Tabloid. Equipped as a landplane towards the end of 1913, this revolutionary aircraft could climb to 1,200 ft. in one minute while carrying pilot, passenger and sufficient fuel for two and a half hours. It was capable of a maximum speed of 92 m.p.h. (148 km./hr.). Its outstanding competitive success was its victory in the second contest for the Schneider Trophy held between Monaco and Cap Martin on 20th April 1914 when, equipped as a floatplane, the aircraft was flown by Howard Pixton over the 280 km. at an average speed of 85·5 m.p.h. (137·6 km./hr.). After completing the race course, Pixton continued for two extra laps to establish a new world speed record for seaplanes at 92 m.p.h. (148 km./hr.).

The first major British aviation competition to be won by an American pilot was the third Aerial Derby, flown in bad weather on 6th June 1914 and won by W. L. Brock in a Morane-Saulnier monoplane powered by an 80-h.p. Le Rhone engine. Apart from the *Daily Mail* trophy, Brock also won a total of £315 in prize money.

The era of unrestricted flying over Great Britain came to an end with the outbreak of the First World War. On 4th August 1914 the Home Office issued the following order severely curtailing the flying of aeroplanes over the country:

"In pursuance of the powers conferred on me by the Aerial Navigation Acts, 1911 and 1913, I hereby make, for the purposes of the safety and defence of the Realm, the following Order:

"I prohibit the navigation of aircraft of every class and description over the whole area of the United Kingdom, and over the whole of the coastline thereof and territorial waters adjacent thereto.

"This order shall not apply to Naval or Military aircraft or to aircraft flying under Naval or Military orders, nor shall it apply to any aircraft flying within three miles of a recognised aerodrome.

R. McKenna.
One of His Majesty's Principal Secretaries of State."

The return of peace was accompanied by the emergence of commercial air travel and on 30th April 1919 was published the British Air Navigation Regulations (1919) which formulated the regulations by which "civil" aviation would in future be governed. Already a Department of Civil Aviation had, on 12th February 1919, been established within the British Air Ministry, and which in effect brought commercial control under the Civil Service, while the Royal Aero Club continued to administer the sport of aviation.

The first King's Cup Air Race was held on 8th-9th September 1922 from Croydon to Glasgow and back; it was won by Capt. Frank Barnard flying a de Havilland D.H.4A, *G-EAMU* (powered by a 350-h.p. Rolls-Royce Eagle engine) at an average speed of 124 m.p.h. (199·5 km./hr.). Second was Fred Raynham in a Martinsyde F.6 (*G-EBDK*) and third Alan Cobham in a de Havilland D.H.9 (*G-EAAC*).

The only Oxford-versus-Cambridge University Air Race ever staged was flown on 16th July 1921 and resulted in a flyaway victory for Cambridge. Each team consisted of three S.E. 5As and the course of three laps lay along the route from Hendon *via* Epping and Hertford, returning to Hendon. Cambridge gained maximum points by achieving the first three places while one of the Oxford aircraft failed to complete the course.

The first flight of the first de Havilland Moth prototype *G-EBKT* was made by Capt. Geoffrey de Havilland on Sunday 22nd February 1925 from Stag Lane Aerodrome, Edgware, Middlesex. Sir Sefton Brancker, Director of Civil Aviation, was so impressed with the new aircraft that he recommended the formation of five Government-subsidised flying clubs to be equipped with Moths, and the first such aircraft, *G-EBLR*, was delivered to the Lancashire Aero Club by Alan Cobham on 21st July 1925. Moths were subsequently manufactured in Australia, Finland, France, America, Canada and Norway.

The first "trans-World" air race was the MacRobertson Race from England to Australia which started on 20th October 1934. In March 1933 the Governing Director of MacRobertson Confectionery Manufacturers of Melbourne, Sir MacPherson Robertson offered £15,000 in prize money for an air race to commemorate the centenary of the foundation of the state of Victoria. (This formed part of a donation of £100,000 placed at the disposal of the Victorian Government in 1933.) The race was won over the 12,300 mile (19,795 km.) course by a de Havilland D.H.88 Comet *Grosvenor House G-ACSS* flown by C. W. A. Scott and Tom Campbell Black which covered the distance in 70 hours 54 minutes 18 seconds. A handicap class was won by a KLM Douglas DC-2 flown by K. D. Paramentier and J. J. Moll.

The first trans-Atlantic air race was sponsored by the *Daily Mail* during 1969 for the fastest journey between the top of the Post Office Tower in London and the top of the Empire State Building in New York. The £5,000 first prize was won by the Royal Navy entry flown by Lt. Cdr. Brian Davies, 35, and Lt. Cdr. Peter Goddard, 32, in a McDonnell Douglas F-4K Phantom II. Flying time was 4 hours 36 minutes 30·4 seconds, and the overall time between terminal points was 5 hours 11 minutes 22 seconds.

AEROBATICS

Aerobatics are almost as old as flying itself, and their development was a measure of the growing confidence in the aeroplane, not only as a flying machine but as a vehicle of sport. The word "aerobatic" is obviously a contraction of the original "aerial acrobatics", and as such found its appeal in the dramatic and spectacular, for, no sooner had a pilot extricated himself from an unusual attitude in the air than he set about perfecting the manoeuvre in such a manner as to impress his grounded spectators. Of course it was not long before fairly complicated manoeuvres came to be developed for necessity—such as, in air combat, the "Immelmann turn"—now thought to have been a climbing half loop with a roll off the top. Yet for many

Top, *the B.A.C. Lightning T.Mk. 55 an export version of the R.A.F.'s two-seat T.Mk 5 trainer, in the insignia of the Kuwaiti Air Force. Deliveries of the Lightning to Kuwait commenced late in 1968; the T.Mk 55 is a fully operational Mach 2 interceptor despite its two-seat configuration. Bottom, Dassault Mirage IIIR reconnaissance fighter-bomber of l'Armée de l'Air, of which some ninety have been built, including export models. The Mirage III "family" constitutes France's main fighter strength, and has been widely exported.*

years aerobatics as such remained no more than a spectacle provided by a skilled, individual pilot, performed to display the manoeuvrability of his aeroplane—or simply his own skill and daring. There were certainly few parameters in aerobatics.

Much more recently aerobatics have been pursued more seriously and even "scientifically", and since the Second World War national prestige has been upheld through fairly lavish displays of aerobatics performed by formations of interceptor fighters, so that almost every major air force in the world has trained squadrons or flights to provide the spectacle of such displays.

Since 1960 nations have competed in world aerobatic championships and so complicated and precise have modern aerobatics become in these championship meetings that only a very small handful of specialist aeroplanes, designed and prepared with extreme precision, have been capable—even in the most expert hands—of competing with any chance of success. It is almost certainly true to state that the successful pilots in these championships are the finest exponents of the pure art of flying.

The first aerobatic manoeuvre was undoubtedly the spin. Though nowadays not regarded as an aerobatic but simply as a manoeuvre in which the aeroplane falls in a stalled condition while rolling, pitching and yawing simultaneously, it was originally performed as a spectacular manoeuvre—once the means of recovery had been discovered.

The first pilot to survive a spin (probably the first pilot in the world) was Fred Raynham who, flying an Avro biplane during 1911, stalled while climbing through fog. The stall occurred after he had stooped to adjust his compass as he thought that it was malfunctioning; the next he knew was that he was standing upright on the rudder pedals with his aeroplane whirling round. Quite how he recovered from the spin will never be known, for his recollection was that he *pulled the stick back*; notwithstanding this he caught sight of the ground and was able to perform a controlled landing.

The first pilot to perform, recover from and demonstrate recovery from a spin was Lt. Wilfred Parke, R.N., on 25th August 1912 on the Avro cabin tractor biplane during the Military Trials of that year. On this occasion Parke and his observer, Lt. Le Breton, R.F.C., were flying at about 600 ft. (200 m.) and commenced a spiral glide prior to landing; finding that the glide was too steep, Parke pulled the stick back, promptly stalled and entered a spin. With no established procedure in mind for recovery he attempted to extricate himself from the danger by pulling the stick further back and applying rudder *into* the direction of spin, and found that the spin merely tightened. After carefully noting this phenomenon he decided, *when only fifty feet from the ground*—and from disaster—to reverse the rudder so that the machine recovered instantly. Parke was able to give a carefully reasoned resumé of his corrective actions thereby contributing immeasurably to the progress of aviation.

The first pilot in the world to perform a loop was Lt. Nesterov of the Imperial Russian Army who, flying a Nieuport, performed the manoeuvre at Kiev on 20th August 1913. (*See photo.*)

The first pilot to fly inverted in sustained flight (as distinct from becoming inverted during the course of the looping manoeuvre) was Adolphe Pégoud who, on 21st September 1913, flew a Blériot monoplane inverted at Buc, France. Notwithstanding the above definition, Pégoud's manoeuvre involved two "halves" of a loop, in that he assumed the inverted position by means of a half-loop, and after sustained inverted flight recovered by means of a "pull-through". He thus did not resort to a roll or half-roll, which manoeuvre had not apparently been achieved at this time. As a means of acclimatising himself for the ordeal of inverted flight, Pégoud had had his Blériot mounted inverted upon trestles and had remained strapped in the cockpit for periods of up to twenty minutes at a time!

The first British pilot to perform a loop was Benjamin C. Hucks who looped a Blériot monoplane, probably at Hendon in September 1913. Like Adolphe Pégoud (see above), Hucks also sought training in his feat by remaining strapped in an inverted cockpit on the ground.

The first woman in the world to experience a loop in an aeroplane was Miss Trehawke Davis, who was taken aloft for the manoeuvre by her protége, Gustav Hamel (son of an English-naturalised German doctor), at Hendon probably in September 1913.

The first hesitation roll was probably performed towards the end of or shortly after the First World War. This manoeuvre was unlikely to have been performed by a wing-warping aeroplane, but in view of the power available may have been first performed by a Sopwith Camel or Snipe, and would have been a "four-point" hesitation roll.

The cartwheel manoeuvre (essentially performed in a twin-engined aeroplane) was first demonstrated by Jan Zurakowski in a de Havilland Hornet fighter (two Rolls-Royce Merlin engines) at Boscombe Down, England, in 1945. The same pilot also later gave demonstrations of the manoeuvre in a Gloster Meteor IV jet fighter at the annual S.B.A.C. Displays at Farnborough, Hants. It was performed during a vertical full-power climb to the point of near-stall by quickly throttling-back one engine and performing a controlled, vertical wing-over.

The only known occasions on which inverted spins by high-performance jet aircraft have been demonstrated publicly, were the S.B.A.C. Displays at Farnborough, Hants, of September 1959 and September 1960. At these displays the Hawker Aircraft Ltd. Chief Test Pilot, A. W. ("Bill") Bedford, flying the demonstration Hunter two-seater *G-APUX*, performed inverted spins of twelve or thirteen turns and used coloured smoke to trace the pattern of his recovery in the sky.

The "Derry Turn" was evolved by John Derry, a test pilot of de Havilland Aircraft Co., Ltd., in 1949–50. It was a positive-G turn initiated by rolling in the opposite direction through 270°. It was a fairly spectacular manoeuvre only ultimately made possible by the availability of sufficient excess engine-power allied with rudder control to keep the nose of the aircraft up at the necessary late stage in the rolling manoeuvre.

PARACHUTING FOR SPECTACLE, SPORT AND NECESSITY

The first demonstration in the world of a quasi-parachute was given by the Frenchman, Sebastien Lenormand, who in 1783 descended from an observation tower at Montpellier France, under a braced conical canopy.

An impression of the Lenormand device

The first parachute descent ever performed successfully by man from a vehicle was accomplished by the Frenchman, André Jacques Garnerin, who jumped from a balloon at about 3,000 ft. (915 m.) having ascended from the Parc Monçeau near Paris on 22nd October 1797.

The Garnerin parachute

The first parachute descent from a balloon in America was that made by Charles Guille who, on 2nd August 1819, jumped from a hydrogen balloon at a height of about 8,000 ft. (2,440 m.) and landed at New Bushwick, Long Island, N.Y.

The first parachute descent from an aeroplane in America was performed by Capt. Albert Berry who on 1st March 1912 jumped from a Benoist aircraft flown by Anthony Jannus at 1,500 ft. (460 m.) over Jefferson Barracks, St. Louis, Mo.

The first parachute descent by a woman from an aeroplane was made by the 18-year-old American girl, Georgia ("Tiny") Broadwick who, using an 11-lb. (5 kg.) silk parachute, jumped from an aircraft flown by Glenn Martin at about 1,000 ft. (305 m.) over Griffith Field, Los Angeles, Calif., on 21st June 1913.

The first parachute drop from an aeroplane over Great Britain was made by W. Newell at Hendon on 9th May 1914 from a Grahame-White Charabanc flown by R. H. Carr. Newell sat on a small rope seat attached to the port undercarriage, clutching his 40-lb. (18-kg.) parachute in his lap; when the aeroplane had climbed to 2,000 ft. (610 m.) F. W. Gooden, seated on the lower wing, prised Newell off his perch with his foot! The parachute was 26 ft. (7·9 m.) in diameter and the drop occupied 2 minutes 22 seconds.

The first successful use of a free parachute (i.e. a "free fall") **from an aeroplane** was made by Leslie Leroy Irvin (1895–1965) on 19th April 1919 using a parachute of the pattern he had developed for the U.S. Army. His descent was at McCook Field, Dayton, Ohio.

The first American to escape from a disabled aeroplane by parachute was Lt. Harold R. Harris, U.S. Army, who on 20th October 1922 jumped from a Loening monoplane at 2,000 ft. (610 m.) over North Dayton, Ohio.

The greatest altitude from which anyone has ever jumped without a parachute and survived is 22,000 ft. (6,706 m.). In January 1942 Lt. (now Lt.-Col.) I. M. Chisov of the U.S.S.R. fell from an Ilyushin Il-4 which had been badly damaged. He struck the ground a glancing blow on the edge of a snow-covered ravine and slid to the bottom, sustaining a fractured pelvis and severe spinal damage. (It is estimated that the human body reaches 99% of its low level terminal velocity after falling 1,880 ft. (573 m.); this is 117–125 m.p.h. (188–201 km./hr.) at normal atmospheric pressure in a random posture, but up to 185 m.p.h. (298 km./hr.) in a head-down position.) **The British record** stands at 18,000 ft. (5,490 m.) by Flt. Sgt. Nicholas Stephen Alkemade, aged 21 of the R.A.F., who jumped from a blazing Lancaster bomber over Germany on 23rd March 1944. His headlong fall was broken by a fir tree, and he landed *without a broken bone* in an 18-in. (45-cm.) snow bank.

The first man to bale out from an aeroplane flying at supersonic speed and live was George Franklin Smith, 31, test pilot for North American Aviation Corporation, who ejected from a North American F-100 Super Sabre on 26th February 1955 off Laguna Beach, Calif. After failure of the controls in a dive, Smith fired his ejector seat at an indicated speed of Mach 1·05 or more than 700 m.p.h. After being unconscious for five days Smith made an almost complete recovery from his injuries which included haemorrhaged eyeballs, damage to lower intestine and liver, knee joints and eye retina. Within nine months he was passed fit to resume flying.

The first member of the Royal Air Force to survive a supersonic ejection (and the second man in the world) was Fg. Off. Hedley Molland who escaped from a Hawker Hunter fighter which had suffered a runaway tailplane during a dive from 40,000 ft. (12,190 m.) on 3rd August 1955. Fg. Off. Molland, by delaying his ejection longer than Smith (see above), left his cockpit at a higher Mach number (estimated at M=1·10) but at a lower altitude, probably about 10,000 ft. (3,050 m.). He was picked up by a tug, and recovered in hospital from his injuries which included a broken arm (caused by flailing in the slipstream) and a fractured pelvis.

The world's first parachute escape from an aeroplane travelling at speed on the ground was achieved by Sqdn. Ldr. J. S. Fifield, D.F.C., A.F.C., on 3rd September 1955 at Chalgrove Airfield, Oxfordshire, when he was ejected from the rear cockpit of a modified Gloster Meteor 7 piloted by Capt. J. E. D. Scott, chief test pilot of Martin-Baker Ltd., manufacturers of the ejector seat. Speed of the aircraft at the moment of ejection was 120 m.p.h. (194 km./hr.) and the maximum height reached by the seat was 70 ft. (21 m.) above the runway.

The greatest altitude from which a successful emergency escape from an aeroplane has been made is 56,000 ft. (17,070 m.). At this altitude on 9th April 1958 an English Electric Canberra bomber exploded over Monyash, Derbyshire, and the crew, Flt. Lt. John de Salis, 29, and Fg. Off. Patrick Lowe, 23, fell free in a temperature of −70°F (−56·7°C) down to an altitude of 10,000 ft. (3,050 m.) at which height their parachutes were deployed automatically by barometric control.

The longest recorded parachute descent was that by Lt. Col. William H. Rankin of the U.S. Marine Corps who, on 26th July 1959, ejected from his LTV F8U Crusader naval jet fighter at 47,000 ft. (14,326 m.). Falling through a violent thunderstorm over North Carolina, his descent took 40 minutes instead of an expected time of 11 minutes as he was repeatedly forced *upwards* by the storm's vertical air currents.

The greatest altitude from which a man has fallen and the longest delayed drop ever achieved by man was that of Capt. Joseph W. Kittinger, D.F.C., aged 32 of the U.S. Air Force, over Tularosa, New Mexico, U.S.A., on 16th August 1960. He stepped out of a balloon gondola at 102,200 ft. (31,150 m.) for a free fall of 84,700 ft. (25,816 m.) lasting 4 minutes 38 seconds, during which he reached a speed of 614 m.p.h. (988 km./hr.) despite a stabilising drogue and experienced a minimum temperature of −94°F (−70°C). His 28-ft. (8·5 m.) parachute deployed at 17,500 ft. (9,334 m.) and he landed after a total time of 13 minutes 45 seconds. The step by the gondola door was inscribed "This is the highest step in the world."*

The longest delayed drop by a woman was 46,250 ft. (14,097 m.) made by the Russian woman parachutist, O. Komissarova, on 21st September 1965.

The world's "speed record" for parachute jumping is held by Michael Davis, 24, and Richard Bingham, 25, who made eighty-one jumps in 8 hours 22 minutes at Columbus, Ohio, U.S.A., on 26th June 1966.

The British record for a delayed drop by a group of parachutists stands at 39,183 ft. (11,942 m.), achieved by five Royal Air Force parachute jumping instructors over Boscombe Down, Wiltshire, on 16th June 1967. They were Sqdn. Ldr. J. Thirtle, Flt. Sgt. A. K. Kidd, and Sgts. L. Hicks, P. P. Keane and K. J. Teesdale. Their jumping altitude was 41,383 ft. (12,615 m.).

The greatest number of parachute jumps made by one man is over 5,000 by Lt. Col. Ivan Savkin of the U.S.S.R., born in 1913, who reached 5,000 on 12th August 1967. It has been calculated that since 1935 Savkin has spent 27 hours in free fall, 587 hours floating and has dropped 7,800 miles (12,550 km.). **The largest number of jumps made by a Briton** is believed to be the 1,601 descents made by Flt. Lt. Charles Agate, A.F.C. (born March 1905), all with packed parachutes, between 1940 and 1946.

The most northerly parachute jump was that by the Canadian, Ray Munro, 47, of Lancaster, Ontario, who on 31st March 1969 descended on to the polar ice cap in 87° 30′ N. His eyes were frozen shut instantly in the temperature of −39°F (−39·5°C).

The greatest landing altitude for a parachute jump was 23,405 ft. (7,134 m.), the height of the summit of Lenina Peak on the borders of Tadzhikistan and Kirgiziya in Kazakhstan, U.S.S.R. It was reported in May 1969 that ten Russians had parachuted on to this mountain peak but that four had been killed.

---

* The speed of 614 m.p.h. (988 km/hr.) reached by Kittinger during his fall represents a Mach No. of 0·93 in the Stratosphere and would have been reached at an altitude of about 60,000 ft. (18,300 m.); thereafter his fall would have been retarded fairly rapidly to less than 200 m.p.h. (322 km./hr.) as he passed through the Tropopause at about 36,000 ft. (11,000 m.). The speed of 614 m.p.h. almost certainly represents the greatest speed ever survived by a human body not contained within a powered vehicle beneath the interface (i.e. within the earth's atmosphere).

CHAPTER 8

ROCKETRY AND SPACEFLIGHT

Cdr. Charles Conrad and LCdr. Richard Gordon, Crew of Gemini XI, after recovery.

One of the oldest known forms of mechanical propulsion, the rocket for hundreds of years possessed one serious drawback, the uncontrollable nature of its combustion; it was essentially a matter of lighting the fuse and standing back. In the seventeenth and eighteenth centuries chemists were able to demonstrate the action of acids as potential propulsive agents, yet still the advance in metallurgy was inadequate to enable these agents to be contained within a suitable combustion chamber. Even today, in the extraordinary development of acceleration associated with space travel, one sees an almost clinical approach to the handling of rocket fuels, so powerful is their interaction.

The first rocket-powered aeroplane in the world was the sailplane *Ente* (Duck) which, powered by two Sander slow-burning rockets and built by the *Rhön-Rossitten Gesellschaft* of Germany, flew just over three-quarters of a mile near the Wasserkuppe mountain in about one minute on 11th June 1928. The rocket-powered glider flown by Fritz von Opel at Rebstock, near Frankfurt, is often stated as being the world's first rocket aeroplane but did not fly until 30th September 1928.

Opel's glider   *The "Duck"*

The first successful liquid-fuel rocket aircraft in the world was the German DFS 194 which, having been conceived by the Sailplane Research Institute in 1938 under Professor Alexander Lippisch, was taken over by Messerschmitt A.G. at Augsburg and flown in 1940 by Heini Dittmar. It was powered by a 600-lb. (272-kg.) thrust Walter rocket.

The world's first operational rocket-powered fighter was the Messerschmitt Me 163 *Komet*, first flown by Heini Dittmar at Peenemünde, Germany, in 1941. On one early flight Dittmar far exceeded the official world's speed record when he recorded a speed of 571 m.p.h.; on 2nd October 1941, after having been towed to 13,000 ft. (4,000 m.), he started the rocket motor and two minutes later recorded a speed of 623 m.p.h. (1,001 km./hr.) in level flight. It was the success of these early trials that led to the Me 163 being developed as an operational rocket-powered interceptor.

Me 163B Komet

The first combat sortie flown by a rocket-powered interceptor is believed to have been flown against Allied bombers over Germany on 16th August 1944. The only Luftwaffe unit equipped with Messerschmitt Me 163B *Komet* aircraft was *Jagdgeschwader 400*, whose first two operational *Staffeln* moved to Brandis, near Leipzig, in July 1944. (See *Military Aviation*.)

The first American rocket-powered military aircraft was the Northrop MX-324, which was first flown under rocket power by Harry Crosby on 5th July 1944. It was powered by an Aerojet XCAL-200 motor fuelled by monoethylaniline. It had originally flown as a glider, being first flown by John Myers on 2nd October 1943.

The first manned supersonic rocket aeroplane in the world was the American Bell XS-1. Its first powered flight was air-launched by a Boeing B-29 Superfortress on 8th December 1946 and was carried out by Chalmers Goodlin. Although this aircraft repeatedly exceeded the world's speed record (then standing at 616 m.p.h.), it never qualified as a record holder as international regulations did not include air-launched flights.

Bell X-1B

The fastest aeroplane in the world is the rocket-powered North American X-15A-2 research aircraft. Three X-15s were built during the late nineteen-fifties and the second of these was extensively modified to extend the design's flight envelope as the X-15A-2. Although these aircraft have been air-launched from modified Boeing B-52 bombers on every occasion, their speed and altitude spectrum is far in excess of any other aeroplane ever built or realistically conceived. The greatest altitude yet reached was 354,200 ft. (67·08 miles) on a flight by J. A. Walker on 22nd August 1963, and the highest speed was 4,534 m.p.h. (Mach 6·72) by W. J. Knight on 3rd October 1967. Power for the X-15 is provided by a Thiokol (Reaction Motors) XLR99-RM-2 single-chamber throttleable rocket rated at 57,000 lb. (25,880 kg.) thrust at 45,000 ft. (13,700 m.). The fuels are liquid oxygen and anhydrous ammonia. A full list of the progressive speeds and altitudes achieved by these aircraft are given in an Appendix.

Bell X-15A-2

ROCKETS AND ROCKET MISSILES

Rockets for research and commerce. During the period 1931–34 a number of Europeans conducted experiments with rockets fired from the ground with the principal object of developing solid- and liquid-fuel motors as reliable powerplants for air and surface vehicles. Some went further to suggest a commercial application. **The first successful firing of a ground-launched rocket in Europe for research measurements** was achieved by the German, Karl Poggensee, on 13th March 1931 who fired a solid-fuelled rocket to a height of 1,500 ft. (450 m.) near Berlin. It carried cameras and an altimeter and was recovered by parachute. Also using solid fuel, Reinhold Tiling, achieved a height of 6,600 ft. (2,010 m.) and a speed of about 700 m.p.h. (1,100 km./hr.) with a rocket launched at Osnabrück in April 1931 and which burned for about eleven seconds. Shortly afterwards he may have achieved an altitude of about 32,000 ft. (9,750 m.) with another solid-fuelled rocket launched from the Frisian Island of Wangerooge. **The first attempt at a ground-to-ground rocket flight in the British Isles** was undertaken by the German, Gerhard Zucker, on 31st July 1934. Attempting to fire a powder rocket from Harris to Scarp, in the Western Isles of Scotland, Zucker failed when the rocket exploded before take-off. He had put forward the idea of sending mail by rocket across the English Channel, but his scheme never materialised.

The initial development work which led to the German V-2 rocket commenced at Kummersdorf, near Berlin, during 1933–34, after Wernher von Braun had been invited to complete a thesis on rocket combustion in 1932. **The first German army rocket,** the A-1, was developed at Kummersdorf in 1933 but this was destroyed in an explosion. Two A-2 rockets were fired from Borkum in December 1934 and achieved altitude of about 6,500 ft. (2,000 m.). In April 1937 the Kummersdorf site was abandoned and von Braun took his team to Peenemünde on the Baltic coast. Here the A-3 and A-5 rockets were developed in preparation for the A-4 (later known as the V-2, or the second retaliatory weapon).

The world's first strategic rocket surface-to-surface missile was the German V-2, developed under the supervision of Wernher von Braun. The first firing of a V-2 took place on 13th June 1942, but the rocket failed, went out of control and crashed. **The first successful launching of a V-2** occurred on 3rd October 1942 when the rocket burned for just under one minute, lifting it to over 50 miles (85 km.) before it returned to earth nearly 120 miles (190 km.) away down range from Peenemünde. The operational V-2 was 46 ft. 2 in. long, weighed 27,000 lb. (12,250 kg.), of which the warhead weighed about one ton, and possessed a range of about 200 miles (320 km.).

The first country in the world to be subjected to an assault by ballistic rocket missiles was France. On the morning of 8th September 1944 the first V.2 rocket was fired against Paris. At about 6.40 p.m. on the same day the **first V.2 to land in Britain** fell in Chiswick, London, killing two people and injuring ten. The last rocket to fall in Britain fell at Orpington, Kent, at 4.54 p.m. on 27th March 1945, killing one person and injuring twenty-three. Between the two dates 1,115 rockets fell on Britain (of which about 500 hit London), killing 2,855 and seriously injuring 6,268. **The worst incident** is believed to have occurred when a V.2 fell upon a Woolworth store at Deptford, killing 160 and injuring 135. **The worst-hit country** was, however, Belgium, more than 1,500 rockets being launched against Antwerp alone.

The first ballistic missile to enter service in the United States was the Firestone SSM-A-17 Corporal, a liquid-fuelled rocket-propelled (unboosted) missile which entered service with the U.S. Army during the early nineteen-fifties and subsequently with the British Army. It had a range of about 75–100 miles (120–160 km.).

The first Swedish surface-to-surface guided missile was the Robot 315 which was conceived in 1946 but on which work did not start until 1949. It was a subsonic weapon, boosted by four solid-fuel rockets and sustained by a pulse-jet. The first test firing of the complete weapon was accomplished from the Swedish destroyer *Halland* in January 1954, and three years later it became operational aboard the *Halland* and *Smaland*.

The first surface-to-surface weapon to enter service with the U.S. Air Force was the Martin TM-61A Matador "flying bomb" which joined Tactical Missile Wings in the U.S.A., Germany and Taiwan during the early nineteen-fifties. By 1957 Martin's Baltimore factory had delivered 1,000 Matadors.

The first British ballistic missile was the Hawker Siddeley Dynamics Blue Streak which, though started in 1955, was cancelled as a military project in 1960. It was, however, adopted as the launch vehicle in the ELDO (European Launcher Development Organisation, or *Conseil Européen pour la Construction de Lanceurs d'Engins Spatiaux* CECLES. Its first test launch was conducted on 5th June 1964, but in 1970 British participation in ELDO was withdrawn.

The first operational sub-surface-to-surface ballistic missile in the world was the American Lockheed Polaris FBMS (Fleet Ballistic Missile System), of which the first test firing was carried out in 1959. Sixteen such missiles were carried aboard each of the special class of nuclear-powered submarines built for the U.S. Navy and Royal Navy.

GROUND-TO-AIR MISSILES

The first British commercial organisation to engage in the development of surface-to-air guided missiles was the Fairey Aviation Company which, in 1944, started work on a missile to counter Japanese suicide aircraft. The outcome of this was a general-purpose test vehicle named Stooge.

The first American surface-to-air anti-aircraft guided missile was the Western Electric SAM-A-7 Nike-Ajax, development of which was started by Bell Telephones Laboratories in 1945. Before the weapon entered service more than 1,500 test rounds were fired and by 1959 10,000 had been delivered. Its place was taken in 1959–60 by the Nike-Hercules.

The first operational pilotless long-range ground-to-air interceptor was the Boeing IM-99 Bomarc. The first prototypes, designated XF-99s, were tested in 1952. Launched vertically, the Bomarc was powered by two Marquardt RJ43-MA ramjets and incorporated a Westinghouse guidance system. Its cruising speed was Mach 2·8 and maximum range varied from 200 miles for the IM-99A to 400 miles for the IM-99B.

The first operational French ground-to-air guided missile was the D.E.F.A. (*Direction des Etude et Fabrications d'Armement*) PARCA (*Projectile Autopropulsé Radioguidé Contre Avions*) liquid-fuel rocket weapon which entered service with the French Army in about 1957. It had an effective ceiling of 82,000 ft. (25,000 m.).

The first British surface-to-air guided missile to enter service was the Bristol/Ferranti Bloodhound (codenamed *Red Duster*), powered by two Bristol Thor ramjets (and four solid fuel booster rockets), which equipped the experimental R.A.F. missile station at North Coates, Lincolnshire, in June 1958. **The first British surface-to-air guided missile ordered for the British Army** was the English Electric Thunderbird (*see left*) (codenamed *Red Shoes*) which entered evaluation service in 1959.

AIR-TO-AIR GUIDED MISSILES

For many years the traditional armament of fighters was the machine gun and, later on, the so-called cannon (20-mm. calibre and over). Generally speaking this type of weapon was effective but demanded that the interceptor close right up to its target, assuming that it possessed the speed, rate of climb and high altitude performance to reach its target before the bomber dropped its bombs. In time bombers, by reason of their greater size, came to carry such equipment as tail warning radar, pressure cabins, and gun-laying radar, and were powered by such powerful engines that on detecting the approach of an interceptor they could fight back or take effective evasive action. As, by the end of the nineteen-fifties, bomber speeds had risen so high that the conventionally-armed interceptor could do little more than perhaps "pick off" an occasional bomber, dependence was placed upon a type of missile that could take over the interception and destruction of the intruder at greater range.

Ever since the early introduction of the first "air-to-air" rockets (of which the first were Le Prieur anti-balloon and anti-airship weapons, used during the First World War), efforts have been made to improve the range and accuracy of the missile, as well as its target-seeking capabilities and destructive power. Today we have the missile which, carried into the approximate area of the incoming bomber, can be released to continue climbing, homing through infra-red detection of the enemy bomber's jet engine exhaust and exploding sufficiently close to ensure the total destruction of its target.

The first successful use of air-to-air rockets against aeroplanes is believed to have taken place on the afternoon of 20th August 1939 when five Polikarpov I–16 Type 10 fighters each fitted with underwing rails for eight 82-mm. RS 82 rockets went into action against Japanese fighters over the Khalkin Gol area of Mongolia. The unit, commanded by Captain Zvonariev, claimed the destruction of two Mitsubishi A5M fighters on this occasion.

The first widespread operational use of air-to-air rockets against aeroplanes was by the *Luftwaffe*, probably by III/JG7 either in late 1944 or early 1945. The R4M unguided rockets, of which twenty-four were carried on racks under the wings of Messerschmitt Me 262A-1b jet fighters, were 55-mm. folding-fin missiles aimed through a standard Revi gunsight. Fired in salvoes their effect was devastating especially against the American formations of B-17 Fortress and B-24 Liberator bombers.

The first air-to-air guided missile to be adopted by the U.S. Air Force was the Hughes GAR-1 Falcon, six of which were carried in wing-tip pods on the Northrop F-89H Scorpion all-weather fighter. They entered operational service in 1956.

The first British air-to-air guided missile to destroy a target aircraft was the Fairey Fireflash (codenamed *Blue Sky*). Work on this started in 1949 but it never achieved operational status; it was however ordered into production and, fitted to Swift Mark 7 fighters, used by an R.A.F. squadron to develop interception tactics using missiles. Fireflash was a "beam-riding" missile which in fact carried no sustainer motor but was boosted by two cordite rockets and then coasted along a coded radar beam.

The first British air-to-air guided missile to achieve operational status was the de Havilland Firestreak (codenamed *Blue Jay*). Incorporating infra-red seeking guidance system the Firestreak equipped squadrons of Gloster Javelin 7s and 8s of the R.A.F. in 1958 and 1959, and also de Havilland Sea Vixens of the Fleet Air Arm.

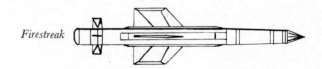

Firestreak

The first-ever firing of a nuclear-tipped air-to-air missile was carried out on 19th July 1956 when a Northrop F-89J Scorpion discharged a Douglas MB-1 Genie at 15,000 ft. (4,500 m.) above Yucca Flat, Nevada, in the U.S.A. This missile incorporated a warhead of about 1·5 kilotons yield and the fighter turned away sharply to avoid the missile's blast. The warhead was detonated after having travelled about three miles horizontally, but U.S.A.F. observers standing directly below the explosion reported no ill-effects from fall-out.

AIR-TO-SURFACE GUIDED MISSILES

Just as recourse to guided weapons was sought to overcome the inherent inaccuracy of the gun in air fighting tactics, so the guided "bomb" was developed to improve on the accuracy available from the conventional bombsight and free-falling bomb. Inevitably the bomb acquired wings and engines, thereby enabling the bomber to "stand off" from its target and avoid the defences.

The first American rocket-powered radar-guided missile was the Bat, a small rocket-powered aircraft developed by Hugh L. Dryden. Carrying a 1,000-lb. warload, the missile was about 20 ft. long and, on being launched from its carrier aircraft, accelerated to about 3,000 m.p.h. (4,830 km./hr.). It possessed a range of about 20 miles (30 km.), and in April 1945 one such missile succeeded in sinking a Japanese destroyer at this range.

The Bat

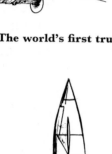

The world's first true stand-off bomb to achieve operational status was the Bell GAM-63 Rascal on which, under the original designation XB-63, work started in 1946. Powered by three liquid-fuel rockets, this bomb was first delivered to the U.S. Strategic Air Command at Pinecastle A.F.B., Florida, on 30th October 1957, and was carried operationally under Boeing DB-47E Stratojet bombers of S.A.C. Its warhead was either atomic or thermonuclear, as required, and its range was about 100 miles (160 km.).

The first operational British stand-off bomb was the Hawker Siddeley Dynamics Blue Steel of which test firings were made from Avro Vulcan and Handley Page Victor bombers in mid-1960. It entered service with Vulcan Mark 2s of No. 617 (Bomber) Squadron in 1962, becoming operational in February the following year. Initially powered by a 16,000-lb. (7,260 kg.) thrust Bristol Siddeley Stentor BSSt.1 liquid-fuel rocket, it had a stand-off range of about 200 miles (320 km.).

Blue Steel

SPACEFLIGHT

From the moment that Dr. Wernher von Braun's first A-4 (V-2) ballistic rocket succeeded in lifting a pay-load into the upper atmosphere above the Baltic during the Second World War, spaceflight by mankind became a realistic possibility. Nevertheless that War left all but two nations, the U.S.A. and the U.S.S.R., so economically exhausted that only they could apply their resources to pursue this hitherto-fictional adventure. Von Braun himself went to America to continue his work while other Germans found themselves working in Russia, yet more than a dozen years were to pass before the first man-made object could be placed in orbit round the Earth. *Only twelve years later, man first placed his foot upon the Moon!*

Dr. Wernher von Braun

Blast-off of Apollo XI, 16th July 1969.

The first man-made satellite, Sputnik I, to enter an orbit round the Earth was rocket-launched from the Soviet Union on 4th October 1957. Weighing 184·3 lb. (83.6 kg.), the satellite was a metal sphere 23 in. (58·42 cm.) in diameter which orbited the Earth in 96 minutes at 142–588 miles' (228·5–945·6 km.) perigee and apogee. Its purpose was to measure and transmit information on the density and temperature of the upper atmosphere as well as to measure the concentration of electrons in the ionosphere. It completed about 1,400 circuits of the Earth before re-entering the lower atmosphere and burning up on 4th January 1958.

The first living creature carried into space from Earth to survive orbital flight was a small Russian bitch, *Laika*, which was carried aloft in the second Russian satellite, launched on 3rd November 1957. The purpose of this satellite was to measure and transmit readings of cosmic radiation and on the behaviour of the creature during space flight. The satellite weighed 1,120·6 lb. (508·3 kg.) and orbited the Earth in 103·7 minutes at 140–1,038 miles' (225–1,670 km.) perigee and apogee. By regulated feeding, supply of oxygen and by other devices, the dog was kept alive for seven days in space, during which time telemetred information on respiration and heart behaviour was transmitted back to Earth. This satellite completed 2,370 orbits of the Earth before it re-entered the denser atmosphere and burned up on 14th April 1958.

The first human to enter space was the Russian cosmonaut, Flt. Maj. Yuriy Alexeyevich Gagarin (aged 27, born Friday, 9th March 1934 near Gzatsk, died in a jet crash on Wednesday, 27th March 1968). Launched at 09.07 a.m., Moscow time on 12th April 1961, from Baikonur, East Kazakhstan, in the 4·5-ton *Vostok 1* spacecraft, Gagarin completed a single orbit of the Earth, making a safe landing in the U.S.S.R. one hour and forty-eight minutes later.

Yuriy Gagarin

The first American to enter space was Alan B. Shepard who was fired in a sub-orbital trajectory lasting fifteen minutes on 5th May 1961 in his spacecraft *Freedom 7*.

Valentina Tereshkova

The first woman to enter space was the Russian cosmonaut Junior Lt. Valentina Vladimirovna Tereshkova, 26, who, in Vostok 6, was placed in Earth orbit on 16th June 1963 and completed forty-eight orbits in 70 hours 50 minutes.

Andrian Nikolayev (left) *and Vitaly Sevastyonov, the crew of the Russian space capsule* Soyuz 9, *whose flight from 1st to 19th June 1970 qualifies as the longest continuous period yet spent in space by any crew.*

The first human to set foot on the Moon was the American astronaut, Mr. Neil Armstrong, 39, late of the U.S. Navy (born on Tuesday, 5th August 1930 at Wapakoneta, Ohio). At 02.56 hours 20 seconds GMT on Monday, 21st July 1969 Armstrong stepped on to the moon's surface from the lunar module *Eagle*, an event watched through television by 600 million viewers 232,000 miles away on Earth. Shortly afterwards his colleague Aldrin joined him on the Moon while Collins remained in moon orbit in the command module *Columbia*. The entire flight to the moon had been a complete success, and the safe return to Earth was terminated with splashdown at 16.49 hours GMT on 24th July 940 miles southwest of Honolulu in the Pacific Ocean.

In his Special State of the Union Message of 25th May 1961, the late President John F. Kennedy addressed to Congress a request for additional funds to accelerate space research:

"I believe that this nation should commit itself to achieving, before this decade is out, of landing a man on the moon and returning him to earth. No single space project in this period will be more exciting, or more impressive, or more important for the long-range exploration of space; and none will be so difficult or expensive to accomplish. Including necessary supporting research, this objective will require an additional $531,000,000 this year and still higher sums in the future. We propose to accelerate development of the appropriate lunar space craft. We propose to develop liquid and solid fuel boosters much larger than any now being developed . . . We propose additional funds for other engine development and for unmanned explorations, which are particularly important for one purpose which this nation will never overlook—the survival of the man who first makes this daring flight. But in a very real sense, it will not be one man going to the moon—it will be an entire nation. For all of us must work to put him there."

After the expenditure of $24,000,000,000 Neil Armstrong brought success to the President's proposal. The following table lists all spaceflights by man to April 1970.

Left: *The three crew members of Apollo XI, l. to r., Neil Armstrong, Lt.-Col. Michael Collins, U.S.A.F., and Col. Edwin E. Aldrin, U.S.A.F.*

Right: *The Moon as seen by the American Astronauts in Apollo XI.*

Left: *The Command Module, "Columbia" as seen from the Lunar Module, "Eagle" above the surface of the Moon.*

Right: *Colonel Aldrin emerges from the Lunar Module, at Tranquillity Base, photographed by Neil Armstrong.*

CHRONOLOGY OF MAN IN SPACE

Date	Country	Spacecraft	Crew Members	Flight Duration Hr. Min.	No. of Orbits	Remarks
12th April 1961	USSR	Vostok 1	Flt. Maj. Yuriy Alexeyevich Gagarin (27).	1 48	1	First man in space. Flight represented progressive world altitude record of 203·2 st. miles (327·0 km.).
5th May 1961	USA	MR-3, Freedom 7	Cdr. Alan B. Shepard (37) U.S. Navy.	15	Sub-orbital	First American in space; launched by Redstone rocket and reached height of 115 miles (185·1 km.).
21st July 1961	USA	MR-4, Liberty Bell 7	Capt. Virgil Ivan Grissom (34) U.S. Air Force.	16	Sub-orbital	Spacecraft sank on splashdown; launched by Redstone rocket and reached height of 118 miles (190·0 km.).
6th–7th Aug. 1961	USSR	Vostok 2	Maj. Gherman Stepanovich Titov (26).	25 18	17	To study effects of prolonged weightlessness; believed to have made final descent by parachute.
20th Feb. 1962	USA	MA-6, Friendship 7	Lt.-Col. John Herschel Glenn (40), U.S. Marine Corps.	4 55	3	First American manned spacecraft to enter earth orbit. Launched by Atlas rocket.
24th May 1962	USA	MA-7, Aurora 7	Lt.-Cdr. Malcolm Scott Carpenter (37), U.S. Navy.	4 56	3	Duplicated Glenn's first flight; reached speed 17,532 m.p.h. (28,215 km./hr.).
11th–15th Aug. 1962	USSR	Vostok 3	Maj. Andrian Grigoryevich Nikolayev (32).	94 22	64	First man-operated television from space; travelled 1,640,000 miles (2,639,320 km.).
12th–15th Aug. 1962	USSR	Vostok 4	Col. Pavel Romanovich Popovich (31).	70 57	48	Among other purposes, flight was to "obtain data on establishing contact" with Vostok 3.
3rd Oct. 1962	USA	MA-8, Sigma 7	Cdr. Walter Marty Schirra (39), U.S. Navy.	9 13	6	Launched by Atlas rocket; splashed down in Pacific north-west of Midway. Near tragedy with spacesuit.
15th–16th May 1963	USA	MA-9, Faith 7	Maj. Leroy Gordon Cooper (36), U.S. Air Force.	34 20	22	Launched by Atlas; manual re-entry after failure of automatic control system. Splashdown in Pacific.
14th–19th June 1963	USSR	Vostok 5	Lt.-Col. Valeriy Fyodorovich Bykovsky (28).	119 66	81	Callsign "Hawk" in two-way communication with Vostok 6 (q.v.).
16th–19th June 1963	USSR	Vostok 6	Junior Lt. Valentina Vladimirovna Tereshkova (26).	70 50	48	First woman in space. Callsign "Seagull". Came within three miles of Vostok 5.
12th–13th Oct. 1964	USSR	Voskhod 1	Col. Vladimir Mihailovich Komarov (37), Commander; Lt. Boris Borisovich Yegorov (37), Space Physician; Konstantin Petrovich Feoktiskov (38), Engineer-scientist.	24 17	16	First three-man crew in space. The purpose of the flight was, inter alia "to examine the capacity for work and interaction during spaceflight of a group of cosmonauts consisting of specialists in different fields of science and technology".
18th–19th Mar. 1965	USSR	Voskhod 2	Lt.-Col. Aleksey Arkhipovich Leonov (30); Col. Pavel Ivanovich Belyayev (39).	26 2	17	Leonov became world's first man to leave his spacecraft and float in outer space (for a total of 20 minutes).
23rd March 1965	USA	GT-3, Gemini 3	Maj. Virgil Ivan Grissom (38); U.S. Air Force; Lt.-Cdr. John Watts Young, U.S. Navy.	4 53	3	First American two-man spaceflight, launched by Titan rocket; splashed down east of the Bahamas in the Atlantic.

Date	Country	Spacecraft	Crew Members	Flight Duration Hr. Min.	No. of Orbits	Remarks
3rd–7th June 1965	USA	GT-4, Gemini 4	Maj. James Alton McDivitt (35), U.S. Air Force; Maj. Edward Higgins White (34), U.S. Air Force.	97 56	62	First American "space walk" by White (which occupied 21 minutes); also longest space-flight by multi-man crew.
21st–29th Aug. 1965	USA	GT-5, Gemini 5	Lt.-Col. Leroy Gordon Cooper (38), U.S. Air Force; Lt.-Cdr. Charles Conrad (35), U.S. Navy.	190 56	120	Longest spaceflight to date. This was Cooper's second earth-orbital flight, thus having spent more time in space than any other man.
4th–18th Dec. 1965	USA	GT-7, Gemini 7	Lt.-Col. Frank Borman (37), U.S. Air Force; Cdr. James Arthur Lovell (37), U.S. Navy.	330 35	206	Longest spaceflight to date; rendezvoused with Gemini 6 which, after one failure to launch on 12th December, was successfully put into orbit on 15th December.
15th–16th Dec. 1965	USA	GT-6, Gemini 6	Cdr. Walter Marty Schirra (43), U.S. Navy; Maj. Thomas P. Stafford (35), U.S. Air Force.	25 51	15	Approached to within ten feet (3 m.) of Gemini 7 and flown for two earth orbits side-by-side. Splashed down in Atlantic south-west of Bermuda.
16th March 1966	USA	GT-8, Gemini 8	Mr. Neil Alden Armstrong (36); Maj. David Randolph Scott (34), U.S. Air Force.	10 42	6½	Intended 3-day flight; first docking between manned and unmanned spacecraft (Agena-7); flight terminated prematurely due to failure of manoeuvring rockets.
3rd–6th June 1966	USA	GT-9, Gemini 9	Lt.-Col. Thomas P. Stafford (36), U.S. Air Force; Lt.-Cdr. Eugene Andrew Cernan (32), U.S. Navy.	72 21	21	Longest space walk to date (129 minutes by Cernan); it had also been intended to attempt a docking with the ATDA (Augmented Target Docking Adapter) but this failed owing to failure of docking mechanism on ATDA.
18th–21st July 1966	USA	GT-10, Gemini 10	Cdr. John Watts Young, U.S. Navy; Maj. Michael Collins, U.S. Air Force.	70 47	43	Space walk by Collins (30 minutes); rendezvous with two Agena craft in different orbits. Flight represented altitude record of 474·6 miles (763·8 km.).
12th–15th Sept. 1966	USA	GT-11, Gemini 11	Cdr. Charles Conrad (36), U.S. Navy; Lt.-Cdr. Richard F. Gordon, U.S. Navy.	71 17	44	Space walk by Gordon (44 minutes); docking tests with Agena. Photographs taken through open hatch of Earth and stars.
11th–15th Nov. 1966	USA	GT-12, Gemini 12	Cdr. James Arthur Lovell (38), U.S. Navy; Maj. Edwin Eugene Aldrin (36), U.S. Air Force.	94 35	59	Record EVA (extra-vehicular activity), 5½ hours by Aldrin; more open-hatch photography; docking with Agena.
22nd–23rd Apr. 1967	USSR	Soyuz 1	Air Engineer Colonel Vladimir Mikhaylovich Komarov (40).	26 45	18	First Russian to make two space flights; was killed, landing parachute tangled. First man killed in space.
11th–22nd Oct. 1968	USA	Apollo VII	Capt. Walter Marty Schirra (45), U.S. Navy; Maj. Donn F. Eisele (38), U.S. Air Force; R. Walter Cunningham (36), civilian scientist.	260 9	163	First American three-man space flight; launched by Saturn 1-B rocket. This was first flight of capsule designed for ultimate seven-day voyage to the moon. Included numerous safety features not previously used.

Date	Country	Spacecraft	Crew Members	Flight Duration Hr. Min.	No. of Orbits	Remarks
26th–30th Oct. 1968	USSR	Soyuz 3	Col. Georgiy T. Beregovoiy (47).	94 51	61	Rendezvous with unmanned Soyuz 2. Col. Beregovoiy was the oldest man yet to travel in space.
21st–27th Dec. 1968	USA	Apollo VIII	Col. Frank Borman (40), U.S. Air Force; Cdr. James Arthur Lovell (40), U.S. Navy; Maj. William A. Anders (35), U.S. Air Force.	147 0	1½ (Earth) 10 (Moon)	The first men in history to break free from the earth's gravitational field and the first to orbit the moon; launched by Saturn-5 rocket. Splash down in mid-Pacific. Christmas radio messages from astronauts while in moon orbit. This flight set up an altitude record of 234,772 miles (377,828 km.).
14th–17th Jan. 1969	USSR	Soyuz 4	Lt.-Col. Vladimir Shatalov (41); Alexei Yeliseyev (34), civilian engineer; Lt.-Col. Yevgeny Khrunov (35);	71 14	48	Successful docking manoeuvre in Earth-orbit with Soyuz 5. Orbits of both spacecraft altered under manual control. This flight provided the first joining of two manned spacecraft in orbit and the first transfer of crew (Yeliseyev and Khrunov transferring to and landing in Soyuz 5).
15th–18th Jan. 1969	USSR	Soyuz 5	Lt.-Col. Col. Boris Volynov (34).	72 46	49	
3rd–13th March 1969	USA	Apollo IX	Col. James Alton McDivitt (39), U.S. Air Force; Col. David Randolph Scott (36), U.S. Air Force; Mr. Russell Louis Schweikart (33), U.S. Air Force Reserve.	241 1	151	First trial of lunar module (manned) in space; transfer of crew through interior connection. Also the first flight of all three components (Command, Service and Lunar). Splash-down in Atlantic.
18th–26th May 1969	USA	Apollo X	Col. Thomas P. Stafford (38), U.S. Air Force; Cdr. John Watts Young (38), U.S. Navy; Cdr. Eugene Andrew Cernan (35), U.S. Navy.	192 3	1½ (Earth) 31 (Moon)	Lunar module ("Snoopy") flown by Stafford and Cernan to within 9·4 miles (15·13 km.) of moon, while Young remained with Command and Service Module ("Charlie Brown"). Flight set up new altitude record of 246,960 miles (397,443 km.).
16th–24th July 1969	USA	Apollo XI	Mr. Neil Alden Armstrong (38), Flight Commander; Col. Edwin Eugene Aldrin, Jr., (39), U.S. Air Force, Lunar Module Pilot; Lt.-Col. Michael Collins, U.S. Air Force, Command Module Pilot.	195 18	1½ (Earth) 30 (Moon)	First moon landing by man (Armstrong, first, EVA, 2 hr. 14 min.; Aldrin, second, EVA, 1 hr. 33 min.). Lunar Module ("Eagle") landed in south-west corner of Sea of Tranquillity at 0256 hr., GMT, on 21st July 1969. Col. Collins remained in Command Module ("Columbia"). 48 lb. Moon rock returned.
11th–16th Oct. 1969	USSR	Soyuz 6	Lt.-Col. Giorgiy Shonin (34); Valery N. Kubasov (34), engineer.	118 42	75	Rendezvous and formation trials and experiments carrying out simulated assembly techniques for manufacture of space stations (including arc welding, electron beam welding and electrode welding in de-pressurised compartment). Total of 31 manoeuvring operations carried out during the flight.
12th–17th Oct. 1969	USSR	Soyuz 7	Lt.-Col. Anatoly V. Filipchenko (41); Lt.-Col. Viktor V. Gorbatko (35); Vladislav N. Volkov (34).	118 41	75	
13th–18th Oct. 1969	USSR	Soyuz 8	Col. Vladimir A. Shatalov (41); Alexei N. Yeliseyev (35), engineer.	118 41	75	

Date	Country	Spacecraft	Crew Members	Flight Duration Hr. Min.	No. of Orbits	Remarks
14th–24th Nov. 1969	USA	Apollo XII	Cdr. Charles Conrad (39), U.S. Navy; Cdr. Richard F. Gordon (40), U.S. Navy; Cdr. Alan L. Bean (37), U.S. Navy.	244 36	1½ (Earth) 45 (Moon)	Second moon landing by man (Conrad, total EVA, 7 hr. 53 min.; Bean, total EVA, 6 hr. 50 min.) Lunar Module ("Intrepid") landed on Ocean of Storms while Command Module ("Yankee Clipper") stayed in moon orbit. 73 lb. Moon soil returned.
11th–17th Apr. 1970	USA	Apollo XIII	Capt. James Arthur Lovell (41), U.S. Navy; Mr. Fred W. Haise; Mr. John L. Swigert.	142 54	1½	Projected moon landing abandoned after near-catastrophic failure of Service Module en route, 205,000 miles (329,915 km.) from Earth. Crew occupied Lunar Module for remainder of flight, but returned to Command Module for splashdown.

APPENDIX A

ADDENDA

The first woman to lose her life in an aerial disaster was Madame Blanchard, widow of the pioneer French aeronaut Jean-Pierre Blanchard (who had died after a heart attack, suffered while ballooning, on 7th March 1809). Madame Blanchard was killed when her hydrogen balloon was ignited during a firework display which she was giving at the Tivoli Gardens, Paris, on 7th July 1819.

The man whose aircraft have probably contributed most to British sporting flying was the late Captain Sir Geoffrey de Havilland, O.M., C.B.E., A.F.C. His first two aircraft, designed while working at the Army Aircraft Factory at Farnborough, were failures, but his third design—the B.E. Tractor Biplane—may be said to have been the forerunner of the world-famous Moth which was introduced during the nineteen-twenties. This first B.E. attended the British Military Aeroplane Trials of 1912 but, although it did not participate, far exceeded the performance of the official entries, and after further improvements carried out during the following six months was timed at 91·4 m.p.h. (147·1 km./hr.) over a measured course. Geoffrey de Havilland joined the Aircraft Manufacturing Co., Ltd., as Chief Designer in 1914 and after the 1914–18 War went on to lead the company which carried his name, and which produced successive generations of sporting and record-breaking light aircraft of the Moth family. He was born in 1882 and died on 21st May 1965.

The first occasion on which four people lost their lives in an air accident was on 25th September 1909 when the French dirigible *Republique* lost a propeller which pierced the gasbag; the craft fell from 400 ft. (120 m.) at Moulins, the crew of four being killed.

The first occasion on which five people lost their lives in an air accident was on 13th July 1910 when a German non-rigid dirigible, of the Erbsloch type, suffered an explosion of the gasbag and fell from high altitude near Opladen, Germany. The crew of five, including Oscar Erbsloch, were killed.

The first gyroscopic automatic stabiliser was successfully demonstrated by the Americans, Lawrence B. Sperry and Lt. Patrick Nelson Lynch Bellinger, in a Curtiss F flying boat in August 1913. The aircraft was longitudinally and laterally stabilised.

The first composite (i.e. "pickaback") aeroplane experiments were conducted in May 1916 in Britain using a Bristol Scout "C" mounted atop a Felixstowe Baby three-engined flying boat with a view to developing a means of intercepting Zeppelin airship raiders. On 17th May the pair of aircraft took off from Felixstowe, Suffolk, the lower component captained by John Cyril Porte and the Bristol occupied by Flt. Lt. M. J. Day, R.N.A.S. When flying at 1,000 ft. (300 m.) over Harwich, Day released the Bristol and climbed away, landing later at Martlesham Heath. Although successful, the experiment was not repeated.

The first Bolivian military pilots were Capitáns José Alarcón and Renato Parejas, and Sub-Lieutenant Horacio Vasquez who were sent to the Argentine to learn their flying at El Palomar in 1916, attending the fifth Flying Course. Capitán Alarcón was however killed on 23rd January 1917 while flying a Farman.

The first flight across Australia was made during the period 16th November-12th December 1919 by a B.E.2e flown by Capt. H. N. Wrigley, D.F.C., accompanied by Lt. A. W. Murphy, D.F.C., from Melbourne to Darwin to meet Ross and Keith Smith. They covered the 2,500 miles (4,000 km.) in 46 hours' flying time.

The first Mexican pilot to be awarded a Mexican pilot's certificate was Samuel C. Rojas who gained Mexican Certificate No. 1 in 1918.

The first variable-incidence variable-geometry aeroplane in the world was the Swedish Pålson Type 1 single-seat sporting aircraft of 1918–19. It is said that the aircraft featured a system of cranks to alter the position of the biplane's top wing as well as its angle of incidence as a means of achieving optimum lift/drag in cruising flight. It is not known what success attended flight trials (if any).

The Australian Air Force was established by Proclamation on 31st March 1921, pending passage of the Air Defence Act. H.M. King George V approved the designation as Royal Australian Air Force on 13th August 1921.

The first commercial operations by the German state airline, Deutsche Lufthansa AG, commenced with passenger flights in Europe on 6th April 1926.

The first occasion on which an heir to the British throne crossed the English Channel by air was on 4th May 1926 when H.R.H. The Prince of Wales flew in an Imperial Airways Handley Page W.10 piloted by Capt. O. P. Jones from Le Bourget, Paris, to London.

The first film (movie picture) shown in an aeroplane in flight was demonstrated in a Ford aircraft of Transcontinental Air Transport Inc., flying at 5,000 ft. (1,600 m.) over land in America on 8th October 1929. The entire film projector and equipment weighed less than 34 lb. (16 kg.).

The first electrical-mechanical flight simulator was the Link Trainer, which represented a replica of an aeroplane with full controls and instruments, but which did not leave the ground; instead it was "attached" to a mechanical crab which traced a path over a large-scale map in such a way as to represent heading, speed and time of the replica aircraft "flown" by its occupant. It was invented by Edward Albert Link who sold his first model in 1929; it was adopted by the U.S. Navy in 1931, and by the U.S. Army in 1934. By 1939 there was scarcely an air force in the world that was not using Link Trainers, and there can be no doubt that they were the forerunners of today's complex flight simulators.

The first commercial British aeroplane to be fitted with a retractable undercarriage was the Airspeed Courier which first flew early in 1933. The second was the General Aircraft Monospar ST-6 which first flew several weeks later.

The first commercial use of composite aeroplanes in the world occurred during 21st–22nd July 1938 when the Short S.21 *Maia* flying boat and the Short S.20 *Mercury* seaplane flew the Atlantic from Foynes, Ireland, the upper component seaplane separating and flying non-stop to Montreal, Canada, with a load of mail and newspapers. It covered 2,930 miles (4,715 km.) in 20 hr. 20 min., at an average speed of 140 m.p.h. (225 km./hr.). The pilot of *Mercury* was Capt. D. C. T. Bennett (later Air Vice-Marshal, C.B., C.B.E., D.S.O.). Numerous composite flights and separations were carried out and the pair of aircraft continued to operate on the Southampton to Alexandria air route until the outbreak of the Second World War. After brief service with a Dutch seaplane squadron (No. 320) serving with the R.A.F., *Mercury* was broken up in 1941; *Maia* was destroyed by a German bomb on the night of 11th May 1941 while moored in Poole Harbour, Dorset.

The first operational use of stand-off bombs was by twelve Dornier Do 217s of II *Gruppe, Kampfgeschwader 100*, commanded by Hauptmann Molinus, on 25th August 1943 in an attack against seven anti-U-Boat ships of the Royal Navy in the vicinity of Cape Finisterre, Spain. The German weapons were the Henschel Hs 293 rocket-boosted glider bomb. On this occasion the bombs were released about six miles from the ships but no hits were scored, only H.M.S. *Bideford* being damaged by a near miss. **The first ship to be sunk in action by the Henschel Hs 293 stand-off bomb** was H.M.S. *Egret*, a corvette of the Royal Navy, which was hit in the same area as the above action two days later, on 27th August 1943. A Canadian destroyer, the *Athabaskan*, and the corvette *Rother* were damaged.

The first documented sighting of an Unidentified Flying Object (UFO or "flying saucer") by a qualified flying person was reported by an American private pilot, Kenneth Arnold, who in June 1947 reported seeing from his cockpit nine "saucer-shaped things" flying among the peaks in the Mount Rainier area.

The first woman in the world to fly faster than the speed of sound was Miss Jacqueline Cochrane, an American cosmetics tycoon, who, flying a North American F-86 Sabre exceeded the speed of sound on 18th May 1953, and on the same day established a world's speed record for women of 652 m.p.h. (1,048 km./hr.).

The world's first aircraft to be fitted with a hinged tail for rear loading, the Canadair CL-44D-4, was flown for the first time on 16th November 1960. Powered by four Rolls-Royce Tyne 515/10 two-shaft two-spool turboprops, each rated at 5,730 e.h.p., it had a range of 5,205 miles (8,381 km.) with a maximum payload of 66,480 lb. (30,191 kg.).

Aviation's richest man. The progress of aviation has been constantly sponsored and nurtured by some of the wealthiest men (and women) of the age. Not surprisingly, aviation has also made many men very wealthy. Without question, the richest man associated with aviation is Howard Hughes, who shares with Paul Getty the distinction of being the richest man in the world. Hughes' assets were recently estimated, conservatively, at $985,500,000 (£369,000,000). Three years ago he sold his shares in Trans World Airlines, realising the sum of $546,549,771 (£227,729,070), which, incidentally stands as a world record for the largest cash sum to be paid to an individual by cheque. His own two major companies,

Hughes Aircraft and Hughes Tool contribute share holdings conservatively estimated in 1968 to $387,500,000 (£161,458,000). Thirteen years older than Hughes, Jean Paul Getty, 78, is also an American citizen but is resident in Surrey, England. With visible assets estimated at $957,404,289 (£398,918,500), Getty's fortune lies principally in oil, although the Sarah C. Getty Trust owns stock valued at $2,832,812 (£1,180,330) in the Spartan Aircraft Company.

The first light plane competition to be organised in Great Britain was that held that at Lympne, Kent, in September 1924, organised by the Royal Aero Club and for which prizes worth £3,000 were offered by the Air Ministry. The lightest aircraft to be entered in this competition was the Hawker Cygnet two-seater whose tare weight was 373lb. (169·3 kg.). In the competition of the following year the Cranwell C.L.A. 3 single-seater had a tare weight of 325 lb. (147·5 kg.)

The lightest aeroplane ever flown was the Beecraft Wee Bee, built in 1948 by four Convair employees at a cost of $200 (then £71) at San Diego, California. With a wing span of 15 ft. (4·57 m.) its tare weight was 170 lb. (77·2 kg.); loaded it weighed 360 lb. (163·4 kg.)

The lightest aeroplane built and flown in Great Britain is the Ward Gnome, built by Michael Ward of North Scarle, Lincolnshire, and flown in April 1969. Empty it weighs 210 lb. (95·3 kg.), loaded 350 lb. (159 kg.). Its ceiling, officially imposed at 10 ft. (3·05 m.) because of the use of materials not covered by air regulations, is probably the **lowest ceiling of any aeroplane!**

The smallest piloted aeroplane ever flown is the Stits Skybaby biplane, designed, built and flown by Ray Stits at Riverside, California, in 1952. It had a wing span of 7 ft. 2 in. (2·19 m.) and a length of 9 ft. 10 in. (3·02 m.). Powered by an 85 h.p. Continental C85 engine, it weighed 452 lb. (205·2 kg.) empty and had a top speed of 185 m.p.h. (298 km./hr.)

The first ascent of a hydrogen-filled balloon (unmanned) was made on 25th August 1783 in Paris when Jacques Alexandre César Charles (1746–1823) launched a 12 ft. diameter balloon. Capable of lifting about 20 lb. (9 kg.), the balloon was filled with hydrogen generated by the action of 498 lb. (225 kg.) of sulphuric acid upon 1,000 lb. (454 kg.) of iron scrap. The balloon was tethered and on the following day was permitted to rise to 100 ft. (30 m.). **The first free ascent of the balloon** (christened the *Globe*) was made from the Champ de Mars, Paris, on 27th August 1783, when it rose to about 3,000 ft. (1,000 m.), drifted for 45 min. and came to earth at Gonesse, 15 miles (25 km.) from Paris, where it was promptly attacked by a frenzied mob of panic-stricken peasants.

The first living occupants of a balloon to ascend were a sheep, a duck and a cock which rode aloft under a 41 ft. (13 m.) diameter Montgolfier hot-air balloon at the Court of Versailles on 19th September 1783 before King Louis XVI, Marie Antionette and their Court. The balloon achieved an altitude of 1,700 ft. (550 m.) before descending in the forest of Vaucresson 8 min. later, having travelled about two miles. The occupants were scarcely affected by their flight or by their landing.

The South African Air Force was formed on 9th August 1920.

The New Zealand Air Force was formed on 14th June 1923. It was re-organised in 1934 and re-styled the Royal New Zealand Air Force on 1st April 1937.

The first practical flights by an aeroplane in England were those carried out by Samuel Cody, then still an American citizen, during February 1909. He achieved one flight of about 400 yards (370 m.) at about 12 ft. (4 m.) in the British Army Aeroplane No. 1, an agglomeration which had been assembled under the direction of Maj. Capper of the Balloon Section, Royal Engineers, at Farnborough, Hants.

The first solo flight round the world was achieved by Wiley Post between 15th and 22nd July 1933 when he flew a Lockheed monoplane from New York for a distance of 15,596 miles (25,099 km.) in 7 days 18 hours 49 minutes. His route was *via* Berlin, Moscow, Irkutsk and Alaska.

The first fighter to enter service with the Royal Air Force capable of a maximum level speed of more than 200 m.p.h. (322 km./hr.) was the Hawker Fury I biplane. Powered by a 525-h.p. Rolls-Royce Kestrel II liquid-cooled engine and armed with two synchronised Vickers machine guns, the Fury had a top speed of 207 m.p.h. at 14,000 ft. (4,270 m.). Designed by the late Sir Sydney Camm, it entered service in May 1931.

The first Schneider Trophy contest for seaplanes was won by the Frenchman Prevost on 15th April 1913. This race was staged at Monaco and the winner was flying a Deperdussin seaplane powered by a 160 h.p. Gnôme engine. The official result is misleading and was recorded as 45·75 m.p.h. (73·63 km./hr.), or 3 hrs. 48 min. 22 sec. to fly the 174 miles (280 km.) circuit; in fact Prevost completed the course in 2 hr. 50 min. 47 sec., an average speed of approximately 61 m.p.h. (98 km./hr.), but the judges decided that the pilot had not crossed the finishing line correctly and instructed him to take off again and repeat the last lap, a process which occupied almost an hour!

The smallest aeroplane in the world is claimed to have been the Stits Sky Baby, built by Ray Stits of the U.S.A. in 1952. With a span of 7 ft. 2 in. (2·19 m.) and a length of 9 ft. 10 in. (3·01 m.), it was powered by a Continental C85 engine which bestowed a reported top speed of 185 m.p.h. (298 km./hr.).

The first flight by a powered and navigable lighter-than-air craft (i.e. a dirigible) was made on 24th September 1852 by Henri Giffard from Paris to Trappes—about 17 miles (27 km.). The craft, coal-gas filled, was powered by a steam engine.

The first rocket-propelled aeroplane to fly with a degree of success was an aircraft designed and flown by the German, Fritz von Opel. He flew his aeroplane on 30th September 1929 for a distance of about 2,000 yards (1,900 m.), attaining a speed of about 85 m.p.h. (136 km./hr.), but crashed on landing.

The first man to lose his life in an aerial disaster was the Frenchman, François Pilâtre de Rozier, who, on 15th June 1785 while attempting to cross the English Channel, died when his "combination" balloon caught fire and fell in flames near Boulogne. This was a double tragedy, for his companion, Jules Romain, also died in the accident.

The first man killed in an aeroplane accident was the American, Lt. Thomas Etholen Selfridge, U.S. Army, killed at Fort Myer when flying as passenger with Mr. Orville Wright in a Wright biplane on 17th September 1908. The aircraft crashed and Wright was badly injured.

APPENDIX B

PROGRESSIVE WORLD ABSOLUTE SPEEDS ACHIEVED BY MAN IN THE ATMOSPHERE

Those entries marked with an asterisk represent accurately-measured speeds not ratified as World records by the *Fédération Aéronautique Internationale*. These speeds were often achieved during one run of several, from which the mean was submitted for ratification as a record; they are included to indicate the progressive highest speed achieved by man.

Speed m.p.h.	Speed km./hr.	Pilot	Nationality	Aircraft	Location of achievement	Date
(25·65)*	41·27	Alberto Santos-Dumont	France	Santos-Dumont 14bis	Bagatelle, France	12th Nov. 1906
(32·73)*	52·66	Henry Farman	France	Voisin biplane	Issy-les-Moulineaux, France	26th Oct. 1907
34·04	54·77	Paul Tissandier	France	Wright Biplane	Pau, France	20th May 1909
43·35	69·75	Glenn Curtiss	U.S.A.	Herring-Curtiss biplane	Rheims, France	23rd Aug. 1909
46·18	74·30	Louis Blériot	France	Blériot monoplane	Rheims, France	24th Aug. 1909
47·85	76·99	Louis Blériot	France	Blériot monoplane	Rheims, France	28th Aug. 1909
48·21	77·57	Hubert Latham	France	Antoinette monoplane	Nice, France	23rd Apr. 1910
66·19	106·50	Léon Morane	France	Blériot monoplane	Rheims, France	10th July 1910
68·20	109·73	Alfred Leblanc	France	Blériot monoplane	Rheims, France	10th July 1910
69·48	111·79	Alfred Leblanc	France	Blériot monoplane	Belmont Park, Long Island, U.S.A.	29th Oct. 1910
74·42	119·74	Edouard Nieuport	France	Nieuport biplane		12th Apr. 1911
77·68	124·99	Alfred Leblanc	France	Blériot monoplane		11th May 1911
80·82	130·04	Edouard Nieuport	France	Nieuport biplane	Châlons, France	12th June 1911
82·73	133·11	Edouard Nieuport	France	Nieuport biplane	Châlons, France	16th June 1911
90·20	145·13	Jules Védrines	France	Deperdussin monoplane	Pau, France	21st June 1911
100·23	161·27	Jules Védrines	France	Deperdussin monoplane	Pau, France	13th Jan. 1912
100·95	162·53	Jules Védrines	France	Deperdussin monoplane	Pau, France	22nd Feb. 1912
103·66	166·79	Jules Védrines	France	Deperdussin monoplane	Pau, France	29th Feb. 1912
104·34	167·88	Jules Védrines	France	Deperdussin monoplane	Pau, France	1st Mar. 1912
106·12	170·75	Jules Védrines	France	Deperdussin monoplane	Pau, France	2nd Mar. 1912
108·18	174·06	Jules Védrines	France	Deperdussin monoplane	Chicago, Illinois, U.S.A.	13th July 1912
111·74	179·79	Maurice Prévost	France	Deperdussin monoplane		9th Sept. 1912
119·25	191·87	Maurice Prévost	France	Deperdussin monoplane	Rheims, France	17th June 1913
126·67	203·81	Maurice Prévost	France	Deperdussin monoplane	Rheims, France	27th Sept. 1913

First World War: No reliable international records

Speed m.p.h.	Speed km./hr.	Pilot	Nationality	Aircraft	Location of achievement	Date
171·05	275·22	Sadi Lecointe	France	Nieuport-Delage 29		7th Feb. 1920
176·15	283·43	Jean Casale	France	Blériot monoplane		28th Feb. 1920
181·87	292·63	Baron de Romanet	France	Spad biplane		9th Oct. 1920
184·36	296·64	Sadi Lecointe	France	Nieuport-Delage 29		10th Oct. 1920
187·99	302·48	Sadi Lecointe	France	Nieuport-Delage 29		20th Oct. 1920
192·02	308·96	Baron de Romanet	France	Spad biplane		4th Nov. 1920
194·53	313·00	Sadi Lecointe	France	Nieuport-Delage 29		12th Dec. 1920
(210·64)*	339·00	Sadi Lecointe	France	Nieuport-Delage 29		25th Dec. 1921
205·24	330·23	Sadi Lecointe	France	Nieuport-Delage 29	Villesauvage, France	26th Sept. 1922
211·91	341·00	Sadi Lecointe	France	Nieuport-Delage 29	Villesauvage, France	21st Sept. 1922
222·98	358·77	Brig. Gen. William A. Mitchell	U.S.A.	Curtiss HS D-12	Detroit, Michigan	13th Oct. 1922
(243·94)*	392·64	Brig. Gen. William A. Mitchell	U.S.A.	Curtiss HS D-12	Detroit, Michigan	18th Oct. 1922

Speed		Pilot	Nationality	Aircraft	Location of achievement	Date
m.p.h.	*km./hr.*					
233·03	374·95	Sadi Lecointe	France	Nieuport-Delage 29		15th Feb. 1923
236·59	380·67	Lt. R. L. Maughan	U.S.A.	Curtiss R-6	Mitchell Field, N.Y., U.S.A.	29th Mar. 1923
259·16	411·04	Lt. A. Brown	U.S.A.	Curtiss HS D-12	Mitchell Field, N.Y., U.S.A.	2nd Nov. 1923
266·60	429·96	Lt. Alford J. Williams	U.S.A.	Curtiss R-2 C-1	Mitchell Field, N.Y., U.S.A.	4th Nov. 1923
(270·50*)	435·30	Lt. Alford J. Williams	U.S.A.	Curtiss R-2 C-1	Mitchell Field, N.Y., U.S.A.	4th Nov. 1923
(274·20*)	441·30	Lt. A. Brown	U.S.A.	Curtiss HS D-12	Mitchell Field, N.Y., U.S.A.	4th Nov. 1923
278·47	448·15	Adj. Chef A. Bonnet	France	Ferbois V-2	Istres, France	11th Dec. 1924
(284·21*)	457·39	Fg. Off. Sidney Webster, AFC	Great Britain	Supermarine S-5	Venice, Italy	26th Sept 1927
297·83	479·21	Maj. Mario de Bernardi	Italy	Macchi M-52	Venice, Italy	4th Nov. 1927
(313·59*)	504·67	Maj. Mario de Bernardi	Italy	Macchi M-52	Venice, Italy	6th Nov. 1927
318·64	512·69	Maj. Mario de Bernardi	Italy	Macchi M-52*bis*	Venice, Italy	30th Mar. 1928
(348·60*)	561·00	Maj. Mario de Bernardi	Italy	Macchi M-52*bis*	Venice, Italy	30th Mar. 1928
(>370·00*)	>595·40	Fg. Off. R. D. Waghorn, AFC	Great Britain	Supermarine S.6	Solent, England	7th Sept. 1929
*		Fg. Off. R. L. R. Atcherley	Great Britain	Supermarine S.6	Solent, England	12th Sept. 1929
357·75	575·62	Sqdn. Ldr. A. H. Orlebar	Great Britain	Supermarine S.6	Ryde, Isle of Wight, England	12th Sept. 1929
(388·00*)	624·00	Flt. Lt. G. H. Stainforth, AFC	Great Britain	Supermarine S.6B	Ryde, Isle of Wight, England	13th Sept. 1931
407·02	654·90	Flt. Lt. G. H. Stainforth, AFC	Great Britain	Supermarine S.6B	Ryde, Isle of Wight, England	29th Sept. 1931
(415·20*)	668·20	Flt. Lt. G. H. Stainforth, AFC	Great Britain	Supermarine S.6B	Ryde, Isle of Wight, England	29th Sept. 1931
423·85	681·97	W/O Francesco Agello	Italy	Macchi-Castoldi 72	Lago di Garda, Italy	10th Apr. 1934
(430·32*)	692·53	W/O Francesco Agello	Italy	Macchi-Castoldi 72	Lago di Garda, Italy	10th Apr. 1934
(>434·96*)	>699·85	Col. Bernascori	Italy	Macchi-Castoldi 72	Desenzano, Italy	18th Apr. 1934
440·69	709·07	Lt. Francesco Agello	Italy	Macchi-Castoldi 72	Lago di Garda, Italy	23rd Oct. 1934
(441·22*)	710·07	Lt. Francesco Agello	Italy	Macchi-Castoldi 72	Lago di Garda, Italy	23rd Oct. 1934
463·92	746·45	Flugkapitän Hans Dieterle	Germany	Heinkel He 100V-8	Oranienburg, Germany	30th Mar. 1939
469·22	754·97	Flugkapitän Fritz Wendel	Germany	Messerschmitt Bf 109R	Augsburg, Germany	26th Apr. 1939
(486·00*)	781·97	Flugkapitän Fritz Wendel	Germany	Messerschmitt Bf 109R	Augsburg, Germany	29th Apr. 1939
Second World War: No reliable international records						
(603·00*)	970·23	Sqdn. Ldr. P. Stanbury, DFC	Great Britain	Gloster Meteor IV	Moreton Valence, England	19th Oct. 1945
606·38	975·67	Gp. Capt. H. J. Wilson, AFC	Great Britain	Gloster Meteor IV	Herne Bay, Kent, England	7th Nov. 1945
(611·20*)	983·42	Gp. Capt. H. J. Wilson, AFC	Great Britain	Gloster Meteor IV	Herne Bay, Kent, England	7th Nov. 1945
615·78	990·79	Gp. Capt. E. M. Donaldson, DSO, AFC	Great Britain	Gloster Meteor IV	Rustington, Sussex, England	7th Sept. 1946
(623·45*)	1003·31	Gp. Capt. E. M. Donaldson, DSO, AFC	Great Britain	Gloster Meteor IV	Rustington, Sussex, England	7th Sept. 1946
623·74	1003·60	Col. Albert Boyd	U.S.A.	Lockheed P-80R Shooting Star	Muroc, California, U.S.A.	19th June 1947
640·74	1030·95	Cdr. Turner F. Caldwell, USN	U.S.A.	Douglas D-558 Skystreak	Muroc, California, U.S.A.	20th Aug. 1947
650·92	1047·33	Maj. Marion E. Carl, USMC	U.S.A.	Douglas D-558 Skystreak	Muroc, California, U.S.A.	25th Aug. 1947
670·98	1079·61	Maj. Richard L. Johnson, USAF	U.S.A.	North American F-86A Sabre	Muroc, California, U.S.A.	15th Sept. 1948
698·50	1123·89	Capt. J. Slade Nash, USAF	U.S.A.	North American F-86D Sabre	Salton Sea, California, U.S.A.	19th Nov. 1952

Speed		Pilot	Nationality	Aircraft	Location of achievement	Date
m.p.h.	*km./hr.*					
(699·94)*	1126·20	Capt. J. Slade Nash, USAF	U.S.A.	North American F-86D Sabre	Salton Sea, California, U.S.A.	19th Nov. 1952
715·75	1151·64	Lt. Col. William F. Barnes, USAF	U.S.A.	North American F-86D Sabre	Salton Sea, California, U.S.A.	16th July 1953
727·63	1170·76	Sqdn. Ldr. Neville Duke, DSO, OBE, DFC, AFC	Great Britain	Hawker Hunter 3	Littlehampton, Sussex, England	7th Sept. 1953
(741·66)*	1193·33	Sqdn. Ldr. Neville Duke, DSO, OBE, DFC, AFC	Great Britain	Hawker Hunter 3	Littlehampton, Sussex, England	31st Aug. 1953
735·70	1183·74	Lt. Cdr. Michael Lithgow, OBE	Great Britain	Supermarine Swift 4	Libya, Africa	25th Sept. 1953
752·94	1211·48	Lt. Cdr. James B. Verdin, USN	U.S.A.	Douglas F4D-1 Skyray	Salton Sea, California, U.S.A.	3rd Oct. 1953
755·15	1215·04	Lt. Col. Frank K. Everest, USAF	U.S.A.	North American YF-100A Super Sabre	Salton Sea, California, U.S.A.	29th Oct. 1953
822·27	1323·03	Col. H. A. Hanes, USAF	U.S.A.	North American F-100C Super Sabre	Edwards AFB, California, U.S.A.	20th Aug. 1955
1132·00	1821·39	L. Peter Twiss, OBE, DSC	Great Britain	Fairey Delta 2	Chichester, Sussex, England	10th Mar. 1956
1207·60	1943·03	Maj. Adrian Drew, USAF	U.S.A.	McDonnell F-101A Voodoo		12th Dec. 1957
1404·09	2259·18	Capt. Walter W. Irvin, USAF	U.S.A.	Lockheed F-104A Starfighter	Southern California, U.S.A.	16th May 1958
1483·83	2387·48	Col. Georgiy Mosolov	U.S.S.R.	Sukhoi Type E-66	Sidorovo, Tyumenskaya, U.S.S.R.	31st Oct. 1959
1525·95	2455·74	Maj. Joseph W. Rogers, USAF	U.S.A.	Convair F-106A Delta Dart	Edwards AFB, California, U.S.A.	15th Dec. 1959
1606·51	2585·43	Lt. Col. Robert B. Robinson	U.S.A.	McDonnell F4H-1F Phantom	Edwards AFB, California, U.S.A.	22nd Nov. 1961
1665·89	2681·00	Col. Georgiy Mosolov	U.S.S.R.	Sukhoi Type E-166	Sidorovo, Tyumenskaya, U.S.S.R.	7th July 1962
2070·10	3331·51	Col. Robert L. Stephens	U.S.A.	Lockheed YF-12A	Edwards AFB, California, U.S.A.	1st May 1965

The record speed achieved by Col. Stephens on 1st May 1965 has survived to date as the highest ratified speed record attained by an aeroplane which took off under its own power from the Earth's surface. Between 1960 and 1967 however the U.S. Air Force conducted a substantial programme of manned flight trials with the North American X-15 and X-15A-2. Powered by a liquid oxygen and ammonia rocket engine, the X-15 was carried to altitude by a Boeing B-52 before embarking upon ultra-high speed and altitude flights, a summary of which is listed below:

Progressive Maximum speeds achieved by the X-15:

m.p.h.	km./hr.	Mach No.	Pilot	Date
2111	3397	3·19	J. A. Walker	12th May 1960
2196	3534	3·31	J. A. Walker	4th Aug. 1960
2275	3613	3·50	R. M. White	7th Feb. 1961
2905	4675	4·43	R. M. White	7th Mar. 1961
3074	4947	4·62	R. M. White	21st Apr. 1961
3300	5311	4·90	J. A. Walker	25th May 1961
3603	5798	5·27	R. M. White	23rd June 1961
3614	5816	5·25	J. A. Walker	12th Sept. 1961
3620	5826	5·25	F. S. Petersen	28th Sept. 1961
3647	5869	5·21	R. M. White	11th Oct. 1961
3900	6276	5·74	J. A. Walker	17th Oct. 1961
4093	6587	6·04	R. M. White	9th Nov. 1961
4104	6605	5·92	J. A. Walker	27th June 1962 (X-15A-2)
4250	6840	6·33	W. J. Knight	18th Nov. 1966 (X-15A-2)
4534	7297	6·72	W. J. Knight	3rd Oct. 1967

APPENDIX C

TWO REMARKABLE AIRCRAFT

The Boeing 747

The Boeing 747, currently referred to as the first of a new generation of "jumbo-jets", is the largest aircraft in commercial airline service in the world. It was conceived in 1965 to cope with the worldwide explosion in the demand for intercontinental passenger travel, as airlines came to realise that saturation of airways and air traffic patterns was rapidly approaching. Apart from its sheer size, its development was something of a technical masterpiece; from the date of first airline orders being placed to that of the first airline deliveries was only three years and eight months, and regular airline service followed only five months later.

The first airline to order the Boeing 747 was Pan American World Airways which ordered twenty-five aircraft on 13th April 1966, at a cost of $525 million(£218,750,000), or $21 million (£8,750,000) each.

The first Boeing 747 made its first flight on 9th February 1969 from Paine Field, near Seattle, Washington. There was no prototype and this first aircraft was representative of the type scheduled for airline delivery. **The first Boeing 747-36 ordered by B.O.A.C. flew for the first time** on 15th March 1970 and was handed over to the airline on 20th April.

At the time of writing, orders for the huge aeroplane totalled 186, of which the first 184 were scheduled for delivery to the following airlines:

KLM . . .	6	Air France . .	4	South African	
Pan American . .	33	BOAC . . .	12	Airways . .	3
American Airlines .	16	Sabena . .	2	Japan Air Lines .	8
United Airlines .	18	Lufthansa . .	5	Western Air Lines .	3
Continental . .	4	Air Canada . .	3	Irish International .	2
Trans-World Airlines .	15	National Airlines .	2	Iberia . . .	3
Eastern Air Lines .	4	Air India . .	2	El Al . . .	2
Braniff . . .	2	Qantas . .	4	World Airways .	3
Delta Air Lines . .	5	Alitalia . . .	4	SAS . . .	2
Northwest Orient .	15	Swissair . .	2		

At the current rate of production of eight aircraft per month, these Boeing 747s will have been delivered by mid-1972.

In terms of size, weight and load-carrying capacity the Boeing 747 is indeed impressive. The standard current passenger version provides accommodation for 374 passengers—66 first class and 308 economy class; other versions include one for 447 economy class passengers seated nine-abreast, and one for 490 seated ten-abreast. Compare this accommodation with that of the Short Sandringham flying-boat of twenty-five years ago (at 25 passengers) and with that of the de Havilland Comet which, with accommodation for 60–81 passengers, entered service on the trans-Atlantic run thirteen years ago.

The weight of the Boeing 747 at maximum take-off load is 775,000 lb. or 346 tons (352,000 kg.). This weight is equivalent to the *total take-off weight of nine Lancaster bombers each loaded with a 22,000 lb."Grand Slam" bomb!* Its fuel capacity of 42,466 Imperial gallons (193,050 litres), is sufficient to run sixty family saloon cars each for 20,000 miles (33,000 km.), or forty cars round the world.

The engines, of which four power the Boeing 747, each develop between 43,500 and 47,000 lb. thrust (19,730 to 21,320 kg.) depending on the aircraft variant. This is more than ten times the power of the jet engines fitted to the first jet fighters which entered service with the R.A.F. and U.S.A.F. twenty-five years ago.

By way of summing up the Boeing 747, it is an aeroplane capable of carrying more than 400 passengers (equivalent to a fairly good attendance at a cinema show) from New York to London in about six hours, together with their baggage, feeding them, and entertaining them with a film show as they cruise at more than 600 m.p.h. (1,000 km./hr.) seven miles above the earth!

The Hawker Siddeley Harrier
In a totally different sphere of aviation lies the Hawker Siddeley Harrier, a British military fighter aircraft capable of vertical and short take-off and landing. Developed directly from the Hawker P.1127 and by way of the Hawker Siddeley Kestrel, **the Harrier was the world's first operational, high performance V/STOL fighter,** entering service with No. 1 (Fighter) Squadron, Royal Air Force, early in 1969. Powered by a single Rolls-Royce Bristol Pegasus vectored-thrust turbofan (developing 19,200 lb., 8,710 kg., thrust), the Harrier is capable of taking off vertically and flying at more than 720 m.p.h. (1,159 km./hr.). At the time of writing more than one hundred Harriers were on order, including a number destined for the U.S. Marine Corps.

The P.1127 was the world's first high performance, fixed-wing aeroplane to achieve vertical take-off and landing. Its first untethered vertical take-off was performed on 19th November 1960, and its first conventional take-off on 13th March 1961. Its first transition from hovering to conventional flight and *vice versa* occurred in September 1961. Supersonic speed was achieved in dives during 1962, the aircraft thus becoming **the world's first VTOL aeroplane to fly faster than the speed of sound**.

The Kestrel was the world's first VTOL high-performance fixed-wing aircraft to be evaluated under service conditions, was the first to be flown by Service pilots of the R.A.F., the Luftwaffe, the U.S.A.F., the U.S. Navy, the U.S. Army and the U.S. Marine Corps, under field conditions. It was the first such aircraft to be exported anywhere in the world when, in 1966, ex-evaluation aircraft were passed to the American Services for further trials in the U.S.A. **It was the first such aircraft to perform night take-offs and landings, and the first to operate to and from an aircraft carrier. The Harrier is the world's first fully-operational fixed-wing high-performance V/STOL military aircraft to achieve worldwide combat capability,** and the two-seat trainer version (the T. Mark 2) is **the first fully-developed fixed-wing high-performance V/STOL trainer in the world.**

The two-seat Harrier trainer, the T.Mk. 2, which recently (August 1970) entered squadron service with the Royal Air Force.

APPENDIX D

AVIATION'S WORST DISASTERS

The following table presents details of all known air disasters involving the loss of more than fifty persons' lives.

Date	Loss of life	Location of Accident	Aircraft involved
24.8.21	62	Hull, Yorkshire, England; airship broke in two and fell in flames.	British airship R-38.
21.12.23	52	Mediterranean Sea; airship crashed in sea.	French airship *Dixmude*.
4.4.33	73	Off New Jersey coast; airship crashed in sea during storm.	U.S. airship *Akron*.
23.8.44	76	Freckleton, Preston, England; bomber hit school in storm.	U.S.A.F. Liberator bomber.
30.5.47	53	Near Fort Deposit, Maryland.	Eastern Air Lines DC-4.
24.10.47	52	Boyce Canyon, Utah; aircraft caught fire and crashed.	United Air Lines DC-6.
1.11.49	55	Washington, D.C.; collided with P-38 fighter.	Eastern Air Lines DC-4.
12.3.50	81	Sigginston, South Wales; crashed while preparing to land at Llandow.	Chartered Avro Tudor V.
24.6.50	58	Lake Michigan; crashed in storm.	Northwest Airlines DC-4.
31.8.50	55	Near Cairo, Egypt; crashed and burned.	TWA Constellation.
23.3.51	53	Atlantic Ocean; only wreckage found.	U.S.A.F. C-124.
16.12.51	56	Elizabeth River, New Jersey.	Miami Airlines C-46.
11.4.52	52	Off San Juan, Puerto Rico.	Pan-American DC-4.
20.12.52	87	Moses Lake, Washington; crashed and burned.	U.S.A.F. C-124.
18.6.53	129	Tachikawa A.F.B., Tokyo, Japan; crashed after engine failure on take-off.	U.S.A.F. C-124.
12.7.53	58	Off Wake Island, Pacific.	Transocean Air Lines DC-6B.
22.3.55	66	Honolulu; aircraft hit cliff.	U.S. Navy DC-6.
11.8.55	66	Near Stuttgart, Germany; two aircraft collided.	Two U.S.A.F. C-119.
6.10.55	66	West of Laramie, Wyoming; hit mountain.	United Air Lines DC-4.
20.2.56	52	In desert near Cairo, Egypt.	T.A.I. (French) DC-6B.
20.6.56	74	In sea off Ashbury Park, New Jersey.	Venezuelan Super Constellation.
30.6.56	128	Grand Canyon, Arizona; two airliners collided.	TWA Super-Constellation and United Air Lines DC-7.
10.10.56	59	Lost at sea about 150 miles north of the Azores.	U.S.A.F. (MATS) C-118.
9.12.56	62	British Columbia; crashed in mountains.	Trans-Canada DC-4.
21.3.57	67	Lost at sea over Pacific Ocean.	U.S.A.F. (MATS) C-97.
16.7.57	56	Off New Guinea.	K.L.M. Super-Constellation.
11.8.57	79	Quebec, Canada; aircraft crashed in swamp.	Maritime Central Airways DC-4.
8.12.57	62	Near Bolivar, Argentina.	Aerolineas Argentinas DC-4.
18.5.58	65	Casablanca, Morocco.	SABENA DC-6B.
14.8.58	99	Lost at sea 130 miles west of Ireland.	K.L.M. Super-Constellation.
17.10.58	75	Kanash, Chuvashskaya A.S.S.R., U.S.S.R.	Aeroflot Tu-104.
16.1.59	51	Mar del Plata, Argentina.	Austral Curtiss Commando.
3.2.59	65	East River, New York City.	American Airlines Electra.
26.6.59	68	Near Milan, Italy; aircraft crashed in storm.	TWA Super-Constellation.

Date	Loss of life	Location of Accident	Aircraft involved
24.9.59	53	Near Bordeaux, France.	Transports Aeriens DC-4.
5.2.60	59	Near Cochabamba, Bolivia.	Bolivian DC-4.
25.2.60	61	Air collision near Rio de Janeiro.	U.S. Navy R6D transport and Brazilian Real aircraft.
17.3.60	63	Air explosion over Tell City, Indiana.	Northwest Airlines Electra.
24.6.60	51	Guanabara Bay, Brazil.	Brazilian Real Convair.
29.8.60	55	Lost at sea off Dakar, Senegal.	Air France Super-Constellation.
19.9.60	78	Burst into flames after take-off at Guam.	World Airways DC-6B.
4.10.60	61	Boston, Massachussetts; crashed on take-off.	Eastern Airlines Electra.
16.12.60	134	Air collision over Brooklyn, New York.	United Air Lines DC-8 and TWA Super-Constellation.
17.12.60	53	Munich, Germany; aircraft hit tramcar.	U.S.A.F. C-131.
15.2.61	73	Berg, Belgium.	SABENA Boeing 707.
28.3.61	52	Rüsselbach, Germany; aircraft exploded and burned.	Ceskoslovenske Aerolinie Il-18.
10.5.61	79	Sahara Desert.	Air France Starliner.
30.5.61	62	Lisbon, Portugal.	Venezuelan DC-8.
12.7.61	72	Casablanca, Morocco; aircraft hit overhead cable.	Ceskoslovenske Aerolinie Il-18.
19.7.61	67	Azul, Brazil.	Aerolineas Argentinas DC-6.
1.9.61	78	Hinsdale, Illinois.	TWA Constellation.
10.9.61	83	Shannon, Ireland.	President Airlines DC-6.
12.9.61	77	Near Rabat, Morocco.	Air France Caravelle.
8.11.61	77	Near Richmond, Virginia.	Imperial Airlines Constellation.
23.11.61	52	Sao Paulo, Brazil.	Aerolineas Argentinas Comet.
1.3.62	95	New York City; crashed after take-off.	American Airlines Boeing 707.
4.3.62	111	Near Douala, Cameroun.	Caledonian DC-7C.
16.3.62	107	Lost at sea, western Pacific.	Flying Tiger Super-Constellation.
3.6.62	130	Crashed on take-off at Paris, France.	Air France Boeing 707.
22.6.62	113	Guadaloupe, West Indies; crashed in storm.	Air France Boeing 707.
7.7.62	94	North-east of Bombay; crashed in storm.	Alitalia airliner.
27.11.62	97	Lima, Peru; aircraft crashed and burned.	Brazilian Varig Boeing 707.
1.2.63	95	Air collision over Ankara, Turkey.	Middle East Airlines Viscount and Turkish C-47.
5.5.63	54	Near Douala, Cameroun.	Air Afrique DC-6.
3.6.63	101	In sea off British Columbia, Canada.	Chartered Northwest Airlines DC-7.
28.7.63	62	In sea off Bombay, India.	UAR Airlines Comet.
2.9.63	80	Zurich, Switzerland; crashed on take-off.	Swissair Caravelle.
29.11.63	118	Montreal, Canada; crashed on take-off.	Trans-Canada Airlines DC-8F.
8.12.63	82	Elkton, Maryland.	Pan-American Boeing 707.
25.2.64	58	Lake Pontchartrain, Louisiana.	Eastern Air Lines DC-8.
29.2.64	83	Near Innsbruck, Austria.	British Eagle Britannia.
1.3.64	85	Lake Tahoe, California; crashed in snow storm.	Paradise Airlines Constellation.
11.5.64	75	Clark Air Force Base, Philippines.	U.S.A.F. (MATS) C-135.
2.10.64	70	Granada, Spain.	U.T.A. (African) DC-6.
8.2.65	84	In sea off New York; crashed after take-off.	Eastern Air Lines DC-7B.
20.5.65	121	Cairo Airport, Egypt.	Pakistan Airlines Boeing 720B.
25.6.65	85	Los Angeles Airport; crashed on take-off.	U.S.A.F. C-135.
24.1.66	117	Mont Blanc, Switzerland.	Air India Boeing 707.
4.2.66	133	Tokyo Bay, Japan.	All-Nippon Boeing 727.
4.3.66	64	Tokyo Airport, Japan; crashed on landing.	Canadian Pacific DC-8.
5.3.66	124	Mount Fuji, Japan.	B.O.A.C. Boeing 707.
22.4.66	82	Near Ardmore, Oklahoma.	Military-chartered Electra.

Date	Loss of life	Location of Accident	Aircraft involved
1.9.66	97	Near Ljubljana, Yugoslavia.	Chartered Britannia.
24.11.66	82	Near Bratislava, Czechoslovakia.	Bulgarian Il-18.
24.12.66	129	Crashed into village in South Vietnam.	Military-chartered CL-44.
20.4.67	126	Nicosia, Cyprus.	Chartered Britannia.
3.6.67	88	Mont Canigou, France.	Chartered DC-4.
4.6.67	72	Stockport, England.	Chartered DC-4 (Argonaut).
19.7.67	82	Air collision over Hendersonville, North Carolina.	Piedmont Boeing 727 and Cessna 310.
12.10.67	66	Into Mediterranean off Turkish coast.	B.E.A. Comet 4.
20.11.67	68	Cincinnati, Ohio; crashed in snowstorm.	TWA Convair 880.
8.12.67	66	Near Huanuco, Peru.	Peruvian Faucett DC-4.
7.2.68	98	Crashed in Himalayan mountains, India.	Indian Air Force transport.
5.3.68	63	Guadeloupe Island; aircraft hit mountain.	Air France Boeing 707.
24.3.68	61	Irish Sea.	Irish International Viscount.
20.4.68	122	Windhoek, South Africa; crashed on take-off.	South African Airways Boeing 707.
3.5.68	85	Dawson, Texas; aircraft crashed in storm.	Braniff Electra.
11.9.68	95	Off Nice, France; caught fire and crashed.	Air France Caravelle.
12.12.68	51	Off Caracas, Venezuela.	Pan American Boeing 707.
16.3.69	155	Maracaibo, Venezuela; crashed after take-off.	Venezuelan Air Lines DC-9.
20.3.69	93	Aswan Airport, Egypt; crashed and burned on landing approach.	United Arab Il-18.
2.4.69	51	Southwest of Kraków, Poland.	Polish LOT An-24.
4.6.69	79	Near Monterrey, Mexico; struck ground on approach to landing.	Mexicana Boeing 727.
9.9.69	84	Air collision near Indianapolis.	Allegheny DC-9 and Piper Cherokee.
20.9.69	77	Air collision near Da Nang, Vietnam; aircraft collided on approach to landing.	Air Vietnam DC-4 and U.S.A.F. Phantom.
26.9.69	74	Southeast of La Paz, Bolivia; struck high ground.	Lloyd Aereo Boliviano DC-6B.
20.11.69	87	On approach to Lagos Airport, Nigeria.	Nigeria Airways VC-10.
3.12.69	62	Dived into sea after take-off from Caracas.	Air France Boeing 707.
8.12.69	90	Athens, Greece; crashed into mountain.	Olympic DC-6B.
22.12.69	100+	Nha Trang, Vietnam; aircraft overran runway and crashed into school. Many ground casualties.	Air Vietnam DC-6B.
16.2.70	102	Into sea off Santo Domingo; engine failure on take-off.	Compania Dominicana DC-9-30.
1.4.70	60	Casablanca, Morocco; crashed on approach.	Royal Air Maroc Caravelle.

SELECTED BIBLIOGRAPHY

ABBAS, A.: *Till We Reach the Stars: The Story of Yuriy Gagarin*; Asia Publishing House, Bombay, 1961.

AIR MINISTRY: *The Rise and Fall of the German Air Force, 1933–1945*; Air Ministry, London, 1948.

AUTHORS, VARIOUS: *Aircraft Profiles* (Seven Volumes, 204 aircraft described); Profile Publications, Leatherhead, England, 1965–67.

BABINGTON-SMITH, CONSTANCE: *Testing Time: The Story of British Test Pilots and their Aircraft*; Harper, New York, 1961.

BARNES, C. H.: *Bristol Aircraft Since 1910*; Putnam, London, 1964.

BARNES, C. H.: *Shorts Aircraft Since 1900*; Putnam, London, 1967.

BENECKE, TH., AND QUICK, A. W.: *History of German Guided Missile Development*; Verlag E. Appelhaus, Brunswick, Germany, 1957.

BERGMAN, JULES: *Ninety Seconds to Space: The X-15 Story*; Doubleday, New York, 1960.

BOWERS, PETER M.: *Boeing Aircraft since 1916*; Putnam, London, 1965.

BRABAZON, OF TARA, LORD: *The Brabazon Story*; Heinemann, London, 1956.

BRAUN, WERNHER VON, AND ORDWAY III, FREDERICK I.: *History of Rocketry and Space Travel*; Thomas Nelson & Sons, Camden, New Jersey, U.S.A., 1966.

BRETT, R. D.: *The History of British Aviation, 1908–1914*; Hamilton, London, 1934.

BREWER, GRIFFITH: *Ballooning and its Application to Kite Balloons*; The Air League of the British Empire, London (11th Edition), 1940.

BROKE-SMITH, BRIGADIER P. W. L.: *The History of Early British Military Aeronautics*; L. A. Academic Reprint, Chivers, Bath, England, 1968.

BRUCE, J. M.: *British Aeroplanes, 1914–1918*; Putnam, London, 1957.

CANBY, C.: *History of Rockets and Space*; Manhasset, New York, 1963.

CARPENTER, M. S. (ET AL.): *We Seven*; Simon and Schuster, New York, 1962.

CHAPMAN, J. L.: *Atlas: The Story of a Missile*; Harper, New York, 1960.

CORNISH III, JOSEPH JENKINS: *The Air Arm of the Confederacy*; Richmond Civil War Centennial Committee, Richmond, Virginia, U.S.A., 1963.

DIXON, C.: *Parachuting*; Sampson Low, London, 1930.

DOLLFUS, CHARLES: *Balloons*; Prentice-Hall International (Transl. Mason), London, 1961.

DORIAN, A.F., AND OSENTON, JAMES (Ed.): *Dictionary of Aeronautics* (Six Languages); Elsevier, London, 1964.

DUVAL, G. R.: *British Flying Boats and Amphibians, 1909–1952*; Putnam, London, 1966.

FEENEY, WILLIAM D.: *In Their Honour*; Duell, Sloan and Pearce, New York, 1963.

FRANCILLON, RENÉ J.: *Japanese Aircraft of the Pacific War*; Putnam, London, 1970.

FRICKER, JOHN, AND GREEN, WILLIAM: *The Air Forces of the World*; Macdonald, London, 1958.

GAGARIN, YURIY: *Road to the Stars*; Foreign Languages Publishing House, Moscow, 1962.

GARBER, PAUL E.: *The National Aeronautical Collections*; The Smithsonian Institution, Washington, 1956.

GATLAND, KENNETH W.: *Development of the Guided Missile*; Philosophical Library, New York, 1952.

GATLAND, KENNETH W.: *Spacecraft and Boosters*; Iliffe, London, 1964.

GIBBS-SMITH, CHARLES: *A History of Flying*; Batsford, London, 1953.

GIBBS-SMITH, CHARLES: *The Aeroplane: An Historical Survey*; Science Museum, London, 1960.

HADDOW, G. W., AND GROSZ, PETER M.: *The German Giants*; Putnam, London, 1961.

HODGSON, J. E.: *The History of Aeronautics in Great Britain*; Oxford University Press, Oxford, England, 1924.

HOEPPNER, VON: *Deutschlands Krieg in der Luft*; Berlin, 1920.

HOWARD, WILLIAM E., AND BARR, JAMES: *Spacecraft and Missiles of the World*; Harcourt, Brace and World, New York, 1966.

INOGUCHI, RIKIHEI; NAKAJIMA, TADASHI, AND PINEAU, ROGER: *The Divine Wind*; Hutchinson, London, 1959.

JACKSON, A. J.: *British Civil Aircraft, 1919–59* (Two Volumes); Putnam, London, 1960.

JACKSON, A. J.: *De Havilland Aircraft Since 1915*; Putnam, London, 1962.

JACKSON, A. J.: *Avro Aircraft Since 1908*; Putnam, London, 1965.

JACKSON, A. J.: *Blackburn Aircraft Since 1909*; Putnam, London, 1968.

JONES, H. A., AND RALEIGH, SIR WALTER: *The War in the Air* (Six Volumes); Oxford University Press, Oxford, England, 1922–37.

KERR, MARK: *Land, Sea and Air*; Longmans, Green, London, 1927.

KING, H. F.: *Aeromarine Origins*; Putnam, London.

KLEE, ERNST, AND MERK, OTTO: *The Birth of the Missile*; Dutton, New York, 1960.

LEWIS, PETER: *British Aircraft, 1809–1914*; Putnam, London, 1962.

LEY, WILLY: *Rockets, Missiles and Space Travel*; Viking, New York, 1961.

MARSH, W. LOCKWOOD: *Aeronautical Prints and Drawings*; Halton and Truscott Smith, London, 1924.

MASON, FRANCIS K.: *Hawker Aircraft Since 1920* (2nd Edition); Putnam, London, 1970.

MASON, FRANCIS K., AND WINDROW, MARTIN C.: *Battle Over Britain*; McWhirter Twins, London, 1969.

MASON, H. M.: *The Lafayette Escadrille*; Random House, New York, 1967.

MCWHIRTER, NORRIS AND ROSS: *The Guinness Book of Records* (and U.S. Edition, *The Guinness Book of World Records*) 17 Editions; Guinness Superlatives Ltd., London, 1955–1970.

MOYES, PHILIP: *Bomber Squadrons of the R.A.F.*; Macdonald, London, 1964.

NEUMANN: *Die deutschen Luftstreitkräfte in Weltkriege*; Berlin, 1920.

OBERMAIER, ERNST: *Die Ritterkreuzträger der Luftwaffe: Jagdflieger, 1939–45*; Verlag Dieter Hoffmann, Mainz, Germany, 1966.

PEASLEE, B. J.: *Heritage of Valor: The Eighth Air Force in the Second World War*; Lippincott, New York, 1964.

PENROSE, HARALD: *British Aviation: The Pioneer Years*; Putnam, London, 1967.

PENROSE, HARALD: *British Aviation: The Great War and Armistice*; Putnam, London, 1969.

PHELAN, JOSEPH A.: *Heroes and Aeroplanes of the Great War, 1914–1918*; Barker, London, 1968.

PIERCE, P. N., AND SCHUON, KARL: *John H. Glenn: Astronaut*; Franklin Watts, New York, 1962.

PRICE, ALFRED: *Instruments of Darkness*; Kimber, London, 1967.

PRICE, ALFRED: *German Bombers of the Second World War* (Two Volumes); Lacy, Windsor, 1969.

PRILLER, JOSEF: *Geschichte eines Jagdgeschwaders: Das JG 26 "Schlageter" 1937–1945*; Kurt Vowinckel Verlag, Heidelberg, Germany, 1956.

RAWLINGS, J.: *Fighter Squadrons of the R.A.F.*; Macdonald, London, 1969.

RICHARDS, DENIS, AND SAUNDERS, H. ST. J.: *Royal Air Force, 1939–1945* (Three Volumes); H.M.S.O., London, 1953–56.

RICHTHOFEN, GENERAL BARON VON: *Personal Diary*; Karlsruhe Collection, Hamburg, 1941–44.

ROLT, L. T. C.: *The Aeronauts: A History of Ballooning, 1783–1903*; Longmans, Green, London, 1966.

SAUNDERS, H. ST. G.: *Per Ardua: The Rise of British Air Power, 1911–1939*; Oxford University Press, Oxford, England, 1944.

SCHWEIBERT, ERNEST G.: *A History of the United States Air Force Ballistic Missiles*; Praeger, New York, 1965.

SEEMEN, GERHARD VON: *Die Ritterkreuzträger, 1939–45*; Podzun-Verlag, Bad Nauheim, Germany, 1955 et seq.

SIMS, EDWARD H.: *American Aces of the Second World War*; Macdonald, London, 1958.

STEWART, O.: *First Flights*; Routledge and Kegan Paul, London, 1957.

STEWART, O.: *Of Flight and Flyers*; Newnes, London, 1964.

STROUD, JOHN: *Annals of British and Commonwealth Air Transport, 1919–1960*; Putnam, London, 1962.

STROUD, JOHN: *European Transport Aircraft Since 1910*; Putnam, London, 1966.

STROUD, JOHN: *Soviet Transport Aircraft Since 1945*; Putnam, London, 1968.

SWANBOROUGH, F. G., AND BOWERS, P. M.: *United States Military Aircraft Since 1909*; Putnam, London, 1963.

SWANBOROUGH, F. G., AND BOWERS, P. M.: *United States Navy Aircraft Since 1911*; Putnam, London, 1968.

TAYLOR, J. W. R.; JANE, FRED T.; GREY, C. G.; BRIDGMAN, LEONARD: (Ed.): *Jane's All The World's Aircraft* (Various Editions, 1909–1970); Sampson Low, et al.

TAYLOR, J. W. R.: *C.F.S.*; Putnam, London, 1958.

TAYLOR, J. W. R. AND ALLWARD, M. F.: *Westland 50*; Ian Allen, London, 1965.

THETFORD, OWEN J.: *Aircraft of the R.A.F. Since 1918* (Four Editions); Putnam, London.

THETFORD, OWEN J.: *British Naval Aircraft Since 1912*; Putnam, London, 1961.

THETFORD, OWEN J., AND GRAY, PETER: *German Aircraft of the First World War*; Putnam, London, 1962.

WALLACE, GRAHAM: *Flying Witness: Harry Harper and the Golden Age of Aviation*; Putnam, London, 1958.

WINDROW, MARTIN C.: *German Fighters of the Second World War* (Two Volumes); Lacy, Windsor, England, 1968–69.

VASSILIEV, M., AND DOBRONRAVOV, V. V.: *Sputnik into Space*; Souvenir Press, London, 1958.

ZIEGLER, MANO: *Rocket Fighter*; Macdonald, London, 1963.

Index

AB Aerotransport (Swedish Air Lines): *130, 137*
Abingdon, England: *137*
Aces, American: *41, 46, 72, 73*; Australian: *65, 72, 73*; Austro-Hungarian: *41, 72*; Belgian: *46, 72*; British: *39, 46, 65, 72, 73, 75*; Canadian: *65, 72, 73*; Czech: *65, 72*; Danish: *72*; Dutch: *72*; Finnish: *72*; French: *40, 46, 72, 73*; German: *40, 46, 72, 75*; Irish: *72, 73*; Italian: *41, 72*; Japanese: *72*; New Zealanders: *65, 72, 73*; Norwegian: *72*; Polish: *65, 72*; Romanian: *72*; South African: *65, 72, 73, 75*
Achernar, U.S. attack cargo ship: *112*
Achmer, Germany: *69*
Ademeit, Major Horst: *85*
Aero A-10 and A-14: *127*
Aero Club of America: *28*
Aero Club of France: *13, 21*
Aero Club of Great Britain (later Royal): *16, 18, 20, 21, 24*
Aero Club of Sweden (*Svenska Aeronautiska Sallskapet*): *22*
Aerodrome aircraft: *10, 12*
Aeromarine West Indies Airways: *126*
Aeronautical Society of Great Britain (later Royal): *11, 16*
Aeronáutica Militar Española (Spanish Air Force), formation of: *96*
Affleck, A.: *131*
Afghanistan, formation of R. Afghan A.F.: *93*; air operations in, 1928–29: *131*
Africa, H.M. battleship: *100, 102*
Aichi D3A ("Val"): *111, 117*
Aircraft and Travel Ltd., London: *122*
aircraft carrier, world's first: *98*
Air Estimates, first British: *150*
Air Force Cross (British), award of: *102* (Samson)
Air Mail, first British internal: *136* (see also under separate countries)
Air Medal (American), award of: *80* (J. E. Johnson), *81* (Bong)
Air Ministry, British: *62, 83*
airscrew, largest in the world: *38*
Air Transport and Travel Ltd, London: *124, 125*
Air Volunteer Group: *73*
Akagi, Japanese aircraft carrier: *110*
Akron, Ohio: *153*
Akron, U.S. airship: *108*
Akyab, Burma: *129*
Alabama, U.S.S.: *106*

Alabaster, Captain R. C., B.O.A.C.: *139*
Alemada, California: *137*
Alamein, Battle of, 1942: *79*
Albanian Air Force, formation of: *93*
Albatros aircraft: B II: *48*; C I: *48, 55*; D I: *37, 49, 50*; D II: *47, 49*; D III: *48*; D V: *51*
Albert Medal, award of: *103* (Rutland)
Albrecht Order: *49*
Alcock, Captain Sir John: *125*
Aldershot, England: *150*
Aleppo, Turkey: *129*
Alexandria, Egypt: *132, 134*
Allahabad, India: *23, 129*
Allison, E. M.: *127*
Allmenröder, Leutnant Karl: *55*
Almirante Cochrane, planned Chilean battleship: *106, 110*
Alpine, U.S. attack transport: *112*
Alps: *134*
Amanullah, H.M. King of Afghanistan: *93*
American Airlines: *137*
American Civil War, 1861–63: *96, 98, 149, 150*
Amiens, France: *30*
Amoy, China: *129*
Amsterdam–Brussels, speed record: *142*
Amsterdam, Holland: *130*
Anchorage (Alaska)–Chicago, speed record: *142*; –London, speed record: *142*
Ancillotto, Teniente Giovanni: *41*
Anders, Major William A., U.S.A.F.: *187*
Anderson, Captain Orvil: *151*
Andes, air crossings of the: *123*
Andreani, Chevalier Paul: *148*
Andrews, Lieutenant Colonel G. A., U.S.A.F.: *142*
Angkatan Udara Republik Indonesia (see Indonesia Air Force)
Anglo-Irish Treaty, 1921: *94*
Anjou, France: *21*
Anne, H.M. seaplane carrier: *102*
Annonay, France: *145*
Antoinette engines: *13, 14, 20, 159*
Antoinette, Marie: *146*
Antoinette monoplanes: *19, 20, 23*
Antwerp, Belgium: *31*; Siege of: *102*
Anzani engines: *20*
Apollo spacecraft: *181, 186, 187*
Arabia, air operations against Turks in: *102*
Arado Ar 234: *69*

Archdeacon, Ernest: *10, 16*
Archdeacon prize: *13, 16*
Archila, Dr. Aristóbulo: *93*
Argentine; Aero Club: *100*; first aeroplane flight in: *22*; first military aviation in: *28*; formation of air services in: *93*
Argueff, Captain P.V.d': *41*
Argus, H.M. aircraft carrier: *105, 110*
Arigi, Offizierstellvertreter Julius: *41*
Arkel, Lieutenant Colonel van: *72*
Ark Royal, H.M. aircraft carrier: *110, 111*
Ark Royal, H.M. seaplane carrier: *102*
Arlandes, Marquis d': *146*
Arma da Aeronâutica (Portuguese Army Air Service), formation of: *95*
Armée de L'Air (previously *Service Aéronautique*): *31, 46, 96*; formation of: *93*; *Escadrilles*: N/MS/SPA.3: *46, 52*; VB.24: *31*; VB.26: *46*; C.47: *51*; N.65: *53*; SPA.103: *46, 51*; VB.106: *53*
Armengand, France: *17*
Armstrong, Commander Neil, U.S. Navy: *183, 186, 187*
Armstrong, Jackson J.: *143*
Armstrong Siddeley Puma engines: *130*
Armstrong Whitworth Argosy (airliner): *132, 134*
Armstrong Whitworth Whitley: *63*
Arnhem, Holland: *80*
Arnold, Lieutenant Leslie P., U.S. Air Service: *128*
Athens, Greece: *134*
Atka, Aleutians: *129*
Atlanta–Paris, speed record: *142*
Atlantic Ocean; first aeroplane crossing: *124*; first east–west attempt to cross: *53*; first non-stop aeroplane crossing: *125*; first non-stop solo crossing by aeroplane: *130*; first solo crossing by woman: *136*; first direct, solo east–west crossing: *137*; first jet passenger service across: *139*; first airship crossing and double crossing: *153*; first aeroplane crossing of the South Atlantic: *131*; first east–west solo crossing of the South Atlantic: *136*; first man to cross both North and South Atlantic by air: *136*
Atomic bomb: *91*
Attu Island: *129*
Auckland, New Zealand: *23*
Audemars, M.: *24*
Australasian, balloon: *150*
Australia; first flight in glider in: *20*; first aeroplane flights in: *20, 22*; highest scoring fighter pilot: *72*; first regular air services in: *126*; inauguration of Flying Doctor Service: *131*; first flight from Australia to the U.S.A.: *137*; first balloon ascent in: *150*
Australian Inland Mission: *131*
Australian National Airways: *137*
Austria; first aeroplane flight in: *14*; highest scoring fighter pilot: *72*; formation of air forces: *93*
Austro-Hungarian Imperial Air Force: *41*
autogiro: *159 et passim*
Automobil und Aviatik A.G.: *38*
Auvours, France: *17*
Auxi-le-Chateau, France: *56*
Aveline Stabiliser: *126*
Avery, William: *12*
Aviação Maritima (Portuguese Naval Air Service), formation of: *95*
Aviatik aircraft: *31, 38, 51*
Aviation meetings; first International: *19*; first in Great Britain: *20*
Aviators' Certificates: American: *24, 26, 28*; Argentinian: *26, 100*; Austrian: *26*; Belgian: *26*; British: *18,*

23, 24, 26, 28, 99, 101, 102; Danish: *26*; Egyptian: *26*; French: *20, 26*; German: *26, 27, 28*; Hungarian: *26*; Italian: *26*; Norwegian: *26*; Russian: *26*; Spanish: *26*; Swedish: *22, 24, 26, 28*
Avro Avian: *131*
Avro Lancaster: *67, 68, 71, 143*
Avro Lincoln: *91*
Avro Vulcan: *142*
Axvall, Sweden: *96*
Ayling, J. R.: *136*
Azores: *124*

B

Baddeck Bay, Nova Scotia: *18*
Baden-Powell, Major B. F. S.: *16*
Bader, Group Captain, D. R. S., C.B.E., D.S.O., D.F.C.: *79*
Bagatelle, France: *17*
Bager, Captain R.: *126*
Baghdad (Mesopotamia): *123, 129*
Baig, A.: *142, 143*
Baikonur, East Kazakhstan, U.S.S.R.: *182*
Bailey, Lady: *131*
Bailey Lighthouse, Howth: *22*
Baillie, W.: *143*
Baldwin, F. W. ("Casey"): *19*
Baleine, Nova Scotia: *137*
Balkan War, 1912–13: *28, 93, 96*
Ball, Captain Albert, V.C., D.S.O.**, M.C., R.F.C.: *39, 49, 50*
balloon flight: *145 et seq.*
Balloon School, British Army: *152*
Baltic Railway Car Factory, Petrograd: *29*
Baltimore–Moscow, speed record: *142*; –Oslo, speed record: *142*; –Stockholm, speed record: *142*
Bandar Abbas, Persia: *123, 129*
Bangkok, Siam: *129*
Bär, Oberstleutnant Heinz: *70, 82, 83, 85, 90*
Baracca, Maggiore Francesco: *41*
Baracchini, Tenente Flavio Torello: *41*
Barber, Horatio: *121*
Barin, Lieutenant L. T.; U.S. Navy: *124*
Barker, Lieutenant Colonel W. G., V.C., D.S.O.*, M.C.**: *39*
Barkhorn, Major Gerhard: *85*
Barling XNBL-1: *57*
Basle, Switzerland: *132*
Basse und Selve engines: *38*
Battaglione Aviatori (Italian Air Battalion): *94*
Batz, Major Wilhelm: *85*
Bauer, Oberst Victor: *87*
Baumer, Leutnant Paul: *40*
Bavarian Order of Military Merit: *49*
Baylies, Second Lieutenant F. L.: *41*
B.E. 2A aircraft: *30*; B.E. 2C: *49*
Beamont, Roland: *142*
Beadmore & Co., Ltd., William: *62*
Beardmore Inflexible: *62*
Béarn, French aircraft carrier: *108, 110*
Beauchamp-Proctor, Captain A. W., V.C., D.S.O., M.C.*, D.F.C.: *39*
Beaumont, Captain F., R.E.: *150*
Beauvais, France: *127, 132, 153*
Bechuanaland, British expedition to: *150*
Bedford, A. W. ("Bill"), O.B.E.: *143, 144*
Beerenbrock, Leutnant Franz-Josef: *87*
Beisswenger, Oberleutnant Hans: *86*
Belfast, Northern Ireland: *20*; to Gander (Newfoundland), speed record: *142*

Belgium, German campaign against, 1940: *64*; highest scoring fighter pilot: *72*; formation of air force: *93*

Bellinger, Lieutenant, Jg. (later Lieutenant Commander) P. N. L., U.S. Navy: *30*, *124*

Belyaev, Colonel Pavel Ivanovich: *185*

Ben-My-Chree, H.M. seaplane carrier: *102*, *103*

Bennett, Harry: *143*

Bentley, Flight Lieutenant R. R., R.A.F.: *131*

Benz engines: *38*

Beregovoiy, Colonel Giorgiy T.: *187*

Berliner Verein fur Luftschiffarht: 151

Berlin, Germany: *136*; speed records to Hanoi, New York and Tokyo, *142*

Bermuda, B. W. I., speed record to London: *142*

Berry, Squadron Leader Joseph, D.F.C.**: *72*

Berson, Professor: *151*

Berthold, Hauptmann Rudolph: *40*

Beta airship: *152*

Bethersden, Kent: *25*

Bettington, Lieutenant C.: *25*

Beurling, Squadron Leader George F., D.S.O., D.F.C., D.F.M.*: *72*, *73*

Bielefeld viaduct: *71*

Bierut to Karachi, speed record: *142*

Birger gang: *139*

Birkner, Leutnant Hans-Joachim: *87*

Birksted, Group Captain Kaj: *72*

Birmingham, U.S.S.: *99*, *101*

Biseo, Attileo: *144*

Bishop, Lieutenant Colonel W. A., V.C., C.B., D.S.O.*, M.C., D.F.C., E.D.: *39*, *53*, *54*

Bitsch, Hauptmann Emil: *87*

Bizerte, Tunisia: *122*

Blackburn Firebrand: *118*

Blackburn Iris: *117*

Blackburn Roc: *117*

Blackburn Skua: *111*

Blackpool, England: *20*

Black, W. van Lear: *130*

Blanchard, Jean-Pierre: *149*

Blanc Nez, Cap, France: *19*

Bland, Dr. William: *150*

Blériot Flying School, Hendon, England: *24*

Blériot Flying School, Pau, France: *22*

Blériot, Louis: *10*, *14*, *15*, *19*, *24*

Blériot monoplanes: *14*, *15*, *19*, *20*, *22*, *24*, *30*, *36*, *93*, *121*, *122*

Blitzkrieg: 64

Boeing Type C aircraft: *124*

Boeing Model 69: *117*

Boeing F4B fighter: *117*

Boeing B-17 Flying Fortress: *67*, *69*, *83*

Boeing B-29 Superfortress: *83*

Boeing B-47 Stratojet: *121*

Boeing B-52 Stratofortress: *91*, *121*, *142*

Boeing C-135 and KC-135: *142*, *143*, *144*

Boeing 707 (and C-137): *139*, *141*, *142*, *143*, *144*

Boeing 720: *142*, *143*

Boelcke, Hauptmann Oswald: *40*, *47*, *48*

Boelcke, Wilhelm: *48*, *49*

Bois de Boulogne, Paris: *146*

Bolivia, formation of air force in: *93*

bombs, first dropped from an aeroplane: *27*

Bong, Major Richard Ira, U.S.A.F.: *72*, *73*, *77*, *80*, *81*

Borchers, Major Adolf: *86*

Bordelon, Lieutenant Guy, U.S. Navy: *115*

Borman, Lieutenant Colonel Frank, U.S.A.F.: *186*, *187*

Borton, Brigadier General A. E.: *123*

Boston, Massachusetts: *129*; speed records to Bonn, London, Moscow, Oslo, Paris, Shannon and Stockholm: *142*

Boulogne, France: *149*

Bournemouth, England: *22*

Boxer, U.S.S.: *115*

Boxkite, Bristol: *24*

Boxted, England: *77*

Boyd, Flight Lieutenant R. F., D.S.O., D.F.C.*: *65*

Boyington, Lieutenant Colonel G., U.S. Marine Corps: *73*

Braham, Wing Commander J. R. D., D.S.O.**, D.F.C.**, A.F.C.: *73*

Brancker, Major General Sir Sefton: *132*

Brand, Captain C. J. Q. (later Air Vice-Marshal Sir Christopher Quintin, K.B.E., D.S.O., M.C., D.F.C., R.A.F.): *126*

Brändle, Major Kurt: *85*

Brasschaet, Belgium: *93*

Bratislava, Czechoslovakia: *127*

Braun, Dr. Wernher von: *180*

Brazil, first aeroplane flight in: *22*; formation of air forces in: *93*

Breguet aircraft, *Nungesser-Coli: 131*

Breguet biplanes, 1911–13: *23*, *25*, *29*

Breguet, Louis: *23*

Bremen, Germany: *128*

Brendel, Hauptmann Joachim: *85*

Brewer, Griffith: *16*

Brewster F2A-1 Buffalo: *117*

Brewster XSB2A-1 Buccaneer: *118*

Brisbane, Australia: *131*, *137*

Brisbane Museum, Australia: *131*

Bristol Aeroplane Co., Ltd.: *23*, *25*

Bristol Blenheim: *62*, *63*

Bristol Britannia: *139*

Bristol Centaurus engines: *112*

Bristol F.2B Fighter: *88–89*, *93*

Bristol M.1 Monoplanes: *93*, *123*

Britain, Battle of, 1940: *65*, *66*, *79*

British Army Aeroplane No. 1: 15, *18*, *19*

British European Airways: *139*

British Marine Air Navigation Co., Ltd.: *128*

British Overseas Airways Corporation: *139*

Brno, Czechoslovakia: *127*

Brompton Hall, Scarborough, Yorkshire: *10* (*footnote*), *11*

Brooklands, Surrey: *24*, *25*, *125*, *126*

Brough, Yorkshire: *129*

Brown, Captain A. Roy, D.F.C., R.A.F.: *48*

Brown, Lieutenant Commander E. M., R.N.: *114*

Brown, Lieutenant Russel J., Jr., U.S.A.F.: *90*

Brown, Lieutenant Sir Arthur Whitten: *125*

Browning, John: *11*

Brumowski, Hauptmann Godwin: *41*

Brussels, speed records to Amsterdam and Paris: *142*

Bucharest, Romania: *129*

Büchner, Leutnant Franz: *40*

Büchner, Oberfeldwebel Hermann: *70*

Budapest, Hungary: *129*

Buedenfeld, Switzerland: *96*

Buenos Aires, speed records to Christchurch (New Zealand) and Washington, D.C.: *142*

Bühligen, Oberstleutnant Kurt: *82*, *83*, *87*

Bulawayo, Southern Rhodesia: *126*

Bulgarian Army Aviation Corps, formation of: *93*

bull, first recorded flight of a: *128*

Burton, L. E.: *142*

Bushire, Persia: *123*, *129*

Butler, Frank Hedges: *16*

Butte-aux-Cailles, Paris: *146*
Butusov, William Paul: *12*
Bykovsky, Lieutenant Colonel Valeriy Fyodorovich: *185*
Byrd, Commander R. E., U.S. Navy: *132*

C

Cairo, Egypt: *126*; speed record to London: *142*
Calabria, Capitano Fulco Ruffo di: *41*
Calais, France: *19*
Calcutta, India: *23*, *131*
Calder, Squadron Leader C. C., R.A.F.: *71*
Caldwell, Group Captain Clive R., D.S.O., D.F.C.*: *72*, *73*
Caledonia, Empire flying boat: *137*
Calgary, Alberta, Canada: *125*
Cambodia, formation of Royal Khmer Aviation: *93*
Campania, H.M. seaplane carrier: *103*
Campbell, Lieutenant Douglas, U.S. Army: *38*, *56*
Camp d'Auvours, France: *16*
Canada: first balloon ascent in: *150*; first non-stop flight to England from: *136*; first aeroplane flight in: *18*; highest scoring fighter pilot: *72*; first official air mail flight in: *123*
Canadian Mounted Rifles: *53*
Canadian Pacific Air Lines: *139*
Candelaria, Teniente Luis C.: *123*
Canopus, Empire flying boat: *137*
Cantacuzino, Captain Prince Constantine: *72*
Cape of Good Hope to London, speed record: *142*
Cape Town, South Africa: *131*, *132*, *134*, *150*
Capper, Colonel John, R.E.: *152*
Carbury, Flying Officer B. J. G., D.F.C.*: *65*
Cardington, Bedford, England (Royal Airship Works): *132*, *153*
Carey, Group Captain F. H. R., D.F.C.**, A.F.C., D.F.M.: *73*
Caribbean, first British air crossing: *134*
Carpenter, Lieutenant Commander Malcolm Scott, U.S. Navy: *185*
Carr, Air Marshal Sir Roderick, K.B.E., C.B., D.F.C., A.F.C.: *130*
Carver, A. C. P.: *142*
Casco Bay, Maine: *129*
Caudron biplanes, 1913: *29*
Caudron G.IIIa: *93*
Caudron G.IV: *51*
Caudron, René: *100*
Caudron Simoun: *144*
Cavendish, Henry: *145*
Caxias, Marquis de: *150*
Cayley, Sir George, 6th Baronet: *9*, *10*, *11*
Cederström, Baron Carl: *22*
Cerman, Lieutenant Commander Eugene Andrew, U.S. Navy: *186*, *187*
Cerutti, Sergente Marziale: *41*
Československé Státní Aerolinie (C.S.A.): *127*
Ceylon; air operations off, 1942: *107*; formation of air force in: *93*
Chahbar, Persia: *123*, *129*
Chalais–Meudon, France: *152*
Chalons, France: *17*, *19*
Champagne, France: *47*
Champ de Mars, Paris: *146*
Chancellorsville, Battle of, 1863: *149*
Chandler, Lieutenant Charles de Forest, U.S. Army: *28*
Chanute, Dr. Octave: *9*, *10*, *11*, *12*
Chapman, Victor Emanuel: *36*
Chard, Somerset, England: *11*
Charles, Jacques Alexandre César: *146*

Charleville, Queensland, Australia: *126*
Chatham, Massachusetts: *124*
Chel Ha'avir (Israeli Air Force): *94*
Chevalier, Lieutenant Commander, U.S. Navy: *107*
Cheyenne, Wyoming: *132*
Chicago, Illinois: *137*, *153*
Chignic, Aleutian Peninsula: *129*
Chilean Air Force, formation of: *93*
China; first aeroplane pilots in: *24*; first aircraft acquired by: *29*; formation of air force in: *93*
Chinese People's Republic Air Force: *90*
Chittagong, India: *129*
Cholmondeley, Lieutenant R., R.F.C.: *29*
Christchurch, New Zealand: *131*; speed record to Honolulu, Hawaii: *142*
Christmas Island: *92*
Church, Ellen, stewardess: *132*
Churchill, the Rt. Hon. Sir Winston: *101*
Cierva, Juan de la: *160*
cigarette, first aeroplane pilot to smoke while flying: *19*
Cigognes, Les, Group de Combat No. 12: *46*, *51*, *52*
Clark, Julie: *25*
Clausen, Major Erwin: *86*
Clifden, Co. Galway, Ireland: *125*
Clipper III, flying boat: *137*
Cloncurry, Queensland, Australia: *126*, *131*
Closterman, Squadron Leader Pierre H., D.F.C.*: *72*, *73*
Clouston, A. E.: *143*, *144*
Clover Field, California: *137*
Clyde, River, Scotland: *12*
Cochrane, Miss Jacqueline: *142*, *143*, *144*
Cody, Mrs. Samuel: *19*
Cody, Samuel F.: *10*, *15*, *18*, *19*, *152*
Coli, Capitaine: *53*
College Park, Maryland: *28*
Collett, Flight Lieutenant, R.N.A.S.: *31*
Collins, General Michael: *94*
Collins, Major Michael, U.S.A.F.: *186*, *187*
Collishaw, Lieutenant Colonel R., C.B., D.S.O.*, O.B.E., D.S.C., D.F.C.: *39*, *54–55*
Colmore, Lieutenant G. C., R.N.: *99*
Cologne, Germany: *31*, *101*
Coltishall, England: *79*
Columbia, space command module: *183*
Columbus, Ohio: *56*
Commonwealth Boomerang: *67*
Coney, Lieutenant William D., U.S. Air Service: *127*
Congressional Medal of Honour (see Medal of Honor, Congressional)
Conolly, H. P.: *143*
Conrad, Lieutenant Commander Charles, U.S. Navy: *186*
Consolidated B-24 Liberator: *83*
Consolidated PBY Catalina: *109*, *117*
Constantinople (Istanbul), Turkey: *52*, *129*
Conte Rosso, planned Italian liner: *105*, *110*
"Continuation War", Russo-Finnish war, 1941: *67*
Cook, Captain Donald, T. W. A.: *141*
Cook, Miss Edith Maud: *21*
Cooper, Major Leroy Gordon: *185*, *186*
Copenhagen–London, speed record: *142*
Coppens, Second Lieutenant Willens, D.S.O.: *46*
Coral Sea, Battle of, 1942: *111*
Cornu, Paul: *159*
Costes, Dieudonné: *131*
Courageous, H.M. aircraft carrier: *110*
Courbet, French battleship: *77*
Courtrai, France: *36*
Coutelle, Capitaine: *149*

Coventry, England: *21*
Cowan, Richard: *150*
cow, first recorded flight by a: *128*
Cranfield, England: *66*
Cranwell, England, the Royal Air Force College: *94, 130, 132, 136*
Cremorne Gardens, Melbourne, Australia: *150*
Crete, invasion of, 1941: *67*
Cricklewood, London: *125, 126*
crime in the sky: *139 et seq.*
Crinius, Leutnant Wilhelm: *87*
Crissy, Lieutenant Myron Sidney, U.S. Army: *27*
Croix de Guerre (French), award of: *51, 55* (Collishaw), *55* (McCudden), *101* (Samson)
Croix de Guerre (Belgian), award of: *51*
Crosby, Minnesota: *151*
Croydon, England: *126, 127, 130, 131, 132, 134, 160*
Crusader, balloon: *150*
Crystal Palace, London: *11, 151*
Cuerpo de Aeronautica del Perú (Peruvian Air Force), formation of: *95*
Cuerpo de Aeronautica Militar (Guatemalan Air Force), formation of: *94*
Cuerpo de Aviación (Bolivian Air Force), formation of: *93*
Cuerpo de Aviadores Militares (Ecuador Air Force), formation of: *93*
Cuffley, Hertfordshire, England: *66*
Culley, Lieutenant Stuart, D.S.O., R.N.A.S.: *102, 105*
Culmhead, Somerset, England: *71*
Cunco, Chile: *123*
Cunningham, John: *142, 143*
Cunningham, R. Walter, astronaut: *186*
Cunningham, Lieutenant Alfred A., U.S. Marine Corps: *100*
Curtiss A-1 seaplane: *99, 100, 101*
Curtiss AB flying boats: *30, 103*
Curtiss Aeroplane and Motor Company: *106*
Curtiss F9C Sparrowhawk: *108*
Curtiss, Glenn Hammond: *15, 16, 17, 27, 98*
Curtiss HS-1 flying boat: *106*
Curtiss (Navy) NC flying boat: *117, 124*
Curtiss SBC Helldiver: *108, 117*
Curtiss XF9C-1: *108*; XF12C-1: *108*
Curtiss XSC-1 Seahawk: *118*
Czechoslovakia; formation of air force in: *93*; first commercial aircraft: *127*; highest scoring fighter pilot: *72*

D

Dacre, Flight Lieutenant G. B., R.N.A.S.: *103*
Daedalus, myth of: *9*
d'Aeth, N. H.: *143*
Dahl, Oberst Walther: *83, 86*
Dahlbeck, Lieutenant C. O.: *24*
Daily Mail prizes and competitions: *18, 21*
Daimler Airways Ltd.: *127, 128*
Dalkeith Hills, Scotland: *63*
Dallas, Texas: *111*
Dammers, Leutnant Hans: *87*
Danger Hill, Hants, England: *18*
Dardenelles campaign, 1916: *101, 103*
Darwin, Australia: *125, 131, 132*
Davenport, Burl B.: *143*
Davies, Lieutenant Commander Brian, R.N.: *143*
Davis, Flying Officer C. R., D.F.C.: *65*
Dawes, Captain George William Patrick, D.S.O., A.F.C., M.B.E., R.F.C.: *20, 28*
Dayton, Ohio: *17, 27, 128*
DB-3, Russian bomber: *67*
Deal, Kent, England: *24*

14—A.F.F.

Dean, Flying Officer, R.A.F.: *71*
Defries, Colin: *20*
de Havilland D.H.2: *47, 55*
de Havilland D.H.4 and variants: *38, 95, 108, 125, 127, 128*
de Havilland D.H.6: *124*
de Havilland D.H.9 and 9A: *96, 124, 126*
de Havilland D.H.18: *127*
de Havilland D.H.50: *131*
de Havilland D.H.60 Moth and variants: *93, 94, 130, 131, 132*
de Havilland D.H.66 Hercules: *132, 134*
de Havilland D.H.80A Puss Moth: *134, 136*
de Havilland D.H.84 Dragon: *136*
de Havilland D.H.88 Comet racer: *139, 142, 143*
de Havilland D.H.89 Rapide: *94*
de Havilland D.H.100 Vampire: *93, 114*
de Havilland D.H.103 Hornet and Sea Hornet: *88, 118, 142*
de Havilland D.H.106 Comet airliner: *139, 142, 143*
de Havilland D.H.110 Sea Vixen: *120*
de Havilland D.H.121 Trident: *143*
de Havilland Ghost engines: *88, 139*
de Havilland, Geoffrey, Jr.: *88*
Delagrange, Leon: *10, 14, 15, 17, 18*
delta wing plan-form: *91*
Denmark; first aeroplane flight in: *13*; formation of Danish Army Air Corps: *93*; highest scoring fighter pilot: *72*
Denver, Colorado: *25, 141*
Dessau, Germany: *122*
Deutschösterreichische Fliegertruppe (Austro-German Flying Troop): *93*
de Vigne, L. C. E.: *143*
Devyataev, Lieutenant Michael, Soviet Air Force: *68*
DFS 230 glider: *67*
Dickfeld, Oberst Adolf: *86*
Dickson, Captain Bertram: *21, 23*
Digger's Rest, Australia: *21*
Distinguished Flying Cross (American), award of: *80* (J. E. Johnson); *81* (Bong); *99* (Ely)
Distinguished Flying Cross (British), award of: *54* (Bishop); *63* (McPherson); *79, 80* (J. E. Johnson); *106* (Ingalls); number of awards: *83*
Distinguished Flying Medal, award of: *65* (František)
Distinguished Service Cross (American), award of: *81* (Bong)
Distinguished Service Cross (British), award of: *55* (Collishaw); *103* (Rutland)
Distinguished Service Medal (American), award of: *106* (Ingalls)
Distinguished Service Order, award of: *50* (Ball); *54* (Bishop); *55* (Collishaw); *80* (J. E. Johnson); *102* (Samson); *105* (Culley)
Dixon, Lieutenant Commander Robert, U.S. Navy: *111*
Doe, Pilot Officer (later Squadron Leader) R. F. T., D.S.O., D.F.C.*: *65*
Donaldson, Group Captain E. M., C.B.E., D.S.O., D.F.C.: *88*
Doncaster, England: *20*
Dons, Lieutenant Hans E.: *25*
Doolittle, Lieutenant James H., U.S. Air Service: *127*
Doran, Flight Lieutenant K. C., D.F.C., R.A.F.: *63*
Dornier Do 17: *62, 64, 79*
Dornier Do 18: *63, 64, 111*
Dornier Do 215: *64*
Dornier Do 217: *70*
Dörr, Hauptmann Franz: *86*
Douai, France: *23, 25, 50*

Douaumont, France: *47*
Doublin, California: *139*
Douglas A3D Skywarrior: *116, 120*
Douglas A4 Skyhawk: *92, 120*
Douglas BT2D-1 Skyraider: *114, 118*
Douglas DC-2: *137*
Douglas DC-3 (and Dakota, etc.): *137*
Douglas DC-6: *139*
Douglas DC-8: *144*
Douglas DWC World Cruiser: *128, 129*
Douglas F3D Skynight: *115, 118*
Douglas F4D Skyray: *120*
Douglas SBD Dauntless: *111*
Douglas TBD Devastator: *111, 112, 117*
Dover, Kent, England: *19, 21, 30, 31, 149*
Driffield, Yorkshire, England: *63*
Duigan, John R.: *22*
Duke, Squadron Leader Neville F., D.S.O., D.F.C.**,
    A.F.C.: *73*
Duke, Robin: *127*
Dune Park, Illinois: *12*
Dunning, Squadron Commander E. H., R.N.A.S.:
    104
Dun-sur-Meuse, France: *57*
Düsseldorf, Germany: *31, 101, 102*
Dutch Harbour, Aleutians: *129*
Düttmann, Leutnant Peter: *86*
Duxford, England: *79*

                            E
E.14, H.M. submarine: *103*
Eagle Farm, Brisbane, Australia: *131*
Eagle, H.M. aircraft carrier: *106, 110*
Eagle, lunar module: *183*
Earhart, Miss Amelia (Mrs. Putnam): *131, 134, 137*
Eastchurch, England: *31, 99, 102*
Eckener, Dr. Hugo: *132*
Ecuador, formation of air force in: *93*
Edmonds, Flight Commander C. H., R.N.A.S.: *103*
Edmondson, Woodrow W.: *142, 144*
Edward VII, H.M. King: *10, 21*
Effimov, M.: *21*
Egypt; first aeroplane flights in: *20*; Egyptian Air Force,
    formation of: *93*; Egypt to India, first aeroplane flight:
    123
Ehrler, Major Heinrich: *85*
Eisele, Major Donn F., U.S.A.F.: *186*
Eisenach, Major Franz: *86*
electric-powered airship: *152*
Ellehammer, J. C. H.: *10, 13, 14, 159*
Elliott-Lynn, Mrs. (see Heath, Lady)
Ellyson, Lieutenant Theodore G., U.S. Navy: 99
Elsham Wolds, Lincolnshire, England: *68*
Elvington, Yorkshire, England: *71*
Ely, Eugene B.: 99
Empress, H.M. seaplane carrier: *101*
endurance records by aeroplanes: *21, 128*
Engadine, H.M. seaplane carrier: *101, 103*
England; first aeroplane flight by an Englishman in: *18*
England to Australia; first aeroplane flight: *125*; first
    solo flight: *131*; first solo flight by a woman: *132*; first
    regular weekly air mail service: *137*; first through
    passenger air service: *137*
England to Egypt; first aeroplane flight: *123*
England to India; first non-stop flight attempt: *130*;
    first light aeroplane flight: *130*; first commercial air
    route: *132*; first non-stop flight: *132*
England to South Africa; first aeroplane flight: *126*;
    first light aeroplane flight: *131*; first solo return flight

by a woman: *131*; first non-stop flight: *136*; first jet
    passenger service: *139*
England to South America; first aeroplane flight: *136*
English Channel; first aeroplane attempt to cross: *19*;
    first successful aeroplane crossing: *19*; first double
    crossing by an aeroplane: *21*; first woman pilot to
    cross *24*; first crossing by a balloon: *149*; first crossing
    by a rotorcraft: *160*
English Electric Canberra: *90, 142, 143, 144*
Enterprise, U.S. aircraft carrier (first vessel): *110*
ENV engines: *23*
Eremea, G. P.: *142, 143*
Escadrille Lafayette: 56
Escola, Teniente de Navio Melchor Z., Argentine Navy:
    100
Escuela de Aviación, Flandes, Colombia: *93*
Escuela de Aviación Militar (see Palomar, El)
Espejo, Lo, Chile: *93*
Essen, Germany: *67*
Essex, U.S. aircraft carrier class: *116*
Ethiopia, formation of air force in (Imperial Ethiopian
    Air Force): *93*
Etrich, Igo: *14*
Ettel, Oberleutnant Wolf: *86*
Eubank, William E.: *144*
Eugene, Oregon, U.S.A.: *129*
Eveley, Major Clyde P., U.S.A.F.: *142, 144*
exhibition, first aeronautical: *11*

                            F
Fabre, Henri: *98*
Fairchild, F-27: *139*
Fairey IIIC: *127*
Fairey Albacore: *117*
Fairey Firefly: *118*
Fairey Fulmar: *118*
Fairey Long-range Monoplane: *132, 136*
Fairey Swordfish: *111*
Fälttelegrafkårens Flygkompani (Swedish Field Telegraph
    Aviation Company): formation of: *96*
Farman biplanes (Henry): *20, 21, 22, 23, 24, 28, 30, 36,
    93, 94, 95*
Farman biplanes (Maurice): *29, 47, 100, 101*
Farman Goliath: *127*
Farman, Henry: *10, 14, 16, 17, 20, 21*
Farnborough, Hants, England: *15, 28*
Fassong, Hauptmann Horst-Günther von: *86*
Faubourg St. Antoine, Paris: *146*
F.E.2b: *37, 47*
F.E.2d: *55*
Fédération Aéronautique Internationale (F.A.I.): *26*
Feldfliegerabteilungen of the *Luftstreitkräfte:* Nr. 13: *48*;
    Nr. 62: *48, 49*; Nr. 69: *47*
Feoktiskov, Konstantin Petrovich: *185*
Ferguson, H. G.: *20*
Fernbrugg, Oberleutnant Benno Fiala, Ritter von: *41*
Fero, Robert W., Jr.: *142, 143*
Ferrol del Caudillo, Spain: *124*
Fiat BR.20: *144*
Fickel, Lieutenant Jacob Earl, U.S. Army: *27*
Fieseler Fi 156: *62, 64*
Fiji Islands: *131, 137*
Filipchenko, Lieutenant Colonel Anatoly V.: *187*
Finch, John: *144*
Finland: *22, 63, 67*; Finnish Air Force: *63, 67*; highest
    scoring fighter pilot: *72*; Squadron HleLv.24: *63*
Finucane, Wing Commander Brendan E., D.S.O.,
    D.F.C.**: *72, 73*
Fisherman's Bend, Australia: *67*

Fiske, Pilot Officer William M. L., R.A.F.: *66*
Flavell, Squadron Leader E. J. G., A.F.C.: *91*
Fleet Air Arm, formation of: *93*
Fleurant, Monsieur: *148*
Fleurus, Battle of, 1794: *149*
Fliegertruppe (Swiss Air Corps), formation of: *96*
flight re-fuelling: *128*
Flyer, Wright brothers' aeroplane: *10, 13, 14, 15, 22*
Flygvapnet (Royal Swedish Air Force): *88*; formation of: *96*
Flying Doctor Service, Australian: *131*
Focke-Wulf Fw 190: *80*
Focke-Wulf Fw 200: *142*
Fokker C.2: *130*
Fokker D VII: *51*
Fokker D VIII: *38*
Fokker D.XXI: *63, 64, 67*
Fokker Dr. I triplane: *38, 47, 48*
Fokker E-series monoplanes: *48, 49*
Fokker F.VIIa: *130*; F.VIIb-3m: *131*
Fokker T-2: *128*
Fonck, Capitaine René Paul: *40, 51, 52, 53*
Fönnekold Oberleutnant Otto: *86*
Foot, Major E. L.: *125*
Forca Aérea Portuguesa (Portuguese Air Force), formation of: *95*
Force Aérienne Belge, La (the Belgian Air Force), formation of: *93*
Forêt de Felmores, France: *149*
Formosa, air operations off: *113*
Fort Worth, Texas; speed records to Madrid, St. Louis (Missouri), and Washington D.C.: *142*
Foss, Major J. J., U.S. Marine Corps: *73*
Foudre, French torpedo boat carrier: *100*
Foyle Bank, H.M.S.: *66*
France; first naval aeroplanes in: *100*; German invasion of, 1940: *64, 65*; highest scoring fighter pilot: *72*
Frankfurt, German cruiser: *106*
Franklin D. Roosevelt, U.S.S.: *114*
František, Sergeant Josef, D.F.M.: *65, 72*
Frantz, Sergent Joseph: *31*
Frederick, South Dakota: *151*
Frederiksdal, Greenland: *129*
Freedom 7 spacecraft: *182*
Fresson, E. E.: *136*
Frewin, Ken: *67*
Frey, Hauptmann Hugo: *83*
Freytag, Major Siegfried: *87*
Friedrich August Medal: *49*
Friedrichshafen, Germany: *132, 152*
Fuchida, Commander Mitsuo: *77*
Fuerza Aérea Colombiana (Colombian Air Force), formation of: *93*
Fuerza Aérea de la Guardia Nacional (Nicaraguan Air Force), formation of: *95*
Fuerza Aérea Mexicana (Mexican Air Force), formation of: *95*
Fuerzas Aéreas Nacionales (Paraguayan Air Forces), formation: *95*
Fullard, Captain P. F., C.B.E., D.S.O., M.C.*, A.F.C.: *39*
Füllgrabe, Oberfeldwebel: *78*
Furious, H.M. aircraft carrier: *103, 104, 110*
Furnas, Charles W.: *16*

G

G-102, German destroyer: *106*
Gabreski, Colonel F. S., U.S.A.F.: *73, 77*
Gagarin, Flight Major Yuriy Alexeyevich: *182, 185*

Galeh-Morghi, Persia: *94*
Galland, Major (later General) Adolf: *79, 82, 87*
Gallipoli, landings at, 1916: *101*
Gamma, airship: *152*
Gander, Newfoundland; speed records to Belfast (Northern Ireland), Bonn (Germany), London, Paris, Shannon (Ireland): *142*
Garden City, New York: *121*
Gardner, Edward V.: *123*
Gardner Field, California: *80*
Garros, Roland: *122*
Gatchina, U.S.S.R.: *96*
Gaudron, A. F.: *151*
Gaydon, Warwickshire, England: *91*
Gayford, Squadron Leader O. R., R.A.F.: *136*
Geisshardt, Hauptmann Friedrich: *87*
Gemini spacecraft: *185, 186*
General Dynamics-Convair B-58 Hustler: *142, 143, 144*
General Dynamics F-111A: *89, 97*
General Electric Co., Ltd., England: *121*
General Electric J-79 engine: *116*
Genoa, Italy: *132*
George V, H.M. King: *24, 100, 126*
George Cross, award of: *66* (Hollowday)
George Medal, award of: *91* (Waterton)
Georgian Bay, Ontario, Canada: *136*
Gerli, brothers Augustin and Charles: *148*
Germany; first aeroplane flight in: *14*; formation of military air force in: *93*; highest scoring fighter pilot: *72*
Geyensdorffer, Captain G. J., K.L.M.: *130*
Ghent, Belgium: *36*
Gibraltar to London, speed record: *142*
Giffard, Henri: *149, 152*
Gillman, Flight Lieutenant L. E. M., R.A.F.: *130*
Gillmore, Captain J., D.S.O., M.C.**: *39*
Glaisher, James: *151*
Glavnoe Upravlenie Raboche-Krestyanskogo Krasnogo Vozdushnogo Flota (GU-RKKVF, Chief Administration of the Workers' and Peasants' Red Air Fleet), formation of: *96*
Glenn, Lieutenant Colonel John Herschel, U.S. Marine Corps: *185*
gliders, early models: *9, 10, 11, 12*; in Australia: *20*
Globe, balloon: *146*
Glorious, H.M. aircraft carrier: *110*
Gloster Gladiator: *75, 84*
Gloster Javelin: *91*
Gloster Meteor: *71, 88, 142, 143*
Gloucester County, New Jersey: *149*
Gnôme engines: *20, 24, 98, 122*
Godoy, Teniente Dagoberto: *123*
Godstow, Oxford, England: *25*
Gollob, Major Gordon: *79, 86*
Gonesse, Paris: *146*
Goodyear F-1 airship: *153*
Gorbatko, Lieutenant Colonel Viktor V.: *187*
Gordon Bennett, James, balloon contest: *151*; results: *154–157*
Gordon, Lieutenant Commander Richard F., U.S. Navy: *186*
Grade, Hans: *14*
Graf, Oberleutnant (later Oberst) Hermann: *78, 85*
Graf Zeppelin, airship: *132*
Grahame-White, Claude: *21, 22*
Grahame-White Flying School, Hendon, England: *24*
Grahame-White Flying School, Pau, France: *21*
Graham, John G.: *139*
Grands Express Aèriens: *127*

Grand, Sikorsky: *29*
"Grand Slam", 22,000-lb (9,988 kg.) bomb: *71, 91*
Gran, Tryggve: *122*
Grasser, Major Hartmann: *87*
Gratz, Leutnant Karl: *86*
Gray, Pilot Officer (later Group Captain) Colin F., D.S.O., D.F.C.**: *65, 72, 73*
Gray, Lieutenant Robert Hampton, V.C., D.S.C., R.C.V.R.: *83*
Greece; formation of air force in: *93*; campaign in:, 1940–41: *75*
Green, Charles: *149*
Green engines: *152*
Gregory, Lieutenant R., R.N.: *99*
Grey, Squadron Commander Spenser D. A., R.N.A.S.: *31*
Griffin, Commander Virgil C., U.S. Navy: *107*
Grimley, Charles: *150*
Grislawski, Feldwebel (later Hauptmann) Alfred: *78, 86*
Grissom, Captain Virgil Ivan, U.S.A.F.: *185*
Grover, Captain G. E., R.E.: *150*
Grumman Albatross: *118*
Grumman A-6 Intruder: *120*
Grumman E-2 Hawkeye: *120*
Grumman F4F Wildcat: *111, 117*
Grumman F6F Hellcat: *77, 118*
Grumman F7F Tigercat: *112, 118*
Grumman F8F Bearcat: *118*
Grumman F9F Panther: *115, 118*
Grumman F9F-6 Cougar: *120*
Grumman F11F Tiger: *115, 120*
Grumman XFF-1 and FF-1: *109*
Grumman XF2F-1: *117*
Grumman XF10F-1 Jaguar: *91*
Grumman XJF-1 Duck: *117*
Grumman XS2F-1 Tracker: *120*
Grumman XTB3F-1 Guardian: *118*
Guadalcanal: *77*
Guantánamo Bay, Cuba: *106*
Guatemala, formation of air force in: *94*
Gudmundsson, M.: *142*
Guidoni, Capitano Alessandro: *101*
guncotton as fuel for internal combustion engines: *10, 11*
Guynemer, Capitaine Georges Marie Ludovic Jules: *40, 52, 53*

H

Hachtel, Oberleutnant August: *70*
Hackett, John W.: *144*
Hackl, Major Anton: *85*
Haerens Flyvåpen (Norwegian Army Air Service), formation of: *95*
Hafner, Oberleutnant Anton: *85*
Hahn, Major Hans "Assi": *87*
Haile Selassie, His Imperial Majesty Emperor: *93*
Haiphong, Indo-China: *129*
Haitian *Corps d'Aviation*, formation of: *94*
Halberstadt aircraft: *57*
Halberstadt Flying School: *48*
Hales bombs: *31*
Halifax, Nova Scotia: *124*
Hamburg, Germany: *31, 128, 130*
Hamburg Hanseatic Cross: *49*
Hamel, Gustav: *24*
Hamilton, Canada: *122*
Hamilton Field, California: *80*
Hammondsport, New York: *18, 27*
Hampton Roads, Virginia: *99*
Handley Page Air Transport Ltd.: *124, 125, 128*

Handley Page Hannibal: *134*
Handley Page Heyford: *62*
Handley Page Hinaidi: *131*
Handley Page 0/7: *125*
Handley Page 0/10: *126*
Handley Page 0/400: *123, 124, 126*
Hannover CL III: *56*
Hanriot HD–1: *106*
Hansa-Brandenburg C I: *122*
Hanson, Lieutenant R. M., U.S. Marine Corps: *73*
Hanworth, England: *134*
Harbour Grace, Newfoundland: *136*
Harding, Lieutenant John, Jr., U.S. Air Service: *129*
Harrow, Middlesex, England: *149*
Hartmann, Major Erich: *72, 75, 78, 81, 82, 85*
Harvey-Kelly, Lieutenant H. D., R.F.C.: *30*
Harvey, Sergeant Alva L., U.S. Air Service: *128*
Harwich, England: *105*
Havana, Cuba: *126, 131*; speed record to Washington, D.C.: *142*
Hawaii: *108, 130, 131, 137*
Hawker Fury/Sea Fury: *118*
Hawker Horsley: *130*
Hawker Hunter: *143, 144*
Hawker Hurricane: *65, 75, 84*
Hawker, Major Lanoe G., V.C., D.S.O., R.F.C.: *47*
Hawker Sea Hawk: *118, 142*
Hawker Siddeley Kestrel: *88–89*
Hawkes Bay, Newfoundland: *129*
Hazell, Major T. F., D.S.O., M.C., D.F.C.*: *39*
Heath, Lady (previously Mrs. Elliot-Lynn): *131*
Hebborn, A. W.: *143*
Hegenberger, Lieutenant Albert F., U.S. Air Service: *130*
Heglund, Flight Lieutenant Svein: *72*
Heimerdinger, A. G.: *143, 144*
Heinkel He 59: *62*
Heinkel He 111: *62, 64, 68*
Heinkel He 162: *71*
Heinkel He 280: *66*
Heinkel Hirth HeS 5A engine: *66*
helicopters, early design attempts: *9, 10*
Heligoland Bight: *67*
Heliopolis, Egypt: *20, 123*
Henderson, G. N.: *142*
Hendon, Middlesex, England: *12* (footnote), *24, 49*
Henke, A.: *142, 143*
Henschel Hs 123: *62, 64*
Henschel Hs 126: *62, 64*
Henson, W. S.: *9, 11*
Heriot's Garden, Edinburgh: *148*
Hermes, H.M. aircraft carrier: *107, 110*
Hermes, H.M. seaplane carrier: *101*
Herndon, Hugh: *134*
Herne Bay, Kent, England: *88*
Herring, Augustus M.: *12*
Hervé, Capitaine: *29*
Hesepe, Germany: *69*
Heston, England: *136*
Hewlett, Mrs. Hilda B.: *24*
Hewlett, Sub-Lieutenant F. E. T., R.N.: *24*
Hibernia, H.M. battleship: *100, 102*
Hiddeson, Leutnant Franz von: *30*
Highland Airways: *136*
Hilsz, Mlle Maryse: *144*
Hindenburg, airship: *153*
Hingham, Norfolk, England: *37*
Hinkler, Squadron Leader H. J. L. ("Bert"): *131, 134*
Hinton, Lieutenant Walter, U.S. Navy: *124*

Hiroshima, Japan: *81*
Hiryu, Japanese aircraft carrier: *110*
Hispano-Suiza engines: *105*
Hittokapu, Japan: *129*
Hobart, Tasmania, Australia: *137*
Hodges, J. M.: *143*
Hoffmann, Leutnant Gerhard: *86*
Hohenzollern Order: *49*
Holland, Robert, M.P.: *149*
Hollowday, Aircraftman Vivian ("Bob"), G.C.: *66*
Holtje, Herr Gerhard: *141*
Holyhead, Anglesey: *22*
Holyman's Airways (Australia): *137*
Hong Kong: *129*
Honolulu, Hawaii: *108, 130, 131, 183*; first solo flight to American mainland: *137*; speed record to London: *142*
Hooghly River, India: *127*
Hornafjord, Iceland: *129*
Hornum, Germany: *63*
Horsham St. Faith, Norfolk, England: *87*
Horta, Azores: *124*
Hosho, Japanese aircraft carrier: *107, 110*
Hotchkiss, Lieutenant E., R.F.C.R.: *25*
Hotchkiss machine gun: *31*
Houdini, Harry (see Weiss, Ehrich)
Hounslow, England: *125*
Hove, Sussex, England: *121*
Howard-Wright biplane: *23*
Howden, Yorkshire, England: *132*
Hoy, Captain Ernest C.: *125*
Hrabak, Oberst Dietrich: *86*
Hubbart Air Service: *124*
Hubbard, Wing Commander K. G., O.B.E., D.F.C., A.F.C.: *92*
Hughes, Flight Lieutenant P. C., D.F.C.: *65*
Hughes H-2 Hercules flying boat: *114*
Hull, Yorkshire, England: *153*
Humber-built aircraft: *23*
Humphrey, A. H.: *142*
Hunaudières race course, France: *15*
Hungary; formation of air force in: *94*; highest scoring fighter pilot: *72*
hydrogen: *145 et passim*
hydrogen bomb: *92*

I

Ibn Saud: *96*
Icarus, myth of: *9*
Ihlefeld, Oberst Herbert: *86*
Ilya Mourametz, Sikorsky: *29*
Ilyushin Il-28: *92*
Imbias Medal: *49*
Immelmann, Leutnant Max: *48, 49*
Imperial Airways: *128, 134, 136, 137*
Imperial Ethiopian Air Force, formation of: *93*
India; early flights in: *23*; formation of air force in: *94*
Indianapolis, Indiana: *128*
Indian Harbour, Labrador: *129*
Indian Trans-Continental Airways: *137*
Indonesian Air Force (*Angkatan Udara Republik Indonesia*), formation of: *94*
Indo-Pakistan confrontation, 1967: *90*
Ingalls, Lieutenant David S., U.S. Navy: *106*
Inouye, Vice-Admiral Shigeyoshi, Imperial Japanese Navy: *111*
Instone Air Lines Ltd.: *128*
insurance, aircraft accident: *136*; crime involving: *139*
Inverness, Scotland: *136*
Iran (Persia), formation of air force in: *94*

Iraqi Air Force: *92*; (see also Royal Iraqi Air Force)
Ireland; first aeroplane flights in: *20*; formation of air force in: *94*; highest scoring fighter pilot: *72*
Irish Sea, first aeroplane crossing of the: *22*
Irkutsk, U.S.S.R.: *136*
Iron Crescent, Order of the: *49*
Iron Cross, award of: *48, 49, 79*
"Iron Hammer", Operation; attack on the Vistula bridges, 1945: *77*
Irwin, Flight Lieutenant H. C., A.F.C., R.A.F.: *132*
Israeli Defence Force/Air Force: *90, 92*; formation of: *94*
Issoudun, France: *56*
Issy-les-Moulineaux, France: *14, 16, 17, 24*
Italia, Italian battleship: *70*
Italo–Turkish war, 1911: *94*
Italy; first aeroplane flight in: *14*; formation of air force in: *94*; highest scoring fighter pilot: *72*; entry of British airliners controlled: *132*
Ivigtut, Greenland: *129*

J

Jabara, Captain James, U.S.A.F.: *90*
Jacksonville, Florida: *127*
Jacobs, Leutnant Josef: *40*
Jacquet, Capitaine Fernand, D.F.C.: *46*
Jagdstaffeln of the *Luftstreitkräfte*; *Jasta* 2: *47, 48, 49*; *Jasta* 4: *48*; *Jasta* 6: *48*; *Jasta* 10: *48*; *Jasta* 11: *47, 48, 55*; *Jasta* 20: *50*
Jahnow, Oberleutnant Reinhold: *28*
Jamaica, West Indies: *134*
Japan; formation of air forces in: *94*; first naval pilots: *100*; highest scoring fighter pilot: *72*
Japanese Air Self Defence Force, formation of: *94*
Japanese Navy, Imperial: *77*
Japan to U.S.A., first non-stop flight: *134*
JAP engines: *20*
Japy, André: *143*
Jeffries, Dr. John: *149*
Jenkins, Flight Lieutenant N. H., O.B.E., D.F.C., D.S.M., R.A.F.: *132*
jet air liner service, world's first: *139*
Jet Clipper Windward, aircraft: *139*
jet-powered airliner, world's first: *139*
Johannisthal, Germany: *31*
Johnson, Group Captain James E., D.S.O.**, D.F.C.*: *72, 73, 75, 79, 80*
Johnson, Lieutenant Colonel R. S., U.S.A.F.: *73*
Johnson, Miss Amy: *132*
Jones, Captain J. I. T., D.S.O., M.C., D.F.C.*, M.M.: *39*
Jones Williams, Squadron Leader A. G., M.C., R.A.F.: *132*
Jope, Major Bernhard: *70*
Jordan, formation of air force in: *94*
Josten, Oberleutnant Günther: *85*
Jullerot, Henri: *23*
Jumna River, India: *23*
June Bug, Curtiss aircraft: *16*
Junkers, Forschungsansalt Professor: *122*
Junkers F-13: *94*
Junkers G-23: *130*
Junkers J-1 ("Tin Donkey"): *122*
Junkers Ju 52/3m: *62, 64, 67, 130*
Junkers Ju 87: *62, 64, 75*
Junkers Ju 88: *64, 71, 77*
Junkers Jumo engines: *68, 69, 88*
Junkers, Professor Hugo: *122*
Jupiter, U.S.S.: *106, 107, 110*
Jutland, Battle of, 1916: *103*

Jutland coast: *31*
Juutualainen, Flight Master E. I.: *72*

K

Kabul, Afghanistan: *131*
Kaga, Japanese aircraft carrier: *109, 110*
Kagoshima, Japan: *129*
Kamikaze (see Shimpu): *112*
Kansas City, Missouri: *128*
Karachi, India (Pakistan): *123, 129, 130, 131, 132, 137, 139*
Kastner, Hauptmann: *48, 49*
Kasumiga Ura, Japan: *129*
Kavanagh, Miss Spenser (see Cook, Miss Edith Maud)
Kawanishi N1K1-J ("George"): *118*
Kazakov, Staff Captain A. A.: *41*
Kazarinova, Major Tamara Aleksandrovna: *68*
Kelb, Oberleutnant Fritz: *70*
Kelly Field, Texas: *127*
Kelly, Lieutenant O. G., U.S. Air Service: *128*
Kenley, England: *80*
Kennedy Airport, New York: *141*
Kennedy, President John F.: *183*
Kenney, General George C., U.S.A.F.: *81*
Kesler, Chief Machinist's Mate C. I., U.S. Navy: *124*
Keuka, Lake, New York: *98*
Key West, Florida: *126, 131*
Khartoum, Sudan: *134, 139*
Khrunov, Lieutenant Colonel Yevgeny: *187*
Kiaochow Bay, China: *101*
Kiel, Germany: *14*
Kiev, U.S.S.R.: *122*
Kill Devil Hills, North Carolina: *10, 13, 17*
Kimberley, South Africa: *96*
Kindley, Captain F. E.: *41*
King, Captain W. A. de C., R.E.: *152*
Kirkwall, Orkneys: *129, 136*
Kirschner, Hauptmann Joachim: *85*
Kiss, Leutnant Josef: *41*
Kittel, Oberleutnant Otto: *85*
K.L.M. (Royal Dutch Airlines): *125, 128, 137*
Knight, Jack: *127*
Knight's Cross, holders of the: *75, 78, 79, 85–87*
Knocke, Hauptmann Heinz: *83*
Komandorski, Kamchatka: *129*
Komarov, Colonel Vladimir Mihailovich: *185, 186*
König, Hauptmann Hans-Heinrich: *83*
Korea, air operations over, 1950–53: *90, 115*
Korean People's Armed Forces Air Corps, formation of: *94*
Korea, Republic of, Air Force, formation of: *94*
Koroto, Uganda: *126*
Korts, Leutnant Berthold: *87*
Kowalski, Oberstleutnant Robert: *69*
Kozhedub, Guards Colonel Ivan N.: *72, 75*
Kraków, Poland: *62, 122*
Krebs, Lieutenant Arthur: *152*
Krupinski, Major Walter: *85*
Kubasov, Valery N.: *187*
Kubetsch, Major S. J.: U.S.A.F.: *142, 144*
Kukkonen, Sergeant, Finnish Air Force: *63*
Kursk, Battle of, 1943: *78*
Kushimoto, Japan: *129*

L

Labeuville, France: *57*
Lacey, Sergeant (later Squadron Leader) J. H., D.F.M.*: *65, 73*
Lae, New Guinea: *77*

Laffan's Plain, Hants, England: *18, 19*
Laika, Russian space dog: *182*
Lakehurst, New Jersey: *132, 153*
La Legion d'Honneur, appointment to: *51, 102*
Lambert, Oberleutnant August: *87*
La Muette, Chateau, Paris: *146*
Lancashire Aero Club: *20*
Landis, Major R. G., U.S. Army: *41*
Landskrona, Sweden: *22*
Lang, Hauptmann Emil: *85*
Langley, Samuel Pierpont: *10, 12*
Langley, U.S.S.: *106, 107, 110*
Laon, France: *51*
Larissa, Greece: *94*
Larkhill, England: *29*
Latham, Hubert: *19, 20, 21*
Lavender, Lieutenant Commander R. A., U.S. Navy: *124*
Lavochkin La 5N: *75*
Lavoisier, Antoine L.: *145*
Lawford, Lieutenant E. H. ("Bill"): *125*
Lebanese Air Force: *92*; formation of: *94*
Le Bourget, Paris: *125, 127*
Le Brix, Lieutenant Joseph: *131*
Leck/Holstein, Germany: *71*
Lee, Captain H. P., R.E.: *150*
Leefe Robinson, Lieutenant W., V.C., R.F.C.: *66*
Lee Lewis Memorial Winzen Research balloon: *151*
Leete, B. S.: *130*
Legagneux, G.: *14, 15*
Legion of Merit, award of: *80* (J. E. Johnson)
Le Gustav, balloon: *148*
Leie, Oberstleutnant Erich: *87*
Le Mans, France: *15, 17*
Le May, General Curtiss E., U.S.A.F.: *142*
Lemke, Hauptmann Wilhelm: *86*
Lenin, Order of: *68*
Lent, Oberst Helmut: *87*
Leonardo da Vinci: *9, 159*
Leonardo da Vinci airport, Rome: *141*
Leonov, Lieutenant Colonel Aleksey Arkhipovich: *185*
Lethbridge, Alberta, Canada: *125*
Levasseur P.L.8: *53*
Levavasseur: *10*
Lévy-Lepen flying boat: *126*
Lewis, Second Lieutenant D. G., R.A.F.: *4*
Lewis machine guns: *28, 30*
Lexington, U.S.S.: *107, 108, 109, 110, 111*
Leysdown, Isle of Sheppey: *18*
Liberty engines: *57, 106*
Lilienthal, Otto: *9, 10, 11, 12*
Lindbergh, Captain Charles: *130*
Ling-Temco-Vought (see LTV)
Linke-Crawford, Oberleutnant Frank: *41*
Linke-Hofman R II: *38*
Lipfert, Hauptmann Helmut: *85*
Lisbon, Portugal: *124*; speed records to Buenos Aires and Frankfurt: *142*
Lisieux, France: *159*
Litchfield, H. A.: *131*
Lithgow, Michael J.: *143, 144*
Little, Captain R. A., D.S.O.*, D.S.C.*: *39*
Litvak, Lieutenant Lydia: *68*
Llangattock, 1st Baron: *22*
Lock, Pilot Officer (later Squadron Leader) E. S., D.S.O., D.F.C.*: *65, 73*
Lockheed Aircraft Corporation, Burbank, California: *81*
Lockheed C-130 Hercules: *142*
Lockheed F-104G Starfighter: *142*

Lockheed Jetstar: *142, 143, 144*
Lockheed P-38 Lightning: *77, 80, 81*
Lockheed P-80 Shooting Star: *81, 90*
Lockheed PV Ventura: *118*
Lockheed P2V Neptune: *114, 118*
Lockheed SR-71A: *97*
Lockheed Vega: *136, 137*
Lockheed YF-12A: *97*
Loerzer, Hauptmann Bruno: *40*
Loewenhardt, Oberleutnant Erich: *40*
London, England; point-to-point speed records to: Aden, Amsterdam, Basra, Bermuda, Bierut, Bonn, Brussels, Buenos Aires, Christchurch (New Zealand): *142*; Colombo, Copenhagen, Darwin, Johannesburg, Karachi, Kuwait, Valetta (Malta), Cairo, Cape Town, Lisbon, Melbourne, Nairobi, New York, Paris, Reykjavik, Rome, Sydney, Tripoli, Wellington: *143*
London to Berlin: first scheduled air service: *128*
Londonderry, Northern Ireland: *136*
London Gazette: *83*
London–Manchester air race: *21*
London–Paris; first non-stop flight: *24*; first scheduled commercial airline flight: *125*; first jet airliner service: *139*
Long Beach, California: *114*
Longmont, Colorado: *139*
Longmore, Lieutenant A. M., R.N. (later Air Chief Marshal Sir Arthur, G.C.B., D.S.O., R.A.F.): *99, 100, 101*
López, Francisco Solano: *150*
Loraine, Robert: *22*
Los Angeles, California: *132, 134*; speed records to New York, Paris, Stockholm and Tokyo: *143*
Los Angeles, U.S. airship: *108*
Louis XVI, King of France: *146*
Lovell, Commander James Arthur, U.S. Navy: *186, 187*
Lowe, Thaddeus Sobieski Coulincourt: *98*
LTV F8U Crusader: *116, 120*
LTV A-7A Corsair II: *120*
Lualdi, M.: *144*
Lucas, Hauptmann Werner: *87*
Lufbery, Major G. Raoul: *41*
Lufthansa (Deutsche Lufthansa): *141*
Luftstreitkräfte: *47, 49*
Luftwaffe: *64, 66, 67*; units of the *Luftwaffe*: *Jagdgeschwader*: JG 1: *48, 71*,; JG 7: *70*; JG 27: *75, 79*; JG 52: *75, 78, 79*; JG 400: *70*; *Kampfgeschwader*: KG 26: *63*; KG 30: *64*; KG 51: *69*; KG 76: *69*; KG 100: *70*; KG 101: *77*; *Küstenfliegergruppe 506*: *63, 111*; *Lehrgeschwader 2*: *79*
Luke, Second Lieutenant Frank, Jr.: *41, 56, 57*
Luke Field, Arizona: *80*
Lunardi, Vincenzo: *148, 149*
Lushington, Lieutenant G. V. W., R.M.A.: *99*
Lützow, Oberst Günther: *87*
Luukkanen, Lieutenant Eino, Finnish Air Force: *63*
Lwów, Poland: *62, 122*
Lym, Art: *93*
Lympne, Kent, England: *134, 136*
Lyon, Harry: *131*
Lyons, France: *148*

M

Macaulay, Theodore: *122*
McCampbell, Captain D., U.S. Navy: *73, 77*
McClean, F. K.: *25*
McClellan, General: *98*
McConnell, Captain Joseph, Jr., U.S.A.F.: *90*
McCubbin, Second Lieutenant G. R., R.F.C.: *49*

McCudden, Major James Thomas Byford, V.C., D.S.O.*, M.C.*, M.M.: *39, 55, 56*
McCullough, Lieutenant David H., U.S. Navy: *124*
McCurdy, John A. Douglas: *18, 19*
McDivitt, Major James Alton, U.S.A.F.: *186, 187*
MacDonald, Colonel C. H., U.S.A.F.: *73*
McDonnell Banshee: *118*
McDonnell Demon: *120*
McDonnell FH-1 Phantom: *114, 118*
McDonnell F4 Phantom II: *120, 143*
McDonnell, Lieutenant Commander Edward O., U.S. Navy: *106*
McDowall, Sergeant (later Wing Commander) A., D.S.O., A.F.C., D.F.M.*: *65, 71*
McElroy, Captain G. E. H., M.C.**, D.F.C.: *39*
Macewicz, Brigadier General: *95*
McGuire, Major T. B., U.S.A.F.: *73*
McKellar, Flight Lieutenant A. A., D.S.O., D.F.C.*: *65*
MacLaren, Major D. R., D.S.O., M.C.*, D.F.C.: *39*
McMaster, Sir Fergus: *126*
Macmillan, Captain (later Wing Commander) Norman, O.B.E., M.C., A.F.C.: *127*
McMullen, Flying Officer D. A. P., D.F.C.**: *65*
Macon, U.S. airship: *108*
McPherson, Flying Officer A., D.F.C.: *62*
Macready, Lieutenant J. A., U.S. Air Services: *128*
McWilliam, T. H.: *131*
Mader, Dr.: *122*
Madon, Capitaine Georges F.: *40*
Madrid, Spain: *134*; speed record to New York: *143*
Magdeburg, Germany: *14*
Maitland, Lieutenant Lester J., U.S. Air Service: *130*
Majendie, Captain A. M., B.O.A.C.: *139*
Malan, Group Captain A. G., D.S.O.*, D.F.C.*: *73*
Malaya; formation of air force in: *95*; Auxiliary Air Force, formation of: *95*
Malmédy, Belgium: *28*
Malmö, Sweden: *130*
Malta, G.C.: *70, 131*
Mammoth, balloon: *151*
Manly, Charles M.: *12*
Mannert L. Abele, U.S.S.: *112*
Mannock, Major Edward, V.C., D.S.O.**, M.C.*: *39, 52*
Manston, England: *71*
Mantle, Acting Seaman J. F., V.C., R.N.: *66*
Manxman, H.M. seaplane carrier: *103*
Maralinga, Australia: *91*
Marconi Wireless Telegraph Co. Ltd.: *124*
Marine Luchtvaartdienst (Netherlands Naval Aviation Arm), formation of: *95*
Marinens Flyvevaesen (Norwegian Naval Air Service), formation of: *95*
Marix, Flight Lieutenant R. L. G., R.N.A.S.: *31, 102*
Markham, Mrs. Beryl: *137*
Marmara, Sea of, air operations over the: *103*
Marne, Battle of the: *53*
Marquardt, Oberfeldwebel Heinz: *87*
Marsden, Captain J. T. A., B.O.A.C.: *139*
Marseille, Oberleutnant Hans-Joachim: *75, 79, 82, 85*
Martigues, France: *98*
Martin, J. L.: *142, 143, 144*
Martin, Major Frederick, U.S. Air Service: *128–129*
Martin M-130: *137*
Martin MB-2: *106*
Martin Marlin: *118*
Martin XBTM-1 Mauler: *118*
Martin XPBM-1 Mariner: *117*

Martinsyde Type A Mark II: *94*
Martlesham Heath, Suffolk, England (Aircraft and Armament Experimental Establishment): *62*
Mason, Monck: *149*
Mathers, Corporal, R.A.F.: *123*
May, Second Lieutenant W. R., R.A.F.: *48*
Mayer, Oberstleutnant Egon: *82, 83, 87*
Meagher, Captain A., B.O.A.C.: *139*
Medal of Honor, Congressional: *41*; award of: *56* (Rickenbacker); *57* (Luke); *80* (Bong)
Medway River, England: *100*
Melbourne, Australia: *22, 137, 150*
Mendoza, Argentine: *123*
Menin, France: *36*
Mercedes engines: *38*
Mercury, Operation; German invasion of Crete, 1941: *66*
Messerschmitt Bf 109: *62, 64, 75, 77, 79, 80*
Messerschmitt Bf 110: *62, 64*
Messerschmitt Me 163 Komet: *70*
Messerschmitt Me 262A: *68, 69*
Metrovick Beryl engines: *115*
Meulemeester, Adjutant André de: *46*
Meuse River, France: *57*
Meusnier, Lieutenant Jean Baptiste Marie: *151*
Mexico; formation of air force in: *95*; first Mexican pilot: *28*; Mexican Military Aviation: *28*; American punitive operations in, 1916: *36, 38*
Mexico City to New York, first non-stop flight: *137*
Mia Mia, Australia: *22*
Michelin prizes: *17, 23*
Midway, Battle of, 1942: *112*
Midway Island: *137*
Midway, U.S. aircraft carrier class: *116*
Miethig, Hauptmann Rudolf: *87*
MiG-15: *90, 115*
MiG-17: *92*
MiG-21: *92*
Milan, Italy: *17, 23, 148*
Military Cross, award of: *50, 51* (Fonck); *52* (Mannock); *54* (Bishop); *55* (McCudden)
Military Medal, award of: *51* (Fonck), *55* (McCudden)
Military Wing, R.F.C.: *25, 55*
Milling, Lieutenant Thomas de Witt, US Army: *28*
Miller, Max: *123*
Minato, Japan: *129*
Mineola, New York: *20, 121, 127*
Minichiello, Lance Corporal Raphael, U.S. Marine Corps: *141*
Mississippi, U.S.S.: *30, 101*
Mistel weapon: *77*
Mitchell, Brigadier General William: *106*
Mitscher, Lieutenant Commander M. A., U.S. Navy: *124*
Mitsubishi A5M ("Claude"): *109, 117*
Mitsubishi A6M Zero-Sen: *77, 111, 112, 117*
Mitsubishi G3M ("Nell"): *117*
Mitsubishi G4M ("Betty"): *117*
Mitsubishi J2M ("Jack"): *118*
MK 108 aircraft cannon: *68, 70*
Mölders, Major (later Oberst) Werner: *79, 87*
Mollison, J. A.: *134, 136*
Moncuco, Italy: *148*
Montalembert, Marchioness de (and Countess): *146*
Montgolfier brothers (Joseph and Etienne): *145*
Montgolfiere (hot-air balloon): *145 et passim*
Montreal, Canada: *123*
Montoya, Guardia Marina Ismael: *36*
Moore, Machinist L. R., U.S. Navy: *124*

Moore-Brabazon, J. T. C. (later Lord Brabazon of Tara): *18*
Moorfields, London: *148*
Morane Bullet: *52*
Morane Saulnier parasol scouts: *31, 48, 55, 122, 123*
Morgan, David: *142*
Morocco: French colonial campaign in: *29*; formation for air force in: *95*
Morris, Second Lieutenant L. B. F., R.F.C.: *47*
Moscow; speed records to Baltimore, Boston, New York, Philadelphia and Washington: *143*
Mulberry, British artificial harbour: *77*
Müller, Oberstleutnant Friedrich-Karl: *86*
Multan, West Pakistan: *129*
Müncheberg, Major Joachim: *82, 86*
Murvaux, France: *57*
Muselli, Gérard: *144*
Musick, Captain Edwin C., PanAm: *137*
Mustafa Kemal Pasha (Ataturk): *102*
Mwanza, Lake Victoria: *134*
Myer, Fort, Virginia: *15, 16, 27*

N

Nakajima B5N ("Kate"): *111, 117*
Nancy, France: *122*
Nanyuen, China, military flying school at: *24*
Napier Lion engine: *132*
Narrabeen Beach, Australia: *20*
Naval Aircraft Factory N3N-3 trainer: *116, 117*; PN-9 flying boat: *108*; TS-1: *106*
Naval Wing, R.F.C.: *24, 100, 102*
Neefs, B. A.: *142*
Nelson, Lieutenant Erik, U.S. Air Service: *129*
Nesles, near Paris, France: *146*
Nesterov, Staff Captain P. N.: *31*
Netheravon, England: *30*
Netherlands; formation of air force in: *95*; German campaign against, 1940: *64*; highest scoring fighter pilot: *72*
Netherlands Indies Air Force: *94*
Neumann, Leutnant Klaus: *70*
Neuve Chapelle offensive, 1915: *36*
New Jersey, U.S.S.: *106*
New Orleans: speed records to Bonn, Boston, Gander, London, New York, Paris, Shannon, Washington: *143*
New South Wales, Australia: *20*
Newton, Maurice: *123*
New York City: *123, 129, 130, 134, 136, 137*
New York: speed records to Berlin, Bonn, London, Los Angeles, Moscow, Oslo, Paris, Shannon and Stockholm: *143*
New York to London; first solo flght by light aeroplane: *134*; first jet passenger service: *139*
New Zealand; first aeroplane flight in: *23*; formation of air force in: *95*; highest scoring fighter pilot: *72*
New Zealand Permanent Air Force, formation of: *95*
New Zealand Territorial Air Force, formation of: *95*
Nha Trang, Vietnam: *96*
Nicaragua; formation of air force in: *95*; air operations against bandits in, 1927: *108*
Nice, France: *21*
Nicholetts, Flight Lieutenant G. E., R.A.F.: *136*
Nicolson, Flight Lieutenant James Brindley, V.C.: *66*
Niehoff, Leutnant Rolf: *63*
Nields, James F.: *144*
Nieuport aircraft: *29, 50, 52*
Nieuport 11: *47*
Nieuport 28: *106*
Nieuport Flying School: *28*

Nijmegen, Holland: *64*
Nikolayev, Major Andrian Grigoryvich: *185*
Nishizawa, Sub-Officer Hiroyoshi: *72*
Nixon, President Richard: *141*
Noakes, Group Captain J., A.F.C., M.M., R.A.F.: *62*
Nordholz, Germany: *31*
Normandie, French battleship class: *108*
Norrköping, Sweden: *88*
North American A-5/RA-5C Vigilante: *116, 118, 120*
North American Buckeye: *120*
North American F-86 Sabre: *90*
North American FJ-1 Fury: *114, 115, 118*
North American FJ-2: *120*
North American FJ-4: *120*
North American OV-10A Bronco: *118*
North American P-51 Mustang: *69, 78, 88–89, 142, 144*
North American Sabreliner: *142*
North American T-28 Trojan: *118*
North Carolina, U.S.S.: *103*
North Island, San Diego, California: *99*
North Mimms, Hertfordshire, England: *147, 148*
North Pole to South Pole, speed record: *144*
North Sea; first crossing by a balloon: *151*; first crossing by an aeroplane: *122*; air operations over the: *111*
Norway; first aeroplane flight by Norwegian in: *25*; formation of air forces in: *95*; German campaign against, 1940: *64*; highest scoring fighter pilot: *72*
Norz, Leutnant Jakob: *87*
Nowotny, Major Walter: *68–69, 70, 72, 85*
Nowotny, Kommando: *68–69, 70*
Nudelman–Suranov machine gun: *88*
Nulli Secundus, airship: *152*
Nungesser, Lieutenant Charles Eugène Jules Marie: *40, 53*
Nungesser-Coli, Breguet aircraft: *131*

O

Oakland, California: *130, 131, 137*
Oberndorf, Germany: *54*
Oberursel engines: *38*
Obleser, Oberleutnant Friedrich: *87*
Ocean, H.M. aircraft carrier: *114*
Odessa, Russia: *15*
Oesau, Oberst Walter: *86*
Ogden, Staff Sergeant Henry H., U.S. Air Service: *129*
O'Hare, Lieutenant Edward Henry, U.S. Navy: *111*
Ohka, Japanese suicide bomb (Yokosuka MXY7): *112, 113, 118*
Oiseau Blanc, Le, aircraft: *53*
Okinawa, air operations off: *112, 113*
Olieslagers, Lieutenant Jan: *46*
Olivari, Tenente Luigi: *41*
Ontario, Canada: *136*
Orchies, Battle of: *102*
Order of St. Heinrich: *49*
Origone, Sub-Teniente Manuel: *28*
Orly, France: *56*
Ornithopters: *9*
Ortmans, Flight Lieutenant Vicki, D.F.C.: *72*
Oscar Fredriksborg, Sweden: *96*
Oslo Fjord, Norway: *25*
Oslo; speed records to Boston, New York, Philadelphia, and Washington: *143*
Osram electric lights: *121*
Osterkamp, Leutnant Theo: *38*
Ostermann, Oberleutnant Max-Hellmuth: *87*
Österreichischen Luftstreitkräfte (Austrian Air Force): *93*
Ostfriesland, German battleship: *106*
Ostrolenka, Poland: *62*

Ottawa to London, speed record: *143*
Overbury, R. S.: *142*
Ovington, Earl L.: *121*
Oxford, England: *24*
oxygen, identification and naming of: *145*

P

Pablo Beach, Florida: *127*
Pacific Airlines: *139*
Pacific Ocean; first flight across: *131*; first scheduled air mail flight across: *137*
Page, Charles: *150*
Pakistan, formation of air force in: *95*
Palestine, operations against Turks in: *102*
Palomar, El, Argentine: *28, 36, 123*
Pan American (World) Airways: *131, 137, 139*
Pangborn, Clyde: *134*
Panhard motor cars: *14* (footnote)
Paraguayan War, 1864–70: *150*
Paraguay–Bolivia War, 1932: *95*
Paraguay; formation of air force in: *95*
Paramashiru, Kuriles: *129*
paratroops, use of: *67*
Paris, France; first bombs dropped on: *30*; first aeroplane flight to Berlin: *24*; speed records to Bonn, Frankfurt and Hanoi: *143*; speed records to London, Nice, Saigon and Tananarive: *144*
Parke Curtis, G. W., barge: *98*
Parmelee, Philip O.: *27*
Parschau, Leutnant: *48*
Pattle, Squadron Leader M. T. St. J., D.F.C.*: *72, 73, 75*
Pau, France: *21, 22*
Paulhan, Louis: *21*
Payne, M. E.: *142*
Payne, William R.: *143, 144*
Pearl Harbour, Japanese attack on: *77, 108*
Peck, Captain Brian A., R.A.F.: *123*
Peltier, Madame Thérèse: *15, 18*
Pennfield, New Brunswick, U.S.A.: *136*
Penn Gaskell, Lieutenant L. de C., R.F.C.: *30*
Pennsylvania, U.S.S.: *99*
Pensacola Bay, Florida: *103, 153*
Pequet, Henri: *23*
Pershing, General John, U.S. Army: *36, 56*
Persia (Iran), formation of air force in: *94*
Peru, formation of air force in: *95*
Pescara, Marquis de: *160*
Pescara, Pateras: *101*
Petawawa, Canada: *19*
Peter, Kapitän, Heinkel Chief Test pilot: *71*
Peterson, Vern F.: *142*
Philadelphia, Pennsylvania: *123, 149*; speed records to Moscow, Oslo and Stockholm: *144*
Philipp, Oberstleutnant Hans: *85*
Philippine Constabulary: *95*
Philippine Islands: *80, 112, 113*; formation of air force in: *95*
Philomel, H.M.S.: *102*
Phlogiston (hydrogen): *145*
Phoenix, Arizona: *56*
Piccio, Tenente-Colonello Pier Ruggiero: *41*
Pictou, Nova Scotia: *129*
Pilcher, Percy S.: *9, 10, 11, 12*
Pioneer, balloon: *150*
Piscnoulok, H.R.H. the Prince of, Siam: *30*
Pitcairn, Harold F.: *160*
Plymouth, England: *124*
PO-2, Russian aircraft: *68*
Poa, Lieutenant: *24*

Pocklington, Yorkshire: *71*
Podenas, Countess of: *146*
Poland; formation of air force in: *95*; German campaign against, 1939: *62, 64*; highest scoring fighter pilot: *72*
Polish Air Force, formation of: *95*
Pomone, H.M.S.: *102*
Pond, Captain C. F., U.S. Navy: *99*
Poniatowski, Jan.: *72*
Ponta Delgada, Azores: *124*
Popovich, Colonel Pavel Romanovich: *185*
Porat, Captain G. von.: *28*
Porte-Felixstowe Fury flying boats: *105*
Porte, John Cyril: *105*
Portland, England: *100, 102*
Portland (Oregon) to Portland (Maine), speed record: *144*
Portmarnock, Dublin, Ireland: *136*
Port Meadow, Oxford, England: *25*
Port Moresby, New Guinea: *111*
Port Natal, Brazil: *131, 134, 136*
Portsmouth, England: *66*
Portugal, formation of air forces in: *95*
Postal Exhibition, Universal, Allahabad, 1911: *23*
Post, Wiley: *136*
Potez XXV: *95*
Potez 63: *65*
Potomac River, U.S.A.: *10, 12, 98*; Army of the Potomac: *149*
Pour le Mérite, Ordre: *40, 47, 49*
Poznan, Poland: *62*
Prague, Czechoslovakia: *127*
Pratt & Whitney J-57 engine: *116*
Pratt & Whitney R-1830 engine: *67*
Pratt & Whitney R-2800 engine: *112*
Preddy, Major G. E., U.S.A.F.: *73*
Prier, Pierre: *24*
Priestley, Dr. Joseph: *145*
Priller, Oberst Josef: *82, 87*
Prince Rupert, British Columbia, Canada: *129*
Protzel, Aspirant Guillermo: *36*
Putnam, Lieutenant D. E.: *41*
P.Z.L. P-11: *62*
P.Z.L. P-24: *66*

Q

QANTAS (Queensland and Northern Territory Aerial Service): *126, 131, 137*
Queen of Heaven gaol, Rome: *141*
Quénault, Caporal: *31*
Quimby, Harriet: *24*

R

R4M rocket projectiles: *68*
R-34, airship: *153*
R-100, airship: *132*
R-101, airship: *132, 153*
Rademacher, Leutnant Rudolf: *70, 86*
Radlett, Hertfordshire: *62, 134*
Rall, Major Günther: *85*
ramming tactics, first aircraft destroyed by: *31*
Ranger, U.S.S.: *110*
Rangoon, Burma: *129, 131*
Ranza, Tenente Ferruccio: *41*
Rapid City, South Dakota: *151*
Rappahannock River, U.S.A.: *149*
Ras Tafari (see Haile Selassie, H.I.M. Emperor)
Raven II, H.M. seaplane carrier: *102*
Rawlinson, A.: *21*
RD-10 engines: *88*

Read, Lieutenant Commander A. C., U.S. Navy: *124*
Reali, Sergente Antonio: *41*
Redoubt, H.M. destroyer: *105*
Rees, Lieutenant T., R.F.C.: *47*
Reid, Captain L.: *136*
Reinert, Oberleutnant Ernst-Wilhelm: *85*
Reisenflugzeug (R-Type) aircraft: *29, 38*
Renard, Capitaine Charles: *152*
Repulse, H.M. battlecruiser: *103*
Reuter, Otto: *122*
Reykjavik, Iceland: *129*; speed record to New York: *144*
Reza Khan, prime minister of Iran: *94*
Rheims, France: *17, 19, 21, 31*
Rhinower Hills, Germany: *11*
Rhoades, Chief Machinist's Mate E. S., U.S. Navy: *124*
Rhodesia, formation of air forces in: *96*
Rhodes-Moorhouse, Lieutenant W. B., V.C., R.F.C.: *25, 36*
Richardson, Commander H. C., U.S. Navy: *124*
Richmond, Sydney, Australia: *131*
Richter, Lieutenant J. P., U.S. Air Service: *128*
Richthofen, Oberleutnant Lothar, Freiherr von: *40, 50*
Richthofen, Rittmeister Manfred, Freiherr von: *38, 40, 47, 48, 55*
Rickenbacker, Captain Edward Vernon: *41, 56*
Ricketts, Dr.: *12*
Riihimäki, Finland: *67*
Rio de Janeiro, Brazil: *93*
Riviera, H.M. seaplane carrier: *101*
Roberts, Lieutenant, U.S. Army: *57*
Roche, La Baronne de la: *20*
Rockaway, New York: *124*
Rockwell Field, California: *127, 128*
Rocky Mountains, first aeroplane crossing of: *125*
Rodd, Ensign H. C., U.S. Navy: *124*
Roe, Alliot Verdon: *10*
Roëland (French airman): *29*
Rohrbach, Dr. Adolf: *62*
Roland C II: *50, 55*
Rolls, The Hon. Charles Stewart: *16, 21, 22*
Rolls-Royce Avon engine: *91*
Rolls-Royce Condor engine: *62*
Rolls-Royce Dart engine: *139*
Rolls-Royce Derwent engine: *88*
Rolls-Royce Eagle engine: *105, 125*
Rolls-Royce Kestrel engine: *62*
Rolls-Royce Merlin engine: *88, 91*
Rollwage, Oberleutnant Herbert: *83, 87*
Romain, Jules: *149*
Roma, Italian battleship: *70*
Romania; first aeroplane flight in: *15*; formation of air force in: *96*; highest scoring fighter pilot: *72*
Rome, Italy: *131, 139, 141*; speed records to Addis Abbaba, London and Rio de Janeiro: *144*
Roosevelt Field, Long Island, U.S.A.: *128*
Rosenthal, Leutnant Baron von: *31*
Ross, Commander Malcolm D., U.S. Navy Reserve: *151*
rotorcraft: *159 et seq.*
Rotterdam, Holland: *64, 128*
Royal Afghan Air Force: *93*
Royal Air Force; formation of: *94*; Squadrons: No. 1: *28*; No. 2: *28, 30, 31, 36*; No. 3: *28, 29, 30, 47, 55*; No. 4: *28*; No. 5: *28, 30*; No. 6: *28*; No. 7: *28, 91*; No. 11: *47, 50*; No. 13: *49*; No. 19: *65, 79*; No. 20: *55*; No. 21: *53*; No. 24: *47*; No. 25: *49*; No. 39: *66*; No. 40: *52*; No. 41: *65*; No. 43: *65*; No. 44: *67*; No. 47: *55*; No. 49: *91, 92*; No. 54: *65*; No. 56: *50, 55*; No. 60: *50, 54*; No. 64: *88*; No. 66: *55*; No. 70: *131*;

Royal Air Force; Squadrons—*cont.*
No. 72: *65*; No. 74: *52*; No. 80: *75*; No. 85: *52*, *54*;
No. 90: *67*, *91*; No. 92: *65*; No. 99: *62*; No. 100: *37*;
No. 102: *63*, *68*; No. 107: *63*; No. 110: *63*; No. 138:
91; No. 148: *91*; No. 207: *91*; No. 209: *48*; No. 213:
106; No. 214: *91*; No. 222: *65*; No. 234: *65*; No. 238:
65; No. 249: *66*; No. 257: *65*; No. 303 (Polish): *65*;
No. 543: *91*; No. 617: *71*
Royal Airship Works, Cardington, England: *132*
Royal Australian Air Force; Nos. 4, 5, 83, 84 and 85
Squadrons: *67*
Royal Auxiliary Air Force; Squadrons: Nos. 501, 601,
603, 603, 605 and 607: *65*; Nos. 610 and 616: *79*
Royal Canadian Air Force: *54*
Royal Canadian Navy: *83*
Royal Ceylon Air Force; formation of: *93*
Royal Engineers: *52*, *55*, *94*
Royal Flying Corps: *24*, *25*, *28 et passim*; formation of: *94*
Royal Flying Corps Squadrons (see Royal Air Force,
Squadrons)
Royal Hellenic Air Force: *66*; formation of: *94*
Royal Hellenic Naval Air Force; formation of: *94*
Royal Iraqi Air Force, formation of: *94*
Royal Jordanian Air Force: *92*; formation of: *94*
Royal Khmer Aviation; formation of: *93*
Royal Marines: *101*; Royal Marine Artillery: *99*
Royal Moroccan Air Force, formation of: *95*
Royal Naval Air Service (R.N.A.S.): *31*, *102*; formation
of: *94*; Squadrons: No. 1 (Naval): *102*; No. 3 (Naval):
54, *55*; No. 10 (Naval): *55*; No. 13 (Naval): *55*
Royal Naval Armoured Car Force: *102*
Royal Naval Review, 1912: *100*, *102*
Royal Netherlands Air Force: *64*; formation of: *95*
Royal New Zealand Air Force, formation of: *95*
Royal Norwegian Army: *95*
Royal Norwegian Navy: *95*
Royal Pakistan Air Force, formation of: *95*
Royal Rhodesian Air Force, formation of: *96*
Royal Siamese Flying Corps, formation of: *96*
Royal Swedish Air Force (see *Flygvapnet*)
Royal Vauxhall Balloon: *149*
Rozier, François Pilâtre de: *146*, *149*
Rudat, Hauptmann Horst: *77*
Rudel, Major Hans-Ulrich: *75*
Rudorffer, Major Erich: *70*, *85*
Ruhrstahl Fritz-X guided bomb, *70*
Ruiz, Second Lieutenant Enrique: *36*
Rumey, Leutnant Fritz: *40*
Rumpler aircraft: *51*
Russia; first aeroplane flight in: *15*; formation of air
forces in: *96*; highest scoring fighter pilot: *72*
Russian Flying Corps, Imperial: *31*, *41*; formation of: *96*
Rutland, Flight Lieutenant F. J., R.N.A.S.: *103*
Ryan aircraft, *Spirit of St. Louis*: *130*
Ryan FR-1 Fireball: *113*
Rymer, Captain Richard, B.E.A.: *139*
Ryujo, Japanese aircraft carrier: *110*

S

SAAB J-29 aircraft: *88*
SABCA S-2: *130*
SABENA: *130*
Sachsenberg, Leutnant Heinz: *87*
Sadenwater, Lieutenant Harry, U.S. Navy: *124*
Safonov, Lieutenant M.: *41*
Sage, Mrs. Letitia Ann: *149*
Saigon, Indo-China: *129*
Sailly-le-Sec, France: *48*
St. André aux Bois, France: *37*

St. Cyr, France: *51*
St. George's Fields, London: *149*
St. John's, Newfoundland: *125*
St. Lo, U.S. escort carrier: *112*
St. Louis, Missouri: *128*
St. Louis, Senegal: *131*
St. Raphael, France: *100*, *122*
Sakai, Petty Officer Saburo: *77*
Salinas, Major Alberto: *28*
Salisbury Plain, England: *24*, *25*
Salisbury, Rhodesia: *96*
Salmond, Major General W. G. H., D.S.O.: *123*
Salyavudh, Major Luang Sakdi: *29*
SAM-2 missile system: *92*
Samson, Lieutenant (later Air Commodore, C.M.G.,
D.S.O., A.F.C.) Charles Rumney, R.N.: *99*, *100*, *101*,
102, *105*
San Diego, California: *99*, *127*, *128*
San Fernando, Argentine: *93*
San Francisco, California: *27*, *99*, *108*, *127*, *132*, *137*
Sangatte, France: *21*
Santa Monica, California: *137*
Santiago, Chile: *123*
Santos-Dumont, Alberto: *10*, *13*, *14*, *17*
Saratoga, U.S.S.: *107*, *108*, *110*
Saudi Arabia, formation of air force in: *96*
Saunders-Roe SR.A/1 flying boat fighter: *115*, *118*
Savanna, U.S.S.: *70*
Savoia-Marchetti SM.79: *144*
SB-2 aircraft: *63*
Scaroni, Tenente Silvio: *41*
Schack, Hauptmann Günther: *85*
Schall, Hauptmann Franz: *70*, *85*
Schenk, Kommando: *85*
Schenk, Major Wolfgang: *69*
Schirra, Major Walter Marty, U.S. Navy: *185*, *186*
Schmidt, Hauptmann Heinz: *85*
Schnauffer, Major Heinz-Wolfgang: *86*
Schnörrer, Leutnant Karl: *70*
Scholte, First Officer J. B., K.L.M.: *130*
Schroer, Major Werner: *82*, *87*
Schuck, Oberleutnant Walter: *70*, *85*
Schutte-Lanz airships: *66*
Schwann, Commander O., R.N.: *100*
Schweikart, Russell Louis, U.S.A.F. Reserve: *187*
Scientific American trophy: *16*, *17*
Scott, Major David Randolph, U.S.A.F.: *186*, *187*
Scott, Squadron Leader G. H., R.A.F.: *153*
S.E.5 aircraft: *50*, *55*; S.E.5A aircraft: *52*
Seattle, Washington: *124*, *128*, *129*; speed records to
Fort Worth and Madrid: *144*
Seelberg, Germany: *152*
Seely, Colonel: *25*
Seiler, Major Reinhard: *87*
Seki, Lieutenant Yukio, Imperial Japanese Navy: *112*
Selfridge, Lieutenant Thomas Etholen, U.S. Signal
Corps: *15*, *27*
Serbian Military Air Service, formation of: *96*
Sergeivsky, Captain B.: *41*
Service Aéronautique (see *Armée de l'Air*)
Servicio Militar de Aerostacion (Spanish Captive Balloon
Section), formation of: *96*
Setz, Major Heinrich: *86*
Sevastopol, U.S.S.R.: *96*
Seversky, Lieutenant Commander A. P.: *41*
Seward, Alaska: *129*
Shakhovskaya, Princess Eugenie Mikhailovna: *31*
Shanghai, China: *129*
Shank, Robert F.: *123*

Shannon, Ireland; speed records to Bonn, London and Paris: *144*
Shatalov, Lieutenant Colonel Vladimir: *187*
Sheepshead Bay, New York: *27*
Sheerness, Isle of Sheppey, England: *100, 102*
Shellbeach, Isle of Sheppey, England: *18*
Shelton gang: *139*
Shenandoah, airship: *153*
Shepard, Alan B.; U.S. Navy: *182, 185*
Sheppey, Isle of, England: *18*
Sherut Avir (planned Israeli military air force): *94*
Sherwood Forresters: *49*
Shimpu Special Attack Corps: *112*
Shoho, Japanese aircraft carrier: *111*
Shokaku, Japanese aircraft carrier: *111*
Shonin, Lieutenant Colonel Giorgiy: *187*
Shoreham, England: *121*
Short biplanes, early: *99, 100, 102*; S. 27: *100*; Type 184: *103*
Short Bros.: *18, 21*
Short Calcutta: *132, 134*
Short C-Type Empire Flying Boats: *137*
Short Rangoon: *117*
Short Sarafand: *117*
Short Seaford: *118*
Short Shetland: *112, 118*
Short Singapore: *117*
Short Sunderland: *117*
Short-Wright biplane: *18*
Siam; first aeroplane flights in: *29*; first military pilots of: *29*; first military flying corps in: *30*
Siamese Army: *29*
Siemens-Halske engines: *38*
Siemens-Schuckert aircraft: *38*
Sikikorn, Captain Luang Avudh: *29*
Sikorsky, Igor: *29*
Sikorsky S-42 *Clipper III*: *137*
Silver Dart aircraft: *18*
Silver Star, award of: *81* (Bong)
Simons, Major David G., U.S.A.F.: *151*
Sinai, operations against Turks in: *102*
Singapore: *136, 137*; speed record to Darwin: *144*
Sinuiju, Yalu River: *90*
Sitka, Alaska: *129*
Six-Day War, Arab-Israeli, 1967: *90, 92*
Skene, Second Lieutenant R. R., R.F.C.: *30*
skyjacking: *141*
Smart, Flight Sub-Lieutenant B. A., R.N.A.S.: *104*
Smirnoff, Lieutenant I. W.: *41*
Smith, Captain Sir Charles Kingsford: *131, 137*
Smith, Lieutenant Sir Keith Macpherson, K.B.E., R.A.F.: *125*
Smith, Captain L. H., U.S. Air Force: *128*
Smith, Lieutenant Lowell H., U.S. Air Service: *128*
Smith, Captain Sir Ross Macpherson, K.B.E., M.C.*, D.F.C.**, A.F.C., R.A.F.: *123, 125*
Smith, Wesley L., U.S. Post Office Department: *130*
Smithsonian Institution, Washington: *129*
Société Anonyme Belge de Constructions Aéronautiques (SABCA): *130*
Soesterburg, Holland: *95*
Somali, H.M.S.: *63*
Sommer biplane: *23*
Sommer, Roger: *23*
Sondergeräte 113A Forstersonde rocket mortar: *67*
Sopwith 1½-Strutter: *54*
Sopwith Camel: *39, 48, 102, 105, 106*
Sopwith Cuckoo: *105*
Sopwith Pup: *54, 103, 104*

Sopwith Tabloid: *31*
Sopwith Triplane: *54–55*
Sopwith, T. O. M. (later Sir Thomas): *23*
Soryu, Japanese aircraft carrier: *110*
South Africa; formation of air force in: *96*; highest scoring fighter pilot: *72*
South Africa to London, first solo flight by woman: *131*
South African Aviation Corps: *96*
Southampton, England: *66*
Southern Cross, aircraft: *131*
Southern Rhodesia, organisation of an air force in: *96*
South Pole, first flight by an aeroplane over: *132*
Soviet Air Force: *68*; 73rd Guards Fighter Air Regiment: *68*; 586th Fighter Air Regiment: *68*; 587th Bomber Air Regiment: *68*; 588th Night Bomber Air Regiment: *68*
Soviet Union, Heroes of the: *68, 75*
Sowers, Robert G.: *143*
Soyuz spacecraft: *186, 187*
SPAD XIII: *57*
Spain, formation of air forces in: *96*
Spandau machine guns: *38*
Spartan, H.M. cruiser: *70*
Späte, Major Wolfgang: *70*
speed records: *20, 142, 143, 144, Appendix B*
Spirit of St. Louis, aircraft: *130*
Springfield, Illinois: *25*
Springs, Captain E. W.: *41*
Sputnik satellites: *182*
Squires Gate, Blackpool, England: *20, 22*
Stack, T. Neville: *130*
Stafford, Major Thomas P., U.S.A.F.: *186, 187*
Stapleford Tawney, England: *79*
Start, aircraft: *25*
steam engines as aircraft powerplants: *9, 10, 11, 12*
Steinbatz, Oberfeldwebel Leopold: *78*
Steinhoff, Oberst Johannes: *70, 85*
Sterr, Oberleutnant Heinrich: *86*
Stevens, Captain Albert: *151*
stewardess, first airline: *132*
Stockholm, Sweden: *15, 22*; speed records to Baltimore, Boston, New York, Philadelphia and Washington: *144*
Stone, Lieutenant E. F., U.S. Navy: *124*
Stotz, Hauptmann Max: *85*
Straits Settlements Volunteer Air Force, formation of: *95*
Strange, Second Lieutenant Louis A., R.F.C.: *30*
Strasbourg, France: *129*
Stringfellow, John: *9, 11*
Sturm, Hauptmann Heinrich: *86*
Sudan, British expedition to the, 1885: *150*
Sudan, formation of an air force in: *96*
suicide operations, Japanese: *112, 113*
Sukhoi-7: *92*
Supermarine Attacker: *118*
Supermarine Baby: *117*
Supermarine Scimitar: *120*
Supermarine Sea Otter: *117*
Supermarine Spitfire: *65, 75, 79, 80, 83, 84*
Supermarine Swift: *142*
Supermarine Walrus: *117*
Suring, Professor: *151*
Süss, Oberfeldwebel: *78*
Svenska Aeronautiska Sallskapet (see Aero Club of Sweden)
Swaab, Captain J. M., U.S. Army: *41*
Sweden, first aeroplane flight in: *15*; formation of air force in: *96*
Swedish Air Lines (see *AB Aerotransport*)
Sweet, Lieutenant George C., U.S. Navy Department: *16*

Swindal, Colonel J. B., U.S.A.F.: *142, 143, 144*
Switzerland, formation of air service in: *96*
Sydney, Australia: *20, 131*; speed record to London: *144*
Syrian Air Force: *92*
Szentgyörgyi, Second Lieutenant Dezjo: *72*

T

Takagi, Vice-Admiral Takeo, Imperial Japanese Navy: *111*
Tangmere, England: *66, 79, 88*
Tanzer, Leutnant Kurt: *86*
Tasmania, Australia: *137*
Tasman Sea, first air crossing of the: *131*
Taube aircraft: *14, 30, 95*
Tavoy, Burma: *129*
Taylor, Mrs. Florence: *20*
Taylor, George Augustus: *20*
Tegtmeier, Leutnant Fritz: *86*
Templer, Captain J. L. B., K.R.R.C.: *150*
Tenedos, Island of: *101*
Tereshkova, Junior Lieutenant Valentina Vladimi-rovna: *182, 185*
Texas, U.S.S.: *106*
Thailand, formation of air force in: *96*
Thible, Madame: *148*
Thiedemann, Leutnant Richard von: *27*
Thieffry, Second Lieutenant Edmond: *46*
Thieuloy-St. Antoine, France: *127*
Thip, Lieutenant, Royal Siamese Army: *29*
Thomas, George Holt: *122*
Thomas, M. (early French pilot): *23*
Thompson, Commander, R.N.: *62*
Thompson, Lieutenant Stephen W.: *37*
Thompson, Lord, Secretary of State for Air: *132*
Thomson, Ensign E. M., Imperial Russian Air Force: *41*
Thulin, Dr. Enoch: *22*
Thyben, Oberleutnant Gerhard: *86*
Titov, Major Gherman Stepanovich: *185*
Tokyo, Japan: *132, 134*; speed records to Anchorage (Alaska), Chicago, Fort Worth (Texas), London, Madrid, Seattle, Washington and Winnipeg: *144*
Toronto, Canada: *122, 123*
torpedo, first dropped by aeroplanes: *101*
Torun, Poland: *62*
Tourane, Indo-China: *129*
Tower Bridge, London: *25*
Towers, Commander John H., U.S. Navy: *124*
Trail of the Caribou, aircraft: *136*
Transcontinental Air Transport Inc.: *130, 134*
Trans-World Airlines (T.W.A.): *141*
Trefgarne, Lord: *143, 144*
Trenkel, Hauptmann Rudolf: *86*
Trepassy Bay, Newfoundland: *124*
Trewin, Assistant Paymaster G. S., R.N.: *103*
Tsai Tao, Prince: *24*
Tsing, Colonel: *24*
Tuck, Flight Lieutenant R. S. S., D.S.O., D.F.C.**: *65, 73*
Tucumcari, New Mexico: *128*
Tuileries, Paris: *146*
Tupolev Tu-2: *88*
Tupolev Tu-12: *88*
Turin, Italy: *15, 18*
Turkey, formation of air force in: *96*
Tyrell, U.S. attack cargo ship: *112*
Tytler, James: *148*

U

U-117, German U-Boat: *106*

Ubben, Major Kurt: *87*
Udet, Oberleutnant Ernst: *40*
Ukagi, Admiral Matone, Imperial Japanese Navy: *113*
Uganda, H.M. cruiser: *70*
Uhlan Regiment Nr. 1, "*Kaiser Alexander III*": *47*
Ulm, C. T. P.: *131*
Umballa, India: *129*
United Air Lines: *132, 139*
United Kingdom, highest scoring fighter pilot: *72*
United States of America; first manned free flight by a balloon: *149*; first international air mail: *124*; first international scheduled passenger service: *126*; first coast-to-coast aeroplane flight: *127*; first coast-to-coast air mail flight: *127*; first coast-to-coast air crossing in a day: *127*; first non-stop air crossing of: *128*; first transcontinental air mail service: *130*; first flight from mainland to Hawaii: *130*; first coast-to-coast all-air passenger service: *134*; first internal air mail carried by U.S. Army Air Corps: *136*; highest scoring fighter pilot: *72*; formation of air forces in: *96*
United States Aeronautical Reserve: *99*
United States Army, first Air Service of the: *30*
United States Marine Corps: *108, 114, 115*
United States Navy: *77 et passim*
United States Post Office Department: *123*
United States Signal Corps: *15, 96*
United States Strategic Air Command: *91*
Uruguay, formation of air force in: *96*
Unwin, Flight Sergeant G. C., D.S.O., D.F.C.: *65*
Upavon, England: *29*
Upper Heyford, Oxfordshire, England: *62*
Upton, Pilot Officer H. C., D.F.C.: *65*
Urbanowicz, Flying Officer W., D.F.C.: *65*
Utrecht, Holland: *64*

V

V-1 flying bombs: *71, 72*
Valkyrie monoplane: *121*
Valley Forge, U.S.S.: *115*
Vance, Claire K., U.S. Post Office Department: *130*
Vancouver, British Columbia, Canada: *125*
van de Haegen, Oberleutnant Otto: *36*
Van den Schkrouff: *15*
Vänern, Lake, Sweden: *151*
van Ryneveld, Colonel Sir Pierre, D.S.O., M.C.: *126*
Vaucresson, forest of, Paris: *146*
Vaughn, Lieutenant G. A., Jr.: *41*
Vauxhall Gardens, London: *149*
V-Bombers: *91*
Van der Spuy, Major: *96*
Vechtel, Oberleutnant Bernhard: *87*
Védrines, Jules: *122*
Velazco, Guardia Marina Roberto: *36*
Venezuela, formation of air force in: *96*
Vera Cruz, military operations against: *30, 101*
Verdun, France: *36*
Versailles, Court of: *146*
Versailles, Treaty of: *94*
Vickers Valiant: *91, 92, 142, 144*
Vickers Victoria: *131*
Vickers Viking amphibian: *125*
Vickers Vimy: *125, 126*
Vickers Viscount: *139, 144*
Victoria and Albert, royal yacht: *100*
Victoria, Australia: *21, 22*
Victoria, British Columbia, Canada: *124*
Victoria Cross, award of the: *25, 36* (Rhodes-Moor-house), *50* (Ball), *52* (Mannock), *54* (Bishop), *66*

Victoria Cross, award of the—*cont.*
  (Mantle), *66* (Leefe Robinson), *66* (Nicolson), *83*
  (Gray); last Victoria Cross won during Second World
  War: *83*
Vienna, Australia: *122, 129*
Vienna-Schwechat: *71*
Vietnam, formation of air force in: *96*
Viipuri, Finland: *63*
Villa, Flying Officer J. W., D.F.C.*: *65*
Villacoublay, France: *29*
Villa Nova da Rainha, Portugal: *95*
Villers-Bretonneux, France: *48*
Virginia, U.S.S.: *106*
Virtuti Militari, award of: *65* (František)
Visconti, Major Adriano: *72*
Vogelflug als Grundlage der Fliegerkunst, Der (treatise by
  Lilienthal, 1889): *9, 11*
Voisin biplane: *14, 15, 16, 17, 18, 20, 21, 22, 31, 53*
Voisin, Charles: *14*
Voisin, Gabriel: *10, 14, 18*
Volkov, Vladislav N., cosmonaut: *187*
Volynov, Lieutenant Colonel Boris: *187*
Voss, Leutnant Werner: *40*
Vostok spacecraft: *182, 185*
Vought Cutlass: *118*
Vought F4U Corsair: *111, 115*
Vought VE-7: *106*
Vought XOS2U-1 Kingfisher: *117*
Vought XSB2U-1 Vindicator: *117*

                          W
Waddington, Lincolnshire: *67*
Waddon, Surrey (see Croydon, Surrey)
Wade, Wing Commander L. C., D.S.O., D.F.C.**:
  73
Wade, Lieutenant Leight, U.S. Air Service: *129*
Wakamiya, Japanese seaplane vessel: *101, 102*
Wake Island: *137*
Wake Island, U.S. escort carrier: *113*
Walden, Dr. Henry W.: *20*
Walden III aircraft: *20*
Waldmann, Oberleutnant Hans: *86*
Wales, H.R.H. the Prince of: *18*
Waller, Corporal J. H., R.F.C.: *49*
Walsh, Leo: *23*
Walsh, Vivian C.: *23*
Walter rocket motors: *70*
Walvis Bay, South-West Africa: *136*
Ward, John R.: *142*
Ware, Hertfordshire, England: *148*
Warner, James: *131*
Warsaw, Poland: *62*
Warrior, H.M. armoured cruiser: *103*
Warspite, H.M.S.: *70*
Washington, D.C.: *123, 129*; speed records to Bonn,
  Boston, Caracas, Gander, Havana, London, New
  York, Moscow, Oslo, Stockholm, Paris and Shannon:
  144
Washington Treaty, 1922: *107*
Washington, U.S.S.: *106*
Waterton, Squadron Leader W. A., G.M.: *91*
Webb, Lieutenant Torrey H., U.S. Army: *123*
Weber, Flight Engineer K. A. O., K.L.M.: *130*
Weber, Hauptmann Karl-Heinz: *86*
Wehner, Lieutenant, U.S. Army: *57*
Weilberg, Duchy of Nassau: *149*
Weiss, Ehrich (Harry Houdini): *21*
Weiss, Hauptmann Robert: *86*
Weissenberger, Major Theodor: *70, 85*

Wellington, New Zealand; speed record to London:
  144
Welsh, Dr. K. H. Vincent, Australian Flying Doctor
  Service: *131*
Wenatchee, Washington: *134*
Wenham, F. H.: *11*
Wernicke, Leutnant Heinz: *87*
Wernitz, Leutnant Ulrich: *87*
West Australian Airways: *126*
West, Ensign Jake C., U.S. Navy: *113*
Western Air Inc.: *134*
Westinghouse engines: *91*
Westland Wapiti: *94*
West Virginia, U.S.S.: *112*
White Lake, South Dakota: *151*
White, Major Edward Higgins, U.S.A.F.: *186*
Whittington, L. M.: *143*
Wickenburg, Arizona: *128*
Wiener-Neustadt, Austria: *14*
Wiese, Major Johannes: *86*
Wigram, Christchurch, New Zealand: *131*
Wilcke, Oberst Wolf-Dietrich: *85*
Wilhelmshaven, Germany: *62, 63, 67*
Williamson County, Illinois: *62, 139*
Willoughby Spit, Virginia: *99*
Wilson, Group Captain H. J.: *88*
Windham, Captain W. G.: *23*
Windsor, England: *24*
wind tunnel, world's first: *11*
"Winter War", 1939–40 (Russo-Finnish): *63*
wireless telegraphy, first use to obtain weather reports:
  19
Wittmundhafen, Germany: *70*
Woidich, Oberleutnant Franz: *87*
Wölfert, Dr. Karl: *152*
Wolf, German commerce raider: *102*
Wolf, Oberleutnant Albin: *86*
Wolfrum, Oberleutnant Walter: *86*
Wolverhampton, England: *28*
Woolwich Arsenal: *94*
Worden, Hector: *95*
world; first round-the-world flight: *128–129*; first round-
  the-world solo flight: *136*; first jet passenger service
  round-the-world: *139*
World newspaper: *98*
Wright biplanes: *15, 16, 20, 21, 22, 28*; *Miss Columbia*:
  27
Wright J-67 engine: *115*
Wright, Orville: *10, 13, 15, 16, 27*
Wright, Wilbur: *10, 13, 15, 16, 17*
Wurmheller, Major Josef: *87*

                          Y
Yak aircraft: *68*; Yak-3: *93*; Yak-11: *93*; Yak-15: *88*;
  Yak-18: *93*
Yakovlev, Alexander S.: *88*
Yalu River, North Korea: *90*
Yarmouth, England: *31*
Yarmouth, H.M. light cruiser: *103, 104*
Yegorov, Lieutenant Boris Borisovich: *185*
Yeliseyev, Alexei, cosmonaut: *187*
Yoa, Lieutenant: *24*
Yokosuka D4Y: *118*
Yososuka MXY7 (see *Ohka*)
Yorktown, U.S.S.: *110, 111*
Young, Lieutenant Commander John Watts, U.S. Navy:
  185, 186, 187
Ypres, Battle of: *102*
Yugoslavia, formation of air force in: *96*

Z

Zapala, Argentine: *123*
Zeebrugge, Belgium: *102*
Zee Yee Lee: *24*
Zeppelin, Count Ferdinand von: *152*
Zeppelins: *93*; *L.3*: *31*; *L.4*: *31*; *L.6*: *31*; *L.23*: *104*;
L.53: *105*; *LZ.37*: *36*; *LZ.38*: *36*; *LZ.39*: *36*; *Z.IX*: *31*, *102*
Zeppelin-Staaken R VI: *38*
Zuikaku, Japanese aircraft carrier: *111*
Zurakowski, Janusz: *142*, *143*
Zwernemann, Oberleutnant Josef: *86*

A Note to Parents

Many years ago, while teaching at a summer Bible camp, I learned how to lead a child to Christ using the colors of nature. God surrounds us with color just as he surrounds us with his love. I decided to write a story about a grandmother who combined the colors of nature with her talent for sewing to explain salvation to her granddaughter.

In my own life, I was blessed with grandparents and parents who loved Jesus and believed firmly in the gospel. When I became a mother, I realized the most important thing I could do for my children was to lead them to Christ.

I pray this story will inspire you to help the children in your life give their hearts to Jesus.

❦

These Scriptures will help you explain the meaning of the colors in the story.

Yellow: Revelation 21:21 tells us that the streets in heaven are of gold.

Gray: Romans 3:23 tells us that everyone has sinned.

Red: Hebrews 9:22 tells us that without the shedding of blood there can be no forgiveness of sin.

White: 1 Corinthians 15:3-4 tells us that Christ died to save us from our sins.

Green: John 1:12 tells us that when we believe in his name, we become children of God. In 1 John 1:9 we read that by admitting we have sinned, we receive forgiveness and cleansing. Hebrews 13:5 promises that he will never leave us.

"Dear Jesus, thank you for loving me. Please come and live in my heart. Thank you for all the colors of the world that show how much you love me. In Jesus' name, Amen."

"*I made it* just for you, Emma," Grammy said, smiling.

"It's the most beautiful coat I've ever seen!"

"It has all the colors of love," said Grammy. "When you wear it, remember how much God loves you, and that I do too."

I hugged my grandmother as tightly as I could. Then I took Grammy's hands, and as we danced around the sewing room, I thought I heard a thousand angels sing.

Suddenly, I woke up. The sun shone high in the sky. I peeked inside the sewing room to find Grammy asleep in her chair. And there, on the little form was a coat just my size.

I tiptoed into the sewing room.

"Oh my!" I whispered as I slipped the coat off the form and put it on. It was soft and warm, and fit perfectly.

"Green for the hills where the horses run, green for the turtles that doze in the sun, green for the life in the heart of the seed, green for the new life he's given me."

As Grammy danced, the stars grew dim and the sun began to rise. My eyelids felt heavy. Soon I fell asleep behind the sewing room door to the sound of my grandmother's sweet melody. I dreamed I was dancing in a coat made of all the colors of earth while a thousand angels sang.

"White for the sugar, white for the cream,

white for the snow on the evergreen,

white for the lilies blooming in spring,

white for the heart made pure and clean."

The white material made all
the other colors seem brighter. After
stitching the collar and cuffs in place,
she brought a piece of green silk down
from the top shelf of her closet. Tossing
the fabric around her shoulders, she
danced around the room.

"Red for the fire keeping us warm,
red for the rooster that calls up the morn,
red for the sky when day begins,
red for the blood that takes away sin."

୶ଡ଼

Grammy sewed the red fabric
to the yellow and gray pieces. Then
she went to the closet and brought
out a form smaller than the others. I
wondered whose it was. She spread the
new garment across its shoulders.

Then she cut a large piece of snow
white fabric to make the collar and
sleeves. Her face changed and she
laughed out loud as she sang.

"Gray for the forest where shadows creep,

gray for the earth dug cold and deep,

gray for the clouds in a stormy sky,

gray for the day that Jesus died."

⁓

I closed my eyes and felt a cold breath of wind on the back of my neck. I turned around and saw Grammy's cat staring at me from the top of the stairs. Grammy then sewed the gray fabric to the yellow. She soon unfolded a new piece of material. Suddenly, the light in the room became warm and red. Tears fell from her eyes as she held the fabric in her hands. Now her song was low and sad.

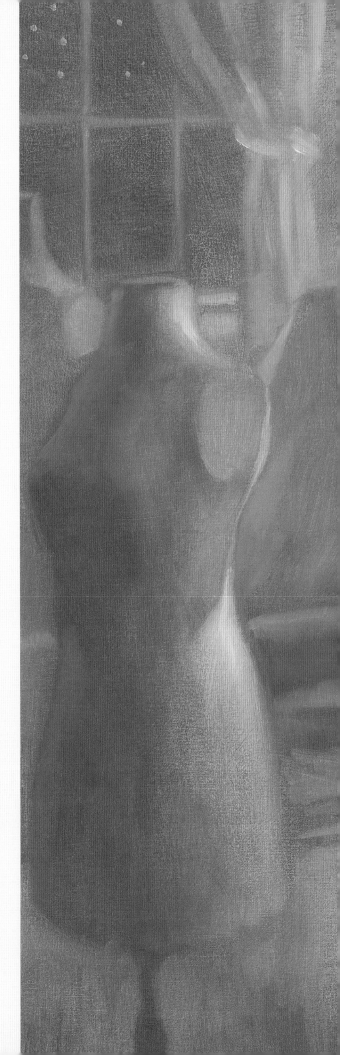

"Yellow for sun at morning's light,

yellow for fireflies dancing at night,

yellow for buttercups' fragrance sweet,

yellow for heaven's golden streets."

∼

The glow from the yellow fabric shone on the walls. Grammy's hands looked like they were dipped in honey as she guided the material under the needle. I leaned against the door and the old dry hinges creaked. I jumped back, hoping Grammy hadn't seen me. When I peeked again, Grammy was cutting a new piece of material. The light in the sewing room changed. As Grammy cut the fabric in pieces, she sang again, but her hands began to tremble.

A few hours later, I awoke to the sound of someone singing. I climbed out of bed and crept downstairs in the darkness. The lovely melody was coming from the sewing room.

I crept closer and hid behind the half open door. Bent over her sewing machine, Grammy sang as she wove the thread into the fabric.

"And dear God, please show me the colors of love," I prayed. Grammy kissed my forehead and slipped out of the room. As I drifted off to sleep, I heard her tiptoe back downstairs.

All day, Grammy worked on her customers' clothes. When
night came she said, "Time for bed, Emma." We climbed the stairs to
my room and Grammy helped me snuggle deep into the covers. She
listened while I said my prayers.

I thought of all the people who visited her sewing room. Each one came with a special request and left with a happy heart.

"What are you making today, Grammy?"

"My masterpiece," Grammy said, winking at me.

"Who's it for?"

"It's for a young lady I care about very much. With this garment I'll wrap her in all the colors of love."

"What are the colors of love?" I asked.

"Soon you will see," she answered.

I loved watching Grammy while she cut odd-shaped pieces of material to fit her pattern. Then, bent over her sewing machine, Grammy sewed the pieces together until they became a garment of perfect shape and design.

The colors made each customer's eyes sparkle. When they wore their new clothes, they stood taller. Their faces were peaceful.

One by one her customers returned, eager to try on their new clothes. Grammy made sure they fit perfectly. She made sure every thread had been knotted and every button had been sewn on snug and tight.

After her customers went home, I watched Grammy make a form of each person from foam rubber and canvas. As she worked, the figure of the person gradually appeared. Soon the sewing room was filled with forms that looked like statues of all her customers. Then she chose fabrics and colors to sew into clothes just right for each person.

People came from all over town
to my grandmother's sewing room.
They walked up her pathway to the gray
wooden stairs of her old front porch, and
stood in line to be measured and fitted.
Slowly and with tenderness, Grammy
took each measurement and listened
as her customers told her their heart's
desires.

Dedicated to my mother Bernie Wyckoff Arnold
and my father, the late Henry O. Arnold, Jr.
You wrapped me in all the colors of love.

~ n.g. ~

For Deb.

~ b.f. ~

Zonder**kidz**®
The children's group of Zondervan

www.zonderkidz.com

What Color Is Love
ISBN: 0-310-70888-5
Copyright © 2005 by Nan Gurley
Illustrations copyright © 2005 by Bill Farnsworth

Requests for information should be addressed to:
Zonderkidz, Grand Rapids, Michigan 49530

Library of Congress Cataloging-in-Publication Data
Gurley, Nan.
    What color is love / by Nan Gurley ; illustrated by Bill Farnsworth.-- 1st ed.
      p. cm.
  Summary: Emma's grandmother, a seamstress, makes a coat for her out of the
"colors of love." Includes Bible references.
    ISBN 0-310-70888-5 (hardcover)
    [1. Grandmothers--Fiction. 2. Christian life--Fiction. 3. Dressmakers--Fiction.]
I. Farnsworth, Bill, ill. II. Title.
  PZ7.G981485Wha 2005
  [E]--dc22

                                         2004000529

Editor: Amy DeVries
Art direction & design: Michelle Lenger

Printed in China
05 06 07/LPC/4 3 2 1

What Color Is Love

A Parable of God's Gifts

Written by Nan Gurley
Illustrated by Bill Farnsworth